I0730470

I TOOK HER FIRST

BOOKS BY SAMANTHA HAYES

The Reunion

Tell Me A Secret

The Liar's Wife

Date Night

The Happy Couple

Single Mother

The Trapped Wife

The Ex-Husband

The Engagement

The Inheritance

Mother of the Bride

Her Housekeeper

The Marriage Rules

I TOOK HER FIRST

SAMANTHA HAYES

bookouture

Published by Bookouture in 2025

An imprint of Storyfire Ltd.
Carmelite House
50 Victoria Embankment
London EC4Y 0DZ

www.bookouture.com

The authorised representative in the EEA is Hachette Ireland
8 Castlecourt Centre
Dublin 15 D15 XTP3
Ireland
(email: info@hbgi.ie)

Copyright © Samantha Hayes, 2025

Samantha Hayes has asserted her right to be identified as the author of this work.

All rights reserved. No part of this publication may be reproduced, stored in any retrieval system, or transmitted, in any form or by any means, electronic, mechanical, photocopying, recording or otherwise, without the prior written permission of the publishers.

ISBN: 978-1-80550-320-0
eBook ISBN: 978-1-80550-319-4

This book is a work of fiction. Names, characters, businesses, organizations, places and events other than those clearly in the public domain, are either the product of the author's imagination or are used fictitiously. Any resemblance to actual persons, living or dead, events or locales is entirely coincidental.

For my beautiful, talented and inspiring daughter, Polly.
With all my love, always
xxx

PROLOGUE

I stand across the road in the rain – watching, waiting, biding my time. There are lights on in the four-storey house, people at home, students coming and going, the hiss of tyres on the wet street, couples with umbrellas hurrying past. I light a cigarette then step back under a tree, squinting up at the top floor where I know she is.

Not long now until the nightmare is over.

Ten minutes later, I stamp out the butt on the pavement. It's now or never. I cross the road and go up to the front door, holding my breath as I turn the knob and push. It's open. *Thank God.*

As I creep inside the hallway, I hear drunken laughter coming from the kitchen. Suddenly, there's a crash as I knock over a bike leaning against the wall. I freeze, cursing silently as I wait for someone to come out, to see who's there. But no one does. I stand the bike up again and head up the stairs – three flights to the top floor.

Breathless from the climb, I push open the door to her

bedroom, knowing I don't have long. It's a mess inside, clothes everywhere, and it smells of perfume – a spicy, sweet, exotic smell that reminds me of *her*, the baby's mother.

I walk around the single bed and go over to the wooden cot, peering down inside. And there she is, gurgling up at me, flapping her arms at the musical mobile turning above her, the doleful notes of the tune coming to an end.

I reach down into the cot and lift the baby out, marvelling at her little face – her plump cheeks, her searching eyes. As she gazes up at me, she has no idea she's being taken. No idea she'll never see her mother again.

'We have to hurry,' I whisper as I cradle her in my arms, praying that no one sees us leave.

ONE
HANNAH

Now

What have I done? What have I *done...*?

What. Have. I. *DONE?*

The queue at the police station is long. I force myself to stay calm, knowing things will get way, *way* worse if I don't. I need to be honest with the police, tell them what I've done. Put everything right and confess. Make this whole dreadful mess go away. Rewind to an hour ago when everything was fine.

'Excuse me... are you in the queue?' I ask a woman. Her arm is being tugged by an impatient child. A child about the same age as... as...

I shudder. I can't stand to think about what happened to her. Her sweet little face staring up at me. Trusting me. Her rosebud mouth. Her long golden hair. Her huge blue eyes.

She's such a special little girl.

Even though I've done a terrible thing, I was only trying to help her. She was mine for such a short while, and now she's gone. Mila – an innocent five-year-old – has vanished into thin air because of me. It feels like history is repeating itself.

'Sorry, what?' the woman says, preoccupied. 'Leave it out, Tommy!' she says to her son.

'Are you in the—'

'Course I'm in the bloomin' queue.'

'Sorry,' I say, my eyes wide, my skin crawling with fear. With shame. With remorse. I can't believe I've been so stupid. 'Is there any chance I could go ahead of you?'

There are three people in front of her, all waiting to be seen. My heart skitters in my chest. If she agrees, it could gain me ten minutes. A whole precious ten minutes to get Mila back.

But the woman just rolls her eyes and turns her back on me.

They say the first hour after an abduction is the most important. I called the police as soon as I realised that Mila was missing, but after the call handler took down the details, telling me they'd send someone out, it felt like wasted time. I had no idea how long they'd be, and I needed to see an officer right away.

So here I am, down at the local police station just a short walk – no, *run* – from where I live, figuring it was quicker to come here myself. Though now, I'm beginning to regret my decision.

Another police officer appears behind the glass barrier at a second window, whispering to the officer already on duty. They shake their heads at the ever-growing line. 'Next!' he calls out.

That's when I take my chance, dashing up to the counter first. My heart pounds as the officer – late twenties with fiery red hair and a smattering of freckles on his forehead – stares at me, an eyebrow raised.

'Please, you've got to help me,' I bluster out.

'Oi!' I hear from behind as someone barges up to the desk. 'What do you think you're doing? I was next!'

I swing round. 'Sorry... please, it's an emergency. A little girl's been taken, she's missing and—'

'God, sorry, love. You carry on,' the man says, backing away with his hands up.

The officer looks at me through the glass. 'You want to make a missing person's report?'

'Yes... yes, I do.' I feel as though I'm going to pass out. 'Urgently!' Still in my paint-covered work clothes from school – black trousers and a navy top – I wrap my arms around myself as a shiver courses through me. 'Though she's not *missing* as such... well, no, she *is*. I mean, I knew where she was – but now I don't.' I touch my temple, tucking back a strand of my mousy-brown hair. 'She's been taken. Stolen, abducted and—'

'Miss, slow down,' he says. 'You're not making much sense.'

My knees feel as though they're going to buckle when I think about Mila being grabbed by a stranger, taken from my kitchen. The ringing sound in my ears grows louder.

'It's *Mrs*,' I whisper, stupidly concerned that the police officer will smell it on me – my singledom. My aloneness. That he somehow senses my husband has upped and left me, that my marriage, along with everything else in my life, is a big fat failure. 'It's *Mrs* Marlowe,' I say, wanting him to know that someone married me. That despite the dreadful thing I've done, someone once loved me enough to say *I do*. 'Hannah Marlowe,' I add.

'Righto, so do you want to start at the beginning, Hannah? Tell me what's happened as clearly and concisely as you can.'

'It's Mila... a little girl. She's five years old. And she's gone.' I feel as though I'm underwater. I can't breathe. 'She's been taken. Stolen.'

'Is Mila your daughter?' he asks, hands poised over the computer keyboard.

I shake my head. 'No, no, you don't understand. She... she was abducted and... and...'

I cover my face as I attempt to curate the right words. Words that won't immediately land me in a cell, but words still strong enough to get him to take me seriously.

'I'm not Mila's mother. I'm her teacher.'

'Where is her mother then?' the officer asks, tapping something into the computer. 'And what is the child's surname?'

'I... I don't know where her mother is, but she was late to pick her up from school. Mila's surname is Weston.' I drag my fingers down my cheeks, pulling at the skin. I don't care if I get eye bags or scratches. I deserve everything I get. 'W-E-S-T-O-N,' I spell out.

'Did you call the emergency services when you realised she was missing? Which school was she taken from?'

All these questions. Wasting time.

I recite the school's address, repeating the postcode when he gets it wrong. Then I screw up my eyes again, seeing Mila's pale cheeks with just a dot of colour on each in the softest peach – as though she'd been painted in watercolour. A moment framed in my mind forever. She'd held my hand. Skipped across the road as I took her home from school. To *my* home, where I'd given her milk and cookies in the kitchen. She only said three words the entire time she was with me. *Where's my mummy?*

'And yes, *yes* I called the police. Of course I did!' I recite the crime reference number I was given.

The officer nods, tapping at the computer. But then he stops – his expression freezing. There's a slight frown – or even a look of disdain on his face. An almost pitying look. He glances at me again. Frowning.

'So, you're saying the little girl, Mila Weston, aged five, was abducted today?'

'Yes... yes, for God's sake that's what I'm saying!'

I feel too stupid to tell him that at first I just wanted to know what it would feel like to have a child her age to care for, a little sister for Jodie – the child that would have made my life whole, my marriage not broken. A child that would put my life back to normal.

For a brief moment, I imagined that she was my flesh and blood with her milky moustache and chocolatey crumbs on her lips, that we'd sing songs together as I cooked her tea, then I'd give her a bath and read her a bedtime story and plant a kiss on her forehead as her eyelids drooped closed. But mainly, I wanted to take care of her, to make life better for her. It broke my heart to see her so neglected.

A sweet little five-year-old whose real mother didn't deserve her.

'Do you have any idea who took her from school?'

'*Yes!*' I lean forward on the counter, my fingers gripping the laminate. 'I know exactly who took her from the playground!'

The officer shakes his head a couple of times, glancing down at his computer screen before giving the other desk sergeant a look, pointing at something. I can't tell if he's about to arrest me or send me on my way. Both officers are giving me daggers now.

'And who would that be?' he says, standing back and sighing out.

I hesitate before answering, knowing how this is going to sound. Knowing my life will never be the same again once the words are out of my mouth.

I take a deep breath and screw up my eyes, gripping the countertop harder.

'*Me,*' I whisper, so ashamed of what I've done. 'I took Mila first. I took her back to my house from school. But then someone took her from *me.*'

TWO

HANNAH

The police interview room feels cold compared to outside – a sunny Friday in June, four weeks from the end of term. I'm struggling to read the blank expressions of the two plain clothes officers – both men – sitting opposite me.

'Let me get this perfectly clear, Mrs Marlowe. You're turning yourself in for kidnapping a child?'

'Yes. I mean...' I pause, thinking carefully about my wording. I want the little girl to be safe, to be found, but I need to protect myself, too. 'No. It wasn't kidnapping *exactly*. I did take Mila, yes – but not in that way...'

They'll never understand why I took her, why I did what I did. I'm not even certain myself. It was like I was acting on impulse, doing what I thought was the right thing for the little girl, though part of me wonders if it was also for me. The only thing I *am* certain of is that however I say it, it doesn't sound good. And that's not the real problem here, anyway.

'Look, you've got to listen. I'm not the one you should be worried about! I took Mila first – from school – and then someone took her from *me*. From my house. Someone's taken her for *real*,' I explain. 'You've got to believe me.'

'Did you take her against her will? Did you have permission to take her?' Both officers still look unconvinced.

The hot sting of tears blurs my vision. I blink a few times.

'She didn't put up a fight, if that's what you mean. And no, I didn't exactly have permission as such. I'm an art teacher at St Peter's Preparatory School on Castle Street. She comes to my art group once a week on a Friday.'

The older officer jots something down. Rests his chin in his hand. Stares at me.

'Do you have any idea where Mila is now?' the younger officer, DC Ed Bright as he previously introduced himself, asks.

'No! She's been kidnapped. It's what I've been trying to tell you.'

'So, you kidnapped – sorry, *took* – the child from school. Then what happened?'

'Someone *else* took her from me!' I say, exasperated at all the time they're wasting. 'But please, don't keep saying that I kidnapped her because it wasn't like that.'

The fact is, my desire to care for Mila overrode good sense and judgement. That poor little girl, standing there alone at the end of the day – I'd only wanted to help her feel better, let her know she was wanted, that someone really cared about her. I suppose a part of me believed it might also help *me* – make me feel a little less wretched about my marriage falling apart, just for a moment. But all I've done is make everything worse. I swear I was going to take her back once I'd made sure she was clean and fed and happy.

'That's bad luck,' the older detective says, curling up his lip. In my panicked state, I've forgotten his name.

'Why aren't you out searching for her? Why are you asking me the same questions over and over?' I knit my fingers together under my chin, imploring them. 'Look, I know I did a stupid thing... But you've *got* to believe me. There was an intruder in my house and they stole Mila from my kitchen.'

'Would this be the same intruder that broke into your house two weeks ago, do you think?' he asks. 'The one where there was no evidence of anyone entering your property whatsoever, and the one where, by your own admission, nothing was taken?'

'I don't know. Maybe...' I say in a shaky voice. A shudder spirals through me as I remember coming home that evening, knowing – just *knowing* – that someone had been in my house. I may not have had hard proof, and I didn't see anyone, but my senses told me otherwise. I could almost *smell* the intruder's presence as though they'd not long left. It was utterly terrifying.

'Or maybe it was the person you reported for sitting in their car outside your property on your street?' DC Bright offers, glancing at the screen of his laptop.

'But it was virtually the middle of the night. You can't tell me that's not suspicious behaviour! What was I supposed to do?' I grip the edge of the table, my knuckles turning white. I didn't sleep a wink, certain someone was watching me outside my house.

'Our records indicate that two officers attended at nine-twenty p.m., but no one was found sitting in a car – and no one else locally had made reports or seen anything suspicious, and nothing was found on neighbours' video doorbells. Not that it's a crime to sit in a car, but we also understand that a woman such as you living alone may feel more... on edge and alert to threats.' DC Bright offers up what can only be described as a pitying smile. 'Hence why our officers attended.'

A woman such as me...

'I don't live alone,' I say, frowning. 'I have a fifteen-year-old daughter.'

They try to hide the pitying looks, but I see through their blank expressions. They think I'm an over-anxious busybody who likes to call the police as a hobby.

'Does that somehow make me more of a target?' I ask, feeling annoyed. 'Make me incapable of good judgement? Make me...' I trail off. I was going to say *neurotic*, but I can see that's exactly what DC Bright is thinking and, by suggesting it, I will be proving him correct.

'I see that we've had fourteen calls and reports from your address in the last three months,' the officer continues. 'All false alarms or claims of incidents and crimes that simply can't be proved. What makes this incident different, Mrs Marlowe? Why should we take you seriously?'

'Oh my God, I can't believe you actually said that!' I'm barely able to contain my frustration. 'Sorry,' I say to the older detective, 'I didn't catch your name, but please, tell your colleague that I'm totally serious. Mila Weston, who attends St Peter's School where I work, was kidnapped from my kitchen this afternoon. Do you understand me?'

'If that makes me a kidnapper, too, then I'll face the consequences. My main concern right now is the child's welfare, which, if you must know, is why I took her home in the first place. No one had come to collect her and...' I pause, remembering the tearful look on Mila's face as she stood all alone at the edge of the playground in her grubby uniform. All the other children had gone home. There was an on-duty member of staff, but she'd been distracted and had headed back towards the school building. It's not the first time this has happened – Mila being forgotten.

I also remember the blue van parked across the street, visible through the six-foot-high metal railings from where I was watching out of the art room window. It might have been the same vehicle that I reported that night a couple of weeks ago, though I can't be certain.

But that aside, it was Mila I'd been worried about. I'd been washing paint brushes when I'd spotted her alone in the playground. *Again.* Her long blonde hair was matted at the back (how I longed to brush it out for her), and I'd noticed earlier in class how the cuffs of her blue cardigan were grubby and frayed.

Her shoes were scuffed and looked too small, plus she had an unwashed scent about her.

To me, it seemed that no one cared for Mila, and since she'd started at the school last September, her neglect was becoming more obvious. Just the sight of her activated my maternal instincts, and I desperately wanted to help her, to take care of her as if she was my own.

'My name is DC Starkey,' the older officer says in response to my previous comment. 'I agree with DC Bright that there have been an unusually large number of calls made to the police by yourself about various incidents lately. Is everything OK at home, Mrs Marlowe?' he asks in a voice that puts me on the edge of tears. 'You seem quite... stressed.'

I stare at him. *No, everything is not OK at home...* I want to yell at him. *My husband, Rory, left me out of the blue ten months ago – most likely because I couldn't give him the child we so badly wanted together – and my teenage daughter, whose father has been absent since she was born, barely speaks to me these days. Apart from that, I'm fine!*

'I'm fine...' I say quietly. 'Totally fine,' I repeat before pulling a wodge of tissues from the box on the table and breaking down in tears.

THREE

HANNAH

At my front door, I rummage in my bag for my house keys. Rory suggested years ago not to keep my car key on the same fob. 'This way, if you lose your house keys, you'll still be able to drive somewhere for help,' he'd said with a grin. 'And if you lose your car keys, then you know there's a spare one inside the house.' He always cared for me so much – looking after the little things, as well as the big stuff.

The next day, he came home from work with a new key ring for me – a little fluffy gonk that he joked would always remind me of him.

'It's green with googly eyes,' I'd said, laughing, attaching my house keys to it.

'Don't you remember? It's exactly what *I* looked like the very first time we met.'

It was at a mutual friend's house party during my first year at university in Plymouth that we encountered each other – me aged eighteen and studying for a fine art degree, Rory, nineteen, and in the second year of his four-year architecture BSc, after which he planned to do a Masters. Though it was another year or two before we started dating.

Natalie, our mutual friend and also on my course, was a tortured artist type of soul, and she'd intrigued me from the start. There was something about her that I lacked, something that I envied, almost. I felt like a dull, monochrome version of her flamboyance, convincing myself that if I spent enough time in her company, whatever her secret essence was, it would rub off on me.

Natalie's invitation stated that everyone must wear 'fancy dress, alien-style for no particular reason', and Rory had decided that layering himself in swathes of luminous green fur plus a lurid green wig constituted what our nearest planetary neighbours might look like.

I'd gone for the silver spacesuit look, sewing a tight-fitting mini dress from sequinned fabric with knee-high silver boots. Rory and I had obviously bought our googly eye antennae headbands from the same fancy-dress shop, although his fell into the toilet at the exact moment we met.

'Oh, yuk!' were my first words to a rather lanky and very green in all senses of the word Rory as he knelt beside the toilet bowl in Natalie's student house. Plop went the googly eyes on springy stalks.

Rory had merely grunted in reply before throwing up again. I'd gone back to the kitchen to find Natalie mixing drinks that she'd named 'Out of This World' and 'In Space, No One Can Hear You Scream'. They were mostly just neat vodka, each with a different coloured liqueur splashed in over a ton of ice.

'Some guy's spray painting your bog,' I told Natalie. She was well on her way to being wasted herself.

'Not a proper party without lashings of vom,' she'd said, handing over another evil-looking cocktail to a guy on our course.

We chatted for a few minutes until I nudged her. 'That's him over there, vom-boy. Shit costume,' I'd said, laughing as the guy wrapped in green fur staggered over to us.

'Oh, that's Rory,' she said. 'Raucous Rory, the guys on his course call him. He's harmless. A posh twat, but a real sweetie. Actually, his family home is near yours in Dorset. Something in common, eh?' Natalie nudged me back. 'He helped me with a technical drawing project for one of my modules. Can you believe he tried it on with me? He was pretty insistent. Like, duh.'

Everyone knew Natalie was a lesbian, and she frequently broadcasted that she'd never slept with a guy, as if it was a badge of honour. Something inside me bristled at the thought of a boy, of the *posh twat*, coming on to her. I felt oddly protective.

While others knew Natalie as confident, wildly creative and often dramatic, I'd seen a sensitive and vulnerable side to her that made me think she'd be easy to take advantage of. Perhaps it was the way she got lost in her paintings, or how she'd sometimes turn up to class barefoot because her mind had been elsewhere and she'd forgotten to put shoes on, that made me want to mother her.

So when Rory lurched over and draped an arm around Natalie as she mixed drinks, dislodging the shoulder pads of her elaborate gold jumpsuit, it made me want to thump him.

'Nice hair, alien girl.' He tugged at Natalie's white-blonde wig, which wasn't too dissimilar to her current hair colour. Natalie seemed to dye or bleach her hair at least once a month, and since I'd known her, it had been every colour of the rainbow – unlike my safe shoulder-length bob, which remained a dull, mousy brown.

Rory planted a wet kiss on her cheek, making me feel even more disgusted given what had just come out of his mouth. 'How's my favourite artist?' he slurred, taking one of her cocktails as he lolled against her.

'Fuck off, Rory,' Nat said, pulling away and rolling her eyes at me.

'Oh, you're such a spoilsport,' Rory said, though it came out as *shoilshport*.

'Think I'll head off now, Nat. Great party, thanks.' I glared at Rory, put my drink down and turned to go.

'Wait... Hannah,' a voice said – Nat's voice – as she followed me to the door. 'Let's get together for a coffee soon, yeah?' she said, a hand on my arm. 'I'd really love that.'

'Me too,' I'd said, giving her a brief hug, noticing Rory watching us from the other side of the room.

I sigh, forcing those early memories of Rory from my mind as I shove the key in my front door and go inside, having finally found my house keys – still attached to the luminous furry gonk Rory gave me a few years ago. 'Hello! Jodie, I'm back. Are you home?' I call out to my daughter.

I head through to the kitchen, having been met with silence from upstairs. After what happened earlier with Mila, the house feels different – as though something menacing is hanging in the air. Surely the police should be here right now, investigating. It could be the scene of a crime, after all.

I sigh, my heart aching as I look around the empty room, imagining Mila sitting at the kitchen table nibbling on her cookie, sipping her milk, but then I shake my head and wash my hands before filling the kettle.

'Hey, Mum,' I hear from behind me, making me jump as two hands come down on my shoulders. 'How was work?'

I spin round. 'Jodie, hi, love.' I try to act normal, though it's been far from a normal day. I don't want my daughter knowing anything about what happened earlier. What I *did* earlier. Thankfully she was at athletics practice when I brought Mila home – God, I can't even stand to think about my stupidity – and given Jodie's unusually cheery hello just now, I don't want to put a downer on her good mood. Every time I think about it, my heart thunders in my chest. *Dear God, let Mila be OK.*

'Work was fine, thanks,' I say, crossing my fingers behind my back. 'How was school – and athletics?'

'Same, same,' she says, opening the fridge. 'What's for dinner? I'm starving.'

'I was going to do some chicken in the air fryer. And some chips.'

'Coleslaw and garlic peas too?' she says with a half-smile, half-pout while clasping her fingers under her chin. I don't know what's got into her – this isn't the sullen and aloof Jodie I've come to know these last few months, but I'm not complaining. I remind myself that she's had it tough, too. Rory might not be her biological dad – Jodie's real father left me before she was even born – but he's the only dad she's ever known. It's nice to see her happy for a change.

'Of course,' I say, though there's no way I'll be able to eat anything. My appetite's disappeared after today.

I load the dishwasher and think back to earlier when I left the police station – on foot, as my car is at the garage for a few days – uncertain about what would happen next. I'd fully expected to be arrested and detained, but the officers had sent me on my way.

'Obviously we can't ignore what you've reported, Mrs Marlowe, and we've got your statement of events. We'll be contacting Mila's family immediately and conducting a welfare check on the child as a matter of urgency,' DC Bright had informed me during my interview. 'And we'll take things from there.'

'But Mila won't be with them!' I insisted, sensing they didn't believe that I'd taken the little girl in the first place, let alone that someone had subsequently stolen her from me. The poor child – abducted twice in one day. And the repercussions that would follow at school didn't bear thinking about – me hauled into the head's office on Monday morning and having to face Mila's distraught parents while simultaneously being fired. 'Should I contact her mother myself?' I'd asked, hating the thought of making the call, but if it helped in any way, then I would do it. Being at the police station... the panic rising within me – it all felt far too similar to a past I thought I'd finally left behind.

'Absolutely not,' the officer had replied. 'We have your version of events now, and we will endeavour to get that of the child's parents, too. Please, leave the matter to us.'

I'd nodded, somewhat relieved, but then my skin had prickled as I told them about the man in his car across the road from school, watching Mila with a clear line of sight, his elbow poking out of the window. How he'd just sat there, outside the entrance to the playground, watching, waiting. His eyes seeming to track the little girl as she walked slowly up and down, her feet dragging as she waited to be collected. Whoever was meant to be fetching her was almost half an hour late.

'I suggest you go home now,' DC Starkey chipped in. 'One of my officers will be in touch. And in the morning, do you think it might be worth phoning your GP? It's best not to ignore anxiety.'

'I'm not anxious!' I said, hearing the lie as soon as it left my lips. I might have done something utterly stupid, but the more I tried to convince them that I didn't need help, the more it seemed like I did.

'You think I've made the whole thing up, don't you?' I'd protested at least a dozen times during the interview. 'Mila was taken from my kitchen! Someone was in my house!'

'Whenever reports of a missing child are made, they're always high priority for us. Be assured that my officers are already on it,' DC Starkey said, leading me back to the reception area. 'Allegations such as these are taken very seriously, Miss Marlowe.'

I saw red then. 'It's *Mrs*, for Christ's sake... I'm *Mrs* Hannah Marlowe.' I jabbed my ring finger towards the officer to show him my gold wedding band. He visibly recoiled.

'Like I suggested,' he said, 'I'd give your GP a call in the morning.' Then he turned and walked off.

Tears blurred my vision as I left the building, making me trip on the top step as I went back out into the sunlight. Was the officer right – was I overly anxious? Was I going mad? It's true that in the months since Rory left, I haven't been feeling myself. Everything just feels so much heavier having to do it alone, as though the weight of life has doubled – no, *quadrupled* – in his absence.

'Maybe it is me...' I whispered to myself. 'Maybe the police are right, and I am imagining all these things. The break-in at home, the man who followed me, the car outside school, the weird phone calls I've been getting, the shadows I swear I see around every corner... Oh *God*...' I whimpered as I walked at a brisk pace home, just managing to pull myself together by the time I reached the end of our street.

'Want a hand with dinner?' Jodie asks now, snapping me out of my thoughts.

'Thanks,' I say. 'You get some seasoning on the chicken, and I'll go and get the chips.'

I head out of the back door and round to the garage at the side of the house where we keep the chest freezer as there's no room for it in the kitchen. Our end-terrace Victorian house is on a corner plot, and we had the garage built a couple of years after Rory moved in with us, though I don't think we've ever put our cars in it. Instead, it's filled with bikes and Rory's tools and God knows what else. Plus, there's easy access to the side alley from the back garden through the gate near where we keep the bins.

I flick on the garage light and go inside, grabbing the bag of chips from the freezer. It's only on my way out that I notice something lying on the paving slabs near the side gate – a little pink hair scrunchie, the type a child might wear.

I bend down to pick it up, turning it over and over in my hands. It's a bit grubby and, when I inspect it closer, I see there are a few strands of blonde hair caught up in the folds of fabric. I try to remember if I've seen Mila wearing something similar.

Then I catch my breath when I see the blobs of black and red paint on one side – the only two colours that Mila will use in my Friday art group. The sight of it is enough to convince me that I'm not going mad, that Mila *was* here, that someone *did* take her. I can't help the shudder when I imagine it falling from her hair as she was manhandled from my house.

FOUR
JODIE

Mum thinks I went to athletics club straight after school, but I didn't. I couldn't face it since those two new girls joined. They think they're so cool with their designer sports gear and flash trainers, pretending they're better than everyone else. Better than *me*. If only they knew how much their cruel words stung, adding to my loneliness.

In my bedroom, my laptop pings with another message. It's the only thing that makes me smile these days – knowing I've got one friend at least.

Will you be around later?

Sure, I type back. So far, our chat's been squeaky clean, with him being so supportive and kind – not at all like other boys I know. They can be so immature and stupid – though ShadowKnight184 isn't like the lads at school. That's his gaming name, though he's told me to call him Shadow. It's kind of an unspoken safety thing that no one gives out their real names online. Mum would be proud of me.

I'll be here, I quickly add, making my heart race. It's been a few weeks now since he first private messaged me out of the blue, and while there's not been any flirting between us, I'm hopeful things might go that way in the future – though I don't even know what he looks like yet.

Then I'll be here too, Jodeenoodle09, he types back with a smiling emoji.

Can't wait, I reply, feeling brave and adding a heart eyes emoji. That's my screen name – Jodeenoodle09 – and we first got chatting on a Twitch channel that we both follow. Unashamed Fortnite fan here, following all the big streamers.

Where you off to now? I ask, though he doesn't reply. I watch the space on my screen where the little bubbles would appear if he was typing something back, but it's just blank. A week or two after we started talking, we figured out that we both live super local to each other, which was enough to convince me that us chatting was fate at play. He asked for my phone number, but he was super chill when I said it would be best to wait until we'd *actually* met. I'm not an idiot.

He's been such a good friend, listening when I've been down, offering advice when I've typed out my problems. It gives me hope to know there are good guys out there. It's been hard to watch Mum going through it after Rory left us last year, turning our lives upside down. I haven't spoken to her much about it, though I've heard her crying in her room at night.

'Jodie, you in there?'

I snap my laptop lid shut, shove it under the duvet. Then I grab my book from the bedside table, hoisting myself upright in bed. 'Yeah, Mum, of course I am.' I smile to myself. Mums say the stupidest things.

'Can I come in?'

'Sure.'

Great timing, Mum. I swear Shadow was about to say something... well, something *nice* about the pic I just sent him. I blush at the thought. It was only a shot of my face, of course, but the lighting was good, and I looked really pretty.

She comes in, sitting down on the edge of my bed. Her eyes flick around my room, as if she's on the hunt for evidence to catch me out. Or maybe it's just my guilty conscience.

'Is it spicy?' she asks, eyeing my book with a smile. 'You're blushing.'

'Oh my God, Mum. Like, *literally*?' I roll my eyes. 'Only if you count dragons as spicy.' I flash her a look at the black and gold cover of my romantasy novel. For some reason, my mind is filled with the photo Shadow sent me earlier this evening – the only picture I've ever seen of him. Though to be fair, I couldn't see his face because of his red baseball cap. It had something printed on the front, but I couldn't make out what it said. *Took this in Brighton*, he told me. *On the pier.* Then he put a few laughing emojis.

Very cool, I'd typed back. I suppose I found his shyness kind of alluring. I imagined he had sultry brown eyes and that he'd taken the photo just for me, even though I knew he hadn't.

'It's nice that you love reading,' Mum says. 'I always used to like to get lost in a book.' She sighs. 'I can't seem to concentrate these days.'

'You've had a lot to deal with.' I reach out and touch her hand. I know I've not been there for her lately, but I've had my reasons. Though since chatting with Shadow, I'm feeling more positive. His words from earlier are still playing on my mind: *Let's meet soon...*

'I can't mope about forever though, can I?' Mum replies, though I sense there's something else she wants to get off her chest. 'Rory might not be here anymore, but we're coping OK, aren't we? We're doing all right?'

I squeeze her hand. I doubt she'll ever get over Rory walking out on her so suddenly. They'd been together going on fourteen years – *this* time round – and he's the only man I've ever known as a dad. But the pair of them go way back to when they first met at university.

Either way, I know Mum is still besotted with him and her heart hurts like hell. It might have been easier for her to accept the situation if he *had* had another woman on the side, but by all accounts, there's no one else involved.

'Yeah, Mum, we're doing great. Just the two of us. We really are.' I give her a smile – one of many since she got home earlier, given my good mood. But the thing with Mum is, she has this way of sniffing things out, like she's peeling back all my layers.

'What's up with you then?' She gives me a playful prod. 'You seem unusually happy.'

'Nothing,' I say, hoping she'll let it drop. There's no way on earth I'm telling her about Shadow.

'And you're sure you went straight to athletics after school today? You didn't pop home first?' It's the third time she's asked me since we ate supper.

'Yeah, of course. I went straight to the track. Why?' My tone and blush immediately signal something is off. Damn her sixth sense. And damn my guilty conscience.

'No reason,' she says, her eyes narrowing in concern.

Thing is, I know she has a guilty conscience of her own.

FIVE
HANNAH

The pink hair scrunchie is tucked inside my handbag when I arrive at work on Monday morning. I've got classes most of the day, so if I'm going to get a roasting in the head's office, they'll need to find a stand-in teacher to cover me.

I usually drive to St Peter's School – never seeming organised enough to walk the short distance – and very often Jodie is running late for her bus, so I drop her off at school first. Today, though, with my car *still* at the garage, I had no choice but to walk, and Jodie had to scramble to be on time for her school bus.

On the way to the art department, I'm expecting to be accosted in the corridor as I walk past the main office, manned by Alma, our eagle-eyed receptionist, but she smiles and gives me a little wave through the open hatch. 'I love your scarf,' she calls out, making my heart thump for a moment as her eyes flick up and down me – a 'fit check' as some of the older girls at school call it. Although by older, I mean thirteen – the maximum age of the pupils here. And 'fit' in my case means loose black cotton trousers and a plain grey T-shirt with a huge printed scarf I've had forever wound around my neck. Practical clothes, given my messy work – I usually go home covered in glue, paint or clay.

'Thanks, Alma,' I reply with a brief wave back, making sure to keep walking.

Next, I run the gauntlet of the head teacher's office, front-lined by her secretary, Connie – but again, I slip by unnoticed. Not what I was expecting after Friday afternoon's events. The weight of what I did has hung over me like a black cloud all weekend, making me feel sick and unable to focus on anything as I waited for the police to knock on my door, arrest me and take me away. But they didn't – and what's stranger still is that I haven't had an email from Madeline, the head teacher, demanding that I come and see her first thing this morning either. Surely the police will have informed her of what happened.

In my art room, I flick on the lights – a large and well-equipped studio attached to the side of the main school building – and dump my bag on my desk. I glimpse the pink scrunchie inside, my stomach knotting as I wonder what it means. Did it fall from Mila's hair as she was snatched from my kitchen, through the side gate and out into the alley? Whoever took her could only have come in and out of the back door – I'd have seen or heard them otherwise. I'd only popped upstairs to get something when she vanished.

I take a breath, wishing above all else that I could rewind the clock to Friday morning – no, to last September when Mila started at St Peter's. I'd known from the start that she was a special little girl – there was just something about her that was different to the other children. Perhaps it was her vivid imagina-tion, the thoughtful and innocent way she painted the world, the stories she told in her pictures. Or it could have been that I felt... *sorry* for her, I suppose. She never had quite the right uniform, and she always looked so thin compared to the other children. Several times I brought in snacks for her to eat at break time, and she often came to school without a coat. I ended up buying her a cheap padded anorak from the supermarket to keep at school when the weather turned cold. While I didn't want her mother to think I was interfering, I couldn't stand to see her shivering, either.

But now – God, how I wish I'd kept my nose out and alerted the head teacher about my concerns. Instead, I allowed my instincts to get the better of me. I'd just wanted to take care of her and, coupled with my longing for another child after Rory and I tried to conceive for so long, all my good judgement went out of the window. In my line of work, that's not OK.

I crouch down beside a set of plastic storage trays, opening the one that contains the picture painted by Mila at Friday's art session, a couple of hours before everything went wrong. I pull out a stack of paintings and look through them – most are daubed with bright and bold images of whatever was on the children's minds – trees, the park, a house, Mummy and Daddy, the beach...

But Mila's picture is easy to pick out of the pile. She chose dark grey paper for her painting and spent the next hour carefully applying jet-black paint in vertical lines.

'That's interesting, Mila,' I'd said, thinking they looked a lot like prison bars.

'It's a forest,' she replied quietly, concentrating on her work.

As I study it again now, I notice something that I'd not spotted on Friday. Amongst the black tree trunks is a figure. No, *two* figures – and one is smaller than the other with a triangle for a skirt. A short way behind is someone else, much taller and striding through the trees with outstretched arms.

But more disturbing is the patch of dark red paint on the forest floor between them, which looks a lot like it's meant to be blood. And when I look closer still, I see that Mila has painted a splotch of red on the child's body, right over her heart.

SIX

HANNAH

'Morning, Madeline,' I say, going into the head teacher's office. I'm surprised I've lasted until break time before being hauled in front of her, presumably to be given my marching orders.

I stand in front her desk. She's mid-fifties and has a some-times-stern-sometimes-soft look to her angular face, making her almost unreadable. Whatever her mood, I wish that I'd made arrangements for Jodie to stay with my parents if the worst should happen and I'm arrested and thrown in a police cell.

But then she smiles, flicking a hand at the chair opposite. 'Please, sit down.' Another smile.

My mind is spinning. Why does she look so agreeable, so normal? And why does she almost seem pleased to see me?

'I wanted to pick your brains about a pupil,' Madeline begins. 'Mila Weston. You know her, right?'

Here we go, I think, making me wonder if this is some kind of trick to make me admit my guilt.

'Look, I can totally explain,' I say. 'No one came to pick her up, and it's not the first time she's been forgotten. She was waiting for going on forty-five minutes and there was a man in a car across the street, and—'

'Right... exactly that,' Madeline interrupts, nodding and steepling her fingers under her chin. 'You've noticed it too – the neglect?' She glances across at her computer, tapping something on the keyboard.

'Yes, I have. That's why I—'

'It's so sad, poor little mite.' A shake of her head. 'I'm just gathering evidence at this point. The police were in touch first thing this morning.'

I freeze, staring at her as she types, clicking her mouse occasionally, biting her bottom lip as she concentrates.

'So,' she continues, turning to me. 'Can you tell me any other concerns you've had about Mila's welfare?'

'The police...' I say quietly. 'What... what did they say?'

Madeline takes a few glugs of coffee. 'It was only a quick chat, but apparently, they've had cause to do a welfare check on Mila after some kind of incident on Friday. They wouldn't say exactly what it was about.'

A strange squeak bubbles up my throat.

'They went to the child's home late on Friday afternoon and spoke to the nanny, but Mila wasn't there. Apparently, she was on a sleepover playdate, but the officers still insisted on seeing the child for themselves. The nanny agreed to go and fetch her from the playdate and take her to the police station to confirm that she was fine, which she did. After that, the police were satisfied. Anna Weston, her mother, is away overseas on business, it would seem.'

'Mila was at a *sleepover* on Friday?' I manage to say, stunned by this revelation. 'Who... who with?'

'That, I don't know. The police wouldn't reveal much, but the very fact that she's on their radar is enough for me. At least she's been confirmed as safe and fine for now, which was what was concerning them last week. Social services will follow up.'

'Yes, that's... that's good news...' I say, not sounding as relieved as I should. 'I didn't know she had a nanny.'

A nanny who can't be bothered to fetch her on time, or put her in clean clothes, I think, wondering if Mila's mother knows about her daughter's neglect – though right now, I'm more concerned about how Mila got to the sleepover in the first place. From *my* kitchen...

Something doesn't sit right with me, yet if I tell Madeline I'm still concerned, then I risk her finding out what I did. My chest feels so tight from anxiety I can hardly breathe. My mind whirs through the possibilities. Perhaps the mother of the sleepover child spotted me taking Mila from the school playground, and then she followed me home to collect Mila as she was always meant to. Or maybe a staff member had seen me with Mila, and they gave the sleepover mum my address. If I hadn't heard her knocking at the front door, perhaps she'd gone round the back, maybe calling out to me and, when I didn't reply, she just came in and took Mila. But what mother would do that – take a child without letting anyone know?

I'm suddenly teary when it occurs to me that that's exactly what *I* did, especially when I realise that someone else now knows my secret – that I took Mila without permission.

'I'll be following up with social services,' Madeline tells me. 'The police make a referral as a matter of course.' She pulls a sympathetic expression when she sees I look upset. 'Oh, Hannah... I know how good you are with the younger classes, how much you relate to the kids. It's hard not to get involved when things like this are flagged, but try not to worry for now. They said the child is currently safe, and school will fully co-operate.'

I nod, trying to appear unaffected. Madeline's no fool. For the next ten minutes, I recount a few instances of Mila coming into school in grubby uniform with unbrushed hair and food round her mouth, or not being picked up on time, wracking my brains for anything odd she might have said.

'The truth is, she's very quiet in class and doesn't seem to have a particular best friend.' Which also makes me curious whose house it was she went to for the sleepover. 'Her artwork is rather dark and... well, a bit disturbing, if I'm honest.'

Madeline seems interested in this and, when she's finished typing up what I've told her, she gets me to come round to check what she's written is correct. 'We can't afford to make errors.'

I check over the file on her screen, nodding as I read through. Then I catch sight of Mila's mother's name at the top of her online file – Anna Weston. I've not had a chance to meet her yet. There doesn't seem to be a father's name on file, though I spot a secondary contact number for Mila's nanny, but don't catch her name before Madeline clicks off the screen. All this information is available to me on the system anyway, but seeing it here now, in the head's office, adds gravity to the scrape I got myself into on Friday.

'It's a shame that Mila's not in school today.' Madeline continues, 'or we could ask her a few gentle questions. The nanny called in first thing to say she's sick. She's got that stomach bug, apparently. Probably picked it up at the sleepover.'

'She's absent?' I say, my thoughts racing as the panic rises inside me again. I can't help thinking that it's a strange coincidence for her to be off school today – just a couple of days after she went missing. Could the police have made a mistake with the welfare check?

'There's something going around,' Madeline replies. 'A twenty-four-hour thing. Seems like half the school's had it lately.'

We exchange a few more words, with me trying to stay calm, and Madeline telling me she'll liaise with Kim, Mila's class teacher, again to fill her in on what we've discussed. As I leave her office, still shaking, I can't believe how stupid I've been, knowing I won't relax until I know that Mila really is fine, until I've set eyes on her myself. My gut is telling me that something isn't adding up – that her absence can't simply be because of sickness after everything that's happened. As I head down the corridor, I wonder if I should go back to the police to make certain it was Mila they saw, though I know they'll tell me I'm overreacting, being irrational. The police don't get things like that wrong, and they're unlikely to take me seriously when I'm forced to explain that my concern is based on nothing much more than a hunch.

I'd just wanted to take care of her, I try to convince myself as I go back into the art room. *And to see what it felt like to have another child in the house.* A little boy or a little girl – I wasn't fussy, but the lure of knowing I could help make Mila's life just a little bit more comfortable in the face of neglect was a pull I couldn't resist. It seemed so unfair that Mila's mother didn't care about her.

After all the years of trying for a child of our own, the countless rounds of failed IVF, the soul-crushing disappointment when the pregnancy test was negative or, if it was positive, only to miscarry a few weeks later, I swear our infertility was what tore Rory and me apart. What drove him to leave me without a backward glance.

SEVEN

The day Rory disappeared was just a normal Friday, ten months ago. No drama. No blazing rows or simmering resentment that had reached boiling point. No forewarning or anything at all that she could later piece together and think *Ahh, yes, I should have seen that one coming*. In fact, her relationship with Rory had always been open and honest, with the pair of them valuing how quick they were to iron out any wrinkles in the fabric of their marriage.

Hannah came home from work with a couple of bags of shopping, struggling with the load as she unlocked the front door, thinking that perhaps they could both sit out the back with a glass of wine or a beer and enjoy the last of the sunshine. The final rays of the day flooded a spot at the end of their garden where Rory had laid a patio, along with the help of his mate Mitch, a couple of summers ago. Hannah knew Rory was working from home today and, being the end of the working week, he could probably knock off a bit early.

'It's only me,' she sang out from the hallway. It was one of those silly couple's habits. *Only meee...* was the echo she'd expected to hear from upstairs where Rory had a desk in the box bedroom, but nothing was forthcoming. She figured he was probably on a call.

In the kitchen, Hannah unpacked the shopping and pulled an already chilled bottle of wine from the fridge. It was almost 5 p.m., and it had been a long week. Looking back, she supposed she'd sensed *something* about the feel of the house that afternoon, though she wasn't sure exactly what was different, couldn't quite pinpoint it, even with hindsight. Just that something was... *off*. Out of kilter. As if the thrum of life, the vibration of their familiar routine, had shifted.

Hannah took a beer from the fridge and popped off the cap, taking it upstairs to Rory. On the landing, she listened outside the door to see if she could hear his voice on a call, but when it was silent, she went in. Jodie was at swim club and wouldn't be back for another hour or so.

'I come bearing gifts,' she said, her eyes searching around.

Strange. Rory was not there.

His office chair was pushed in, and his laptop wasn't on his desk, but Hannah thought nothing much of it at that point. She went downstairs to check her phone, putting the beer back in the fridge. He'd obviously been called into the office for a last-minute face to face meeting, and she'd probably missed his message letting her know.

But there were no texts and no missed calls.

'Odd,' she mumbled, tapping out a message asking when he'd be back. Then she got on with preparing dinner – a Mexican tonight.

It was half an hour later, after she'd washed her hands and was checking her phone to see if Rory had at least read her message, that she spotted it hadn't even delivered. One grey tick sat next to her words. And it took her a moment longer to realise that his profile photo had disappeared at the top of the screen. It was only after a bit of googling that she discovered what it meant – that in all likeliness, Rory had blocked her.

'What the *hell*?' She sent another message to see if it went through. It didn't. 'Surely there's been some kind of mistake,' she said to Jan, Mitch's wife and her good friend, when she phoned to see if they'd heard anything from Rory, or if he'd gone round to theirs.

They were Rory's friends originally, but Hannah had known them for as long as she'd been with Rory this time round – going on fourteen years now – having holidayed and hung out together loads. They had a son, Harry, several years older than Jodie and away at university. They lived in a large 1950s house on the edge of town that was Jan's pride and joy and at the heart of her design business, and sometimes they'd all head to the pub after work for a couple of pints and a catch-up. The two couples' friendships were solid.

'Oh God, yeah, it's a mistake for sure,' Jan had said dismissively. 'If Ror's anything like Mitch, he's crap with technology. He's probably been fat-fingered while on his phone and has no idea he's blocked you. The silly goose.'

'So, he's definitely not with you?' Hannah had asked, sounding unconvinced.

'Han, I swear he's not here. I promise I'm not covering for him. Mitch isn't harbouring him, either. He's outside giving the shed a long-overdue coat of wood stain if you must know. I can see him now,' she said cheerily.

Hannah thanked her and hung up, deciding to call Jodie. She wouldn't be able to answer her phone until swim club was over, but thought she'd try her anyway to see if there'd been a change of plan. Perhaps Rory had arranged to fetch her from the pool early and then gone on to pick up a takeaway, not remembering that Hannah was cooking Mexican. But as she expected, there was no answer from Jodie, so she sent her a message for when she came back to the changing rooms.

Then Hannah called the office where Rory worked as an architect – Draper Ford, one of the most well-known and well-respected firms in the area, known for designing the sort of homes Hannah could only dream about. She never liked bothering him when he was at the office. While Rory earnt a decent amount as an architect, he'd been saddled with huge debt from his previous marriage that had only come to light in the last couple of years – he didn't like to talk about the details much, and Hannah didn't like to pry, but he told her that the divorce settlement had dragged on forever.

He worked long hours and promised Hannah that once it was all paid off and he was back on his feet financially, they'd begin saving in earnest and planning their own dream house build – hopefully a plot at Ocean Heights, their favourite spot up on the headland. Hannah wasn't sure how they'd ever get close to saving what they'd need for that development, especially as Rory never seemed to have any spare cash to put aside, and her teacher's salary didn't go very far. But it was a dream they both aspired to.

'Bea, hi, it's Hannah Marlowe,' she began, exchanging a few pleasantries. 'Sorry to bother you, but did Rory come into the office this afternoon? I'm suspecting the answer is yes,' she added hopefully. 'He was working from home earlier but he's not here right now.'

'Oh, erm, let me just check, Mrs Marlowe, hang on.'

The line went silent for a few minutes, then Bea returned, her well-spoken yet still young voice chiming out what Hannah didn't want to hear.

'Sorry, no. He's not been in today. I asked around and everyone here seems to think he was working from home. Hope he's not missing for too long!'

They said their cheery goodbyes. Bea liked Hannah because when she visited the office she often took in home-baked brownies for everyone – and it was only later, much,

much later when Jodie had long since returned from swim club, eaten her dinner and was asleep in bed, when Hannah had exhausted all the options of calling round their friends, family, and contacts, with Rory still not home, that she replayed Bea's words over and over in her mind, a glass of wine in hand as she glanced at the time – 11.29 p.m.

Hope he's not missing for too long!

EIGHT

HANNAH

'What do you mean, someone's already picked up my car?' I'm confused by what the mechanic, mid-twenties and dressed in oily overalls, is telling me. 'I got a text yesterday afternoon saying it was fixed, that I could fetch it first thing today, Wednesday.' I check my phone to prove I'm not going mad. 'See, a message from Malc Barnes Motors.'

'Hang on, let me ask Malc,' he says with a non-committal sigh, sloping back off into the workshop behind the waiting area.

'Thank you!' I call out after him, concerned I'll be late for work. Maybe he doesn't realise that Malc has been fixing our cars for years. My Toyota is probably parked out the back behind a load of other vehicles that the lad can't be bothered to move. If nothing else, his attitude could certainly do with a tune-up.

'Sorry to keep you waiting,' the young mechanic says on his return. 'Malc says your car was definitely picked up earlier. He said they had a spare key and you'd given permission for them to fetch it.' He glances behind me at another customer who's just come in.

'But... that's not right!' I squeak. 'Who picked it up?' For some reason, my mind immediately goes to Rory, wondering if it's him messing with me – perhaps letting me know that after all these months he still exists, somewhere, out there. I still have no idea where he's living – though I do know for a fact that he's still alive. 'The man who picked it up,' I ask, 'did he have sort of dark curly hair, a bit tousled and windswept?' I ask. 'And a stubbly beard? Quite tall and maybe wearing a green bomber jacket and jeans?'

A wave of sadness creeps through me as I realise that I don't have a clue what Rory might be wearing these days, or if he even has stubble anymore. For all I know, he might have taken all his clothes to a charity shop and bought himself a whole new wardrobe, reinventing himself entirely. Stepping out of his old life and into a new one. Not getting any kind of closure has been almost unbearable.

'No, not at all like that,' the mechanic replies, looking puzzled. 'Malc said it was a woman who picked up your car.'

'Maybe Rory has a new woman and she took it,' I say to Kim through gritted teeth several hours later at break time. Not that I even know if he's seeing anyone else, or what his life looks like these days.

It's a stretch, but I've often wondered if Rory has been behind the odd things that have happened over the last few months. And if he's been inside my house, he could have easily taken my spare car key. I should have listened to Dad's advice and changed the locks, but a part of me still longs for my husband to come home, that maybe he's had a mental break-down or something to explain what he's done. Forgiveness wouldn't seem quite so impossible then.

Kim, a year one class teacher, is going above and beyond in her friendship duties this morning, allowing me to have a rant while we're in the playground supervising the lower years' midmorning break time, each of us scanning around the junior play area as we walk about.

'Anyway, they have a CCTV camera on the garage forecourt, so Malc is going to email me some clips.' I pull my phone from my pocket to check if anything has come in, even though it's only been a couple of hours. There's nothing in my inbox apart from an Amazon email. If the camera footage doesn't show anything, and if there's not a damn good reason for whoever it was taking my car, then I'll be reporting it to the police. Though my stomach churns at the thought of them not believing me again.

'What have I always told you?' Kim says predictably. '*Cherchez la femme* and that'll tell you everything you need to know.'

I make a noise in the back of my throat, still none the wiser ten months on from that dreadful night when I literally sat up until dawn waiting for the police to arrive, for them to take me seriously about Rory's disappearance. I'd always refused to believe there was anyone else involved. That he'd ditched me for another woman. I thought we were rock solid.

The police investigation culminated a couple of months later with an overly sympathetic female officer, her head tipped patronisingly to one side, informing me that they can't force someone to be found – even if they'd technically found them. When she left my house, I was left with a sinking feeling that they had indeed located Rory, but he'd chosen not to reveal his whereabouts and the police had to respect his privacy.

At the time, Rory having run off with another woman was simply not on my radar, nor something I believed could be true. Before it happened, there were literally no signs of his impending disappearance, yet as time wore on I tried to piece together any small clues he'd left behind, desperate for a reason, an explanation, a motive. I wondered if his leaving had been a precise and planned operation, perhaps over several months.

Had someone else been behind that – someone egging him on, professing their love for him, promising a better life than he had with me and Jodie?

But I still couldn't accept he'd left because of another woman. If he had, I'd surely have noticed *something* – perfume on his clothing or in his car, lipstick on his collar, condoms hidden in his work bag, or him spending loads of time at the gym or being late home from 'important work meetings' that didn't add up. All the infidelity clichés. But there were none. Until the morning of the day he left, Rory's behaviour had seemed pretty much normal.

'Even if he is in another relationship now, what would his new woman want with my car anyway?' I say to Kim as we pace about. 'It's not exactly a Porsche.'

'If there is someone else, maybe she's operating under strict orders,' Kim replies. '*His* orders. You've had some weird things happen over the last few months – just enough to put you on edge and make you suspicious, but never enough for the police to do anything about.' Kim knows all about the strange goings-on that have happened to me – unprovable whenever I've reported them. I have no concrete evidence it's Rory, and no idea why he'd want to unsettle me like that given he's the one who left me, but I can't think of anyone else it could be. 'Have you reported your car as stolen?'

At the mention of the police, my stomach knots. 'Not yet, but I will. I'm sure they'll think I'm a time waster yet again.'

Kim, along with the rest of the world, has no idea about my latest run-in with them last Friday after I took Mila. And it's going to stay that way. Similarly, the police haven't found evidence of any crimes when I've reported my concerns over the last few months, leaving me frustrated and scared when there's nothing they can do. It's one thing Rory letting himself into my house at night, watching my house from his car, or rummaging through my rubbish bins... all these things are bad enough if it's him – though I have no idea why he'd want to. But what's starting to concern me more is if it isn't Rory messing with my mind for some cheap thrill – not content to have ruined my life enough already – then who *is* it?

'How does Mila Weston seem today?' I ask as we walk along the side of the playground closest to the road. She's in Kim's class. I glance through the small section of six-foot railings in case that van is parked out there again, but thankfully it's not. 'Hey, Marcus, stop that now!' I call out to a year three boy about to hurl a football at another pupil's face. 'Final warning!' I add, shaking my head when he looks over.

'The poor kid is still off school sick,' Kim tells me, instantly causing a surge of adrenaline in my stomach.

'*Still?* I thought it was a twenty-four-hour bug.' I try to sound nonchalant, but it's her third day absent now. I've not seen her since she was in my kitchen last Friday. I try to stay calm, but something about this doesn't sit right with me.

'I think it depends if the parents are both working and need their child back at school ASAP,' Kim says with a laugh. 'Though maybe Zayla is doing the right thing and waiting until Mila is fully better before sending her back.'

'Zayla is her nanny?'

Kim nods. 'Yeah. She seems OK. Quite young, but then everyone under the age of forty seems young to me these days.'

'What does Mila's mum do?' I don't get to know the parents of the younger children as well as their class teachers do. Ten minutes at parents' evenings twice a year is the most I can hope for, plus our annual school art exhibition where I may get to chat with a few more parents.

'Not entirely sure, but she seems to be away quite a lot. I had to look up her address not so long ago to send out a letter. They live up on the headland, you know, one of those super grand houses they've recently built? Dead posh, they are.' Kim's Yorkshire accent always brings a smile to my face.

'You mean Ocean Heights?' I ask, even though I know exactly where she means. A wave of wistfulness surges through me, followed by a chill. Then my mind is back on Rory again.

Kim nods before crouching down to deal with a little girl in a uniform that seems to drown her. 'Got an ouchie!' she says, holding up her finger.

'All better now!' Kim tells her, giving her a clean tissue to wrap around it. The child runs off to play again.

'Whatever Mila's mother does for work, she must be well paid,' I say, feeling sad all over again that any dreams Rory and I had of living up there have been firmly dashed. The plots are all long-since sold. There was no way that prime clifftop real estate on the Dorset coast would sit around forever, despite the hefty price tags. They were the same plots that Rory and I once dreamt of building our perfect family home on.

'Darling, as soon as I'm done paying off the debts that my ex-wife so kindly left behind, we'll be back on track financially,' Rory had told me. 'I mean... there might be one or two other big expenses coming up, but I'll deal with it. Trust me?' He'd looked into my eyes, held my hands, sounded so earnest. 'And I'm up for that promotion soon, don't forget.'

I believed him – even when he told me that he'd soon be able to make an offer on the smallest plot at Ocean Heights to secure it. 'It might mean living in a caravan on-site until I can raise funds for the actual build, but that's half the adventure, right?' He was so convincing, telling me he had contacts through work who knew the landowner, reckoning he could pull strings to keep one plot back in reserve.

Had it all been lies?

I hated the thought, but I was almost certain that Rory was banking on his mother passing away to secure his financial future and fund our dreams. Frank, his father, had died five years ago, leaving everything to Marion, Frank's beloved wife and Rory's mum. With Rory having power of attorney since his mother's dementia got worse eighteen months ago when she moved into a nursing home, I'm pretty sure he was planning on dipping into his future inheritance to build our dream home ahead of time. An inheritance he believed would, as an only child, soon be his anyway.

But developers wait for no one and, with Draper Ford designing all but two of the four thousand square foot glass-fronted homes up at Ocean Heights, we watched with dismay when the last plot was sold off and our dreams of a grand design with sea views were over, our pipe dream having gone up in a delusional smoke. And it seems Rory has since made other life plans, anyway – plans that didn't include me.

The playground bell rings, and the children obediently line up ready to go back into class. I give Kim a friendly salute as she leads class K1 back towards their form room, while I head off back to the art department to prepare for my next lesson.

It's as I'm going inside the building that I turn, catching sight of that van parked on the street outside the school again. My heart pounds in my chest at the sight of it, and my hand comes up to my mouth to stifle a gasp. I *knew* I wasn't imagining it!

The sun is glinting off the windscreen, making it hard to see who's inside, and as I grab my phone from my pocket, fumbling to unlock it so I can take a photo, I only catch a quick glimpse of a man in the driver's seat, hidden in the shadows. He's wearing dark glasses and has a baseball cap pulled low over his face, and I swear he's staring right at me. But when I point my phone in his direction to take a picture, the window slides up and he speeds off down the street.

NINE
JODIE

Mum thinks I don't know what she did – that she brought some kid home from school at the end of last week.

I didn't take much notice at first, but I'm beginning to think that she's done something pretty dumb. If she hadn't kept asking me all weekend where I was after school on Friday, her anxiety virtually seeping from her as she grilled me to find out if I'd been home or seen anything, checking and double checking that I'd gone straight to athletics, then I wouldn't have thought much of it. But the way she went *on and on and on*, asking me my whereabouts, got the red flags waving.

As it happens, I usually do go straight to athletics after school, but last Friday I'd come home to change before heading to the park to meet my mates instead. I thought Mum would still be at work supervising the after-school club, but it turned out I'd got my days muddled. Skipping athletics was a bit of a last-minute decision, which is why I didn't have a change of clothes at school. Mum's weird questions continued over the weekend, making me wonder if she knew I'd been hiding out in my room upstairs and was trying to catch me out. That, or her conscience was on fire with something else... Something far more sinister.

Anyway, turned out she wasn't working late on Friday at all, and when I was getting changed in my bedroom, I heard her come back, chatting away to someone. Mum keeps reminding me how much all these sports clubs cost her, so me bunking off wouldn't have gone down well.

I had no idea who she was talking to, and it's not like her to have friends round. Well, not since Rory left, anyway, but especially not straight after school. So I crept to the top of the stairs to listen, to see if I could figure out who it was, but they either couldn't speak or didn't like chatting because whoever was down there literally didn't say a word. Then I heard Mum say she was going to put *Peppa Pig* on the TV, meaning it must have been a child.

'Is this yours?' Mum asks me now as I come into the kitchen for tea.

The week's half over already and I've got a ton of homework to get done by Friday. Technically, maths is my favourite subject, that and design and technology, but since I've been chatting to Shadow, I've fallen behind so much, staying up late to talk to him rather than studying, thinking about him constantly, and basically not focusing on school stuff.

Mum is holding something out to me.

'No, sorry, it's not mine,' I say, giving the red baseball cap a quick glance. 'Wait, give it to me,' I say, reading the words *Sea Ya* embroidered across the front. 'Where did you get this?'

I swear it's the same colour as the cap Shadow was wearing in the photo he sent me. Could he have been here, at my *house*?

'It was hanging on the back gate post when I went out to the dustbins,' Mum says, handing it over. 'Do you know whose it is?'

I shake my head. 'No.'

'I guess someone found it on the street and hung it there in case the owner came back.'

We both know that's unlikely, given the position of our side gate in the pedestrian alley. It's far more likely that someone would have lost it on the main road out the front. And there are far more obvious places to leave it than the gate to our back garden – unless they were hanging around in the alley.

'Yeah, probably,' I say, trying to sound chill, even though it's giving me a weird feeling knowing that Shadow might have been here. A part of me wants to press the hat to my face and breathe in his scent – connect with him in a small way – but I stop myself. I can't wait to meet him, though I know Mum would totally flip if she knew it was someone I'd met online. She spouts on about all that safety awareness stuff to the kids at her school.

'Stick it out on the front garden wall then, would you, love, while I serve up,' Mum says, grabbing some plates from the cupboard. 'Someone might come back for it.'

I nod and head out of the front door, pressing the cap to my nose, drinking in Shadow's scent, hoping to detect his aftershave or shampoo or his natural scent. But all I can smell is cigarette smoke. It's a bit rank, to be honest, but I still shove the cap up under my baggy sweatshirt, tucking it inside the waistband of my trackie bottoms to keep it from falling out, then I head back inside to eat my dinner.

Later, in my room as my eyes grow heavy trying to solve a maths problem, my laptop pings with a message. I switch windows to Discord, disappointed that it's a message from another gaming friend. She wants to know if I fancy playing Fortnite.

Not rn, I shoot back. *Homework...* I add a couple of skull emojis then I switch back to my chat with Shadow – my last message from just after dinner still unread by him. *Weirdest thing happened*, I'd written. *Found a cap just like yours in my garden. Were you here?* I put a silly wonky-eyed emoji to make it seem like I appreciated his random visit, even though, if I'm honest, I'm a bit creeped out by it.

Then, as I sit staring at his screen name, a green dot flashes up beside his name. He's online. I sit up straight, certain he's about to reply. Minutes pass and I don't take my eyes off his name and his silly cartoon profile pic, the green dot almost sending me cross-eyed as I stare at it. Thankfully, in that moment of deep concentration, the solution to the maths problem comes to mind, but any satisfaction I get from solving it is wiped out by the green dot turning red again.

ShadowKnight184 is offline.

'Damn!' I curse, covering my mouth because I don't want to wake Mum. It's close to midnight. What the *actual*...?

He found time to come online and chat to someone else, but not reply to me. I don't like the simmering feeling inside me – but what I like even less is that it drives me to send him a photo of myself in my swimsuit that one of my friends at swim club took the other day. I don't care that it's got my face in as well as my body, I just want to get his attention.

But after it's sent, as I sit there staring at the red dot by his screen name, the thought that's been on my mind since Mum found the red cap grows even heavier.

How the hell did Shadow know where I live?

TEN
HANNAH

'At last,' I say when the email from Malc Barnes Motors appears in my inbox the moment I get home from work. I was checking in every spare moment during lessons, and it's finally arrived – along with several attached video clips from Malc's CCTV footage.

Hi Hannah, not a mega clear view of the person who fetched your car earlier, but hope this helps. She said she'd got permission and had a spare key. Sorry, we assumed you knew. Account for the repairs is also attached for your attention. Say hi to Rory for me! Malc.

I lean back in my chair. *Say hi to Rory for me.* I've lost count of the number of people who have said similar over the last ten months – most not knowing about the situation, while some forget that Rory has left me. Everyone was so used to us coming as a pair, a matching set, Hannah and Rory. Han and Ror. Mr and Mrs.

I click play on the video, seeing the camera is aimed down at the garage forecourt.

'There,' I say as a car comes into view on the left-hand side of the screen – *my* car.

The black and white footage is grainy and not very clear as I watch my Toyota being driven round from the back of the building.

I squint, trying to catch sight of whoever's at the wheel, but it's difficult to make out because of the camera angle. A woman suddenly becomes visible through the open window but only for a couple of seconds, and it's hard to see her face. I zoom in and play the clip again, this time stopping at the exact moment she turns her head towards the camera.

There... even though the footage isn't in colour, I can see that her hair is blonde – long and slightly wavy. But her features are hard to see. She has on a dark jacket but that's about all I can make out. I press play again and watch her turn left out of the garage and drive off down the street.

I'm disappointed; all I'm able to glean from the video clip is that she could be one of countless women with long blonde hair. But what does she want with *my* car? It's not as though it's valuable. Whatever she's up to, it's made me feel creeped out and violated. It feels like she's targeted me specifically and I have no idea why. Not to mention that I'm still without transport.

I've no idea how I'll convince the police to take me seriously, especially after what happened last Friday with Mila, not to mention all the other times I've had to call them recently about incidents I can't prove. Though at least I have video evidence this time to show that I'm not going completely mad.

Then it occurs to me. The spare key – of *course*!

I leap to my feet and open the kitchen drawer, the one that's stuffed with all kinds of bits and pieces, rummaging through everything, scooping stuff out onto the counter to get a better look. 'I *know* it was in here, right at the back.'

But with the drawer now empty, the spare car key is nowhere to be found. Someone has taken it. My heart thumps and my hand comes up to my mouth when I realise that the woman in the video must have been inside my house.

I never usually drink wine on a school night, but I figure tonight is an exception. It's not like I can drive anywhere. After I made dinner for Jodie, I watched the CCTV video clip a few more times, then I plucked up the courage and reported my car stolen via the non-emergency police line. If nothing else, I'll need a crime reference number for insurance purposes. The call handler took my details, hesitating for a few moments after I gave my name and address, eventually telling me, with a weary tone, that someone would be in touch. I'm not holding my breath – especially not after the last few times I reported incidents when I was made to feel like a nuisance or as if I was losing my mind.

It was the sense that someone had been in my house that drove me to call the police late one night a month ago. However, explaining to the attending officers that I *knew* things had been moved – the pillows rearranged on my bed, food eaten from my fridge, the curtains closed when I swore I'd left them open – had simply made me sound neurotic. 'What is it you want us to do, exactly, Mrs Marlowe?' the officer had asked, arms folded as he stared at me, not having found a scrap of evidence.

And I kicked myself for not getting photos of the car sitting across the street from my house for several nights in a row, the vehicle speeding off the moment I came outside. I never caught sight of the number plate.

As I draw the curtains in the living room now, I glance out at the front garden. 'Oh, good, it's gone,' I say, spotting that someone has claimed the baseball cap from the front wall. I grab my wine glass and drop onto the sofa, desperately needing to relax.

Jodie went back upstairs after dinner – nothing unusual

there. Her brighter mood of the last few days seems to have worn off again. Perhaps the aftershocks of Rory leaving us are still affecting her. The pair were close, and Jodie saw him as her father in all ways apart from genetics. They were into the same things – swimming, maths, designing things. Him leaving so unexpectedly is bound to have left a hole in her life.

I settle on an episode of *Grand Designs* but quickly mute the volume when I hear a noise outside – the sound of a car pulling up. I go to the window, peeling back the curtains, not quite able to see the street because of the hedge. Stupidly, and despite everything that he's done, I don't suppose I'll ever stop hoping that it'll be Rory when I hear a noise – that he wants to come home, maybe sort things out, realising he made a terrible mistake or has had a midlife crisis or some other kind of mental breakdown. I don't know how I'd feel or what I'd do if he ever did knock at my door, but it might provide me with closure at least, the answers I've been longing for.

I freeze, cocking my head to the front door. Someone is definitely out there, fiddling with the letterbox. My heart thumps as I put down my wine and go to the hallway, about to peer through the spyhole, when I tread on something hard, making me squeal and jump back. A single black car key with the Toyota logo on the key fob is lying on the doormat.

'What the hell?' I rush to the front window again, standing on the armchair to see if I can get a glimpse of anyone, but all I can see is the roof of a metallic blue car outside my house – a car that looks very much like mine.

I shove on my shoes and unlock the front door, dashing down the front path, looking up and down the street and confirming that my car is indeed parked right outside my house. But there's no one to be seen, just the flap of a dark coloured coat disappearing around the corner.

'Wait! Hey you, stop!' I yell out, flinging open the front gate and chasing after them, praying I don't fall flat on my face in these slip-on clogs – not ideal footwear for a pursuit. But when I get around the corner, there's no one there. Only the tail lights of another car disappearing down the street.

I drop forwards, breathless, hands on my knees as my heart pounds in my chest. I'm shaking and panting, desperate to know who it was yet terrified that this person, whoever they are, is intent on messing with my mind. And they're doing a good job. I walk slowly back to my house, clutching my arms around my body, looking back over my shoulder and scanning around to see if anyone is following or watching me. I won't sleep a wink tonight now.

'Mrs Kirk?' I say, spotting the old lady who lives in the house next to mine peeking out of her front door, looking nervous.

'Hello, dear,' she says, her eyes flashing around. 'Is everything OK? I heard someone out here, then there was shouting.'

'Someone was at my door,' I say, trying to hide the tremor in my voice, not wanting to worry her. 'You didn't see anyone, did you?'

'You mean that woman?'

I nod. 'What did she look like?'

'I only got a glimpse, but she was quite tall with blonde hair. She rushed off before I saw her properly, sorry.'

Mrs Kirk's description matches that of the woman on the CCTV. I have no idea who she is, let alone any clue why she took my car. But whatever the reason, I'll be double-checking all the windows and doors before I go up to bed tonight.

I head out onto the street again and walk around my car, checking it for damage. Oddly, it's the opposite – the bodywork is gleaming and seems newly polished. It was muddy and dirty when I dropped it off at Malc's last week.

I peer inside the window, cupping my hands to the glass. It

takes me a moment to focus, but I can't help the gasp when I see a single white rose left on the driver's seat, its head snapped off and the petals scattered around the thorny stem.

ELEVEN
HANNAH

Since Rory left, I've become something of a recluse. Thinking back over our time together, analysing and picking apart what might have gone wrong, what I could have done differently, has become my new pastime. It's night times that are worst, or early evening when Jodie is out at an activity and I'm left with nothing but the washing-up and my thoughts.

The white rose left in my car reminds me of when Rory and I first met – or should I say, *re*-met in our early thirties after we'd dated briefly at university – because he often bought me roses, always accompanied by a new reason for loving me. As I sit in my living room now, the sinister rose petals and thorny stalk from my car lying on the sofa beside me, I can't stop the memories flooding back.

'You look so beautiful pregnant...' he said to me once, even though I wasn't showing at that point. He held me so gently, hardly daring to touch me or even breathe on me. *In case you break...* he'd said.

It was hard to believe that that particular baby had started life in a Petri dish – the first time we'd had an IVF embryo implanted successfully. But soon after, I had indeed broken, and I was left searching for a reason why our little baby had decided to leave my body in such a heart-breaking and messy way.

I'd been teaching my year fives when I felt it – a loosening of my insides. A series of increasingly painful cramps followed by a feeling of desolation and emptiness. A quiet resignation that something wasn't right. I phoned reception. Asked for them to send someone to supervise my class while I slipped out to the toilets. I didn't say that I suspected I was miscarrying because we hadn't told anyone I was pregnant yet. One of the young PE teachers came sauntering into the classroom to fill in for me, a weary look on his face because I'd interrupted his break.

I phoned Rory. He was at the school within half an hour, and I was lying on a couch in the hospital having an ultrasound scan an hour after that.

'I'm so sorry,' the sonographer said without looking either of us in the eye. 'I can't find a heartbeat.'

Later that night as we lay in bed, me with a heat pack on my belly, Rory staring up at the ceiling in the dark, he said, 'Do you think it's the combination of us together that nature doesn't like? My DNA and your DNA – a toxic mix?'

I couldn't even begin to answer, but he triggered a cascade of thoughts as I lay there, a tear rolling down my cheek. How was it that Lewis and I were able to conceive all those years ago when we hadn't even planned to have a baby – yes, I admit, Jodie was a drunken mistake that I loved dearly from the moment I knew of her existence – yet Rory and I, who had been trying to conceive for years now, could not even produce a single embryo that wanted to stick around? What were we doing wrong?

Being practical, I suppose I wasn't getting any younger as the doctor kept reminding us, and when we were trying to conceive naturally, we'd been told that Rory's sperm count wasn't ideal either. Several years before, Jodie had arrived without complication after I'd been pursued relentlessly by her cocksure yet infuriatingly attractive father. Lewis was the type who charmed the snake *and* the snake charmer. All through my pregnancy with Jodie, while I'd lived with my parents and worked shifts at the supermarket and the pub (my art degree had, at that point in my life, proved worthless), Lewis had flitted in and out of my life, leaving me not knowing if or when I'd see him next.

'All depends, chick,' was his stock phrase as he kissed me goodbye on my doorstep after gracing me with his presence for a couple of days, my ever-growing bump becoming a bolster between us.

'Depends on *what*?' I used to ask, but I never got a serious reply.

It could be later that day, the next week or another two months before I'd see him again, and as I got close to my due date and gave up work for maternity leave, I warned him that our baby would be here soon. I'd pretty much resigned myself to giving birth without him and was considering asking my mum and a friend to be with me when the time came.

'I'll be there, I'll *be* there...' he insisted. 'But I've got this job up north...' He'd bent down and kissed my tummy, whispering to our baby all the things he was going to buy her. We already knew we were having a girl. 'Daddy's little angel, that's what you're going to be. I'm going to spoil you rotten,' were Lewis's words to her before he disappeared into the night leaving a trail of cigarette smoke behind him.

And indeed, he did spoil things for Jodie, though not in the way he originally intended. Three days later, while I was panting my way through my first meticulously timed contractions, frantically trying to reach Lewis, I eventually gave up and called Mum and my friend instead. In my heart of hearts, I always knew Lewis would never be present at Jodie's birth. Just like I figured he would never be present in her life.

As I held our little girl in my arms for the first time, I felt so sad that her daddy would never see our little angel grow up, that beer and cash-in-hand jobs wherever the wind took him were his main priority. I promised my baby that we would do just fine alone – me and her. A happy little team of two.

And indeed, we did do well – with Mum childminding while I worked hard, saving up, eventually securing the job of my dreams as an art teacher at St Peter's, a prep school in my hometown. It was just a junior role back then, but it was a start – a start I was proud of – and it wasn't long before I was able to put a down payment on a home for Jodie and me, albeit a modest terraced house. We still live there today.

When Jodie was two and a half, by pure chance and not long after we'd moved in here, I bumped into Rory while on a rare night out with a friend. We hadn't seen each other since our early twenties when we graduated from university – a period of my life I prefer not to think about after everything that happened – but he'd moved back to the area to be close to his ageing parents. Our relationship picked up so naturally from where we'd left off that it seemed like fate had brought us back together – though I'd done my best to block out the reasons why we'd parted company in the first place.

Despite him being something of a reminder of those times, dating Rory for a second time almost a decade later still felt like slipping into a comfy pair of slippers. It was another chance at a familiar love, yet still had the excitement of a new relationship. Though in those early days of getting to know each other again, neither of us mentioned the *terrible thing* that had happened a couple of months before graduation. It sat like a dark shadow between us.

I sigh, gathering up the rose petals and crushing them in my fist before dumping them in the bin. I should probably tell the police that my car has mysteriously come back, that someone left a torn-up rose on the driver's seat – but they'll just think I'm mad like they did before, suggesting that I need to get some help. And as I flick off all the lights and head up to bed, I can't help wondering if they'd be right.

TWELVE
HANNAH

I drove into work this morning, though I'd been reluctant to use my car with that woman being the last person to drive it. I racked my brains, desperate to work out who she is, if she's someone I know. The thought of a friend – or even an acquaintance – doing this to me makes me feel on edge and violated. I've gone through everyone I know, even the mums at school, wondering if I've upset anyone, as well as distant relatives who I've perhaps forgotten to send a Christmas card to, but no one springs to mind.

Even though the car had been valeted and is spotless (strange in itself), it still feels contaminated. When I arrived at school earlier, I convinced myself that I could smell her perfume, and when I found one of her blonde hairs on the head-rest, I felt repulsed. Stupidly, I'd plucked it off and dropped it on the ground, not thinking that the police might want it.

'Have you heard anything else from Mila's nanny... or her mother?' I ask Kim at the end of the school day, stopping in at her classroom on my way out. Mila hasn't been in school *again*. I can't stop thinking about her. I just need answers... who took her from my house? And what is wrong with her?

'Sorry, no. The office might have had a call,' Kim says, only half listening as she's focused on her laptop. 'Why?' She glances up, peering at me over the top of her glasses.

'I've got some of her paintings in the art room, that's all.'

Kim tips her head at me, a wrinkle forming at the top of her nose. 'Are you worried?'

'A little,' I say, knowing that's an understatement. 'Madeline's on a fact-finding mission.' I pull a face. We both know our head teacher doesn't let up when she has the bit between her teeth. 'She was asking me what I knew for the social services referral following the police welfare check.'

I'm praying it doesn't come out that the check was triggered because of me.

'Shame, poor little mite,' Kim says, swinging round in her chair to face me. 'Best to be overcautious in these cases. I don't think there's a dad on the scene. Seems like a massive house for just the two of them.'

'Does the nanny live in with them?'

'I suppose she must,' Kim says. 'I've heard Mila's mum is often away for work. What money can buy, eh?' She snorts a laugh, though we both know that many of the families who send their children to St Peter's live lives that we can only dream of – massive houses, chauffeurs, nannies, holiday homes.

'See you tomorrow then,' I say to Kim, giving her a half-hearted wave as I leave, thinking that no amount of money can buy a loving mother for Mila.

She's such a sweet little girl with a vivid imagination, and many times I've had to fight my motherly instincts in class not to pick her up, give her a cuddle, wash her face and brush her hair. When I've been on lunch duty, I've made sure she's had an extra-large portion because she looks like she needs feeding up. And I always choose her to ring the hand bell at the end of playtime. She loves doing it, giving me a beaming smile as it chimes – a moment of happiness for her.

If only I'd fought my instincts harder and not taken her home that afternoon.

I sigh, knowing I should have reported my concerns about Mila, adhering to procedure rather than acting on my emotions. If I had, then maybe she'd be back in school now and... I shake my head, knowing these thoughts aren't helpful as I go out of the main school building towards the staff car park, faltering as I spot the navy-blue van outside the playground entrance again. The sun is reflecting off the windscreen, and whoever's inside quickly winds the window up. A rush of adrenaline surges through me.

'Hey, you!' I call out, charging over to confront the driver, but before I get there, the engine starts and the car pulls away, speeding off before I can make a note of the number plate. As I get my breath back, I can't help wondering that with Mila still not in school, and the way the driver seemed to be looking in my direction, it's not Mila he's interested in at all. I can't help thinking it might be *me*.

Back at my car, my mind is made up. I can't just do nothing – with everything else that's happened, that van lurking around is freaking me out. Besides, if anything happened to one of the kids at school, I'd never forgive myself. This time, I make the police report anonymously, dialling 141 to conceal my phone number, and I don't give out my name when asked.

After I hang up, I drive off in the same direction as the blue van, just in case it stopped up ahead or is parked on a driveway somewhere along the route out of town. Though I don't know what I plan on doing if I spot it. I can hardly confront a male driver alone. But it feels as if I'm doing *something* at least, and I'll send an email to the head teacher to let her know, too.

I grip the wheel tightly, my eyes scanning the road ahead. There are only a couple of side turns down no-through residential streets in this area, so he's unlikely to have gone down there unless he's hiding, waiting until I've gone. But instinct tells me to continue on, and it's not long before I'm on the edge of town and heading out towards the coastal route – a beautiful drive where, in a few miles, the road skirts closer to the cliffs. It's also where Ocean Heights is located – the gated community that Rory and I had our sights set on.

'God, what if the van is heading up there?' I say to myself, thinking that if he *is* interested in Mila, then maybe he knows where she lives?

I press the accelerator harder, skimming the upper end of the speed limit until I'm on the open road, where I properly put my foot down. The juddering in the steering wheel seems to have been fixed by the garage – the reason it went for repairs in the first place – but the engine now seems to be making a strange noise, not running as smoothly as usual.

It's only three miles or so to the new houses, and I take the sweeping bends as fast as I dare, hoping I'll catch up with the van. As I approach the headland that juts out, forming the wide bay below Ocean Heights, I slow down before turning right and heading towards the coast.

There's no sign of the blue van as I approach the grand entrance to Ocean Heights – double-width wrought-iron gates at least seven feet high. I pull into the entryway and sit with the engine ticking over, wondering what to do. The gates are flanked by sweeping stone walls and there's an intercom system where visitors can buzz whoever they're visiting. I'm not sure which one is Mila's house.

Beyond the gates, I see the wide road weaving through the development, past the large glass-fronted properties, each one angled towards the coast and carefully designed so that every plot has an uninterrupted view of the sea. I can't help wondering which ones Rory had a hand in designing.

'Imagine living here,' I whisper, suddenly feeling tearful.

Then, just as I'm about to reverse out of the gateway to head home, I spot another car about to leave Ocean Heights, the gates slowly swinging open as it approaches. A shiny black Mercedes cruises through, making me slide down in my seat in the hope the driver doesn't notice me. There's enough room for them to pass without me having to move, but as the car draws up along-side me, the blonde-haired woman behind the wheel stops, lowering her window and shouting something in my direction.

THIRTEEN

Before

Hannah could count on one hand the number of bad or sullen moods Rory had got himself into during the time they were together – fourteen years, three months and twenty-seven days this time, if you count the day he walked out on her, which she did (though they'd known each other since they were at university).

In those early days last year when the police were looking for him, she couldn't bring herself to say 'disappeared' or 'missing' because that made it sound as if death was a possibility. In those first terrifying hours, days and weeks of Rory's absence, it felt as though the discovery of his body was imminent.

Stop it! Stop it! Stop it!

Every time the catastrophic thoughts came, Hannah had to force them from her mind to dispel the living nightmare.

But it was the lack of prior blots in Rory's copybook that troubled Hannah the most. If he'd had previous form for being moody or unstable or selfish or even capable of having an affair and betraying her, then it would go some way to explaining him leaving without warning. But as things stood, there were only a few times that she could remember when Rory had been properly upset or angry.

The first that she could remember was one evening about six years ago after he'd come home from a work conference. He'd been away for three days with the other partners at Draper Ford, schmoozing clients and presenting their latest designs. While she didn't say anything initially, Hannah sensed there was something *off* about her husband's behaviour on his return, as though he had something on his mind – and not because of work. Something that was weighing him down, yet hard to pinpoint.

Hannah never once suspected it was another woman – she knew Rory would never cheat on her. For a start, she was able to read him like a book, and he'd never be able to hide the guilt. No, what Hannah sensed in her husband was *fear*. A raw and primal threat to the very fabric of his life. She had no idea why, and when she probed him, he immediately shut her down, making her feel paranoid and silly.

There was another instance around that time, when they were processing the empty and desolate feelings they'd been left with after yet another round of IVF had failed, and they'd decided to freeze their embryos. In fact, it was as Hannah was trying to explain how she was feeling that Rory had turned on her.

'I think of them every day,' was all she'd said to trigger the outburst, referring to their embryos as they'd been eating lunch at their favourite café.

'For God's sake, Hannah,' Rory had said, leaning forwards across the table. 'I really don't want to waste yet another Saturday discussing IV bloody F. Can't we just talk about something else?'

Hannah had stared at him. This was the first time she'd seen him so... bitter about their attempts to conceive. They'd decided to wait a year before trying again, and she'd always believed Rory to be on her side, of never giving up hope, of always holding out for one more attempt at getting pregnant before they gave up entirely. These remaining embryos were their final chance. They just needed to save up enough money for one more attempt.

The rest of their lunch had been filled with awkward small talk about anything other than babies with Rory grunting in reply, followed by an outburst when they were back in the car.

'Why is it always the women, eh?' he'd snapped, thumping the driver's side window as he sat at the wheel. 'The women who get all the attention and sympathy and the condolences. You think this is only about *you*? How are men supposed to deal with this?'

'Rory, I know—'

'But that's the thing, you *don't* know, do you? You don't have a bloody clue how it feels to be me in this situation.' More thumping the car with his fists, a deep growl resonating in his throat – so much so that Hannah had felt compelled to get out and walk the short distance home. She needed to clear her head.

If this was what freezing their embryos had done to him, she wondered how he would be if, when the time came, they failed to go full term yet again. It would be their last chance. She wasn't getting any younger and it was the clinician who'd advised they take a temporary break from IVF, not to mention the many tens of thousands of pounds they'd so far spent and the strain that had put on their relationship. Every year that passed was one year closer to having to face facts – that they'd never conceive a child together.

Three days of the silent treatment had followed that particular upset, followed by a couple of weeks of unusually sullen behaviour from Rory.

'You're going out again?' Hannah had queried one evening. It was 7 p.m. several months later, and she'd just put dinner on the table. Rory had come downstairs in a suit and tie, grabbing his car keys and wallet.

'I already told you. Client dinner.' Then he turned and left.

Hannah was certain he hadn't told her. She never forgot things like that. She hadn't forgotten that they were still saving up for the next round of IVF, either, though it seemed Rory had when, a couple of days later, she happened to check their joint account to see how far away from the target they were. But the money had all gone – four and a half thousand pounds transferred out of their account the week before.

'Relax,' was all Rory said when she confronted him the next morning. 'I moved it to an account with a better interest rate.'

'Without telling me?' Hannah knew she'd not filled out any forms to open a new joint one. 'What account?'

'An account I already had before we met,' Rory replied, shaking his head and getting on with pumping up his bike tyres before heading out on a ride. 'I'm getting nearly five per cent interest now instead of the three and a half in our joint account. What do you think I'm going to do, run off with it?' He'd laughed before tearing off on his bike.

The only other incident she could recall that might possibly have a bearing on him leaving was a phone call early last year about six months before he vanished for good. In hindsight, Hannah wondered if he'd been a bit different since then – different with *her*, not anyone else. As though there was something on his mind. Though she might have been clutching at straws, knowing how desperate she was for answers since Rory had left.

It was the final words of that phone call, though – the call he'd gone outside the restaurant to take the night they were having dinner with Mitch and Jan to celebrate the couple's anniversary – that played on her mind. Rory had been gone a while, ducking outside when No Caller ID had flashed up on his phone. The others were ordering desserts, wanting to know

Rory's choice, so on the way back from the ladies' room, Hannah had nipped outside to find him.

The freezing January air hit her face, making her wrap her arms around her body. Her coat was in the restaurant. At first, she didn't spot Rory as he'd wandered further up the street, his back to her. It was the foggy puffs of air coming from his mouth, illuminated by the streetlight, that she noticed first, wondering if they were the result of angry words given the heavy gesticulating of his right arm.

She approached Rory's shadowy figure, dressed all in black, as he paced about the edge of the harbour. Hannah grinned, thinking how tall and handsome he looked against the backdrop of twinkling harbour lights, the familiar chorus of the sailing boat ropes clanking against the masts in the breeze. Such a perfect scene.

She sidled up to him – him still unaware of her presence as he pressed his phone to his ear – and she was about to wrap her arms around his waist from behind, surprise him, but then the words shot out of his mouth like bullets. Bullets that hit her right in the heart. Bullets that are still lodged there today.

'OK, OK... but I've got to go now. I love you so much, my darling...'

FOURTEEN

HANNAH

I put down my car window so I can hear what the woman who has just come through the Ocean Heights gates is saying. But judging by the expression on her face, I don't think it's pleasant.

'This is a private road!' she calls through her open window, scowling at me. 'What are you doing here?' Her face is perfectly made-up and she's wearing a soft peach lip gloss. Her cheekbones high and her sharp jaw defined, while her long blonde hair hangs over her shoulders. Even though I can only see the top half of her, it's clear she's well turned-out.

'I'm sorry,' is all I can manage in reply as her eyes scan over me and my car.

'Do you have a reason for being here?' she says, still sounding haughty.

'I... I...'

Maybe I should tell her that I'm just admiring the houses, that my husband and I once had a crazy dream to build our home up here – the plot tucked away at the back with the wooded area behind it was the one we had our sights set on – but that she mustn't worry, I'm leaving now...

'Oh... are you OK?' she asks. Then, to my horror, she opens

her car door and gets out. And to even more of my horror, I realise that I have tears in my eyes. 'You seem upset.'

I sniff, wiping a finger under my eye. 'Sorry, no, I'm fine. Just a bad day, that's all.' I let out a little laugh. 'And... and hay fever.'

'Sorry to hear that,' the woman says, sounding far less confrontational now. 'Who have you come to visit?' she asks. 'I'll buzz you through.'

'I'm visiting the Westons,' I blurt out.

You idiot! I scream in my head.

'I'm... I'm Mila's godmother,' I add, only making things worse. My stomach churns as I inwardly curse myself – she could be Mila's mother for all I know! I have no idea what she looks like.

But the woman's face relaxes. 'Oh... little Mila is just adorable!' she says. 'My Saffy loves it when she comes to play. Last time she was over, they baked cookies together. She's always so polite. But it must be so hard, you know...' She pulls a pained face, as though she's said too much.

Relief floods through me. I should have realised that everyone is bound to know everyone in such a small, exclusive development. Then I wonder if this is the woman who had Mila over for a sleepover – perhaps the woman who took her from my house. Goosebumps spread up my arms.

'In what way?' I ask, hoping she'll continue. Any extra information about Mila could be useful and help explain her absence from school all week. I want to believe she's still poorly, but I'm not convinced. The more time that passes without the police believing my story, the more guilty I will appear if something *has* happened to her. Despite the welfare check, part of me wonders if they somehow located the wrong child given there's been no sign of her since.

'It must be hard with no father on the scene,' the woman says, lowering her voice even though no one else is about.

'Well, no one *consistent*, anyway,' she says with a disapproving face.

'Must be tough,' I reply, hoping she'll continue with her drip feed.

She pulls a cashmere cardigan around her tiny waist, her blonde hair whipping about in the breeze. 'Poor Mila seems quite troubled sometimes,' she says. 'I think she feels a bit different to the other kids.'

'It's tough for her,' I chip in, thinking it sounds like the right thing to say. Though I really want to tell her that I've noticed it too, that she seems troubled, especially when an image of Mila's painting flashes into my mind. The two dark figures in the woods, the bright red blood... I look over at the wooded area behind the development, wondering if it's the forest in Mila's picture.

'And that nanny of theirs...' the woman continues, blowing out through perfectly straight, white teeth, shaking her head. 'Anyway, look. I've said far too much already. Do you want me to buzz Eastcliff House for you? They're number six on the panel.' She points to the intercom system.

'Oh... um, sure, thanks. Though they're not really expecting me.' I grip the steering wheel until my knuckles turn white, shocked at how easily the lies come.

The woman smiles and presses buzzer number six. Then it strikes me. I think it's the same plot of land that Rory and I were set on buying – the only plot that we could possibly even think of affording as it was set a bit further back from the sea and slightly smaller than the others. We loved the seclusion of the woodland behind it, but it still had amazing views of the channel.

'No reply,' the woman says, waiting for a voice to come through the speaker. 'Maybe they're in the garden. I'll let you in with the code anyway, and you can ring her doorbell when you're at the house.'

'Thank you,' I say, feeling apprehensive. Ridiculously, I'll have to pretend to know where I'm going in case she watches me drive in. It all seems so different now that the houses have been built.

Before the development was fenced off for building, Rory and I used to come up and imagine ourselves living here. We'd bring a picnic and a bottle of wine and stroll around the site, laying out with twigs and stones where we'd build our house – planning which would be our room, Jodie's room (or entire teenage pad as she'd requested), and of course we planned out where the nursery would go. Then we'd amble over towards the clifftop and spread out our picnic blanket, sitting and taking in the views as we ate.

I watch as the woman punches in the four-digit code with a perfectly manicured finger.

Seven one eight nine.

I say the numbers over and over in my head several times – 7189, 7189, 7189 – forcing myself to remember.

'Say hi to Mila and her mum from me,' the woman chimes, getting back in her car. '*If the poor child's mother is even there...*' she mutters under her breath. 'I'm Nicole, by the way.'

'I'll tell her,' I say, giving her a brief wave as the huge wrought-iron gates swing open and I drive on through.

FIFTEEN

I cruise down the road between the exclusive houses of Ocean Heights. Each property is different, but all have sea views and sweeping in-and-out driveways.

I don't know what Rory and I were thinking, aspiring to live up here. The homes seem about as far out of reach for us as living on the dark side of the moon. Rory is – *was...?* I don't know anymore – on a good salary, though in the last few years of our relationship he always ran short each month, blaming his ex-wife's past debts and other financial commitments for his money never lasting. His photo and bio are still on the Draper Ford website, so I assume he still works there, but despite checking a few times as well as calling and trying to get information out of the partners, who were reluctant to tell me anything, I've never spotted his car in their car park.

While my teacher's pay has never been huge, between us we'd hoped to secure a self-build mortgage. I'd planned on selling my little house to put towards the deposit and Rory was banking on his inheritance to add to the pot, but still... seeing these grand homes with my own eyes now, there's no way on this earth that we'd have been able to keep up with the Joneses. Or the *Nicoles*, I think.

I scan the property names – *Westwood House... White Cliff Lodge... Oakmoor...* each one worth, at a guess, anything upward of a million pounds. Rory and I would have been way out of our depth, even with him designing the house himself.

I glance in my rear-view mirror, seeing that Nicole has driven off. Up ahead, where the road curves round towards the woods, the final house on the development comes into view. It's a little less grand than the others, though still gorgeous, and probably my favourite with its white picket fence surrounding the neat front lawn. It still has amazing sea views, but the frontage appears much more... homely, with its traditional-style windows and canopied front porch.

'Eastcliff House,' I read. Mila and her mother's house. And Mila's nanny, Zayla, I think, wondering if she lives here, too. There's a small white Fiat parked on the drive – the only car there – perhaps belonging to the nanny. I imagine Mila's mother would drive something much flasher – a big four-wheel drive or maybe something sportier like a BMW.

As it happens, I don't have to wait long to find out. A young woman comes out of the house – early to mid-twenties by the looks of it – and walks towards the Fiat while staring down at her phone. She's got shoulder-length jet-black hair with blonde and pink streaks running through it. It whips around her face in the sea breeze, making her swipe it out of the way. She's wearing black lacy fingerless gloves, ripped jeans, Doc Marten boots that reach halfway up her calves, and a tasselled suede waistcoat over a faded grey T-shirt. Her forearms are covered in tattoos and bangles.

It's then that I realise I've stopped right across the driveway, blocking her exit. I put my car into reverse to drive off before she spots me, but, in my panic, my foot slips off the clutch and I stall the engine. Cursing, I quickly start it up again, turning the key a second time when it doesn't catch immediately. Then a third, and a fourth...

'Not now, not *now*,' I groan, closing my eyes. I turn the key again, praying the engine will start, but this time it barely makes any sound at all. Just a clicking noise as I turn the key. 'Dammit!' I thump the steering wheel and check out of the window to see if there's enough room for the Fiat to squeeze past. But there isn't, as proven when she pulls up to the edge of the drive, tooting her horn for me to move.

I hold up a palm to tell her to hang on as I try to get my car going again, realising that I'll have to go and speak to her. My car has no intention of starting. If she's the nanny, I'm hoping that she won't recognise me from school, especially as I don't remember her from the playground pick-ups.

I go up to her open window. 'Hi... I'm so sorry,' I begin. 'I was... well, I got a bit lost and was about to leave, but then my car stalled and now the stupid thing won't start. It's been at the garage recently and they can't have fixed it properly and—'

'It's cool,' she says, looking up at me through eyes ringed heavily with dark eyeliner. 'I'll wait. I'm not in a hurry.'

'OK, thank you, I'm so sorry,' I say once more, rushing back to my car to try again. Perhaps it will start this time. But no – as I sit half in and half out of the driver's seat, the key just clicks when I turn it. I pop the bonnet and open it up, peering into the engine as if whatever is wrong with it will become obvious when I have no idea what I'm looking for.

'Sounds like the starter motor to me,' a voice says. I swing round to see the girl peering over my shoulder.

'You know about engines?'

'It helps having a mechanic for a boyfriend.' She smiles, showing me she's pretty beneath all the make-up.

'That's handy,' I say, eyeing her vehicle. 'For when you need repairs.'

'That's not actually my car. It's my boss's.'

'Oh?' I say, wondering if she's going to be as chatty as Nicole at the gate. 'A company car?'

'No, it's to run the kid around in,' she says, her mouth breaking into a sly smile as she points back at the house. 'I'm the nanny,' she quickly adds. 'To a little girl.'

'I'm probably keeping you from fetching her,' I say, frowning down at the engine again. 'I don't want you to get into trouble.'

'It's fine,' the nanny replies. 'The kid's at after-school club. And... and her mum's away on business.'

'I see...' I say thoughtfully, my dead car now the least important thing on my mind. 'Does after-school club finish soon?' I ask, knowing exactly what time it ends – 6 p.m. And I also know that Mila isn't *in* after-school club today because she wasn't even at school in the first place. 'I'll have to call a breakdown service to sort my car,' I say. 'But so you can get out, would you help me push it out of the way for now?'

'School is pretty chill about what time I fetch her,' the nanny tells me. 'Look, I've got an idea. Pop your boot open,' she says, striding round to the back of my car.

Knowing that's not true, that the school has a strict policy on pick-up times, I follow her round to my boot. She roots around inside, lifting the carpeted floor to reveal the spare tyre and tool kit.

'This should do it,' she says, pulling out a wrench and holding it up. 'Get in and turn the key when I tell you.'

'Ok*aay*,' I say, willing to give anything a try. The last thing I want is for anyone to know that I was hanging around outside the house of the child I took from school.

From inside the car, I hear a clanking and banging sound coming from under the bonnet. 'Try now!' the nanny calls out. 'Start her up!'

I do as I'm told and, surprisingly, the engine sounds a bit more life-like.

'Hold on,' she calls out. More clanking, then she yells for me to try again.

This time, my car starts. It sounds a bit rough at first – but *thank God*, it's going.

'You're a genius!' I say when she comes round to the driver's door.

'A tip I picked up from my boyfriend. He works down at Malc's Motors in town. They're really good. I think you're gonna need a new starter motor, but this will tide you over for now. Pop in and see Dave and tell him Zayla sent you.' The girl gives me a broad grin, exposing a tongue piercing, and waves as she walks back to her Fiat.

Before she gets inside, she stops and turns. 'Which house were you looking for, anyway?' she calls out. 'Maybe I can help.'

There's no way I'm explaining what I'm doing here, so without replying, I ram my car into reverse, taking extra care not to stall it this time, and drive off towards the entrance gates, relieved when they open automatically.

In my mirror, I see Zayla following me in her white Fiat, but, once we're up at the junction with the main road, she turns the opposite direction to the way I'm heading – the way back to town, the way back home, and the exact same way she should be heading, too, if she had any intention of picking Mila up from school.

SIXTEEN
JODIE

I want to see you is the message that I wake to from Shadow. It's taken him long enough to reply, and I'm tempted to make him wait for my answer, though if I do that I won't be able to concentrate at school. It's maths test day today – the test that I've done pretty much zero revision for. Death by algebra.

Me too... I start typing, sitting at my desk in my pyjama shorts and T-shirt. I'm desperate to know what he thought of the photo, though I did feel a bit silly after sending it. What if he shows his mates? I mean, it's no different to him seeing me at the beach or the pool, but out of context it could be taken the wrong way.

When are you free? I type just as I see Shadow come online. *Where shall we hook up?* But I quickly delete the 'hook up' bit and replace it with 'meet'. I bite my nails as I wait for his reply. *Was that red baseball cap yours?* I add, because he still hasn't told me.

You shouldn't send pics like that, you know... Shadow replies, instantly making me feel stupid.

You didn't like it?

It's not that, he types. *Don't share pics like that. Who else have you sent it to?*

No one! I type fast. *I was in my swimsuit fgs.*

Promise me you won't do it again. Ever?

I stare at my screen, wondering whether to feel annoyed with him – he's not the boss of me and can't tell me what to do – or if I should feel grateful that he cares about me so much.

Sorry, I type. *I thought you'd like it.*

It's a dangerous world out there. You've got to protect your-self. I can teach you.

And that's when I crush on Shadow just a little bit more.

Thank you, I type, desperate to tell him how I feel, though I figure that's best saved for when we meet in person.

Mum's going out tonight. Why don't you come round here?

I don't go to maths class. There's no way I'll pass the test. In fact, I decide not to go into school full stop. Instead, I wait for Mum to go to work, convincing her I'll get the bus, then I head off down to the row of shops a couple of streets away. I buy a sandwich and a drink for later, then walk down to the river in town, following the path all the way to where it runs behind the industrial estate on the northern edge of town.

The consequences of bunking off school are bad, I know that, especially on the day of an important test. I grabbed my school bag on the way out – maybe I'll sit by the river and try to catch up with some work – but also to make it look like I'm going in if anyone sees me. Mum would have a shit fit if she knew. But that's not as bad as being unable to answer a single question in the subject I'm meant to be good at and getting a roasting at the parents' evening next week.

Mum and Rory have always had high hopes that I'd do well in my A levels, go on to study architecture or design or something like that. I think Mum had a secret hankering that I'd follow in her foot-steps and do art, but here I am throwing stones into the river because there's not much else to do around here when you're skipping school and need to keep a low profile for the day. And I daren't go home in case Mum comes back unexpectedly like last Friday.

I wander around, so bored, and end up at the back of a disused warehouse, rattling the metal doors to see what's inside. But they're padlocked, so there's no way I'm getting in to have a nose about or find shelter if it rains. The sky has turned a murky shade of grey in the last half hour.

I spot a couple of plastic crates so drag them over to the warehouse wall, stacking them on top of each other, balancing on top to peer in through a small window. It's covered in cobwebs and is dark inside, but I can just make out a massive space with old machinery and conveyor belts, as well as piles of timber. In one area, there's a load of cardboard boxes stacked up.

I jump down and walk around the side of the warehouse, finding a concrete forecourt covered in weeds, litter and old pallets. Then I spot a narrow passageway down the other side of the warehouse, so I duck down it, expecting to emerge back somewhere near the water. But there's a six-foot metal fence at the end stopping me from getting through. As I turn to head back, I see another door in the side of the warehouse – this time without a padlock. In fact, there isn't even a handle on the outside, and when I kick it, it springs open with a loud clank, slamming back against the warehouse wall.

I freeze, listening out. Nothing – apart from the reverberations. Then silence.

I go inside, my eyes slowly growing used to the dark.

'Oo-oh!' I call out, listening to my echo. '*Ooh! Ooh! Oooh!*' I cry again in sharp bursts, laughing at the sound of my own voice bouncing back at me in the vast space. I walk over to what looks like a sleeping dinosaur but is actually some kind of abandoned machinery.

Then I freeze, my feet scuffing to a stop on the dusty concrete floor.

I cock my ears, listening out. I heard something. No mistake.

There. Again.

My heart beats fast as I hurry towards the machine, ducking down and hiding behind it. It's coming from the opposite side of the building to where I came in.

There – over there...

I peek out of my hiding place, squinting over to an area of the warehouse that's been partitioned off, forming what was probably once an office or staff room.

And there it is again – the noise, coming from inside the room, and it sounds like... like someone is crying. Someone thumping and banging and sobbing.

But way worse than that – the *someone* sounds just like a child.

SEVENTEEN
HANNAH

I drive down into town feeling shaken up from being caught red-handed at Mila's house. What an idiot I was to go to Ocean Heights in the first place. But I'm mainly feeling shaken because Zayla lied about Mila's whereabouts – and she didn't seem that bothered about fetching her. I know for a fact that she wasn't in school today, and therefore she can't be at after-school club, which all adds to my theory that something isn't right. I have no idea what to make of it all.

I can't help thinking that Zayla is covering something up, but if so, what? Or was she simply muddled with the days, meaning that Mila is at another club this afternoon? With all the classes and activities that kids go to, it's a possibility.

I glance at the car clock – 5.40 p.m. There's still time to check. I indicate left and turn down a side street, and in a few minutes I pull up outside school. I dash inside, heading down the corridor towards the assembly hall where the after-school club for Mila's age group is located, suddenly realising that even though I'm staff, I'm still going to need a reason for bursting in when I've already left work.

'Oh, hi,' I say to one of the supervisors, Elaine. I don't know her well but recognise her from the staff room. 'You haven't seen, um, a... a grey coat lying about, have you? I think I left it in here the other day... in assembly.'

'I've not seen one, sorry,' she says, her eyes scanning around. 'You're from the art department, right?'

Thankfully, a couple of the girls come up to me, chiming, 'Hello, Mrs Marlowe,' in a cute way, making me turn and give them a smile – putting the supervisor's mind at rest that they know me. I scan around the room, pretending to look for my jacket, when really, I'm scouring the kids' faces for Mila. I check again. There are about twenty or so children here – but none are Mila.

'I must have left it at home,' I say, giving one last sweep around the large hall. Definitely no Mila. 'It's a good-sized group you've got. Is... is everyone here?'

The supervisor looks surprised by my question.

'A parent asked me about wraparound care the other day, that's all,' I say. 'I promised I'd ask about it for her.'

'They'd need to go through the office for details,' she replies. 'We're generally full at this time of year. Parents need to apply in advance of the September term.'

She doesn't exactly answer my question. 'Is everyone here today?' I ask, pushing my luck, pointing around the children.

A puzzled expression sweeps over her face as she shrugs. 'A couple of absences,' she tells me in a way that's clear she wants me to leave.

On the way out, I duck into the girls' toilets to check if anyone is in there, but the cubicles are all empty. I head back to my car feeling concerned, guilty and torn as to what to do. Should I go back to the police and tell them I suspect Mila is still missing, that it must have been the wrong child they saw at their welfare check? I can't think of another explanation – though why would Zayla do that? More to the point, *how* would she do that?

I hold my breath as I turn the key, praying my car will start. Mila was not in after-school club. Mila has not been at school since last Friday, almost a week ago now. And Mila was not at home with her nanny, who lied about her whereabouts.

Relieved when my car starts first time, I sit there thinking, finally knowing what I must do.

'Mrs Marlowe,' DC Starkey says an hour later. 'What brings you here again?' His voice is weary and resigned as we stand in a corridor at the police station. His officer ID hangs around his neck on a lanyard, and the sleeves of his pale blue shirt are rolled up, exposing hairy forearms folded across his body. In one hand, he's holding a file, as if he was on his way somewhere when the desk sergeant took me through.

'It's about Mila. Do you remember, the little girl I told you about?'

He nods once.

'She's... I'm concerned that she's still missing.'

'More worried than you were last week just before our officers did a welfare check on her, reporting that she was safe and well?'

'Yes,' I say, falling into his verbal trap before I realise. 'Look, I know it sounds stupid, but I don't think it could have been Mila Weston that your officers saw. There's no other explanation for it. She hasn't been in school all week, and her nanny said she was at after-school club today, but she wasn't. I checked. The nanny is lying.'

DC Starkey stifles a sigh. 'You want me to search for a child who hasn't been reported missing by her family? A child that two of my officers set eyes on last week? You think the child's nanny is lying, even though she was the one to assist with the welfare check?'

'Yes.'

'Mrs Marlowe—'

'Something's not right, *please*... you've got to believe me.' I shift from one foot to the other, wishing we could go into a private room to sit down, but I sense the detective's patience with me is not simply wearing thin, but is non-existent.

'There's been a routine referral to social services,' DC Starkey says calmly. 'They will be conducting the necessary enquiries, if they haven't already. I'm not sure what else you want me to do.'

'What about the man in the blue van? He was watching the school again. And my car – it was stolen from the garage the other day.'

'Did you report your vehicle stolen?'

'Of course.'

The detective glances down at my hands, his eyebrows raised as he sees me nervously jangling my car keys.

'My car... it came back that evening. Someone left it outside my house.'

'Perhaps it turned up the same way that Mila Weston showed up exactly where she was meant to be?'

He waits for me to reply, but I can't. I'll break down if I say another word.

'Look, I read the officer's report myself. Mila's nanny went to fetch her from her playdate and presented her here at the police station. We have the station's CCTV footage on record for a start, not to mention the child happily chatting away to the PCs and confirming who she is.' Another sigh as the detective walks towards the door leading to the reception area, holding it open for me. 'Did you make that GP appointment yet, Mrs Marlowe? If not, I strongly suggest that you do.'

EIGHTEEN
HANNAH

Jan's text comes in as I'm getting into my car in the police station car park. *Still on for food at 6.30?* I'd totally forgotten we'd planned to go out for a catch-up tonight. How could I forget a plan with one of my best friends? Once upon a time, it would be the four of us going out – her and Mitch, Rory and me.

While it's the last thing I feel like doing, it will be good to get out of my head and think of something else other than Mila, blue vans and suspicious nannies. *Yes!* I tap out in reply. *See you there.*

'Jan, hi,' I greet her half an hour later, giving her a hug in our favourite lounge bar. Mismatched chairs and rustic wooden tables, huge chandeliers and eclectic paintings are the vibe of the place, which suits Jan's character and love of interiors.

I'm not sure what *my* character is anymore – I think it used to be arty and a bit alternative once, though at university I always felt outshone by Natalie and her bubbly personality, her unique dress sense, and her wild artwork. These days, I'm happy in black or grey easily-washed gear for work – looking a bit like a grieving widow, if I'm honest. At the weekend I seem to slop about in oversized sweatshirts and leggings. I've not had a colour or cut in ages, and I end up just tying back my long, mousy hair.

'So good to see you, Hannah.' Jan's tight embrace squeezes the air from my lungs. 'I took the liberty,' she says, tapping a bottle of white wine sitting in a cooler. There are two glasses, and, as I sit down and settle in, she pours. 'Busy day?' she enquires, noticing my flustered state.

'A bit,' I lie, wanting nothing more than to spill everything out to her. 'I dropped my car home first and walked so I can have a drink.' I lift my glass and clink it against hers. 'Cheers!'

'Mitch is being a darling and picking me up later. How's that gorgeous girl of yours?'

At mention of Jodie, I check my phone in case she's messaged. 'Missing in action, right now,' I say, wishing I'd chosen a different expression. 'Not literally, of course, but she wasn't home when I popped back, so our paths haven't crossed tonight.'

When I got back from the police station, I ducked inside to quickly freshen up. But there was no sign of Jodie. I seem to remember her saying she was hanging out with a friend after school tonight, but I send her a text to check.

The next hour flies by with a round-up of what we've each been up to – Jan gathering another ten-thousand followers on Instagram for her garden and lifestyle videos after she was featured on breakfast TV a couple of weeks ago, and subsequently being offered two prominent brand deals in the last week.

As an interior designer, she still takes on a few high-end clients locally, but she mainly focuses on making content about her home, style and life. Not that her and Mitch's house is some kind of stately home or anything, but Jan has transformed their 1950s place on a budget, including the garden, which her followers love – that, and her rawness and vulnerability when things don't go to plan. Being utterly gorgeous with her slender frame, blonde hair and olive skin helps enormously too, though she's similarly humble about her looks. Some people are just born getting everything right.

'I signed with a new design client earlier,' she tells me proudly. 'Up at Ocean Heights. You know where I mean?'

I stop, wine glass halfway to my mouth. Jan knows perfectly well I know where she means. In fact, she was the one who suggested I start a mood board for mine and Rory's dreams. *What you put out into the universe you attract back tenfold*, she once told me. So I did just that, taking up the entire front of the refrigerator with my clippings and images. Rory hadn't exactly mocked me for it, but he did keep reminding me that until Marion died, or we won the lottery, Ocean Heights was always going to stay stuck on the front of the fridge.

Anyway, it all went in the bin after Rory left. I couldn't stand to be reminded of our broken dreams, nor his mercenary views regarding his poor mum. I'd always got along fine with Marion, visiting her weekly at the care home, and I think she saw me as more of a daughter than she did Rory a son. I still visit her every couple of weeks, though each time I go, her dementia means I have to relive the agony of telling her that Rory and I aren't together anymore.

'That's great news,' I say to Jan about her new design contract. 'Congratulations!' I sip some wine to disguise how I'm really feeling. I love hearing about her success, of course, but it only reminds me of my failures. That, and the universe seems to be ramming Ocean Heights down my throat lately. 'They've sold all the plots up there now, haven't they?'

'The last house was finished only a few months ago,' she confirms. Mitch, Jan's husband, owns the local estate agency, getting all the property gossip first.

'My new client travels a lot for work, so it's going to be a challenge to learn her tastes. She's away at the moment.'

Jan once explained that she does her best work when she gets under the skin of her clients, being as nosey as possible and prying deep into their lives, learning all their foibles and habits, likes and dislikes.

'I'm going to have to do a lot of snooping around her house for clues. See how she lives, what the space provides and lacks, experience the lighting and the views. She's a busy single mum so doesn't have a lot of free time.' Jan flashes a straight white smile, a passionate look sweeping across her face.

I nod, trying not to show my shock as the penny drops. *Single mum... away for work.* My mind whirrs, wondering how many single mothers are likely to live at Ocean Heights. What if she's talking about Anna Weston, Mila's mother?

'How the other half live, eh?' I say, taking a long sip of wine. Then I check my phone. Nothing back from Jodie yet. 'Do you know which house it is?' I can't help asking, the sinking feeling growing inside me. I've so far managed to resist mentioning Rory, though my face must have revealed my thoughts because Jan grabs my hand, giving it a squeeze.

'You're better off without him,' she says without answering my question. 'Thank your lucky stars he showed you his true colours before you ended up neck-deep in house-building debt and having a child with him.'

I feel as though I've been kicked in the guts.

'Oh, God, Hannah... I didn't mean it like that. I'm so sorry.'

'It's OK.' I say quietly, grateful that my phone pings. When I grab it, hoping it's Jodie, I'm disappointed that it's not. It's just a message from the art department group chat about a school trip next term.

'Excuse me a second,' I say, tapping out another message to Jodie while my phone is open. *Let me know you're home safe xxx.* I glance at my watch – while it's only half past seven and still light outside, it's not like Jodie to not message, even if it's just a thumbs up emoji. She might have been a bit aloof and distant lately, but she always lets me know her plans and where she is.

'Everything OK?' Jan picks up a menu.

'Still nothing from Jodie. She's not been in touch all day.' I explain that I've been a bit worried about her lately, that her mood has been up and down over the last few weeks.

'Hardly surprising,' Jan rightly says. 'What with mock exams coming up, she's bound to be feeling the pressure.'

We order food – Jan gets a vegan wholegrain salad bowl, while I go for a cheeseburger and chips with a side order of guilt.

'I'm stuffed,' I say half an hour later, putting down my knife and fork. I check my phone yet again, apologising to Jan as I call Jodie's number. It rings out then goes to voicemail. 'I think I'm going to call it a night,' I say, my stomach churning, and not because of the food. 'I can't relax until I know Jodie's OK. She's never gone this long without being in touch, especially if she knows I'm trying to reach her.'

We pay and head outside, where Jan phones Mitch to collect her, and I set off for home on foot, my heart rate quickening the closer I get.

What if Jodie's not home? What if I can't reach her? What if something terrible has happened to her? What if...? What if...? What if...?

I shove my key into the front door and go inside as my anxiety peaks.

'Jodie, it's me, I'm back!' I call up the stairs, imagining myself explaining to the police that this time it's *my* daughter who's missing, begging them to believe me as they usher me out of the station, telling me to get a doctor's appointment, that I'm mad, stressed, anxious...

I run up the stairs, bursting into Jodie's bedroom, my eyes darting around, taking in her unmade bed, the pile of clothes on her dressing table stool, her stack of schoolbooks on her nightstand. Everything as it usually is – slightly messy, slightly chaotic.

But there's no Jodie to greet me. No Jodie lying on her bed with her headphones on, her foot tapping to the beat of whatever she's listening to as she chews on her pencil, maths books balanced on her stomach.

'Oh, Christ,' I say, forcing myself to stay calm. 'Where the hell *is* she?'

I run downstairs again, dashing through the living room, though it's in here that I come to an abrupt stop, sniffing the air.

Smoke. I smell cigarette smoke – that unmistakable acrid tang that gets stuck on smokers' clothing and hair and seems to exude from their skin. And then I see it. The red baseball cap again, lying on the corner of the sofa. It's just as I pick it up that the front door opens and someone comes inside.

I spin around.

'*Jodie!*' I gasp. 'Oh, oh... thank *God* you're back.'

But her eyes grow wide with shock – and something else, something anxious and fearful – when she sees the baseball cap in my hands.

NINETEEN

HANNAH

'Hi, Mum,' Jodie says, trying to sound light and breezy, though she looks anything but. Her voice wavers and her cheeks pink up. As her mother, I know every little quirk, expression and tell-tale sign, and right now, she's a walking beacon of guilt with her jaw twitch and ear lobe pulling.

'Hi, love,' I say, deciding I won't tell her off for not replying to my messages – not yet anyway. 'Silly question, but you haven't been smoking, have you?' I instantly regret asking.

'No, Mum!' she replies indignantly. 'It's disgusting. You know I'd never do that.'

I nod, believing her. She's too into her sport to be bothered with cigarettes. 'Sorry, love, it's just that... can you smell it too? Cigarette smoke?'

Jodie makes a show of sniffing the air. 'No, I can't. You OK, Mum? You seem a bit... flustered.'

I fake a laugh. If only she knew. 'I'm fine. I had a quick bite with Jan, and we had some wine. You know me, I'm a lightweight.'

Jodie nods, sliding past me to get to the kitchen. Her eyes

flick to the baseball cap I'm holding again, but she doesn't say anything.

I follow her through. 'Where have you been?'

'At Becca's house, like I told you,' she replies, staring inside the fridge. 'I'm starving.'

I think back to this morning – it was such a rush to get out of the house – vaguely recalling her saying something about going to a friend's place. With Mila constantly on my mind, I've dropped the ball with my own daughter.

'There's some leftover pasta if you fancy it,' I say, going over to her. 'I can heat it up.' And that's when I smell the unmistakable smell of cigarette smoke on her clothing. Not only that, but down the back of her pale grey sweatshirt are dirty marks as if she's fallen over, as well as a patch of what looks like cobwebs stuck to her hair and clothing. I'm about to lay into her properly for lying and not answering my texts, demanding to know where she's been, when she turns and hurls herself at me, hugging me tightly.

'Thanks, Mum,' she says, pressing her face into my shoulder. 'I love you,' and then she breaks down in tears.

The next morning, Saturday, I wake early. I roll over and pull the pillow over my head. But it's no good – I won't get back to sleep now, not with everything on my mind. It's been over a week since I last saw Mila, and I'm desperately worried something bad has happened. I wish the police had listened to me.

Downstairs, I'm surprised to find Jodie up already. She swings round from the cooker. 'Hi, Mum! I was going to bring you breakfast in bed.'

She turns some rashers of bacon over and lifts the edges of two fried eggs with a spatula. The welcome smell of coffee fills my nose.

'Wow, what's all this for?' I ask. 'It's not Mother's Day, is it?'

She gives me a glimmer of a smile. 'Just because...' Then she shrugs and breaks down in tears again, her hair flopping forward as she bows her head, dropping the spatula into the frying pan and breaking an egg yolk.

'Hey, *love*...' I cradle her shoulders. 'What is it?' I can't help thinking that it's to do with last night.

'I'm such an idiot,' she says through a few sobs. 'I thought he liked me.'

'Thought who liked you, darling?'

A boy... of *course*. I should have guessed.

'You'll think I'm an idiot and please don't be mad, but there's this lad I met online through gaming. He's local and seemed really nice. He wanted to meet up and hang out, but then he cancelled and didn't arrange another time and...' Jodie trails off in a flurry of sobs and sniffs, while I get a sinking feeling in my stomach that everything I've ever said about online safety and protecting herself has fallen on deaf ears.

'Oh love, I'm so sorry,' I begin, forcing myself to hold back a tirade of warnings. 'But you know what? It's probably for the best. If he can't be bothered to meet, he's not worthy of you.' *And he's probably a fifty-year-old bloke in his childhood bedroom*, I can't help wondering, but shudder the thought away.

'Yeah,' she says, sniffing and turning back to the bacon as the rashers pop and spit in the pan. 'You're right.'

'Is that where you'd gone before you came home last night?'

Another surge of dread washes through me as I think about my teenage daughter arranging to meet up with a stranger from the internet during the evening. I've never wanted to clip her wings, and we live within walking distance of most of her activities in town, and she and her friends all look out for each other – plus there's CCTV everywhere. But it only takes a second to bundle someone into a car, to drive off, to take them somewhere secluded. Then Mila is on my mind again as I realise, when it comes down to it, I did exactly the same to her.

*That's it, sweetheart... hold my hand and come with me...
Good girl...*

'No...' Jodie says, hanging her head as she turns the bacon.
'I... I was with Becca last night. I told you.'

'Does Becca smoke?'

'No! Mum, we were just hanging out in her bedroom
listening to music and chatting. I went to her house after that
boy cancelled. I was supposed to meet him before that at... at
the chippy.' She grabs a tissue and blows her nose. 'God, why
don't you put a tracker on me if you're that paranoid?'

Her tone smarts. She's not spoken to me like that in ages –
not since she blamed me in a fit of upset about a week after
Rory left when she realised he really wasn't coming back.

'Maybe a Find My Friends type of app *is* a good idea?' I say,
knowing that some of the parents at school use it for the older
kids who have phones. At this precise moment, teenagers don't
seem that different to the twelve-year-olds I teach. 'Then you'll
be able to see where I am, too,' I say, hoping that will sweeten
the deal.

To my surprise, Jodie pulls her phone from her pocket and
unlocks it, handing it over. 'Here, take it. Do whatever you
want.'

TWENTY

OK, OK... but I have to go now. I love you so much, my darling...

Hannah never told a soul what she overheard Rory say on the phone that night outside the restaurant when they were celebrating with Jan and Mitch early last year. She'd since played the words over and over in her mind, and there was something about his tone that didn't make her suspect another woman necessarily, but it definitely made her feel uneasy – as though he was more *fond* of the person than anything else.

Standing beside the harbour, Rory had ended his call and swung around, coming face to face with Hannah a few feet behind him. She was rooted to the spot, her mouth hanging open as she hugged her bare shoulders. They'd all dressed up for the evening.

'Oh, hi, love,' Rory said, smooth as silk. He walked over to her and wrapped an arm around her, noticing the shiver run through her. 'Are you cold?' He led her back towards the restaurant.

'Who was that?' she managed to ask as they got near the door. Her voice was fragile. 'On the phone?'

I love you so much, my darling...

'Just a work thing,' he said breezily, giving her a squeeze before pulling the door open and allowing Hannah to go inside first.

The words were there, right inside her mouth sitting on the tip of her tongue. *Who were you saying 'I love you so much, my darling' to? That wasn't a work call, was it? Be honest, Rory. Who was it on the phone?* But nothing came out and, before she knew it, she was sitting down at the table again with Mitch recounting a funny story that had happened with the waiter while they were gone.

Then dessert came and Rory and Mitch had brandies and after that the bill arrived, followed by their taxis and goodbyes out on the harbourside. Hannah had sat next to Rory in the back of the cab having swallowed down what she wanted to say until it gave her indigestion. Back home, they'd made love, and suddenly everything felt perfect just as it always had been, so she'd let those questions pass through her, knowing everything would seem better in the morning. And anyway, she wasn't sure the answers would do anyone any good.

But over the next few days, she still couldn't get Rory's words out of her head. *I love you so much, my darling.* He'd said the same words on repeat after she miscarried, waiting on her hand and foot, nursing her through her grief while choking down his.

I love you so much, my darling...

She remembered one hospital appointment when the doctor explained that sometimes there's no good reason why a couple can't conceive.

'The thing is, I have a daughter already... so I know I can,' Hannah replied. 'Like, my body knows what it's supposed to do.' She'd always assumed it was her fault somehow – she was the one rejecting the embryos, after all – though she knew that if it wasn't her fault, then Rory would shoulder the blame.

'It can just go like that,' Mr Flemming, the NHS consultant, had said when their first round of IVF had failed. 'No rhyme or reason to it. Sometimes nature makes poor decisions.'

Afterwards, they'd gone back to West Bradport and walked along the beach. Their shadows were long on the sand, seeming to stride ahead of them as they held hands – like another couple that was them but also not them.

Perhaps us in another life, Hannah mused.

Maybe that version of her was pregnant, and so that she could see what she'd look like with a bump standing beside Rory, she'd unwound her scarf and stuffed it up her sweater, turning slightly so the sun caught her belly, making her shadow seem pregnant.

'There,' she said to Rory. 'Not long until my due date,' she said, managing a small laugh. Rory also laughed, then he grabbed her and pulled her close, squashing the scarf-baby between them.

'It'll happen,' he said, planting a kiss on her mouth. 'A baby will come soon; I feel sure of it.'

They didn't know it then, but there would be many more tears and miscarriages before they decided to put three embryos into frozen storage and take a break. Time to save up again. Time to regroup and mend their broken hearts. It would be five years filled with pain and joy and disappointment and hope, and, at the end, all they had to show for it was a few cells on ice and an empty bank account.

As they set off on their walk again, the scarf fell out from beneath Hannah's sweater, trailing along the beach until she pulled it out completely.

'I suppose the pain of not having a baby is nothing compared to the pain of having one for two months and *then* losing it.' Hannah sighed out into the sunset, shocked that she'd even mentioned it.

'God, for sure,' Rory had replied in agreement. 'Totally.'

Silence fell between them. Since meeting for a second time ten years after graduating, neither of them had mentioned what happened that night a few months before the end of their final year. And that was mainly down to Hannah – she was the one who couldn't stand to think or talk about it, preferring to believe that it hadn't happened, that it hadn't all been her fault.

Now she was older and with a daughter of her own, somehow it didn't seem right not to at least bring it up occasionally, and maybe ease the pain in her heart.

No one had expected Natalie, of *all* people, to have a baby – let alone while she was still a student. It happened sometimes, of course, but not to people like *her*. Free-spirited and independent, Natalie getting pregnant so young had sent ripples of raised eyebrows around their friendship group – not least because she was a lesbian – but especially when she decided to keep the baby, staying on at university to finish her degree after it was born.

Good luck doing any work with a kid in tow, came some sarcastic remarks, while others simply avoided her, never offering to help even when Natalie looked gaunt and tired and a wisp of her former self because she'd not slept in weeks.

But she was determined to graduate, determined to make a good future for her and her child. 'My life isn't over,' she told anyone who pitied her. 'It's just different now.'

As Hannah and Rory walked along the beach, heading back to fetch Jodie from a playdate, Hannah closed her eyes for a moment. She couldn't stand to think about what had happened to two-month-old Fleur, how Natalie had fallen apart over the subsequent weeks, her grief melting her into a puddle that seemingly evaporated when she quit university early.

No one heard from her after that, but then no one went in

search of her, either. Hannah had lived with the guilt ever since, the weight of it pressing down on her since that terrible night when she'd only been trying to help.

She stamped her feet to get the sand off her trainers as they walked up through the town. Even after all these years, it was impossible to comprehend that Natalie's baby had been stolen. That it was all *her* fault. And she knew, in her heart of hearts, it was why she'd been able to have a child with Lewis – the man who was never going to stick around or be a decent husband and father – but not with Rory, the man she adored most in the world.

The universe had a way of settling the score.

TWENTY-ONE

JODIE

I didn't mean to break down in front of Mum about Shadow cancelling on me yesterday, but it turned out to be a good cover for everything else. I'd rather she thought that I was upset about a boy, rather than me bunking off school. And she'd go mental if she knew I'd broken into that old warehouse. That industrial estate has been on the local news recently for arson, attracting gangs and anti-social behaviour. If Mum knew the truth, she'd have grounded me for a year. For *life*.

Since Dad... *Rory*... left, she's been even more strict about what I can and can't do, as though she's playing dad as well as mum. I suppose I understand but this tracking app nonsense is a step too far. What she doesn't realise is that I can easily disable it whenever I want – which is why I handed her my phone so readily in the first place.

Anyway, I rarely skip school. It's important to me that I do well, but like I said, with talking to Shadow late at night these last few weeks, I've fallen behind. I just need to catch up then everything will be OK.

But now I have another problem. Someone *else* came into

that warehouse yesterday – someone other than the child I'd heard crying in the office. Panicking, I spotted a gap under the machinery and dived onto the filthy floor, wriggling underneath in the nick of time. Then I realised I'd left my school backpack lying on the ground nearby. I couldn't risk making a noise by dragging it over, but I was terrified whoever it was would see it. I stayed squashed under the machine for what seemed like ages, my face pressed up against greasy cogs. I heard two people talking in low voices as they came further into the warehouse, the sound of footsteps drawing closer. I held my breath as two pairs of trainers stopped about four feet away from where I was hiding. Eventually, I had to take a breath, but something caught in my throat, making me want to cough. I tried to stifle it.

'What was that?' a hushed male voice said. That's when I smelled cigarette smoke and heard a long exhale.

'Nothing,' a female voice replied. 'Just this old place creaking.'

Silence for a few moments, followed by the more distant sound of sobbing again.

'We'd better get this shit taken care of, yeah?' the male growled quietly.

'Yeah, right,' the female said, followed by a series of quick puffs. Then, suddenly, two half-finished cigarette butts, still smouldering, landed on the warehouse floor about six inches away from where I was hiding under the machine.

Slowly, I turned my head. The smoke wound up from the butts in grey and white twists, the plume suddenly blowing sideways in a draft – coming directly at me. I screwed up my eyes and held my breath again because the stink of smoke always made me cough and feel ill. Mum should have known better, grilling me like that, but I could hardly tell her why I reeked.

The pair walked off and then I heard keys rattling, something being unlocked – that office, I figured – and then the sound of a door being opened. Momentarily, the cries grew louder, followed by the man's angry voice telling whoever it was to shut up.

After that, I didn't hear much, because they must have shut the door again. All I knew was that I had to get out before they came back. Slowly, I shuffled and wriggled and slid my way out, getting into a crouch as I peered around the side of the machine. I struggled to focus in the semi-darkness, but about fifty feet away, through a grimy window in the partition wall of the office, I saw two shadowy figures moving about.

Knowing I might not get another chance, I made a run for it across the warehouse to the door where I came in. I kept bent and low as I set off, praying that the pair wouldn't see me through the internal window. I held my breath, keeping my sweatshirt hood up, my shoulders hunched. I felt like a commando soldier on a mission as I approached the door, curling my fingers around the edge of it.

Just as I was about to open it, I heard someone shout out.

Oi, you! Stop, come back! Wait!

Panicking, I burst through the door and stumbled outside. Then I tore down the alley, charging towards the river, heading along the path, grateful that a gang of older lads was loitering up ahead. Normally, I'd have given the group a wide berth, but if I was being followed, whoever it was wouldn't try anything on with witnesses about.

Ten minutes later and I was back in the centre of town, panting and relieved. I looked back over my shoulder, but there was no one chasing after me – almost making me wonder if I'd imagined it all. As I got my breath back, I headed into a shop to get a bottle of water. It was only when I went to pay that I realised my purse was inside my school backpack – the same backpack that I'd left on the warehouse floor. *Shit.*

I sat on a low wall near the fountain wondering what to do.

I'd still got my phone, but losing a load of schoolbooks and my purse was a nightmare I could do without. I'd have to go back to get it at some point, and I prayed that no one stole it in the meantime. Though at least it had my name and address inside if someone honest found it. Feeling shaky, wishing I'd gone into school after all, I opened the app where Shadow and I chatted. There was one new message.

Can't meet up after all soz. Something's come up.

That was it. No kiss like he usually put. And no offer to rearrange. Like, literally, could the day get any worse?

Fuck him, I thought, not even bothering with a reply. I shoved my phone back in my pocket. *He's not into you, you idiot*, I told myself over and over as I stared at the fountain. Especially since he'd been the one to suggest meeting in town rather than at my house, saying that would be better for a first meet. I figured someone as cool as Shadow would be super popular, and he'd probably got a date with a girl he knew in real life, not some saddo off a gaming site.

I looked at my watch. I'd already told Mum that I was going to Becca's tonight – a lie because I'd hoped my meeting with Shadow might run into the evening, but it was also so she didn't worry, thinking I was bored and alone at home, which would have made her come back early from her night out with Jan to keep me company. That's the sort of thing she'd do. She was far more likely to stay out late if she knew I was having fun round at a friend's place.

But then somehow, my day did manage to go from really bad to even worse when, as I dragged my feet away from the town square to go and lick my wounds at the park for a couple of hours, my phone rang with No Caller ID on the screen.

For a second, I hoped that it was Shadow, that he'd somehow got hold of my number and was phoning to change his mind about meeting up, so I answered it. The person was indeed male, though he sounded deep and growly like he was trying to disguise his voice, and he only said one thing before hanging up, making my blood run cold.

Do as I say, or you'll never see your mother again.

TWENTY-TWO

HANNAH

Weekends are the hardest. Even though Rory and I used to blitz through our chores on a Saturday morning, we still managed to squeeze in a coffee in town or duck into the bookshop on the way back from the market. Heading into town alone isn't the same anymore.

I go into the dry cleaners, rummaging in my bag for my ticket while I wait in line. I could have sworn it was tucked in a side pocket from when I dropped the evening dress off well over a month ago now. I've been meaning to pick it up for ages.

Bringing the dress in to be cleaned in the first place was one of those jobs that I'd been putting off. I'd only worn it once, when Rory and I were invited to a party at the home of one of Draper Ford's top clients.

'You'll need a new frock,' Rory had said with a wink. I'd been feeling less than attractive at that time – age seeming to creep up on me, and the chances of ever having a baby rapidly diminishing – so I'd not particularly leapt at the chance to go shopping. While I was intrigued to see the house Rory and his colleagues had designed for their super-wealthy client, I'd rather have gone in my jeans and a hoodie, had a quick drink and a nose around, and been back home by nine.

'I'm sorry, I can't seem to find my ticket,' I tell the woman in the dry cleaners, remembering how the red wine had spilt down the front of my new dress. 'Can you manage without it?'

The woman nods, taking down my details, making me grateful that they cross-reference every drop-off with a phone number.

'I hope the stain came out OK,' I say as she taps at the computer then heads to the back of the shop to hunt through a rail of plastic-bagged garments.

She turns around, calling over her shoulder. 'When did you drop it off again?'

'About five, maybe six weeks ago now? Sorry, I should have come back sooner.' It had taken all my resolve to even bring it in the first place – it was reminder of Rory and me being together. Part of me had wanted to shove it in the dustbin.

The woman hunts through a different rail and then disappears out the back. When she returns, she taps at the keyboard again, biting her lip. 'Sorry, I was mistaken. It says the dress was picked up a few days ago... on Wednesday,' she tells me, glancing up.

'But...' I shake my head. 'No. No, I haven't picked it up. That's why I'm here. Can you check again? It was a long peach-coloured skirt with a sequinned bodice. It had a red wine stain on it and—'

'Ahh, yes, I dealt with that dress,' another woman behind the counter chips in, overhearing our conversation. 'The stain came out a treat!'

'What?' I edge closer to her.

'The woman who picked it up, she was well pleased. It was me who served her.'

'You gave my dress to... to another *woman*?' Even as I'm saying it, my mouth is dry, my throat closing up. *Not again*, I think, my heart rate speeding up. I steady myself on the counter, wide-eyed as I stare at the assistant.

'She had the ticket, so why wouldn't I?' She sounds defensive. 'It was a blonde woman, about the same age as you, I guess. A bit taller.'

'Name – what was her name?' I blurt out, hardly able to speak. 'Did you get her details?'

'Sorry, no.' The assistant shrugs and shakes her head before turning to serve another customer.

'Wait...' I push my way across the counter so I'm in front of her. 'You must know *something* about her? I've no idea how she got my ticket, but she had no right to collect my dress!' I feel my voice caving in.

It must be the same woman who took my car. I can't think of any other explanation. And the same woman who came inside my house and took my spare key. She must have rummaged through my handbag to find the ticket, which would mean... Oh God, I can't stand to think that she was in the house while Jodie and I were at home, maybe breaking in at night as we slept. I stifle a whimper as it occurs to me she might not be working alone.

'Sorry I can't help more,' the assistant says, giving me a pitying look.

'OK, thanks,' I say flatly, turning to leave. I consider going to the police station, but quickly dismiss that idea. If I dilute my concerns about Mila with tales of lost evening dresses and mislaid dry cleaning tickets, they'll never take me seriously. No, I need to figure this out myself and find out who is infiltrating my life. Because this is getting more than scary now. This is stalking, home invasion, theft and potential kidnapping – and the police haven't done a damn thing to help me!

It makes me wonder if this woman is building herself up to something – something even more sinister. I shudder as I think what might come next, glancing around to check for CCTV cameras as I leave, but there are none. I head out of the shop, feeling more scared than ever, wondering how the hell I'm going to sleep at night after this.

'Oh... sorry!' I say, stumbling on the step and bumping into another customer coming through the door.

'Hannah?' the woman says.

It takes me a moment to realise who it is – Becca's mum. I've not seen her in ages, though our daughters hang out all the time. 'Toni, hi... nice to see you,' I say, too distracted to get embroiled in a chat right now. 'Thanks for having Jodie over last night. She'd have been sat at home on her own otherwise.'

Toni hesitates then looks at me in an almost pitying way, her dark brown eyes widening beneath a compassionate frown. She sweeps back her fringe that sits diagonally over her heart-shaped face. Even if you didn't know her, you'd feel you could be friends with Toni Lawrence. She's all kind eyes and laughter.

'Lovely to see you too, Hannah,' she says with a smile, guiding me back down the step by the elbow so we're not in the way. Then the frown again. 'But Jodie wasn't at ours last night. We went to the cinema – a rare occurrence, getting the whole family together.' She ends on another smile, her concern bracketed by kindness.

'Oh...' Another surge of adrenaline rushes through me. I mean... I know Jodie is safe, that she came home last night – *eventually* – after ignoring my texts all evening, but something isn't adding up. 'I guess I must have misheard her then,' I say, not wanting her to think I didn't know where my fifteen-year-old daughter was. But I can't let it go. 'So... so she definitely didn't come to the cinema with you then?'

Toni's hand rests on my arm. 'No, she wasn't with us.' A sideways tip of her head. 'Are you concerned about her?'

'God, no!' I say. 'Just a misunderstanding. She's been studying so hard, she was probably in her room and...' I trail off, realising I've basically admitted I didn't know where my child was last night. 'And forgot to check her messages.'

'Becca would love to have her stay over soon though,' Toni continues. 'I'll get her to organise something.' The way she says it makes me feel as if she'd be doing me a favour, helping out with my single parenting because I'm clearly not coping. Like everyone else, I imagine she knows Rory upped and left without a word.

'Sure, let's make it happen,' I reply as cheerfully as I can while feeling punched in the guts. 'Good to see you.' I give her a little wave as I head off, hopping on the bus home for a couple of stops, wondering why the hell my daughter lied to me.

Once I've got a seat, I call Jodie to see if she fancies a walk later. It'll give us a chance to chat, to see if I can prise out of her what's going on, and besides, I could do with blowing away some cobwebs. It's been a while since we've spent any proper time together. Annoyingly, her phone goes to voicemail.

I send a quick message telling her I'm nearly home, that we should hang out this afternoon, but even after I get off the bus, walk the short distance home – discovering she's not in the house – and call her again, she still doesn't answer. Then I remember the tracking app. But when I open it, clicking on her icon to see where she is, a message pops up stating *Jodie cannot be located right now*.

TWENTY-THREE

HANNAH

I was so relieved that Jodie came home last night, I didn't think to ask her about the baseball cap that keeps turning up like a bad penny – and especially not when she seemed so upset. It's still sitting on the coffee table where I left it. Instead of leaving it out on the front wall, she must have taken a shine to it, knowing its owner probably wouldn't come back to collect it. I smile at the *Sea Ya* slogan, knowing it would appeal to Jodie, then I hang it in the hallway before unpacking the groceries.

It's as I'm wondering what to do with the rest of the day, trying not to feel concerned that Jodie hasn't replied yet, that the doorbell rings.

'Jan, hi,' I say, pleased to see her so soon after our meal last night, but also concerned. It's not like her to call round unannounced. 'Is everything OK?'

I hold the door open as she steps inside, her face giving nothing away. In the kitchen, she spins round and whips something from her bag. 'Ta-da!' she sings, her made-up face breaking into a grin.

I shake my head, confused. 'What's that?' I mean, I know *what* it is she's jangling in my face, I'm just not sure *why*.

'Keys, my darling! Keys to a fabulous afternoon out if you'd care to join me. Mitch is playing golf, and *I* have a very important job to do. I thought we could make an afternoon of it. I have a picnic basket in my car, and I nicked a bottle of champers from Mitch's collection. What do you say? Will you come?'

'Come where?'

I know she's trying to be kind, but I'm too distracted by everything to enjoy a picnic right now. And I certainly won't relax until I know where Jodie is. I can't believe she's not replying to me again.

'Ocean Heights, of course!' Jan says. 'I need to get a mood board together before my new client returns in a few days. I thought you might enjoy a nosy around the house, then we can go and sit on the clifftop and have our picnic. I know you love it there. Or we can go down the path to the beach if—'

'Jan... I know you mean well, but...' I stop. Stirring up memories is the last thing I want to do today – but then if it *is* Mila's mother's house as I suspect, it would give me a chance to have a look around inside. See if there's any trace of Mila.

'Come on,' Jan says, clasping her hands together. 'I'd really value your input. The client isn't particularly easy to deal with and being a high-value contract, I need to get this one right.'

'OK...' I say, wondering what she means by *not easy to deal with*. 'Let me get my stuff together and we'll head off.' I dash upstairs and grab a jacket, sending another text to Jodie. The tracking app is still showing her as offline.

'Truth is, I was quite worried about you last night,' Jan says as we set off in her car. It's a beautiful day so she's put the top down, making me glad I've tied back my hair. Compared to Jan, I feel a bit shabby in my ripped jeans and old T-shirt, and I shoved on my huge sunglasses to cover up the dark circles around my eyes. 'You didn't seem yourself. What's going on, Hannah?' She quickly glances over at me.

'Nothing!' I shoot back with a fake laugh. 'I'm fine.'

I so want to tell her about Mila – how I did a stupid, *stupid* thing and, because of that, someone took her from my house, that I haven't seen a trace of her for over a week. Should I mention that despite the police insisting she's fine, I'm worried she's still missing? What with her weird paintings, her grubby uniform, her sweet but timid nature, I'm growing more and more concerned for her.

And that's without mentioning the other weird things that have been going on in my life – my car, the dress... the man watching me at school.

'Really, everything's fine,' I add quite calmly despite the turmoil in my head.

Ten minutes later, we arrive at the entry gates to Ocean Heights. I watch Jan enter the security code at the gates, getting it wrong the first try. I only just stop myself blurting out that the last digit should be a nine not a six, her fingernail having caught the number above by mistake.

'Right,' she says, cruising down the wide avenue. 'Welcome to how the other half lives.'

'You're sure no one's going to be home?' I double check. If the nanny is there, she's bound to recognise me from when I broke down here the other day.

'Relax,' Jan assures me, pulling onto the drive of Eastcliff House. 'My client texted me earlier saying that it was a great time to go because the house will be empty. She's away on a work trip and told me that her daughter and the nanny won't be home all weekend either.'

'Really?' I whip my head round. 'Did she say where they are?' If they've gone away, it would explain Mila's absence from school, ending my immediate worries about her. They should have told the school, but I just want to know she's OK.

Jan raises her eyebrows, pulling on the handbrake and turning off the engine. 'How would I know?' She pauses, staring at me with a frown, then unbuckles her seatbelt. 'Right, come on. Let's go inside for an hour or two, then it's a glass of fizz on the beach.'

TWENTY-FOUR
JODIE

Dear God, don't let him hurt Mum...

I have no choice but to follow the instructions of that weird man on the phone yesterday evening. I've felt sick from worry ever since he called but have no idea who he is. He must have got my phone number from the details inside my bag, but I have no idea how he knows about my mum. As soon as he threatened her, I knew I had to do exactly what he said. I don't know what kind of trouble I've got myself into, but I don't like it one bit. I just want to get my stuff back from the warehouse and go home. I pray this will be the end of it.

'No police, no telling anyone where you're going, and no asking questions,' he'd growled down the line in a creepy voice. He almost sounded like an old man as he gave me precise instructions, telling me to be back at the warehouse at eleven o'clock the next morning – *today* – saying someone would hand over my bag. Then he said I had a job to do and that I'd get further instructions. By his gruff tone, I got the feeling it was very much *or else*. With the threat against my mum, I'm not taking any chances.

My stomach knots and twists as I head back along the river

to the industrial estate with a deep sense of dread that there's much more to this than I realise. There's no one about, which makes this place even scarier. Everywhere is littered with fag butts, beer bottles and other rubbish – the only sign that anyone ever comes here. The empty warehouses attract all the wrong types.

'Oi, over here,' I hear a voice suddenly call out – a female voice. I whip around, scanning the area. 'Psst, here! Behind the tree!'

I spin around the other way, spotting a shadowy figure lurking behind a clump of bushes near the back entrance of the warehouse that I broke into.

Slowly, I walk over to where she's standing. It's a young woman, who looks to be in her early twenties. She has black hair, though most of it is hidden under a purple bandana that's tied at the nape of her neck, and she has on mirrored wrap-around sunglasses, ripped jeans and a faded T-shirt with a long black cardigan on top. If she's trying to be discreet, her vibe isn't helping her blend in.

'Have... have you got my backpack?' I ask nervously.

'Maybe,' she says in a terse whisper, beckoning me closer into the thicket.

'I'll stay here, thanks. Where's my bag?' I glance around but she seems to be alone.

'You'll get your bag, but you've got to do something first.'

'Like what?' I say incredulously. This is stupid. 'Just give me my bag. All my exam stuff is in it. I'll be in deep trouble if I don't finish my work and—'

Suddenly, the girl leaps out of the bushes and lunges at me, dragging me back into the thicket by my arm.

'Oi!' I cry out, lashing out at her with my free hand. 'Get off me!'

'Sorry,' she says, releasing me. She's panting, her eyes scanning around between the warehouses, with a worried – no, *terri-*

fied – look on her face. 'We'll be seen otherwise. Don't want trouble.'

'Who are you?' I ask, losing my cool. 'And where is my bag? You'd better tell me what's going on, or I'm out of here.'

A deeper frown sweeps over her face. I wish I hadn't come now – I've already cancelled my bank card, but it's the books and school notes I couldn't stand to lose. I'll be in deep shit with my teachers. At least my laptop was safe at home. I glance around, worried I've been lured into some kind of trap.

'Just tell me who you are. What do you want?' I take a step away.

'Stop, wait! Look, if you want your bag back, you've got to do something. He meant it when he said your mum would get hurt.' She picks at her fingernails, her eyes flicking about. 'You really shouldn't have gone into the warehouse, yeah? He went right mental about it.'

'Who? *Who* went mental?' I'm so confused right now, though the girl almost seems as scared as I am.

'That don't matter. You've got to deliver a letter, that's all. Then you can have your stuff.'

'I want my bag *now*! If you don't give it to me, I'm going to call the police.' I fish my phone from my pocket and start to video her. I'm going to need some kind of proof.

'What the hell are you doing?' She swipes at my arm, trying to knock the phone from my hand, but I leap back just in time. 'Oi, give it to me!' she yells out, though suddenly claps a hand over her mouth, looking terrified that someone has heard her.

'I'll stop recording when you give me my stuff back!' My heart is pounding, but I stand my ground. 'Look, I'll post the letter for you when I'm back in town. Is that OK?' Perhaps that will be enough for them to leave Mum out of this.

'No, it needs to be hand delivered. And you've got to get a photo of the letter inside the house as proof you did it. Understood?'

'Is someone making you do this?' I look around, sensing we're being watched. I've heard about things like this, where young women are blackmailed into setting up crimes, doing the dirty work so the real criminals further up the chain are less traceable.

The girl shakes her head unconvincingly.

'Are you asking me to break into someone's house?'

'No, it's not like that. I'm going to give you a key.'

'If you have a key, then why don't *you* just deliver the letter?'

'Cos... cos he told me not to.' She scuffs the ground with her foot. 'Said someone else had to do it.'

'Look, I have no idea who you are or why that guy on the phone threatened my mum, but he told me that if I came here, I could have my bag back. Now you want me to deliver something and won't tell me why. I'm not an idiot. Something's not right here and—'

'Honestly, it's gonna be OK. But... but you don't want your mum to get hurt, do you?' She pulls the sleeves of her cardigan down over her hands, chewing the cuff, her eyes nervously flicking about.

'How does he even know about my mum or where to find her?' I'm so confused, not to mention scared. My heart is pounding so hard. 'Tell me who you are, and I'll think about it,' I say, calling her bluff, though I can't risk Mum being hurt.

'It doesn't matter who I am. Look, here's the letter,' she says, pulling a crumpled white envelope from her back pocket. 'The address is on it.' She holds it out so I can read it.

'Wait, that's out of town. I'm not old enough to drive. Just give me my schoolbag back, yeah, and I promise I won't go to the cops.' I'm getting annoyed now, pacing about the bushes, kicking the undergrowth as I hunt about for my bag. It must be around here somewhere.

'I'll drive you up to the house.' She shoves the letter at me, forcing me to take it. 'My car's just around the corner.' She points across the potholed track. 'Once we're there, you go inside, leave the letter in the kitchen and take a photo of it. Then you send me the evidence, I'll drive you back, and you get your bag. It's in the boot of my car. Deal?'

'Fuck's sake. OK, deal. But I'm not happy,' I eventually say, swiping the envelope from her with a trembling hand. I stop filming and put my phone back in my pocket 'What's your name, anyway?' I ask as we walk towards her car. It doesn't feel right, getting into it with a stranger. I certainly wouldn't do it with a man.

'Zayla,' she says in a low voice, looking around again. 'Now get in. I want this job done.'

It's as we're driving off, heading out of the industrial estate and back towards town, that I remember the tracking app. Mum made me put it back on last night, but I turned it off again this morning before I left for the warehouse. She'd have a proper rage if she knew what I was doing, and I figured that what she doesn't know can't hurt her.

TWENTY-FIVE

HANNAH

It's like stepping inside another world – a world that exists only in my dreams. Eastcliff House is all space and light, luxury and comfort.

'Wow,' I say, gazing around the hallway while Jan turns off the alarm. She comes out of the cloakroom where the security panel is located. 'It's gorgeous.'

'Decent, right?' she says, beaming. 'I love having a blank canvas.' She grabs my hand. 'Come on, let me show you around.'

We pass through the large square entrance hall with a sweeping staircase that rises to a galleried landing, and on through wide double doors into a vast open-plan living room running along the side of the house.

'Just wait...' Jan says, pressing a switch on the wall, triggering a huge expanse of glass to turn from frosted to clear, exposing a view that dreams are literally made of.

I gasp. 'Wow again!' I walk over to the forty-foot-wide floor-to-ceiling wall of glass. 'It's incredible. If I lived here, I literally wouldn't get anything done. I'd just be staring out of this window the whole time.'

I gaze out, my eyes drinking in the wide expanse of horizon over an azure sea. The sun sparkles off the waves, and there's a ship in the distance. I fight back the tears, telling myself I'm being a spoilt and privileged brat by even considering feeling hard done by that I don't live here, that Rory and I were going to do everything in our power to buy this very plot, even if it meant pitching a tent on it for five years until we could afford to build.

'Come this way,' Jan says, leading me around the corner. I'm hardly able to take my eyes off the cliffs and the sea beyond, but we go through to a dining area with a large table. A vase of white roses catches my eye, a few petals having dropped around the base of it.

There's a similarly spectacular view along one side of the dining room, which opens into a large kitchen at the other end. Again, it's all neutrally decorated with white kitchen cabinets and an off-white marble floor, and looks out onto a private back garden with a dark woodland looming behind it.

'It needs landscaping out there, of course,' Jan explains. 'But if I lived here, it would barely get a glance. It's all about the sea view.'

'Right?' I say, nodding. I'm trying not to sound flat, but that's how I'm feeling.

'Let me show you the rest of the house,' Jan says, leading me through the remaining rooms – a large boot room behind the kitchen, a study, another snug living room, and then we go upstairs and check out the four bedrooms and family bathroom.

I only get a glimpse inside, but one of the bedrooms clearly belongs to a little girl – a little girl whose name begins with 'M', going by the pretty painted letter plaque stuck on the door. My heart thumps as I try to get a proper look, but I don't want Jan to get suspicious.

Mila's room, I think, spotting a little pair of ballet shoes on the floor at the end of her bed. There's a fluffy bunny wearing a tutu resting on her pillow.

Where are you, Mila? I plead in my head, wishing I could hear her reply...

'The main bedroom is this way,' Jan says, leading me down a corridor. On the way, I get a quick look inside one of the smaller bedrooms, though it's still bigger than mine at home. There are skincare items on the dressing table, plus a few black clothes strewn on the bed. The nanny's room, I presume.

But it's when we're in Anna Weston's room that I find myself feeling overwhelmed – so much so that I pretend I need the toilet so Jan doesn't see how upset I am. I wish I'd never agreed to come.

'Just use the en suite,' she tells me. 'I'll see you back downstairs.'

I close the door and lock it, even though I know no one will come in. Immediately, I'm hit by the sultry notes of an expensive perfume. The vanity unit is littered with upmarket products and a few make-up items, and plush white towels hang from a heated rail beside the marble and gold walk-in shower.

'Incredible,' I say, sniffing, realising that even if Rory and I had raised the funds to buy and build here, we'd never have fitted in. Our tastes, lifestyle and values are wildly different to what seems to be the norm at Ocean Heights. We're just not marble and gold people.

I don't need to use the toilet, so instead I open the cabinet above the double vanity unit to have a quick snoop. Inside are more expensive products, along with the usual items found in a bathroom cabinet – paracetamol, antiseptic wipes, various creams. Then I spot a blister pack of what looks like contraceptive pills – not the box, just the tablets with the days of the week printed on the foil backing. I take it out, seeing a few tablets are missing.

Weird. Surely if she's away for work, she would have taken them with her. But then, maybe she wouldn't if she was trying to get pregnant again. My mind whirs through the possibilities.

With only one robe hanging on the back of the door, and one hand towel beside the double basin, Anna Weston does seem to be a single parent, and not of the struggling financially type, either. Then I tell myself to stop speculating and shove the pills back in the cabinet.

Jan calls out from downstairs, making me jump. Quickly, I flush the toilet and run the tap, not daring to actually wash my hands for fear of messing up the pristine hand towel. Then I go back into the bedroom, glancing around, wondering if there are any more clues about Mila's mother, apart from that she's obviously very successful.

'Tea won't be long!' I hear Jan call out from the kitchen.

Before I go down, I quickly open another door off the bedroom, finding myself in a dressing room. I can't help sliding back one of the mirrored wardrobe doors. Everything is neatly ordered, all her tops and trousers and skirts grouped together in colour order. There's an entire cupboard for shoes and handbags, then the final sliding door reveals longer garments – evening dresses, with one or two still in their plastic coverings from the dry cleaners.

I don't know what it is that makes me check the garment nearest to me – instinct or nosiness – but either way, I lift the plastic cover, realising from the logo that it's the same dry cleaner I use, which is hardly a surprise, given there's only one in town.

It takes me a moment to realise what I'm looking at, but once my brain kicks in and the initial shock subsides, once I pluck up the courage to remove the evening dress entirely from its protective cover, I see that, without a doubt, the peach-coloured dress beneath is mine.

TWENTY-SIX
HANNAH

'I made us a cup of—' Jan halts abruptly in the dressing room doorway. 'Oh,' she says, eyeing the dress draped over my arms. 'Probably best we don't look at my client's personal stuff,' she adds, coming up to me.

I don't move. *Can't* move. If I tell Jan why I'm so shocked – that Mila's mother has, for some reason, stolen my dry cleaning ticket and picked up my dress – it'll open the floodgates to everything else that's been building up inside me. I don't trust myself not to break down and blurt everything out. It seems far too huge a coincidence for Anna Weston to have been given the wrong item at the cleaners.

'Hannah?' I hear a voice say. 'Are you OK? Come on now, let's put this away.'

I feel the dress being lifted from my arms and hear the scrape of the hanger as Jan puts it back in the wardrobe. She flicks off the light as she leads me from the dressing room, plucking a tissue from the box on the bedside table as we pass. 'Here, wipe your face, love. Let's go and have that cuppa and a chat.'

In the kitchen, Jan sits me at the table and stirs two sugars into my tea even though she knows I don't take it.

'Sorry, I don't know what came over me,' I tell her, taking the mug as I stare down at the floor.

Jan holds up a palm. 'No, no, look, it's entirely understandable. You've been through so much. Emotions leak out when you're least expecting them.'

I snort a snotty laugh. 'You know that Rory and I used to have this silly dream about living here... I guess being at Ocean Heights is a bit of a trigger. I'll be fine.' I'm hoping that's enough to avert a full-on Jan questioning session. I can't face explaining about Mila or my dress or me suspecting that Anna Weston's nanny was lying. And I know that to anyone else, what I did last Friday would look insane... it's even starting to feel that way to me.

'You will indeed be fine,' she says kindly, staring at me for a moment. 'And as a distraction, you can give me your thoughts on a colour for the dining room. I'm thinking of this powder blue shade, what do you reckon?' She opens her iPad and pulls up a mood board on Pinterest.

'It's beautiful,' I say, meaning it, relieved she's changed topic.

We chat a while longer about the colourways she's put together for each room, with me adding my thoughts, when Jan's phone rings.

'It's Harry,' she says, checking the screen. 'I'd better see what he wants.'

I browse through the mood board while she answers her son's call. Harry is almost twenty, going on thirteen – an only child away at university. It seems he needs something from her several times a week, usually money.

'What do you mean, you're at the station?' Jan says.

I hear the urgent tones of a male voice coming down the line.

'Can't you call your dad?' A pause. 'Oh, typical. Well, he's out on the golf course so his phone is probably in the clubhouse locker.' A sigh. 'OK, give me ten or fifteen minutes and I'll be there,' Jan says before hanging up. 'Harry is at the station in town. An impromptu visit for the weekend,' she tells me, rolling her eyes. 'He wants a lift home. And probably money.' She shakes her head and glances at her watch. 'I'll only be gone half an hour. Come with me if you like, or feel free to stay here and get some inspiration. I'll leave my iPad so you can add to the mood board.'

'Couldn't he walk to yours from the station or get a taxi?' I ask, knowing how Jan always jumps the moment her son demands anything.

'He hurt his ankle playing rugby, apparently, and he said there weren't any taxis at the station. Besides, he doesn't have keys to the house, and I can't let him just sit in the garden.'

I don't bother suggesting he could wait in a café in town, because I know, deep down, Jan wants to drive him the mile to her house. And I also know I'd do the same for Jodie, which reminds me to check for messages. Nothing back from her yet.

'I'll wait here,' I tell her. 'I'm quite happy staring at this view for half an hour.' And it's true – as soon as Jan leaves, I plant myself in the hanging egg chair by the large window and stare out across the sea.

I rock myself gently back and forth as the white-topped waves roll towards the shore, feeling more relaxed just by staring out at the ocean. Once I hear Jan's car pull away from the house, I call Jodie again, hoping she'll pick up, though predictably, she doesn't. I'm going to have to have a word with her later about checking in with me more often. I get so anxious when she doesn't reply. I send her another brief message and put my phone away, rocking in the chair and hugging a soft cushion.

I have no idea what prompts the thought, but I'm suddenly

imagining myself sitting here holding a baby, rocking gently as the tide comes in, waiting for Rory to come home from work. I've got our favourite dinner in the oven, Jodie has a friend around, and my little baby is content and happy in my arms. As I stare down at my son or daughter's rosebud lips, I'm so grateful that the IVF finally worked... that the embryos we had frozen were successfully implanted and grew into our beautiful little—

Suddenly, I startle awake. I must have nodded off, but only for a moment. Despite the relaxing chair and view, I'm far too on edge to sleep, especially while in *this* house – the house where Mila lives. I can't believe I'm here alone, not to mention that Anna Weston stole my dress. And I'm almost certain it was her who stole my car, too. Something is very wrong, and now is my chance to find out what.

I need the bathroom for real now so head for the downstairs cloakroom. Afterwards, I pass by the study, the door still open from when Jan showed me around. Stopping and peering inside, I decide a quick look can't hurt – just to see if I can find anything out about Mila and her nanny's whereabouts. That's what I tell myself, anyway, as I glance out of the hallway window to check for cars. Jan will be gone for a little while yet.

TWENTY-SEVEN
HANNAH

My heart pounds at the thought of getting caught as I creep into the study. There's a bookshelf along one wall, so I quickly scan the titles to see if they give me any clues about Mila's mother. So far, the only evidence I've seen of a child living here is the pretty pink bedroom upstairs, though it was very tidy, and I barely saw any toys.

'*Your Healthy Pregnancy*,' I read out from a book's spine, my head turned sideways.

My chest tightens – I have a few similar books at home. There are some other pregnancy and childcare books beside it, their spines well-bent as though they've been read several times.

'*Investments Made Easy*,' I read, scanning another shelf that's filled with books about being successful in life and various self-help titles. I can't help but be impressed by Anna Weston's small library.

Then I spot a book that makes my heart race – I have the exact same one myself. *The IVF Bible: all you need to know for a healthy birth and beyond.* I take it off the shelf, thumbing through the well-worn pages. It makes me wonder if Mila's mother has had a similar journey to me, and I can't help the sudden pang of sympathy towards her.

I put it back on the shelf and head to a wooden filing cabinet, pulling open the top drawer. All the folders inside are neatly arranged with clearly printed labels such as *Car, Mortgage, Health, Insurance, School Reports.*

I take out the school reports folder and put it on the desk, one ear open for Jan coming back as I quickly leaf through the contents. 'Mila is a conscientious little girl, who enjoys writing stories and drawing,' I read. 'A little quiet in class discussions sometimes, she is thoughtful around her friends and a valued member of K1.' I smile, knowing that Kim, her form teacher, wrote these words – standard fare to sum up a sweet girl who's a bit shy.

I spot my own summary of Mila's artwork on the next sheet where her extra-curricular activities are logged. 'Mila has some interesting ideas and is clearly able to express her inner emotions well. She's competent with a paintbrush and imaginative for her age.' I nod, standing by what I wrote at the end of last term. Then her macabre picture is on my mind again – the one she painted at the last art group. It's hard to imagine such darkness coming from the mind of a child who lives in this neat and ordered home.

I shove the school folder back in the cabinet, quickly checking outside again. No sign of Jan coming back, and no one else around at all as far as I can see. Everyone seems to keep themselves to themselves at Ocean Heights.

I go back to the filing cabinet, deciding I have time to look inside one more file, and that's when I spot it, a file simply labelled 'Mila'. My hands are shaking as I take it out, as if I've just found the holy grail. I lay it flat on the desk and open it up.

On the top of the file is Mila's passport, seemingly unused and, I see by the date, only obtained last year. Her familiar little face stares back at me from the small photo, confirming that wherever she might be, she's not overseas.

I quickly flick through the other papers in the file, arranged in date order with the most recent at the top. There's some paperwork relating to childhood vaccinations, and a leaflet from the hospital about caring for a fracture. I remember Mila having her wrist in plaster for a few weeks not long after she started at St Peter's. There are a couple of achievement certificates too – a twenty-five-metre swimming award and a Grade 1 ballet exam. I smile briefly, imagining Mila in little pink ballet shoes.

Though none of these things are helping me find out where she is now. I glance over my shoulder to the door as a wave of guilt runs through me – Jan would flip if she knew what I was doing, snooping around her client's house. But it's as I get to the final documents that I start to wish I hadn't been quite so nosey. Some things you can't unsee.

My eyes widen in disbelief and my mouth drops open as I see the name *Mayfield Clinic* printed at the top of a bundle of papers. I suddenly feel lightheaded as the words blur in front of my eyes.

'What the hell...?' I whisper, recognising the familiar logo. My heart thumps even harder. It's the same clinic that Rory and I went to for our IVF treatment.

A wave of sadness engulfs me as the familiar paperwork triggers a cascade of emotions. I have similar at home, though I've since hidden it all away in a box in the spare room, not wanting to be reminded of my failings.

Anna had a different doctor to me though, I notice, not recognising the consultant's name. I quickly scan through all the medical papers and information sheets relating to implantation and pregnancy – though of course my paperwork trail ends with a record of miscarriage every time. I know I'm hurting myself by looking, but I can't help it.

I flip back to the start, finding the consent forms with two almost illegible parent signatures scrawled at the bottom of the page, alongside that of the doctor.

But it's not the doctor's name that makes me catch my breath. No, it's the names of the baby's mother and father that causes me to drop down into the desk chair, feeling as if I'm about to throw up.

Dear God no, this can't be right...

I stare down at the wording, reading it over and over to make sure I'm not imagining things. But however many times I check, it's still true.

The baby's father is named as Rory James Marlowe. And the mother, clearly printed in black and white, is named as *me* – Hannah Elizabeth Marlowe.

I don't feel real – as if I've stumbled into some kind of alternate reality. A reality that seems as if it should be *mine*, yet here it is in someone else's house. I hear my breath heaving in and out of my chest and see my hands shake as they come up to my face, covering my mouth as I try to absorb what I'm looking at.

Why the hell are mine and Rory's names on these IVF papers? The question screams through my head on a loop.

Suddenly, I snap to attention. I listen out, holding my breath, my whole body shaking now as I sit at Anna Weston's desk. I swear I heard something.

There – definitely a noise. A car coming down the street.

Hardly able to stand, I stagger to the hallway on legs that feel like jelly to check out of the window. I gasp, recognising Mila's nanny's white Fiat parked a little way down the street. For some reason, she appears to have stopped short of the house.

'Shit shit *shit*...' Feeling like I'm about to have a heart attack, I dart back into the study, quickly snap some photos of the clinic documents before shoving it all back in the folder and slamming the filing cabinet closed.

Then, in a panic, still reeling from what I've just found out, I grab a pointed silver letter opener from the desk, ducking behind the study door at the same moment I hear the front lock turning. I stare down at the dagger-like implement clutched in my shaking hands, wondering what the hell I'm doing.

I wait, trying not to move as I hold my breath, my thoughts in turmoil after seeing mine and Rory's names on those clinic papers, the words *'Three viable embryos of Mr Rory Marlowe and Mrs Hannah Marlowe successfully implanted on 3rd March 2019'* emblazoned on my mind.

Mila Weston is my daughter.

TWENTY-EIGHT

Before

'Tell me, Hannah,' the woman, late fifties, smartly dressed and with a neat blonde bob, said at the start of each therapy session.

Her voice, Hannah thought, was unnecessarily saccharine. She was almost twenty-seven, for God's sake. She didn't want platitudes and pity. She hated the niceness and etiquette of turning up on time. Turning up at *all*. She wanted to be force-fed the guilt she'd dragged around with her for six years since that night at university not long before they'd graduated. Have someone tell her in no uncertain terms that what happened to Natalie was all because of her. That she was evil. Deserved everything bad. That her penance for her crime was feeling like this for the rest of her life. The rawness of it still hit her in waves of crushing guilt and sadness every single day. Even in the immediate weeks afterwards, when repercussions, conse-quences and blame had begun the settling process, she knew that life would never be the same again.

But every session began the same way... 'Tell me, Hannah, how has this week been for you?'

'The same as the last one,' Hannah said without looking at her. 'And the same as the one before that and that and that. It's been the same *all* the weeks, right back to when I was at university. Satisfied?'

The therapist knew about her life as far back as 'that night', as Hannah had come to label it. But she'd not been able to go any back further in time – not even in her own mind, let alone spewing it out for someone else to hear. Blocking it out had become something of an art form.

'That sounds frustrating,' the woman said. 'All the weeks seeming the same. Is that what you're telling me?'

'Sounds like, sounds like, *sounds like...*' Hannah spat back, glaring at her. Her arms were folded, and her legs crossed, her feet aimed at the door. The escape route. 'Who cares what it sounds like?'

'I'm sensing a lot of anger,' she then said, followed by some other stuff that Hannah ignored. One session, they'd sat in virtual silence the whole time with Hannah breaking down in tears after forty-five minutes, only to blurt out that she hated herself just as her hand was reaching for the doorknob to leave.

'We'll pick up from here next week,' the counsellor had said, and indeed, next time, she'd kept to her word.

'Tell me what it is that makes you hate yourself.'

'Everything.' She looked away.

It hadn't been a good day at work, and she was exhausted from her evening job at the pub. Plus, Lewis, the guy she was supposed to be seeing, hadn't been in touch for well over a week. He'd got a mobile phone, but it never seemed to be turned on, and her mum didn't like her calling from the landline because it was expensive. Hannah had phoned the guesthouse where Lewis was staying, the one near the building site in Manchester, but the landlady said he'd left for another job further north.

'It's like... like I don't deserve to be here,' Hannah told the counsellor, pressing her lips together. *Not since that night*, she'd wanted to add, but stopped herself. She'd be damned if it was all coming out – not here, not *ever*. Not with this silly woman with her perfectly painted nails and shiny shoes who was just making everything worse.

'Life was OK once, you know,' she said, skipping back to the time before *that night*. She stared at the clouds through the window, the grey coming together in dark swirls. 'I was happy, studying for an art degree, doing what I loved. I had some kind of future mapped out.'

The woman nodded, focusing on her notepad. Hannah hated that she wrote things down about her. What was she saying? *Mad, unhinged, closed-off, compulsive liar?* Or maybe she was writing her shopping list or a meal plan for her family.

'Everything was going great – until I fell in love for the first time.'

And that was where Hannah firmly shut the door in her mind. What came after was no one else's business. She pressed the fast forward button to a safe place again.

'I'm sort of seeing a guy now, but...' She trailed off. 'You know.' A shrug. 'It's just casual.' She added the last bit to make herself feel better about Lewis being rubbish at phoning her. He'd kept spinning her lines about his job, about being busy.

'And this new guy doesn't feel the same as that first love you had at university?' the therapist asked.

Fuck you, Hannah thought. But she must also have shaken her head because the therapist continued.

'When first loves end, it can feel as though nothing will ever be as... as special or intense again. If I'm wrong, please tell me, Hannah. But I'd love to know what your first love felt like for you.'

Hannah paused, closing her eyes briefly, finding herself swept up in a reply. 'It was raw and exciting. Like someone had... had carbonated me. Do you get what I mean?' She turned to the therapist, looking her in the eye, thinking that she probably wouldn't understand. Hannah felt something loosen inside her. 'I felt fizzy from it. As if someone was shaking me up and was about to uncork me.' She laughed, unable to help the grin, the smile in her eyes. 'It was a beautiful, innocent, delicious and greedy love. We couldn't get enough of each other. Like, honestly, I never wanted those days to end.'

Except they did...

'It sounds very special. I don't think the feelings of our first love ever leave us.'

Hannah nodded. 'I guess. There were a couple of lads I crushed on at school, but that wasn't true love.'

'I like to think of those feelings as a kind of souvenir that you get to keep forever,' the therapist said. 'First loves rarely last, but they leave us with something to keep forever. A special memento to take on our journey. Would it help to see your feelings that way?'

Hannah closed herself off again. Despite wanting to lie her way through the session, she'd inadvertently found herself skirting close to the truth. She didn't want souvenirs and she didn't want memories. What she wanted was to take time back to when they'd first met, before they'd fallen in love. Then she'd have made sure it never happened. That they'd never even given each other a second glance.

TWENTY-NINE

JODIE

I'm sitting nervously in the passenger seat of Zayla's car on the way up to Ocean Heights, wondering what the hell I've got myself into. Can't lie, my heart has been thumping in my throat since we left the industrial estate. Getting into a car with a stranger, even if it is a girl, doesn't feel right.

At the entry gates to the new development, she stops and punches a number into a keypad, making me think she's been here before. She's not said a word all the way here.

I peer out at the huge houses. 'Do you know someone who lives here, is that it?'

Silence.

'Is that man from the warehouse making you do stuff? I saw him, you know.' It's a lie – I only saw his feet and legs, and barely heard his growly voice, but she doesn't know that.

Her forearms suddenly tense up, her knuckles turning white as she drives through the gates. 'Keep your nose out of it.' She gives me a sideways glance. 'Not your business.'

'But it *is* my business now,' I say, feeling more confident now we're actually here. She's driving so slowly I could leap out of the car if I had to.

'Look, I'm warning you,' Zayla hisses through pursed lips. She shakes her head, shooting me a quick glance as we pass by the big houses. 'Don't ask questions, OK? Just deliver the letter, get the photo, get back in the car. Then we'll go.'

She stops the car at the side of the road.

'Is that the house?' I point over to a large brick and timber place to my left with an immaculate front lawn. 'You want me to go in there?'

'No, it's that one,' she says, pointing further up ahead. 'The one with the white fence. I don't want to get too close.' Then she hands me a set of keys. 'This is for the front door. The burglar alarm will be triggered when you open it. Go to the cloakroom, where you'll find a control panel with—'

'What? Wait a minute. This isn't just dropping off a party invitation at a mate's house, is it?' I say, a sick feeling growing in my stomach. 'This really *is* breaking in.'

'Yeah, right. Breaking in with a key.' Zayla rolls her heavily made-up eyes. 'Hardly. It's... look, it's fine. The letter is nothing bad.' She takes the envelope from the central console, shoving it at me along with the key, telling me the four-digit alarm code. I don't take either of them. 'When you leave, put the alarm on again. Just enter the number, press the green button, then lock the front door. It's easy.'

'No,' I say firmly, putting my hand on the door handle to get out. 'No way am I doing that. I'm going home. This is all crap. You can keep my backpack, I don't care. I'm not breaking into someone's house for you.'

I pull the handle and open the door, half getting out.

'You want your mother to get hurt?' Zayla says with a wobble in her voice. 'He was dead serious, you know...'

I stop, turning to face her, one foot on the pavement. Zayla draws a line across her neck with her finger, giving me a pleading look.

'I'm trying to be a friend here,' she says earnestly. 'Trying to warn you.'

I see the fear in her eyes. See how her hands shake as she clasps them in her lap. 'I don't like it either, but please, just do it and then I'll take you back.'

'Fine,' I say after a moment, feeling as if I'm about to puke. I grab the letter and the keys and get out of the car, walking nervously towards the big house.

I repeat the alarm code to myself all the way up to the front door, glancing back at Zayla's white Fiat, wondering if I should run away or knock on someone else's door to get help. But I can't take any chances. What if those threats about Mum are true? If I just do as she says, I'll be back in town within twenty minutes, then it'll all be over.

I head up the front drive – Eastcliff House, the sign says – thinking that whoever lives here must be loaded. Taking a deep breath, I shove the key in the lock of the pristine white front door. Despite my shaking hands, it slides in easily and turns with a satisfying clunk. Then I push the door open just an inch, holding my breath as I wait for the alarm to be triggered like Zayla said. But there's nothing – no beeping or any other sound. I push the door open a bit more, wide enough for me to slip inside, but there's still nothing. Standing in the spacious hallway, I wave my arms about in case there's a sensor I need to set off – but again, silence.

Whoever lives here must have forgotten to put the alarm on when they went out. Or worse, they're still at home.

Nervously, I take the letter from my back pocket, wondering why the full address is written on it given it's being hand delivered. I don't recognise the handwriting – the plain capitals give nothing away – and I'm thinking about opening it, to see what I'm getting myself involved in here, when I suddenly hear a noise, like a door creaking.

Shit – there is someone here.

'Hello?' I call out nervously, instantly wishing I hadn't. 'Um... delivery here...' I add to make it sound vaguely plausible in case I'm caught. I'll just say no one answered when I knocked.

There are several doors leading off the hallway with a staircase in the middle. I slip through a set of double doors, hoping it's the way to the kitchen, and find myself in a living room with literally the most amazing sea view that I've ever seen. But I can't stop to gawp now. My instructions were clear: leave the letter in the kitchen, get a photo, then get out.

I keep walking, finding myself in a dining room and, beyond that, thank God, is a fancy white kitchen with a fridge almost the size of a car.

There – that noise again. Definitely a creaking sound. I don't like it. I swear there's someone else here. I freeze, listening out, then quickly drop the letter onto the worktop beside the kettle, snap a couple of photos on my phone, then head back the way I came as silently as I can manage.

It's just as I'm just going through the hallway, wondering if I should put the alarm on or leave it switched off, that I swear I see a shadow move under the door of one of the other rooms as if someone is lurking in there. My heart is thumping so fast I can barely put one foot in front of the other. Any second now, I'm going to have a lot of explaining to do.

Holding my breath, I walk over to the door and raise my hand, slowly pushing it open. First glance tells me it's a study – there's a desk by the window and a bookcase over on the other wall – and, initially, there doesn't seem to be anyone in there.

I sigh out from relief, going further inside and looking around, but I don't get much chance to see anything else as suddenly the door slams shut behind me and someone grabs my shoulders, spinning me round to face them.

'Oh my God, Jodie! What the hell are you doing here?'

'*Mum?*' I say, my voice barely working as she brandishes what looks like a knife at my throat.

THIRTY

HANNAH

'You scared me witless!' I say, releasing my daughter and quickly hiding the letter opener behind my back. Relief surges through me that she's safe, but I'm left with a question. 'What on earth are you doing in Mila's house?'

'Who's Mila?' Jodie says, scowling at me as she straightens her clothing.

I... I think she's my daughter... your half-sister... I want to blurt out, but I manage to stay silent.

I haven't even come close to processing what I just discovered myself, let alone be able to explain it to someone else. None of it makes sense... yet I saw it with my own eyes in black and white. Rory and I are Mila's biological parents... The thought sends spirals of disbelief through my body. How the hell did such a thing happen?

'No one... it doesn't matter. I'm sorry, love, I didn't mean to scare you.' It's all I can manage under the circumstances.

Jodie stares at my hands as I quickly place the letter opener back on the desk. I'm concerned Jan will be back at any moment.

'Anyway, what on earth are you doing here?' I ask, more harshly than I intended.

'Nothing much. Just... helping a friend,' Jodie replies with a nervous look in her eyes.

'What friend?' I feel terrible that my way of avoiding her asking me the same question is to get angry with her. 'And why isn't the tracking app working? I've been trying to reach you all morning, yet you ignore all my texts and calls and—'

'Sorry, Mum. Like I said, I've been helping a friend. She was in some bother.'

For some reason, Jodie suddenly sounds utterly believable. There's a tremor in her voice and an earnest look in her eyes as if she really is on a mission to help someone. For a moment, it even makes me forget all my own worries.

'My friend is called Zayla before you grill me about that too,' she says without missing a beat, though mention of Mila's nanny makes my heart thump. I had no idea they knew each other.

'Oh... I see. How did you two meet?' I try to sound casual. 'You've never mentioned her name before.'

'Playing Fortnite,' she replies with a shrug.

Plausible, I suppose. Having met the nanny, she does look the type to be into gaming.

'She... she asked me to pop in here... to pick something up for her.' Jodie scratches her nose and fiddles with her hair, shifting from one foot to the other.

'Such as?' I take her arm and guide her back to the hallway.

'Um... just her coat. Yeah, she wanted me to grab a jacket for her.'

'Right,' I say, spotting the white Fiat still parked further down the road through the hall window. 'In that case, go and give your friend her coat but then come back here. You can come home with me now, love. I'd like you to stay in for the afternoon and evening.'

All I want is for us both to be at home, knowing that Jodie's safe with me while I think over what I've discovered and decide what to do. Being a Saturday, it's not like I can call the fertility clinic for answers.

'But Mum—'

'Anyway, why didn't Zayla come inside herself?' I ask, sensing something feels off as I keep my eye on her car.

Jodie shrugs and gives me a concerned look. 'I don't know, Mum, but please... just let me grab her coat and go back into town with her. Then I promise I'll go straight home—'

'Jodie, no. Stop.' I rest my hands on her shoulders. 'I'm pretty lenient with your freedom, but today, you're going to do as you're told. Go and give the coat to your friend, say goodbye and tell her you're coming home with me. Understood?'

'Yes, Mum,' Jodie says. 'Anyway, what are *you* doing here—'

'*Now*, Jodie. OK?'

Jodie gives me a reluctant nod and looks around. 'You don't know where the coats are kept, do you?' she asks, almost in tears. I see a familiar furrow on her brow, her glistening eyes. She hugs her arms around herself.

'Try in here, love,' I say, flicking on the cloakroom light. I watch as Jodie grabs the nearest garment from a hook – a small blue waterproof jacket that doesn't look anything like the sort of thing Zayla would wear, let alone the right size. It looks more suited to a child – more suited to *Mila*.

'I won't be long,' she says, giving me a glance before opening the front door and rushing back to the Fiat. I watch as she opens the passenger door and chucks in the coat, but then, to my horror, Jodie also gets into the car. A second later, it swings around in the wide avenue and speeds off back towards the entry gates.

'Jodie! Wait!' I call, rushing outside, waving my arms about. But it's no use, the car is gone. I immediately phone her but get her voicemail. I can't believe she's done this. I let out a big sigh, knowing Jan will be back at any moment, so I head back inside and turn the cloakroom light off, but something else in there catches my eye. It's a man's coat hanging on the hook next to where the little blue jacket was.

I take it down. It's brown and way too big for a woman. Probably for a man at least six foot in height and broad across the chest too. The label isn't one I've heard of but looks quite expensive. Perhaps Anna Weston isn't as single as I'd been led to believe.

I stare at it for a moment then shake my head, quickly putting it back. The coat could just belong to a friend or male relative. Not that it's any of my business, I remind myself, feeling wrung out and drained from everything that's happened. There's simply no space in my head for anything else today – not until I find out why the hell those IVF papers with my name on are in Anna Weston's study.

The sea breeze whips my hair around my face as Jan and I sit near the clifftop sipping champagne an hour later.

'To us and... and good fortune,' Jan says, chinking her plastic flute against mine. Then she smooths out the tartan picnic rug we're sitting on. 'Don't worry, I'll only have one,' she adds, raising her glass, not realising that with everything on my mind, I hadn't given her drink a second thought.

I have another large sip, knowing that alcohol in the afternoon is going to give me a terrible headache, but right now I don't care. If it takes away the hurricane of feelings inside me, then that's fine by me. I'm not sure how long I can keep quiet about what I saw in the study, not knowing if I should go back to the police and insist they do another welfare check on Mila, or tell Jan about what I found – that mine and Rory's names were on her client's IVF papers. Or maybe I should just wait to contact the fertility clinic first thing on Monday. I could keep everything to myself and hope I've just had a bad dream. A terrible, *terrible* nightmare.

How can Mila possibly be my daughter? Nothing makes sense.

'Go on, your turn to spill,' Jan says after regaling me about Harry's swollen ankle, how she thinks it might be broken. She leans sideways and nudges me with her shoulder. 'I've known you long enough to figure there's something on your mind.'

'I'm fine,' I reply, my hand shaking as I bring the glass to my lips. 'Honestly.'

Jan takes the champagne from me and puts it down on the cheeseboard where it won't topple. 'You need some food inside you,' she says. 'You're shaking. When did you last eat?'

'I'm fine, honestly.' But Jan hands me a plate of cheese, biscuits, cold meats and a homemade Scotch egg from the deli in town. 'It's just that...'

'Just that what?'

'You'll probably think I'm mad, but I'm really worried about a little girl at school,' I tell her, annoyed with myself that I've even revealed that much, but it does feel good to have shared a tiny bit at least.

'Go on.'

'She was poorly. She's been off school for a whole week now. She has a nanny, but no one's heard from her for over a week.' I hate lying, but there's no way I'm telling anyone that I've spoken to Zayla, that she fixed my car, that she lied about Mila's whereabouts, that she gave my daughter a lift only half an hour ago. Some secrets are best kept... well, secret.

'So where's the girl's mother?' Jan asks.

'Away on business,' I say, thinking I probably shouldn't say any more, not when I'm talking about Jan's actual client. 'Thing is, they did a welfare check on the little girl recently, and that was all fine. Now there's a social services follow-up.' I really, *really* shouldn't be saying all these things but can't help myself.

I wring my hands in my lap, cursing myself, yet desperately needing advice. Not having Rory to confide in anymore really hits home how alone I am.

Jan remains silent for a while, having some food and a few sips of her drink. Then she frowns and says, 'Hannah, apologies if I'm missing something here—'

'It's Mila, your client's daughter!' I blurt out, kicking myself the moment the words come out. 'I don't know what to do. She's in my art class at school, and I think she's gone missing.'

THIRTY-ONE
HANNAH

'I'm sorry I ruined the picnic,' I say as Jan drives us back towards town, but she instantly tells me I haven't. Thankfully, there's no judgement from her, and I'm grateful she doesn't question me too much about Mila – just one or two sympathetic comments about letting the school and police deal with it. She senses how fragile I am.

I haven't revealed to her what I found in Anna Weston's study, or that I have no idea how I'm going to get through until Monday morning when I can phone the fertility clinic to find out why another woman's IVF papers have mine and my estranged husband's names on them. It simply doesn't make sense. Well, not any sense that I'm prepared to consider, anyway. What it *might* mean is utterly unthinkable.

'Do you want me to come in with you?' Jan says when she pulls up outside my house. I haven't told her that Jodie is friends with Mila's nanny, Zayla, either, or that Jodie just happened to turn up at Ocean Heights while she was fetching Harry.

It all seems such a mess, and until I've worked out what's going on myself, I don't want to complicate things for Jan when all she'd wanted was to get a bit of work done then have us enjoy a picnic together. Somehow, I've managed to ruin it all.

'No, you get off home and see Harry,' I tell her. 'I'll be fine.'

Jan gives my hand a squeeze before I get out of the car. 'I'll call you later, OK?'

I nod, grateful to have such a good friend, and head inside. The house seems dark and cold, despite the lovely day outside, and there's no sign of Jodie back yet. I put the kettle on and make a cup of tea, but between phoning and messaging my daughter, checking the tracking app in case it locates her, and searching for information about the fertility clinic, my drink goes completely cold.

I sit at the kitchen table, shivering and staring into space, with no idea where Jodie is, and no idea why my paperwork might have got mixed up at the clinic. When I searched online about errors at fertility clinics, some shocking stories came up in the results – clinics implanting embryos into the wrong women. Though thankfully it seems the chances of this happening are extremely rare.

I drag myself upstairs and, even though I know she's not home, I still knock on Jodie's bedroom door out of habit before going inside. It's messy, as usual, and I catch a whiff of the body spray she uses every day – a coconut scent that reminds me of family holidays. Of times long gone.

I stand beside her unmade bed, looking around. There's a pile of dirty clothes on the floor in the corner, and an equally large pile of worn stuff on her chair by the window. The top of her chest of drawers is littered with all her beauty and make-up products, and her hairbrush is a tangle of hairs.

On her desk is a pile of schoolbooks, a folder with scribbles all over the cover, plus various pens and rulers and highlighters. Her laptop is also there, the lid covered in peeling stickers. On a whim, I open it up and, as expected, there's a login screen asking for her password. I sit down at her desk, thinking for a moment, typing in a couple of guesses, but the screen judders when they fail. I'm worried that if I keep getting it wrong, the system will lock entirely, alerting Jodie to my snooping when she comes back. I'm about to give up and gather up all her laundry when I see some jottings on her open notepad.

In among a few notes about homework, I see *Shadow-Knight184* scribbled over and over, decorated with hearts and swirls and Xs all around. She's noted down a couple of dates and times – Fortnite, 8 p.m. Elden Ring Sat morn. Shadow-Knight184's name is written alongside Fortnite, which I know is a game she likes to play.

They must be the times she's arranged to game with her online pals, and how she met Zayla. Though as I gather up her dirty clothes, I can't help thinking what a coincidence it was to find someone so local on a gaming platform that has people from all over the world on it. And not only that, but she just happens to be Mila's nanny. It makes me suspect it's not much of a coincidence at all.

Downstairs, I shove the laundry in the washing machine and set it running. Then I grab my laptop to see what I can find out about whoever this ShadowKnight184 person is. For a start, I want to know why Jodie has seen fit to decorate her notebook with the name, covering it in love hearts, though I'm pretty sure it will turn out to be the username of the lad she mentioned she likes – the one who cancelled on her the other night. If nothing else, it'll make me feel like I'm doing something useful until she gets home. She's still not answering her phone and after everything that's happened today, my nerves are in tatters.

I enter ShadowKnight184 into the search bar and scan the results. The first page is filled with links to games and books about Shadows and Dark Knights and all kinds of forum posts and articles about superheroes and comic-collecting websites. The next page seems similar, though halfway down there's a more specific hit on a gaming discussion forum.

I click the link and end up on what appears to be a chat board with one particular post referring to gamers in this area. Someone has posted a question about a meetup at a gaming convention, and while there's no one replying with the username ShadowKnight184, his name is mentioned within someone else's post.

Can't make the meet but paging @ShadowKnight184 in case he wants to go.

Then I spot the name of the person who wrote the comment – Jodeenoodle09. My eyes well up as I recognise my daughter's gaming handle. Rory's nickname for her was *noodle*. I drop my head down on the table, finally letting the tears flood out as I wonder what the hell has become of my little family.

After I've gathered myself again, it only takes a moment to set up a user account on the gaming chat forum, and another minute to realise that as a newbie account, I can't contact another poster directly until I've got ten 'thumbs ups' from people ranking my forum contributions. I suppose to prove I'm a real person with good intentions.

'Damn,' I say, running a username search for Shadow-Knight184. All it shows me is that he has an account, but his full details aren't visible to me because I've only just signed up. A good thing, I suppose, in that anyone can't just start chatting with members given that most of the accounts on this site probably belong to kids.

I shut my laptop lid, feeling a bit creepy for wanting to track down the boy Jodie likes. She wouldn't be happy if she knew I was snooping. But since Rory left, I need to be doubly vigilant about her safety online as well as in the real world – which I should probably be more concerned about right now given that she still isn't home.

She's probably just lost track of time, but I call her again, then send her another message telling her where I'm going this afternoon and, like a broken record, I ask her to phone me back. The tracking app still isn't locating her. Instead of sitting here fretting, I head out for my fortnightly visit to see Marion at the Elms Nursing home in Upper Bredon, a village about three miles west of here.

Before Rory left, I visited his mum several times a week when she lived at Chapelfields, Marion and Frank's family home and the place where Rory grew up. For the last eighteen months, though, I've been visiting her at the Elms Nursing Home where she now lives. Before he left, Rory would sometimes come with me, but more often than not he would have an excuse why he couldn't visit his eighty-three-year-old mum. He wanted to go cycling, mow the lawn, watch the football, do some work – leaving me to make up lies to tell her. In the end, I think poor Marion began to think she had a daughter rather than a son and would often get muddled. Or should I say, *more* muddled. Her dementia has really taken hold this last year or so.

Most of the carers and nursing staff at the Elms know me well, and when Rory first disappeared, I told them that he'd gone away on an extended work trip. I fed Marion the same story for a few months, too. But when the nursing home's manager started wondering why Marion's only son wasn't visiting, I came clean and admitted that we'd separated, telling them that Rory would be seeing his mother on his own from now on.

They asked me for his new address, so I had to pretend that I didn't know it. Actually, it wasn't a pretence – I really *didn't* know where he was living. In fact, in the early days, I wasn't even sure he was still alive. It was four months after he vanished when I finally got physical proof that Rory still existed – and that was during one of my visits to Marion when I spotted a bunch of fresh flowers in her room. There was a card beside them that simply said, in handwriting that made my stomach churn, *Happy Birthday, Mum. Love Rory xx*

I'd sat there staring at the flowers and the card, barely listening to Marion as she told me about the dry lamb chops she'd had for dinner last night, how the new hairdresser wasn't as good as the old one, and how Rory had told her that she'd have to move from her ground-floor bedroom with doors onto the terrace into a much cheaper room on the third floor.

'Rory said it's because of the money,' she'd whispered with a frown, her bony hands constantly moving in her lap. My ears had pricked up then, confirming again that my husband had been to visit his mother.

I tried so hard not to grill Marion about her son.

How did he seem? Did he look healthy? Was anyone with him – a woman, perhaps? Was he wearing his wedding ring? Did he say where he was living now? Is he still working at Draper Ford? Did he mention me? Did he mention Jodie? Did he say anything... anything at all... that might give a clue as to why the hell he upended our lives and walked out on me?

But all I'd said in response was, 'I'm sure it'll still be a nice room, Marion.'

I park the car and go inside the Elms, finding Rory's mother sitting in an armchair in the communal living room with a magazine on her lap and her head resting to one side. Her mouth is slightly open, and her glasses are about to fall off the end of her nose. I sit down beside her and touch her arm.

'Marion, it's me... Hannah,' I say softly.

One of the carers smiles as she walks past. 'She went for a stroll earlier,' she tells me. 'Tired herself out, she has.'

I smile back, waiting as Marion stirs. 'Oh...' she says in a croak. 'Hello, Jodie. Am I dreaming?'

I laugh. 'No, Marion, I'm really here. You were having a little nap. Sorry to wake you.' I don't bother correcting her about my name.

'No, no that's OK. Is it time?'

'Time for what?' I ask.

Marion thinks for a moment, frowning and staring around the room as if she's looking for someone. Then she looks at her watch. 'Time for Rory to come. Is Daddy with you, love?'

I freeze, not knowing what to say, glancing at the door in case Rory should come striding in.

I've gone over this scenario many times before, working out a plan in case he turns up while I'm here. If I'm honest, I suppose it's part of the reason why I still visit Marion – in case I *should* bump into him now that I have confirmation he's still alive. Though I already knew that much from the police when the only thing they were able to tell me was that *some people don't want to be found.*

'I'm Hannah,' I remind Marion, taking her hand in mine. 'Rory and I aren't together anymore, do you remember?' I look at her, wondering what on earth she'd make of what I found in Anna Weston's study earlier – that she very likely has another grandchild. I just need to make it through to Monday morning when I can phone the clinic and hopefully get answers. Marion gives me a look that breaks my heart, as if she's finding out for the first time that her son has left me.

'Oh no,' she says in a deep, disapproving voice. 'But where's his little daughter then? Such a lovely baby girl.'

'Jodie is...' I hesitate, not actually able to answer that right now given she still hasn't messaged me. And I don't bother correcting her that Rory isn't actually Jodie's father because for all intents and purposes, he was. 'Jodie is nearly sixteen now, Marion,' I say patiently. 'Not a baby anymore. She's out with a friend today,' I tell her, figuring it's sort of the truth.

'Well,' Marion says, sounding shocked. 'She's all grown up.

What on earth would Frank say about you and Rory? God rest his soul.'

'I know, Marion, it's not what I wanted, but Jodie and I are doing fine.' I don't want her to worry. 'Rory's been in to see you, hasn't he?'

Marion looks at me blankly, her eyes narrowing. 'I... I don't know, dear. Has he?' The magazine on her lap slides onto the floor, so I pick it up and put it on the side table.

'He brought you flowers and a card for your birthday a few months ago. Has he been to visit you since?'

'Yes, yes that's right, dear,' she says vaguely, which tells me nothing apart from that she's still confused. 'I need to spend a penny now. Will you take me?'

'Of course,' I say, helping her stand up and get a good grip on her walking frame.

I take her back to her room and wait outside the unlocked bathroom door in case she needs help. Afterwards, she shuffles over to her chair and sits down, looking at the door expectantly.

'Rory shouldn't be long now,' she says, making me wonder if it's some kind of set-up between them, that Rory has orchestrated a visit while I'm here. 'He's gone to deal with my money,' she adds. 'He's going to take care of everything for me. He said that he'll make good investments so that I can get my nice room back on the ground floor.'

'Marion, wait... Rory's doing *what*?' I say, my heart kicking up a gear.

Anything to do with Marion and Frank's house or finances sets me on edge, knowing that Rory has had his sights set on his parents' property for a long while. It was the one thing about him that didn't sit right with me – him getting ready to pounce on the estate the moment his parents passed away, if not before. There was a paddock attached to the property with barns that were ripe for planning and development, and it seemed he'd already spent the proceeds in his mind.

'What do you mean, he's gone to deal with your money?' I want to remind her that she's already rich, that she shouldn't have to move rooms to cut costs, but I hold back.

'Don't worry, dear. Rory said he will make everything better. He's going to have to sell Chapelfields so that I can carry on living here. He said the bills were getting too much for him, that Frank didn't provide enough money for me like I thought.' She shakes her head and sighs. 'The silly old fool,' she adds with a fond yet wistful smile. 'Rory says my money is almost gone.' Marion wrings her bony hands in her lap. 'But he says I'll be OK if I sign a few papers.'

This is all hard to believe. Frank left a huge sum in trust for Marion when he died, easily enough to cover her nursing home fees for life if need be. And it was stated in his will that Chapelfields should not be sold to fund her care.

In fact, Frank was keen for Rory to inherit the family home and live there himself. It had belonged to his grandfather before Frank took it over, and he loved the idea of it being passed down the generations. He was as sentimental as they came, and Chapelfields was his happy place – an old farmhouse on the edge of a village three miles from the coast. I never wanted to push things with Rory as it wasn't my place to do so, but I'd have much preferred to live there than struggle to afford building up at Ocean Heights. But he'd always been against it, especially more recently, claiming it was a money pit that needed a fortune in repairs, that his father had been stuck in the past.

'Are you certain, Marion?' I say, wondering if she's confused. 'Where are your house keys now?' Not that that would stop Rory getting in or having the locks changed. He'd always had a sense of entitlement when it came to his parents' wealth. And being Marion's only son with power of attorney, it's doubtful anyone would question or challenge him. It feels even more like I never knew my husband at all.

'Oh dear, I don't know,' she says, touching her forehead. 'I thought I gave them to Rory, but maybe I forgot. He'll be cross with me, won't he?'

'No one is cross with you, Marion,' I say, going over to her dressing table. 'Are they still in here with your other bits and pieces?'

When she first came to the Elms, we wanted Marion to feel as if she still had a sense of control, agency over her affairs so the move didn't feel too permanent. She wasn't coping alone at Chapelfields physically anymore, so it was a way to get her to come to a care home in the first place. She liked the idea of having keys to go back at any time, to still have a say in her life. But gradually, over the months, her health had declined further.

'I don't know, dear, if I'm perfectly honest,' she says, sounding lost and confused. 'Would Hannah know?'

I sigh, letting her mistake pass, and open the dressing table drawer, hunting around inside. I pull out various papers and trinkets before finding a bunch of keys.

Marion's face lights up when she sees them. 'I told Rory I'm not selling the house, that I want my granddaughter to grow up at Chapelfields just like he did.' She chuckles and looks down at my stomach. 'Can we expect the patter of tiny feet any time soon, dear? Rory told me he can't wait to be a father again.'

Something inside me folds up in agony, and instead of replying, I just give her a nod and a smile, muttering 'perhaps' and 'soon' under my breath. Marion's confusion gets worse each time I see her.

'Now, I want you to do me a favour, dear,' she says, pressing her hand around mine, making me grip her house keys harder. 'In the spare bedroom at Chapelfields there's a special little something I've been keeping for you and your new baby. Something you're going to love.' I see the excitement in her eyes while feeling the pain behind my own. 'I want you to go and get it for me and bring it back here, do you understand? It's under the bed in the spare bedroom in a small brown suitcase. I want to give it to you personally. It's so special – it used to belong to Rory, but I want you to have it now for your precious little cherub.'

Then Marion places her hands on my flat stomach, making my heart ache with sadness.

THIRTY-THREE
JODIE

'What the hell's *that?*' Zayla had said as soon as I leapt back in the car at Ocean Heights, eyeing the coat. 'Did you deliver the note?'

'Just drive!' I'd replied, breathless as I spotted Mum running towards us. She'll go mental that I disobeyed her, but I figured I'd deal with that later. It was just my luck to have run into her, though I've no idea what she was doing up at Ocean Heights.

As we sped off, Zayla swore at me, not believing my story about why I'd taken the coat. Then, halfway back to town along the coastal road, she'd stopped at a picnic spot and ordered me to get out. 'Chuck it over the cliff edge,' she said. 'Make sure it goes right into the sea.'

After I'd done it – my hair whipping around my face as I stood at the barrier watching the pale blue coat fall to the rocks below – Zayla carried on driving, remaining silent the rest of the way back. I didn't tell her I'd seen Mum at the house – not after all the threats against her. I'd just wanted to get this whole thing over with and go home.

But instead of dropping me in town, Zayla had driven along

the bypass, then back down the potholed road to the industrial estate – which is where we are now.

'Your bag is in the warehouse,' Zayla says, pulling up outside the dilapidated building. 'I'll go and get it.'

'I thought you said it was in your car boot?'

She shrugs. 'I've told you a lot of things that aren't true. You'd do well not to ask any more questions.' Then she tells me to get out of the car and wait here, giving me a stern look as she slopes off.

Fifteen minutes later, as I'm about to give up and leave, thinking I'll never get my stuff back, she returns. 'Be more careful next time,' she says, thrusting my backpack at me. Then, in a low voice, she adds, 'And don't ever come here again, yeah? He says that if you do...' She draws another line across her neck, making me recoil. 'He fucking means it, right?'

'Who is he?' I whisper back, wishing I'd got a proper look at him now when I was hiding under the machinery.

'Just go, you idiot, before it's too late,' Zayla replies, glancing over her shoulder. 'And don't even think about going to the police.'

My heart pounds when I see how panicked she is. 'Look, why don't you come back to town with me?' I suggest, hating that she's obviously being forced to do stuff she doesn't want to. She seems a decent sort. 'If you've got mixed up in... in something bad, then you can leave, you know.' I look over at the warehouse just as there's a loud smashing sound coming from within. It makes me jump.

'You don't understand,' she hisses. 'Just get the hell out of here, yeah?' She gives me a shove.

I pause for a second, hoping she'll change her mind, but when I hear another loud crash from inside the warehouse, I take her advice and walk briskly back up the hill towards town, taking the quicker road route this time instead of the river path.

I look back over my shoulder a few times, but Zayla has gone, and when I'm almost back in town, just as I reach the roundabout near the supermarket, I feel my phone buzz in my pocket. I must have just picked up reception again. My screen shows another missed call and a message from Mum – in addition to the many notifications from earlier all saying the same thing: *call me, go home, where are you?* – but it's the gaming chat app alert that catches my eye.

ShadowKnight184 has sent you a message.

Something inside me skitters as I open the app and read his words – sent only ten minutes ago.

Want to meet now? I'm parked up opposite the fountain in town. Look for the dark blue van.

Back in town, the fruit and veg market is packing up in the square with lots of noise and bustle as the traders take down their stalls. When I reach the fountain end of the marketplace, I scan the road running alongside it, looking for a dark blue van. Shadow didn't say what kind of van, but at least he knows what I look like, so he'll probably spot me first.

My stomach flutters when I think that if he's old enough to drive, he must be at least seventeen or eighteen. I guess that's OK – it's not long until I'm sixteen. It's been a crazy day so far and I feel wrung out and hyper from everything that's happened, but I'm just glad to have my stuff back. And now I finally get to meet the boy who has become such a good friend online. I hope he likes me. Perhaps life is finally looking up.

'Oh, sorry,' I say, bumping into a stallholder carting a load of boxes across the square. I spin around as I walk towards the road, shielding my eyes against the sun.

And then I spot it: the blue van. At least, I presume it's Shadow's van because it's the only one around. He'd better tell me his real name now that we're meeting in real life – he already knows mine. I suppose I was stupid to include it in my username, but I've used that one since forever. I wasn't about to lie when he asked if Jodie was my real name.

I stand on tiptoe and raise my hand, waving madly and grinning as I get closer to the busy road. A passing bus blocks my view momentarily, but I think I saw the shape of someone sitting in the driver's seat. I cross the road, darting between cars to get over, and the door of the van opens and... and oh my God, this is so exciting – I can hardly contain myself, I'm literally full of butterflies...

Then someone gets out. Someone tall and muscular and broad... dressed in jeans and a T-shirt, a thick overshirt on top. My heart skips a few beats when I see him, trying to process what's going on.

What the hell...?

'Hello, Jodie,' he says as I approach.

We stand facing each other near the back of his van – me having suddenly stopped, still half-standing in the road, and him with a grin on his face. All I can think as I stare up at him, as he slides his big hands into mine, as the wrinkles crease around his eyes, as I notice the dense stubble on his strong jaw, how thickset his neck and shoulders and thighs are... all I can think of is that Shadow isn't a *lad* at all.

He's a grown man. An adult. Old enough to be my... I shudder at the thought.

Has he been lying to me all this time? I pray to God there's an explanation for this, that this is Shadow's dad come to pick me up... and not actually Shadow at all.

'You're... you're...' I say, taking a step backwards to release my hands from his. But he keeps a firm hold on them. *You're ancient...* is what I want to say, but it won't come out. The way he's looking at me – it feels like an arm closing around my throat, choking me up.

I try to pull free, but his grip on me tightens. And then, in a few easy moves, he grabs me and bundles me into the back of his van.

THIRTY-FOUR

Before

Hannah thought the man in the pub had smiley eyes. She could hardly believe that she'd been stuck in dead end jobs for the last six years since university had finished. So much for her art degree. Here she was – living back at home doing a supermarket daytime shift during the week, plus a part-time job pulling pints in the evenings at the Sailor's Arms, a small pub mainly frequented by locals about her parents' age. In fact, Jeannie and George Bailey, Hannah's mum and dad, were part of the furniture on a Friday night between seven and nine. They came in every week for their fish and chip supper.

Hannah watched the man with the smiley eyes as she angled the pint glass, allowing the head to form on the beer as she pulled the tap. He was a couple of years older than her, she reckoned, and it was the second Friday night in a row that she'd spotted him in the pub. He was with a group of four or five other guys, all sinking their pints, laughing and chatting about God knows what.

'Another round, love,' one of the group said after depositing a tray of glasses on the bar. He winked and looked back over his shoulder at the TV on the wall. The football was on – not loudly, but enough for customers to watch what was going on.

'*Yesss*, get in!' the man standing at the bar suddenly yelled, pumping his arm in the air. The group he was sitting with suddenly stood up, cheering – all except the guy Hannah had been watching. Instead, he caught her eye and smiled.

Later, when the others were outside smoking, the man with the smiley eyes came up to the bar. 'I'll have a whisky, please,' he said, taking a brown leather wallet from his back pocket. He pulled out a ten-pound note.

'Your mates gone home?' Hannah asked over her shoulder, pressing the glass under the optic. She knew they hadn't, but it was a way to start a conversation. She put his drink on the bar.

'Gone outside for a smoke,' the man said. 'Grudgingly, I might add.' He laughed.

'It's about time,' she said in reply. 'Means I don't have to breathe it in.' She pointed at the yellowed ceiling between the beams. The smoking ban had come into force a month ago and customers still hadn't stopped grumbling about having to stand outside if it was raining. Thankfully, being August, it was at least mild.

'You don't smoke?'

'Nah, I quit,' he told Hannah with a cheeky grin. '*Again*,' he added, laughing. Hannah gave him his change, watching as he knocked back his whisky in one go. 'Another, please, love. And get one for yourself.' He slid the change back towards her.

She gave him his drink and then poured herself a Coke. 'Are you new around here? Not seen you before.' *Apart from last week*, she thought, but wasn't about to let on that she'd noticed him. He knew how attractive he was, she could tell by the way he leant on the bar, the way his green eyes followed her about as she worked – not because he was checking her out, but more to see if she was checking *him* out. And she was.

'I'm working up on the bypass,' he told her. 'Eight-week contract building the bridge over the river just north of town. Near the industrial estate.'

'Nice,' Hannah said, not knowing if it really was or not.

'They put us up in the High View Guesthouse.' Hannah knew of it. It was only a couple of streets away. 'It's what I do – contract building work around the country. Takes me all over.' He downed his second whisky.

'A bit of a nomad then?' Hannah asked, looking over to him as she took a card payment from an older couple. She felt a twang of disappointment.

'For now,' he said, sliding his pint glass towards her. 'Until I meet the right one and settle down.'

He held Hannah's gaze for as long as it took her to pour him another pint, to take his money, to serve many other customers during the course of the evening, to clear up the bar, then walk back to his guesthouse and peel off her clothes after he'd shut the door to his attic room. He didn't let go of her gaze even once.

'I'll call you,' were Lewis's parting words when he left early the next morning for work, holding up a pretend phone to his ear. Hannah was still in his bed – a lumpy single mattress in a room with a sloping roof and creaky floorboards – with the sheets pulled up under her arms. He told her to let herself out when she was ready.

When he'd gone, she got up feeling a warmth inside her that she'd not experienced in ages. She hadn't allowed herself to get involved with anyone since moving back home from university – six years now. Hannah pulled on last night's clothes and, after leaving the guesthouse, she went for a walk along the beach, tipping her face to the sun and feeling... feeling... almost *happy* for the first time in ages.

Lewis never did call. Not that day, nor the rest of the week.

A couple of the lads he'd been with last Friday came in for fish and chips and a few beers the week after, but there was no sign of Lewis. Before they left, Hannah asked if they'd seen him, if they knew where he was, but they didn't. She'd given him her number, not thinking to take his. He said he'd call and she'd believed him.

It was two months before she saw Lewis again. Him turning up at the bar out of the blue as if no time at all had passed. His cheeky grin and smiley eyes winning her over as she pulled his pints, shaking her head and trying not to smile as he led her back to High View Guesthouse after she'd closed up the bar. She couldn't help the fluttering inside. This time before he left for work in the morning, she made sure she took down his number.

'Lewis... *Lewis*, fucking call me back...' Hannah screamed down the phone. Her mum was rubbing her back.

'Leave it be, for God's sake, Han,' she said, sounding impatient now. The contractions were growing closer, and Hannah had called him about a dozen times, always getting his voicemail. 'I could have told you this would happen months ago. Forget him and focus on getting this baby out, OK?'

'Owww... *oww*, it hurts so bad, Mum... I can't do this. Where *is* he? He promised.' More sobs.

Jeannie rolled her eyes, though Hannah didn't see. 'Love, you've got no choice. This baby is coming whether you like it or not.'

They'd already been to the hospital earlier but were sent home by the midwife, who said that Hannah was only two centimetres dilated and it would likely be hours yet. Jeannie hadn't wanted to say *I told you so* to her daughter, though she certainly felt like it now when it came to getting hold of that loser who'd got her pregnant. Hannah had only known him a year and a half, and in that time, he'd gone off and left her without a word more times than Jeannie had fingers to count. She and George were at their wits' end with it. And now, at their age, they'd have a baby in the house again. Lewis had shown no signs of stepping up as a responsible father and getting them a place of their own.

Five hours later, Jeannie decided it was time to go back to the hospital, so she got George to drive her and Hannah, plus Hannah's friend from work, Julie, to the maternity ward. Another eight hours, copious amounts of gas and air, a begged-for epidural plus a narrowly avoided emergency C-section, and Jodie Alicia Dunn was born.

'I love you, little one,' Hannah crooned over the swaddled bundle in her arms, exhausted and sweaty, yet pumped with the glow of true happiness.

Jeannie never said anything, but secretly she wished Hannah had given Jodie her own surname, Bailey, and not that of the loser.

'It keeps me feeling close to him,' Hannah said a week later when her mother asked if she was certain she wanted Lewis named on the birth certificate. He still hadn't been in touch let alone met his baby daughter. 'Knowing I'll always have a piece of him with me wherever he is. It's some comfort.'

As if she already knows he's never coming back, Jeannie thought but kept it to herself.

THIRTY-FIVE

HANNAH

After I say goodbye to Marion at the Elms, I take a quick detour to Chapelfields before going home. Marion was quite insistent about me fetching the baby stuff she wants to give me so to stop her getting upset, I promised her that I'd go and get the suitcase now and bring it with me next time I visit her. Besides, it also gives me a chance to do a quick check on the place. I shouldn't be so mistrusting of Rory and his intentions, but I can't help it. This time a year ago, these thoughts would have been unimaginable.

Rory's family home smells musty and unlived-in when I go inside. It looks as though the gardener still comes because the lawn is cut and the borders neat, but I don't have time to sort out any other practical issues right now.

I head upstairs, hoping I can find the suitcase easily. Marion is a borderline hoarder, and I can't face rooting through a load of old stuff from when Rory was a baby, pretending to be grateful for whatever she wants to give me when all it will do is remind me of him. It was bad enough that I played along with her belief that I'm pregnant, that she'll have a grandchild soon. I hadn't got the heart to shatter her dreams, even though her son shattered mine.

There are several spare bedrooms at Chapelfields, but it's second time lucky where, in the room with the pink and white roses on the wallpaper – the room that Rory and I have slept in many times – that I spot a battered brown leather suitcase under the bed. I slide it out and brush off the dust and cobwebs. It's not huge, but it's stuffed full and, when I pick it up, one of the metal catches pops open. I force it shut again and take it downstairs, locking up the house and shoving it on the passenger seat of my car.

As I drive home, my stomach knots when I think back to earlier at Ocean Heights, what I found in Anna Weston's study. I've just got to get through today and tomorrow, and then I can phone Mayfield Clinic on Monday to find out what the hell has happened, why another of their clients has got paperwork with *my* name on it in her house. A paperwork mix-up is bad enough – I suppose that can be rectified – but I just want to know that my embryos are safe. My mind keeps going to dark places, fast-forwarding to a custody battle where I'm fighting for Mila, watching as another woman brings up my daughter. The daughter Rory and I wanted so badly.

If nothing else, it's been a wake-up call – that now might be the right time for one last attempt to get pregnant, even though I'll have to go it alone – *again*. Mum and Dad have said they'd lend me some cash for the procedure, and with a personal loan from the bank, maybe even borrowing a bit more against the house, I think I'll be able to raise the funds. I'll mention it to the clinic when I call on Monday.

I pull up outside home, going over and over what's happened these last few days, trying to make sense of it. If Mila isn't at school on Monday, and if the office can't reach her mother or her nanny to confirm that she's OK, then I'm a hundred per cent going back to the police, which will likely mean everything spilling out at work. What with that and the thought of calling the clinic looming over me, I'm really dreading the start of the week.

I lock my car and head up the garden path. Next door, Mrs Kirk is deadheading an early flush of roses and gives me a little wave followed by a look that's... well, if I'm honest, it's a bit pitying. She nods and goes back to her gardening.

Inside, I kick off my shoes and dump my bag, calling up the stairs. 'Jodie, are you home?'

I wait a moment, praying for a reply, but then relief floods through me when I spot my daughter's white and blue trainers on the hallway floor. I remember she was wearing them earlier when she came up to Ocean Heights.

'Thank heavens,' I say, going through to the kitchen, hearing her mumbling to herself in her room upstairs, probably with her headphones on while chatting to her gaming mates.

I make two mugs of tea and take them up, hoping that the peace offering will allow us to talk. She's been secretive lately, and at fifteen, she might think that she's all grown up, but to me she's still my little girl.

But on the landing, I suddenly stop. Voices – I hear voices and laughter coming from Jodie's room. My first thought is that it's one of her gaming pals coming through the computer speakers, but it sounds too loud for that, and I hear movements, too, as though... as though she's got someone in there.

My next thought is that it's Zayla, which will be awkward when I have to explain to Jodie that I've already met her, that she helped me out with my car when it wouldn't start the other day – *when I was snooping.*

But then I hear a deep voice – a *man's* voice – followed by the sound of the bed creaking. I press my ear to the door, listening, but all I hear are Jodie's giggles and a few unintelligible words from the male voice which, worryingly, does *not* sound like a teenage boy.

Still holding the mugs, I nudge the door with my foot, knowing that it will open if I hit exactly the right spot. When it doesn't budge, I kick it harder, sending it slamming back into Jodie's chest of drawers. I stand there, frozen, staring at the scene in front of me.

Jodie is sitting on the bed in shorts and strappy T-shirt engulfed by a fully grown man. His arms are wrapped tightly around her, his face pressed against her neck. Her skinny arms reach around his broad back as she rests her head on his shoulder in return.

Jodie suddenly jumps, her eyes growing huge as she sees me standing in the doorway, my mouth hanging open. She stiffens, tries to pull away, but the man keeps a firm hold of her.

'Jodie, what the *hell*?'

Her expression goes from terrified to nervous grin as the man slowly unfurls his beefy arms from around her. That's when I see his browny-blond hair is slightly thinning on top and his square jaw is covered in stubble.

'What in God's name is going on?' I cry just as he turns around to face me.

'Hello, Hannah,' he says with a grin that exposes straight white teeth within his handsome, unshaven face. 'How the devil are you?'

And that's when I drop both mugs of tea onto the floor.

THIRTY-SIX

'*Lewis?*' I croak, my mouth hanging open. Despite the years that have passed, I instantly recognise him. Then I glance down at the mess on the carpet and dash to the bathroom to grab a towel. Seeming to have lost the use of my voice, I drop to my knees and start mopping up the tea.

When the worst of the mess is soaked up, I look up to find Lewis towering above me, hands on hips and with a self-satisfied grin on his face that takes me right back. The same grin that I used to think was charming and sexy.

'What the hell are you doing here?' I say, finally finding my voice. Then I glance over at Jodie, who's now sitting cross-legged on her bed, scrolling on her phone and totally unbothered by the situation. 'Jodie, what's going on?'

I grab the doorframe as I stand up, suddenly feeling light-headed, but a pair of strong hands grip onto mine, steadying me as I get up. 'Thank you,' I say reluctantly, shrugging him off. I can't even remember the last time I saw him, but it was before Jodie was born. 'Does someone want to explain what is going on?'

'Mum, chill. It's *Dad*! Can you believe it?' She leaps up off the bed and attaches herself to Lewis's side, leaning her head against his shoulder. 'It's really him! He's back!'

Seeing father and daughter standing side by side triggers a cascade of emotions. There's no denying they're alike – Jodie is a female version of her dad. Sporty, muscular and strong, not to mention they have the same dimple on their chins. And there's a quiet elegance about each of them, too. The pattern of freckles across Jodie's nose almost exactly matches those on Lewis's face, though his skin is ruddier and lined from working outside in all weathers. While Lewis's hair is a bit thinner than I remember, it's the same shade of dark blonde as Jodie's long hair, lightening easily in the sun.

'You...' I croak, glancing between them both. 'I mean, *how...*'

'You're looking good, Hannah,' Lewis says, sweeping his eyes up and down me, which, for some reason, infuriates me. 'That might need some hot soapy water though,' he adds, pointing to the floor. 'Be a shame to ruin the carpet.' He shoves his hands in his pockets and grins.

Jesus, stop it, Hannah, I tell myself when his smile does something to me – a feeling I do not want to have. 'A shame to ruin the *carpet?*' I say, barely able to get the words out I'm fuming so much.

Not... a shame to ruin my life? Or a shame to ruin your daughter's *life? No... just a shame to ruin the bloody carpet.*

'It's fine,' I say through gritted teeth, forcing myself not to rise to the bait. 'I'll sort it later...' Lewis and I stare at each other – him with a glint in his eye, and me with a hole in my heart. *Another* hole.

'Suit yourself,' Lewis says, breaking the moment. Then he grabs the empty mugs off the floor. 'Come on, I think we could all use a cup of tea.'

'A cup of vodka,' I mumble as he heads down the stairs. I follow on... shaking my head at the surreal sight of Lewis in my house. Nothing feels real right now. Surely I'm dreaming...

Surely this whole day is some kind of ghastly, wretched night-mare, and any moment now I will wake up.

'So do you understand now, Mum?' Jodie says, explaining as if I'm an idiot, as if it's all perfectly normal. 'I had my real name searchable on the gaming site, which showed up online when Dad was looking for me. That's what led him to my gaming profile and to join the site. He's been watching over me all this time. He's so awesome.'

I sit there, head in hands, trying to process what she's just told me. I turn to my ex. 'And you didn't think simply adding her as a friend on Facebook or Instagram might have been a better idea?'

'No one uses Facebook these days, Mum,' Jodie chips in.

Lewis holds up his hands. 'No social media here,' he admits. 'Call me a Luddite, but navigating the gaming site was hard enough.'

I shake my head. 'I can think of more accurate things to call you than a Luddite,' I spit back. 'So, you've been befriending and chatting to my daughter online while pretending to be a boy her own age and asking to meet up? It sounds more like grooming if you ask me.'

'Don't say that, Han,' Lewis replies, tipping his head to one side. We're sitting around the table and suddenly my kitchen feels cramped and invaded with Lewis in it. 'Remember, she's our daughter. I just want to get to know her. It's time now. Is that so wrong?'

'Oh, so you didn't feel that being in her life regularly and paying child support for the last fifteen years would have been quite the same?' I can't face drinking the tea Jodie made. I don't trust myself not to chuck it in his face.

'Han, that makes me sound—'

'It makes you sound exactly like you are!' I shoot back,

trying to keep a lid on my emotions but failing. 'You can't pretend to be someone else online, gaining her trust, luring her to meet up with you. It's... it's... so *wrong*!'

'Mum, stop,' Jodie interjects, sounding more grown up than she has any right to. 'It's not like that. Shadow's been... I mean, *Dad's* been there for me these last few weeks. A good friend when I needed one. I like having someone to chat to online. And now I know he's my dad, that he's moving to Bradport... it's like...' She looks across at Lewis and grins. 'It's just so awesome.'

'Moving to Bradport?' I squeak.

'I mean, it's not fully confirmed yet, Jode,' Lewis says, shifting in his chair, scratching his stubble. 'But I'm pretty sure it's going to happen. I just need to check a few—'

'Love,' I say, putting a hand on Jodie's arm. 'Please, don't get your hopes up.' I glare at Lewis again. 'And what's with this Shadow business?' Then I remember the name Shadow-Knight184 jotted all over her school notepad.

'It's his gaming handle. Cool, eh?'

I shake my head slowly, realising that 184 is the eighteenth of the fourth month... his birthday. Lewis will never change. On the outside he might be a six foot two muscular man who's afraid of precisely nothing and is used to women falling at his feet, but on the inside, he has the same level of responsibility as an eight-year-old boy. Hapless, chaotic and free-spirited, Lewis Dunn is about as likely to settle down in our town as I am to win the lottery. I drop my head into my hands again, wondering why I've always been so terrible at picking men.

'OK, OK, I get the hint. I know when I'm not wanted.' In a classic guilt trip move, Lewis stands up, scraping back his chair.

'No! Dad, don't go. Please...' Jodie stands up, grabbing his arm. 'I want to do all those things we talked about... *please*. And you'll still come to my athletics competition next Saturday, right? I'm doing high jump and—'

'*Next* Saturday?' Lewis pulls a pained expression. 'Actually,

I think I've got a job in Birmingham that weekend. I'll come to the one after, though, I prom—'

'But, Dad, you said—'

'Stop!' I shout, wondering how to make this right for my daughter. I hate to see her upset like this within a short time of meeting him. My mind scrambles, wondering if I should suggest that Lewis joins us for Sunday lunch tomorrow, or maybe he'd like to stay for a takeaway tonight, and we can work something out so he can see Jodie on a regular basis.

But the decision is taken away from me as Lewis strides to the front door with my daughter trailing behind him, begging him to stay. He plants a kiss on her head.

'I'll give you a call sometime, sweetie,' he says in a voice that takes me right back to High View Guesthouse all those years ago. Then comes the sound of the front door opening and closing, followed by the hot, angry, frustrated sobs of my daughter.

'I hate you! I hate you! I *hate* you!' she screams at me from the hallway. I'm about to go and comfort her, suggest that we order our favourite pizza this evening and chat about what's happened, but suddenly the front door opens and bangs shut again. In the hallway, I see her trainers are gone and, when I go outside to chase after her, Jodie is nowhere to be seen.

THIRTY-SEVEN

JODIE

If Mum phones me one more time, I swear I'm going to throw my phone in the river and never go home again. I'm sitting on a bench down by the river, angry as hell at her for driving Dad away, as well as wishing I'd brought a sweater with me. All I've got on are my gym shorts and a T-shirt that I changed into when Dad brought me home. Knowing that he'll be in my life from now on gives me some kind of comfort, makes me feel loved by someone at least – cos it's obvious that Mum doesn't care. All she cares about is herself.

I scuff the ground and hurl a stone into the river, wishing I could sink all my feelings the same way. My disappointment that Shadow wasn't a lad my age was quickly replaced by disbelief and then joy when he told me he was my dad.

I mean... like wtf? My Dad!

I'm not stupid, and I asked him about stuff only my real dad would know, things Mum has told me about him to check he was for real. Then her subsequent shit fit when she saw him confirmed who he was anyway. Mind blown. Can't lie, it was a bit freaky when he grabbed me and bundled me into his van, but it was only because I was still standing in the road, frozen at the sight of him being a grown man. But he was getting me out of the way of a bus – saving my life, in fact.

Then he'd climbed into the van too, and we just sat and chatted for a bit, him explaining everything, about where he'd been, and even showing me some crumpled old photos of him and Mum from when they were younger. Then I asked him if he wanted to come back to mine.

I feel the first spots of rain. Deep down I just want to go home and say sorry to Mum, tell her I shouldn't have stormed out like that, maybe get a pizza like we sometimes do on a Saturday night and watch something trashy on TV.

But I'm not doing that this time; I'm not giving in. Not when it was her fault that Dad took off again only a couple of hours after meeting him. She can learn a lesson and maybe start to appreciate me a bit more. I have a right to be in touch with my father, and staying out a few more hours should rattle her cage enough. I know how much she frets when I don't get in touch.

I start walking to try and warm up. Hugging my arms around me, I set a brisk pace along the stretch of the river that will eventually bring me out at the disused warehouses. It could be a good place to hang out until after dark, until Mum is properly freaking out. Though I'll give the one with Zayla and that man a swerve.

Dad put his number in my phone earlier, but it goes to his voicemail when I ring him.

'Hey Dad, it's me. Jodie. Like, can you give me a call? I really want to see you again soon. Love you,' I add as an afterthought, even though I don't know if I do. Are you supposed to love a parent you've only just met?

The rain gets heavier, so I keep walking, skirting away from the water, when I spot a couple of lads up ahead smoking weed. By the time I get to the industrial estate, it's pissing down and I'm soaked. The first warehouse I come to is only small, but when I rattle the metal door, I find it's locked and there are security grilles at the windows. Most of the buildings are covered in graffiti and have old mattresses, beer bottles and other litter slung about outside.

I wipe my face to get my wet hair out of my eyes. There's no one about, but still, I keep close to the cover of the buildings, checking around each corner before trying other doors. I've got to get out of this rain. I'm shivering and absolutely freezing now.

The next building along looks like an old label-making factory, going by the sign above the door. But again, it's locked. I stand under the eaves, trying to shield myself from the rain, but the guttering is overflowing, making it seem more like a shower than a shelter, so I head further down the road and turn right at the end, knowing I'm getting nearer to the warehouse where Zayla and that man were.

'I hope they're long gone,' I say to myself as I approach, spotting the alley where I got in last time. I skirt round the entire building, looking for Zayla's car – or any other cars for that matter – but there's nothing. Thank God, they're not here.

I swallow nervously, glancing around, deciding that I'm going to do it. I'm going in. I need *somewhere* to hang out for a few hours, and it'll give me a chance to get dry before I go home. If I stay out until midnight, I reckon that'll be enough time to teach Mum a lesson, make her realise that now Dad is back on the scene, she doesn't get to call all the shots.

I go down the alley, forcing open the same door. It makes a loud clanking noise that echoes throughout the factory. I hold my breath, then, when it's silent again – the only noise being the rain on the tin roof – I creep inside. This time, I notice stacks of timber piled up around the place. It looks like it was some kind of woodworking factory, and the massive machinery I hid under looks like a load of huge saws and lathes and other weird cutting tools.

There's no way I'm hiding under there again, so I keep close to the walls, skirting around the edge to see if I can find a different spot to hunker down. It's dusk outside, making it pretty much dark in here. It's weird, but a surge of... of something almost thrilling speeds through me, making my stomach churn. It reminds me of something Dad said earlier.

'There's nothing quite like the excitement of disappearing. I mean, like, properly being gone – almost as if you never existed. It's a buzz having no one in the entire world know where you are. It's what freedom tastes like, Jodie. *True* freedom. Make sure you experience it at least once in your life.'

Then he'd gone on to explain how disappearing also hurt people; how he'd hurt Mum so many times it had got so he didn't think he could come back into her life to make amends like he usually did because by then, he'd convinced himself that she'd never have him.

'So I kept on being disappeared,' he told me. 'It seemed the best way not to hurt her anymore. I really did love her, you know.' Then I swear he mumbled *do love her* under his breath.

Suddenly, there's a noise. A loud clunk coming from the other side of the warehouse. Then silence again. I stand on a plastic crate, peering out at the car park. But there's nothing there – no cars and no sign of anyone. It must just have been the...

There. Another noise. A loud bang or thud this time. Then it's quiet again.

I scuttle over to the other side of the warehouse, crouching down behind a stack of timber. There are some old sacks to sit on at least.

Shit... another noise...

With shaking hands, I pull my phone from my shorts pocket and open Snapchat, checking that it's still on ghost mode so no one knows where I am.

But then I think... *No one knows where I am.*

Suddenly, there's a scream. Piercing and shrill coming from

the other end of the warehouse – from that partitioned-off office.

Oh God, why did I think coming in here was a good idea? I'm such an idiot!

A moment later, headlights sweep around the walls as a car pulls up outside, briefly lighting up the cobwebby rafters of the factory. Then I hear the metal doors being unlocked. Someone is coming inside.

No one knows where I am... The words echo around my head as I feel myself sinking deeper into trouble. *More* trouble. I can't believe I've been so stupid again.

I burrow under the pile of sacks behind the woodpile, cursing myself for coming in here a second time. Quickly, with my fingers fumbling and shaking, I open the tracking app that Mum put on my phone, holding my breath as I hear the low voices of people entering the warehouse – Zayla, by the sound of it, and that gravelly male voice from before.

They've come back.

On the app, I toggle the button to share my location with Mum, but my heart sinks when I see there's no data here, that I've only just picked up the weakest signal for calls – that even if she *is* looking for me online, I won't be showing up for her. I've never wanted to be at home so badly, never wanted Mum to pull me close and tell me everything's going to be OK so much as now. My body is stiff from fear. I hardly dare breathe, trying to stay as still as I can. I'd do anything to take back my last words to Mum. *I hate you! I hate you! I hate you!*

Then just as the sound of the footsteps finally seem to fade away – with me praying that they're leaving already – the worst thing in the world happens.

My phone buzzes and a shrill ringtone cuts through the air.

'Mum' lights up the screen with a photo of her grinning up at me as I fumble to silence her call.

THIRTY-EIGHT

HANNAH

One moment Jodie's phone was ringing, but then the line cut out. Now, frustratingly, when I call her again it's going straight to voicemail, meaning either she's turned her phone off, she's lost signal, or it's run out of battery. Either way, my heart is thumping as I pace my living room, not knowing what the hell to do. I was sure she'd have simmered down and come home by now. She's been gone three hours.

It's almost dark outside, and I know she stormed off in anger to punish me, as well as chasing after her dad. I pray that she caught up with him, that they're having a nice meal together somewhere cosy because the weather is foul outside right now. I don't have Lewis's number to call him, and Jodie only had her gym shorts and a vest top on.

'Jodie, *please...*' I mumble, dialling her number again. It still doesn't connect. Apart from waiting – which is agony – I don't know what else to do. She's not been gone long enough to call the police, and driving around looking for her feels a bit futile. Besides, I'd rather be here for when she comes back. She hasn't even got her keys.

But I can't help my thoughts racing, tearing my mind apart

as I wait. What if she's still not back by the morning? Or by the next day or the day after that? What if the police don't believe me when I report her missing? What if they think I'm making everything up, that I'm going mad, that I'm stressed and unhinged, not knowing what's real and what's not?

What if they're right?

'Stop it!' I shout at myself. 'Jodie is fine. She's got form for this. She'll be home within the next hour and certainly by ten o'clock. She's just gone off to cool down.'

I decide to call Becca's mum, but she tells me that Jodie isn't at their house. I then message the whole parent group chat, asking them to let me know if Jodie is with any of them or if they've heard from her, pretending that I couldn't remember where she was going tonight. I try to sound light and breezy, but as soon as the 'Oh my gosh you must be so worried' messages start coming back, I can't hold it together any longer. I break down in tears.

There's only one thing for it and it's probably not the wisest move after everything that's happened today, but I can't sit here and do nothing. My hands shake as I call Rory's number – the first time I've done so in almost a year.

During the first four weeks of him being gone, I'd pretty much called him on the hour every hour. Or at least it had seemed like that. But after a month or so, when the police told me in no uncertain terms that he didn't *want* to be found, that I could be done for harassment if I kept trying to contact him, I stopped. If he didn't want me, then I'd have to pretend that I didn't want him, either – until I eventually believed it myself.

But his number rings out. When I try again, it goes to his voicemail, leaving me wondering if he's blocked my phone calls as well as my messages on WhatsApp.

Rory here. I'm busy right now but leave me a message and I'll be in touch...

The sound of his voice makes me feel sick. I chuck my

phone onto the sofa and peel back the curtains, peering out into the night to see if, by fortune shining down on me, I might see Jodie walking up the front path. But there's no one there. Just the rain still coming down, battering the petals on Mrs Kirk's white roses and making them fall into the mud. I'm reminded of the white rose left on the driver's seat of my car last week. With everything else going on, it's slipped to the back of my mind, but it still haunts me.

As I stare out of the window into the darkness, the fat raindrops rolling down the glass, I'm almost certain that Mila's mother took my car – as well as my dress from the dry cleaners – though I have no idea why she'd leave me a dead rose.

Is she tormenting me? Does she know that I took her daughter from school without permission, and now she's trying to scare me, get back at me, perhaps building up to something bigger – payback for taking her child?

It leaves me wondering how she even knew it was me who took her, or that my car was at the garage, or my dress needed picking up from the cleaners. Besides, according to Zayla, Anna Weston has been away for work. Nothing makes sense and all I'm left with is a sense of doom, apprehension and a sick feeling churning around inside me. Though what's worrying me more than anything right now isn't that I took *someone else's* daughter from school. Rather, I'm starting to think that I took my *own*.

I wake with a start. I must have dozed off on the sofa. For a few blissful moments, I don't remember what's happened, and then I do. Lewis being here... Jodie storming off into the night... Mila... the IVF paperwork... My stomach cramps at the thought of it all.

I check the time. *Christ...* it's 11.23 p.m. I leap up, charging upstairs, calling out Jodie's name, bursting into her room. But the bed is still made and she's not there. I phone her again, but it doesn't even ring before going to her message service. Then I try Rory's number again, but the same thing happens.

Is it too late to call Jan? I simply don't know what to do, who to turn to. I can't possibly bother Mum and Dad at this time of night, but then what is Jan going to do even if she does answer? All she'll do is tell me to report it to the police. My thoughts are all over the place. I can't face calling 101 and getting a faceless call handler again promising that someone will be in touch like last time. So, in desperation I grab my jacket and handbag, shove on my trainers, and drive down to the police station in town with no idea if it's even manned at this time of night.

'How may I help?' the duty officer says when I dash up to the counter, breathless and red-faced. Luckily, the station is still open, though the sign outside says it's closed to the public from midnight. I'm relieved it's not busy. The woman at the desk, a little older than me, looks exhausted as she takes down my details.

'Have a seat,' she instructs after I tell her briefly why I've come.

While I'm waiting, I check the tracking app again in the hope Jodie might have turned on her location, but there's nothing except an infuriating message telling me that she can't be located right now. If Lewis hadn't come swanning back into our lives, I'd have had time to chat things over with her, remind her to keep her location turned on, smooth over a few things between us before having a cosy night in together. Instead, the day has been back-to-back stress.

'Mrs Marlowe?' I suddenly hear, snapping me back to the moment. I'm led down a now familiar corridor and into a small side room. A few moments later and a uniformed officer I've not seen before sits down opposite me with an iPad in his hands. He's tall and well-built with neatly cropped auburn hair and a beard to match. From the outset, he's polite and kind, listening to my story intently.

'So, she's been missing... about six hours now would you say?'

I nod. 'Yes, almost.' I swallow down the lump in my throat at the sound of the word *missing*. It sounds so sinister, so serious, so... final. As if nothing short of a miracle can turn its connotations into a happy ending. 'Though I'd say she's *gone off* rather than actually missing,' I add, hoping that it might make things seem better. It doesn't.

'Has she done this sort of thing before?'

I shake my head, even though that's not entirely true. 'She's been a bit bad at keeping in touch lately, I suppose. I put a tracker on her phone last week, but that didn't last long. She's turned off her location as far as I can tell.'

The officer rolls his eyes and makes a sound in his throat. 'Kids, eh?' as if he's had a similar experience, though he looks far too young to have a teenager. 'My little sister,' he adds, seeming to read my mind. 'Drives my mum up the wall, she does.'

I try to smile but it comes out more like a grimace.

'Can you send people out now to find her? Do you have a way of, like, tracking her phone even if it's turned off? I mean... it's nearly midnight. The weather's awful. She's only got shorts and a vest on, and she hasn't eaten dinner. I'm so worried... so bloody worried about her I can barely breathe...'

Then, unable to hold it inside any longer, I drop my head into my hands and sob my heart out.

THIRTY-NINE

Those days at university in Plymouth were the best of Hannah's life. And also the worst. It wasn't that she and Rory broke up exactly – having only got together as a couple just before Christmas six months earlier during the final year of their degrees – it was more that events had got in the way. They'd originally met at Natalie's house party during the very first term of her and Nat's art degree several years ago, but each of them had been seeing other people and enjoying the freedom of university life. And in fact, when they finally started dating, Hannah had only recently broken up with the person she'd always come to think of as her 'first true love', making Rory something of a rebound. But they were happy and enjoyed each other's company and things between them were going well.

Until *that night*.

After that, nothing was the same again. Hannah couldn't face seeing anyone after that, going back to her parents' house and virtually locking herself away.

'I mean, you don't even have to go out partying, if you don't want,' Hannah said, looking across at Natalie. 'You can just catch up on some sleep while I mind the baby if you prefer.'

She didn't know it then, but that moment would become the point to which she wished she could rewind her life. Keep it on pause forever if necessary. Anything to stop Natalie going out. Anything to prevent what happened next.

Natalie was sitting on the end of her single bed in the room she rented on the top floor of the student house with five others. It wasn't the best environment for a baby, but give the girl her dues, she was determined to finish her art degree, scrimping and saving and eking out the money she had from her student loan. Beside the bed was a battered wooden cot, picked up from a second-hand shop that sold baby equipment. To Hannah – to *all* their friendship group, in fact – it still seemed impossible that Natalie, of all people, had a baby. A two-month-old perfect little girl with a heart-shaped pout and huge round eyes. Nat's mantra had always been *no men, no kids, no worries.*

'Fuck sleeping, I'm going out to get shitfaced,' Nat replied, dabbing concealer on the grey circles beneath her eyes. 'I made up a few bottles for her. They're in the fridge downstairs.'

'Fleur will be absolutely fine with me, won't you my little one,' Hannah crooned, leaning over the baby as she lay beside her on the bed, her arms stretched wide and her legs thrashing wildly in the little sleepsuit that was too small for her now.

Natalie had cut the feet off it to make it last a few more weeks, popping socks on her bare toes instead, though they kept coming off. Hannah smiled down at the baby.

'Are you a cute little bunny?' she crooned into the cot, gently rubbing Fleur's tummy over the adorable fabric – white with pink and blue rabbits leaping around. 'Are you? Are you? *Ooh*, you're such a cutie.'

Until a few days ago, Hannah had never held a baby in her life before, let alone looked after one. She watched as Natalie slipped off the silky robe she was wearing, dropping it to the floor. In her lacy bra and pants, with her stomach still gently rounded from pregnancy, she picked her way over to the clothes piled up on a chair under the dormer window.

The view across Plymouth right down to the waterside and marina was the best thing about the dingy room she rented. The house, occupied by five lads and Natalie, was riddled with black mould and damp, and plugging in anything electric felt like Russian roulette, given some of the sockets were hanging off the walls.

'What do you think?' Natalie said, turning and holding up a mauve and green tie-dye dress that came midway down her thighs. Hannah knew she'd wear it with her tan cowboy boots, armfuls of glittery bangles that she'd picked up on a trip to India, and a man's black wool coat that trailed around her ankles. Classic Nat.

The way she was holding the dress up in front of her semi-naked body left little to the imagination, and Hannah couldn't help take a few glances at her belly – the place where Fleur had been safe and snug only eight weeks ago. The few times Hannah had seen Natalie around campus from a distance in the final few months of her pregnancy – during the few months when they weren't speaking – she noticed her bump was neat and small, even up until her due date. In fact, she'd barely even looked pregnant.

With her long, wavy honey-coloured hair, her naturally high cheekbones, huge green eyes that shimmered like sea glass, Natalie was a beauty – and she had an aura about her that Hannah could only dream of. Oh, and to top it all she was the most talented artist in their cohort, having already won several prestigious prizes, catching the attention of several galleries in New York.

And now she had a baby. Which meant she'd also had a man, despite claiming to have only ever been with women. It was Hannah, already shocked by Nat's pregnancy, asking about the baby's father that had caused their falling-out.

'I totally trust you with Fleur,' Natalie said now, slipping into the floaty dress before coming over to Hannah and standing with her back to her, lifting her hair out of the way.

Hannah stared at her lightly tanned back – the weather had been so warm lately and she'd spotted Natalie out and about wearing a skimpy top with denim shorts. She'd had Fleur on her front in a baby sling and a tote bag containing her sketching materials on her shoulder. As she stared at her smooth skin, Hannah had an overwhelming urge to trace her finger down the ladder of Natalie's spine, but she didn't. Instead, she pulled up the zip and turned around to pick up the baby by way of distraction.

'I'll be back by midnight,' Natalie said, shoving a hairbrush and her purse into a slouchy suede bag. 'I promise not to get too drunk,' she said, falling silent. A pensive look swept across her face. 'I'll get a cab back from the club.'

'Get you, being all sensible now you're a mum.' She'd never known Natalie to be back before about 4 a.m. on a night out. 'But really, go and enjoy yourself. Stay out as long as you like,' Hannah said, knowing she and Fleur would probably fall asleep snuggled together anyway. But after everything that had happened between them over the last few months, their falling-out, their recent reconciliation, she wanted to do this for Natalie, give her the opportunity to have a night to herself.

Hannah had been overjoyed when Natalie had accepted her offer to babysit – an olive branch in the aftermath of Fleur's birth. She hoped it would go some way to repairing the fractures between them, knitting together the trust that had been broken, and erasing the lies that were told. She couldn't stand the thought of not having Natalie in her life. 'We'll be more than fine, won't we, Fleur?'

The baby gurgled contentedly as Hannah jiggled from side

to side. A quick peck on her downy head from Natalie, and then they were suddenly alone in the dingy attic room with the evening stretching out before them.

Fleur started grizzling as soon as she woke up about an hour after Natalie had left. Hannah muted the small television set and picked up the baby. 'You want some milk, little one?' she asked, almost expecting a reply as Fleur stopped crying, staring up at her. Then the baby shoved a fist in her mouth and began sucking on it furiously.

Downstairs in the kitchen, a couple of lads from the student house were cooking. One was smoking a joint while the other was standing at the filthy stove stirring something in a saucepan. A plume of smoke suddenly billowed from the grill compartment.

'Shit,' the lad with the joint said, lunging for the grill tray and pulling it out with his bare hand. Then he yelled, whipping his arm away, and the pan fell to the floor, splattering smouldering sausages across the tiles in a shower of hot fat. Hannah jumped back, cradling the baby's head with her hand and turning away to shield her from the chaos and smoke.

'Jesus, guys... what the fuck?'

'Sorry,' the other lad said, stamping on one of the sausages that looked as though it was about to ignite. 'Not great at this.'

'Clearly,' Hannah said, stepping around the mess to get to the fridge. She took out a bottle of baby milk and put it in the microwave, making sure to heat it slowly and giving it multiple shakes and letting it sit for a while, paranoid about burning little Fleur's mouth.

She didn't want to put a foot wrong with looking after the little treasure, especially since yesterday when Natalie asked Hannah if she would be the baby's godmother.

'Really?' she'd replied, almost in tears. '*Me?*'

Natalie had taken her by the hands and looked her in the eye. 'Knowing that Fleur will always have you in her life is a huge comfort. I know things between us have been...' Natalie had trailed off, glancing at the ceiling and sniffing. 'I know that things have been a bit strained lately, that things might feel raw and fragile for a while yet between us, but I promise I still think you're bloody awesome, Hannah Bailey, and I wouldn't want anyone else to take care of Fleur if anything happens to me.'

Hannah had closed in for a hug then, feeling Nat's ribs through her clothes, convinced that she weighed a lot less than she did before she was pregnant.

'I'd be honoured,' Hannah whispered in Nat's ear. 'But nothing is going to happen to you, OK?' She held her at arm's length, looking directly at her.

'OK,' Nat replied in a slow, drawn-out way that made Hannah wonder if it already had.

FORTY

HANNAH

'The police told me to go home and wait,' I say to Dad on the phone as I hurry back to the car, having explained everything that's happened today, including Lewis turning up. I caved in and called him, despite the late hour. I can't wait this out alone. 'I mean, do they expect me to put my feet up and watch a movie or something?'

'Try to stay calm, Hannah,' Dad says, stifling his sleepy state. 'Do you want me to come round?'

'Would that be OK?' I say, thanking God that my car starts. That would have been the icing on the cake.

'Give me twenty minutes and I'll be there.'

I drive home, praying that Jodie will be back when I get there, but when I get inside, she's not. I can't fault the police officer, who was on the case as soon as he'd taken a few details. He said someone would be in touch with me in the next hour or two if there isn't news before.

'Ninety-nine per cent of the time we find runaway teens safe and well,' he'd said before showing me out, though of course my mind had leapt straight to the one per cent that they didn't.

I shudder, having barely filled the kettle, when I hear a key in the front door lock. I rush to the hall, my hopes raised, but then realise that Jodie didn't take her keys with her so it can't be her. 'Hi, Dad,' I say as he lets himself in. 'Still no sign. Come on through.'

He follows me into the kitchen where I hug him, silently sobbing on his shoulder as I have done countless times over the years, feeling like a little girl as I gulp down the grief. 'What... what did you tell Mum?'

'The truth, love. She's worried. I said I'd keep her in the loop. She said there was no need for her to come as well.'

I nod, running my hands down my face. That sounds just like my mother. Rarely showing emotion, she's stoic and practical and only deals with the things that she's able to change. She's always been the same, and the reason I always turned to Dad for comfort as a child.

'Here,' I say, handing him a mug of tea once I've composed myself. I've got a coffee, not wanting to fall asleep even for a second until Jodie is safely home.

'Do you think we should drive around and look for her?' Dad asks.

'PC Gilbert said I should stay here in case she comes back,' I explain. 'They're going to call soon.' I glance at my watch. 'Christ, it's almost 1 a.m. I mean, there's literally nowhere good I can think of that she'd be right now. She's wearing virtually nothing, and her phone battery has probably run out – I've been meaning to get her a better phone, but money's been a bit tight and—'

'Hey, hey, hey...' Dad's hand comes down on mine as he looks at me from beneath his bushy grey eyebrows. 'That kind of talk won't do you any good. She's a smart lass and after everything that's happened today, she's probably gone to hunker down somewhere and lick her wounds. There's been a lot to process with her father coming back on the scene.' He squeezes my hand. 'Do you remember that time *you* went missing?'

I manage a small smile. 'Dad, it was for about eight minutes, and I was only hiding in the garden.'

'Still, it was the worst eight minutes of my life, so I know exactly how you feel. I'm right here with you, OK? I bet you anything they'll find her any moment now and bring her home safe. She'll probably feel a bit—'

We both freeze at the sound of the doorbell, then hammering on the front door.

'Jodie...' I say, looking Dad in the eye. Then I leap up and rush to the hall, fumbling to unlock the door. But my heart sinks.

'Have you found her?' I say to the two officers standing on my doorstep. Dad draws up beside me.

'Mrs Marlowe?' the female officer asks, and I nod. 'May we come in?'

Dreading what they're about to tell me, I lead the pair into the living room, gripping onto Dad's hand. 'Where is she? Have you got her?' I can't stop shaking.

'Not yet,' the young male officer says, silencing the radio at his shoulder. 'We've come to ask a few more questions and take a look around her bedroom if that's OK.'

I look across at Dad, my hand tightening around his. 'That's not good, is it? Do you know something? Do you think something bad has happened to her? Please... I can't stand this. If you know something, you've got to tell me.'

'Like we explained before, this is all precaution and routine. Think of it as us getting ahead of ourselves... just in case,' the female officer says after she's rooted around Jodie's bedroom. Back downstairs and she's holding my daughter's laptop in a large plastic bag, plus a few other items – including a couple of notepads and some receipts by the looks of it.

'In case...?' I hardly dare ask.

'Look, to put your mind at rest, most teens who go missing are only gone a few hours. They decide that running away and fending for themselves isn't such fun after all,' the male officer adds with a smile. 'Usually hunger or their phone needing a charge flushes them out.' Another confident smile.

'But what if she's not back by morning?'

'We're following all our protocols and search criteria for this stage of the investigation, Mrs Marlowe, so I'd strongly recommend that you don't speculate or tear yourself up with worry over something that hasn't happened yet. We've got CCTV cameras in the town, including one at the end of your street, so it's likely we'll have images of her. Officers are scouring footage as we speak, and we have a dog unit on standby. We'll also be conducting door to doors and requesting phone data from her provider as a matter of urgency.'

'But what if—'

'We'll be in touch again soon, Mrs Marlowe,' the female officer says, and the pair head off to the marked police car parked outside my house.

An hour later, at 2.34 a.m., Dad returns from driving around the town. 'Everywhere is dead,' he says, making me wince. 'Sorry,' he says, sensing my discomfort. 'No one about, apart from a few drunks spilling out by the square. Coming from that nightclub, I suppose.'

In case, I try Jodie's phone again, but it goes to voicemail. And the tracking app still isn't picking up a signal.

'My guess is that she's curled up in a shop doorway or bus stop, cursing herself for being bloody-minded and stubborn, wishing she'd never stormed out in the first place. She'll be back in the morning, you'll see. I suppose getting a few hours' sleep is out of the question for you?'

'Dad, *really*?' I grab my car keys. 'You wait here, my turn to drive around now. Call me if there's news.'

'Righto, love,' he says, shutting the front door behind me.

But an hour or two after dawn, after driving around the entire town about ten times, even going out as far as the old industrial estate and the edge of the bypass, my daughter is still not home. It's as I'm making yet another mug of coffee, as the sun creeps up over the rooftops while Dad dozes on the sofa, that my phone rings with a No Caller ID number.

I grab it, my mind reeling through the possibilities – a kidnapper demanding a ransom, Jodie borrowing someone else's phone to let me know she's fine, a doctor in A&E asking if I'm sitting down, that they have bad news. But when I answer it, it's none of these things.

At first, the line is crackly, and I can't make out what the caller is saying, and it's hard to tell if it's even male or female. 'Hello?' I say again, praying that it's Jodie, that she's just got bad reception. 'Who is this? Can you hear me?'

More crackling and then the signal picks up, revealing the voice of the caller – someone I was not expecting to hear from.

'Hello, Hannah? It's me. Rory.'

FORTY-ONE
HANNAH

'Dad!' I scream, charging through to the living room, dropping to my knees beside the sofa. 'Dad! Wake up!' My hands are shaking and I'm still reeling from hearing Rory's voice, but I can't think about that now. I thrust my phone in front of my father's face as he sits up.

'What? Is there news? I dozed off.' Dad sits up, reaching around on the floor for his glasses. He puts them on and looks at my phone. I have another quick glance to make sure I'm not imagining it.

'It's Jodie! Look, her phone is showing up on the tracking app, at the supermarket on the edge of town, the little minx!'

Dad peers at the screen. 'Well, I'll be—'

'I've been checking it loads, but she's only just shown up as active. Maybe she's hungry and gone to get breakfast. The shop opens at 7 a.m., so God knows where she's been all night.'

'Does the app show her past movements?'

'No, it doesn't,' I tell him, not bothering to explain the technology. 'But guess where we're going right now?'

'Supermarket shopping?' Dad says, getting up off the sofa and stretching out.

While Dad quickly goes to the bathroom, I grab my shoes and bag, refreshing the tracking app every few moments to make sure she's still there, checking that the green dot with Jodie's name above it doesn't take off somewhere else.

As I wait for Dad, Rory's voice echoes in my head after his phone call half an hour ago. My stomach was already churned up, but hearing his smarmy tone made everything so much worse, the man I once loved sounding so cold and uncaring. I decide not to tell Dad about it, and now I wish I'd never phoned Rory in the first place, but I was desperate. As it turned out, he was next to useless when it came to helping find Jodie, and all it did was open a load of wounds that were almost starting to heal.

'What do you mean, she's missing?' he'd said scathingly when I explained why I'd phoned him. 'And you thought I would know where she was?' he'd added, almost with a laugh.

In all the years I've known him, he's never sounded so cold and uncaring. It's as though he's had a personality transplant, making me start to think that he *has* now met someone else – someone who's pulling his strings.

'I'm not sure what you want me to do about it, Hannah,' he continued. 'She's your daughter after all.' That bit had stung. 'Anyway, I'm away on a four-day work conference at the moment, so I couldn't help you search even if I wan...' He trailed off, at least having the decency not to say the words 'wanted to'. 'Look, I suggest you go to the police. There's nothing I can do. I'm sorry.'

And that was that. He hung up without me even having a chance to ask him why he'd left me in such a cruel way, or where he was living now, or what he thought he was playing at planning to sell his mother's house... As for any kind of apology, it was obvious that would never happen. He could hardly wait to get off the phone.

'Come on, Dad,' I call up the stairs. 'Hurry! I want to get going before Jodie leaves the shop.' *Or turns her app off again,* I think, wondering why she's chosen now to reactivate it. Maybe she wants to check where *I* am, see if I'm out looking for her or getting close to where she is. After pulling this stunt, she's going to be grounded and locked in her bedroom until she's about twenty-five.

'Ready when you are,' Dad says, slinging on his blue anorak in the hall. 'Want me to drive?'

'Yes, thanks,' I say, handing him the keys. I'm shaking so much I'm not sure I trust myself behind the wheel. I pull open the front door and head out, feeling giddy from relief that this whole nightmare is about to be over, when I stop suddenly on the top step, catching my breath.

A blue and yellow marked police car has just pulled up outside the house with two male uniformed officers, one of which is PC Gilbert from last night – God, that seems like a lifetime ago now – and another officer I don't recognise, getting out of the vehicle. They give each other a quick look and a nod before opening my front gate and coming up the path.

'It's all OK!' I call out to them. 'You can call off the search. I've located Jodie! She's up at Tesco, you know, by the ring road?' I roll my eyes, feeling bad for wasting their time, convinced that if they didn't think I was neurotic before, they certainly will now. As they draw close, I hold out my phone for them to see. 'We're just off to fetch her. She finally logged into the tracking app, look, and she's—'

'Mrs Hannah Marlowe?' the officer I don't recognise asks. His voice is deep and serious.

'Yes.' I flash a look at PC Gilbert, who remains expression-less, then look at Dad beside me. I feel his hand slip into mine. 'We're just going to get Jodie and—'

'Mrs Marlowe, I am arresting you on suspicion of child abduction, contrary to Section 1 of the Child Abduction Act 1984. You do not have to say anything, but it may harm your defence if you do not mention, when questioned, something you later rely on in court. Anything you do say may be given in evidence. Do you understand?'

Before I can even think of replying or processing what the officer is saying to me, Dad steps in. 'What nonsense! You honestly think my daughter abducted her own daughter? We've been out all night searching for her, for goodness' sake. And she's not missing any more, she's at Tesco and—'

'Sir, if you'd step aside, please.' PC Gilbert approaches me with a set of handcuffs and holds them out while the other officer guides my arms behind my back.

'Dad... Dad, wait... I don't think this is about Jodie,' I say, my voice choking up. I twist around to see him. 'It's... it's something else. It's about...' I splutter, not knowing how to explain – though as long as my daughter is OK, that's all that matters right now. 'Dad, listen. I need you to go and fetch Jodie from the shop. Bring her home and give her some food.' I wince as my wrists are cuffed together and I'm led away by the arm. 'And do not let her out of your sight, OK? If you need to go back to your house,' I call back over my shoulder as I'm led down my front path, 'then take her with you!'

'Hannah?' Dad calls back, a deep frown set on his face, his voice wobbling. 'Hannah... what's going on? Stop, bring her back! You're making a terrible mistake. Wait! Hannah!' Dad comes down the path, his cheeks red and his chest heaving.

I stare back at my poor father as I'm bundled into the car, wishing I could explain everything to him – tell him that this is about Mila, that I suspect the police finally believe me about what I did. Though their timing couldn't be worse.

'Please, you've got to listen to me,' I say to the arresting officer and custody sergeant at the police station – a police station that I'm becoming overly familiar with. 'My daughter, Jodie, is... *was* missing, but now she's turned up online. I was about to go and fetch her, but then your officers came and...' I take a breath. I've tried to explain at least five times to various people, but no one is listening to me. 'I just want to know she's safe.'

'Empty your pockets, please,' the custody officer says. 'Do you have anything harmful on you?'

'What?' I stare at him. 'Did you hear what I just said? Your officers are out searching for my daughter. I even had two of them rooting through her bedroom a few hours ago, but I've just located her on the tracking app and—'

'All belongings, please, Mrs Marlowe.'

I sigh, turning out my tracksuit pockets and placing a couple of used tissues, a hair band, and a packet of chewing gum on the counter. They already have my phone, the clips from my hair, the drawstring from my tracksuit bottoms and my shoelaces. After the custody officer has booked me in and gone through all my rights, making sure I understand, he asks if there's anyone I want to be notified of my arrest.

My arrest. The words don't seem real.

'Don't I get to make a phone call?' I ask. 'I want to call my daughter. If you can just give me my phone back... and I'll check the tracking app too, to see if she's back home with Dad and—'

'Not possible, I'm afraid, Mrs Marlowe. Would you like us to inform anyone of your whereabouts?'

'What? You're not listening to me! I need to speak to my daughter.'

'We can try to get hold of her if you like?'

I drop my head into my hands, leaning forwards on the counter. 'I should hope that's what you've been doing since last night when I reported her missing!' I slide my hands down my face.

'You have a right to legal advice, Mrs Marlowe. Would you like the duty solicitor to come, or do you have representation of your own?'

'What?' I squeak. All I can think about is Jodie, and if Dad got to her in time before she left the supermarket. I should have given him my phone so he could refresh the app to see where she went. 'Yes,' I say, suddenly realising how serious my situation is. 'Yes, I want the duty solicitor, please.'

I have a feeling I'm going to need all the help I can get.

FORTY-TWO
HANNAH

I can't believe I was so close to getting Jodie back. It's been the longest night of my life, and now I'm stuck here in a police custody cell with Mila at the forefront of my mind again, terrified of what they've discovered. Why am I being arrested *now*, when I already told them I took her – that someone *else* took her from me – nine whole days ago?

My mind races as I sit on the uncomfortable bench, shivering, trying to work everything out. I don't understand how the police reported that Mila was fine after the welfare check, and now this. Did something happen to her since? It's so worrying that she's not been at school – and after finding the IVF clinic papers, I'm even more concerned about her wellbeing. Things aren't all they seem with that little girl, yet I have no idea what – there's a missing piece of the puzzle that I haven't found yet. I feel so helpless, stuck in here.

I was told that I could be detained for up to twenty-four hours. Then they must charge me or release me. It's towards the end of the second hour at 9.35 a.m. when PC Gilbert opens my cell door and tells me my solicitor is here. I get up off the plastic-covered bunk where I've been sitting cross-legged with a blanket around my shoulders.

'Any chance of a hot drink?' I ask, shivering. As I follow the officer down the corridor, we stop at a machine that spews out a cup of milky tea, which he carries into a side room.

'Take a seat in here and the solicitor will be with you in a moment,' PC Gilbert says, putting my tea on the table. I sit down in the stark, soulless room, and almost immediately, the door opens and a young woman walks in. She's wearing black linen trousers and a white short-sleeved top with a lacy collar. Her smooth skin is make-up free, and her thick hair is tied back in a glossy ponytail. She seems fresh and alert, as if she's had a full eight hours. The opposite of me. PC Gilbert gives her a nod and leaves the room, closing the door behind him.

'Duty solicitor Shivani Mehta,' she says, extending a hand. I shake it lightly and look into her brown eyes, placing all my trust in them. She's my only hope of getting out of this place. 'Right, so I've spoken with the arresting officer, and they've given me an outline of your arrest, but I got a sense they're holding some stuff back.' She pulls a thick notepad and pen from her leather bag, sitting down opposite me. 'But that's not unusual,' she adds in a clipped, business-like voice.

'Thank you. I mean, I don't know what I'm going to do.' I laugh incredulously. 'This is all so wrong... my daughter, she's been missing since yesterday. I'd just found her on the tracking app when they came and arrested me and...' I drag my hands through my hair, feeling utterly helpless.

'First things first,' Shivani says, taking a sip of coffee that must also be from the machine in the corridor, given the face she pulls. 'Let's focus on what's relevant to your arrest.' She glances at her file. 'Everything to do with Mila Weston, in other words. That's not the daughter you just mentioned, right? The one you said was missing?' She looks confused.

The room suddenly starts to spin as I think of Mila and what I saw in the study at Anna Weston's house yesterday – mine and Rory's names on the fertility clinic papers. I should have told Rory about it on the phone earlier, but Jodie was my main priority, and then he'd hung up so suddenly. But I can't afford to think about any of that right now. My brain will not cope with the overload. I need to focus on getting out of here and getting to Jodie. I pray to God that Dad is with her now.

'No, Jodie is my daughter. She's fifteen and has been missing since last night, but I'd just located her on my phone and then…' I take a breath. 'I was arrested before I could get to her.'

'Unfortunate,' Shivani says without emotion. 'Now, tell me about Mila Weston.'

Twenty minutes later and I've recounted to Shivani everything that's happened in the last nine days – *almost* everything – from me being Mila's teacher, her disturbing artwork, to me taking her from school. And finally, how she was stolen from my kitchen during the few minutes I left the room. There's no way I'm telling her or the police that I was snooping around Mila's house or that I found IVF papers with mine and Rory's names on. I need to speak to the fertility clinic first, and I'll never get out of here if I mention all that.

'Quite the story,' Shivani says, putting down her pen.

I stop myself telling her that it's not a story, that it's all true, but I keep quiet. I need her on my side.

'And you have no idea who could have taken her?'

'No,' I say. 'I found a little girl's hair scrunchie outside in the garden. It wasn't mine or Jodie's, so I'm guessing it belonged to her. Honestly, I'd only popped upstairs for a moment.'

I recall my disbelief when I came back down to the kitchen

– thinking that Mila was playing hide and seek at first. But then it became apparent that she wasn't in my house or my garden, and that someone had come in and taken her. The back door was wide open.

Then I remember the red cap hanging on our side gate a few days later and tell Shivani about it. 'I thought it was a strange place for someone to have dropped a hat. I'm now wondering if it belonged to whoever took Mila.'

My heart speeds up a few seconds before my brain catches up. The cap smelt of smoke... Lewis was in our house... he often smoked. Trying to quit and failing. I can't imagine him giving up for good.

Was it *his* cap? It's the sort of thing he'd wear. Maybe he'd been lurking around our house before meeting Jodie yesterday afternoon. I wouldn't put it past him to break in – it would explain some of the weird things that I've reported to the police but couldn't explain. But why would he want to take Mila? It makes no sense.

I decide to keep these speculations to myself. If Jodie ever gets wind of me accusing her father of anything, I doubt she'll ever speak to me again. Not now that he's just swanned back into her life. I know she's desperate for a Rory replacement, for a father figure, but I'm not sure Lewis fits the hole Rory left behind.

'OK, look, we can speculate all we like about hair ties and mysterious caps, but that's for the police to investigate. The fact is you have already admitted to taking the child in question from your school without consent, although you deny the allegations of intent to kidnap or falsely imprison.'

'Yes, I deny them vehemently! I did not want to kidnap Mila, I...' I trail off, not knowing how to explain what was going through my head at the time. Unless she's also experienced the soul-crushing ache of wanting a child, the heart-breaking ordeal of losing pregnancy after pregnancy, then it's impossible for her to understand.

'What you need to demonstrate to the police is that you were acting as Mila's teacher and with her best interests at heart, especially since the child was left alone in the playground. She hadn't been collected by her parent or guardian, there was no member of staff present at the time, and no other arrangements had been made. It was extremely unfortunate that she was taken from your kitchen while under your watch, but that event was beyond your control.

'It would have been preferable if she wasn't at your house in the first place, that you'd remained on school premises,' Shivani continues, 'but perhaps you were intending on taking her straight *back* to school, say, once you'd dealt with something urgent at home. Not ideal, but something for you to consider – as long as it's the truth, of course.'

'Yes, yes, exactly,' I say, suddenly feeling hopeful that if I tweak my story, it's all easily explained as a misunderstanding.

'I'll be with you throughout the interview, and if you wish to take further advice, the interview will be paused, and we can consult together. Given that Mila is still missing—'

My insides turn to stone.

'Wait, *what*...? But... but the police did a welfare check. They said she was fine!' I don't know what to believe anymore, hating that what I've suspected all along – that Mila is still missing – is turning out to be right. 'I mean, Mila's been off school poorly all week, which has made me concerned. I even went back to the police to tell them I was still worried about her. But I thought...' I shake my head, blindsided by the revelation. 'They told me she'd gone to a sleepover, that she was fine.' I touch my head as the room spins, making me feel sick. 'So they're now saying that Mila *isn't* at home sick at all? That she really is missing?' My heart thunders in my chest as my worst fears are confirmed.

Shivani nods, her face expressionless. 'It's time to wake up to the seriousness of this, Mrs Marlowe,' the solicitor replies. 'The child's mother got back from a work trip last night to find that both the nanny and her child are gone.'

FORTY-THREE
JODIE

I am in deep, deep trouble. No doubt about that.

My cheek is pressed against the concrete floor, and there's a gag pulled tight around my mouth – some kind of rag that stinks and tastes of oil. My eyes are bandaged with a blindfold, and my wrists are bound behind my back, the rope cutting into my skin. My ankles are tied together so tightly I can't feel my toes anymore.

There's a whimpering sound coming from the opposite corner. I am not alone in this room – the office at the end of the warehouse. Someone else is tied up in here, too – a child, by the sound of it – though they can't be gagged like me, because occasionally they bleat out a few snotty words.

'*Help... help me... I want... I want to go home...*'

It was Mum's phone call that blew my cover. Normally my phone is set on vibrate, but the volume switch must have got toggled on without me realising. The shrill ringtone literally flooded the entire warehouse, and by the time I'd fumbled with my phone, dropped it cos I was shaking so much, and then, finally, silenced it from where I was hiding under the pile of sacks behind the woodpile, it was too late. The pair who'd come into the warehouse found me. I was hauled out of my hiding place by a pair of strong hands, then dragged out backwards with an arm around my throat. It all happened so quickly, there was no way I had time to answer the call let alone scream for help.

Without saying a word, the man tore my phone from my hands as he forced me upright. I put up a good fight, though not enough to overcome an adult male. I caught a quick glimpse of Zayla – she looked upset and worried – though she still helped him drag me across the warehouse.

'Get off!' I'd screamed, making myself go limp, but he gripped onto me, my legs pedalling and kicking the ground beneath me as he manhandled me into the office.

I twisted round to see his face, but he was wearing a cut-out balaclava, so apart from the thin lines of his mean lips and his dark eyes flashing all around, I couldn't see anything. All I knew was that he was strong and determined and stank of stale sweat.

In the office, he growled something at Zayla in a low voice, but I couldn't make out what. I watched on, terrified as she grabbed some heavy-duty tape, rope, and ties from a metal cupboard in the cluttered room, while balaclava man pinned me down on the floor. I thrashed and kicked as much as I could, but eventually, between them, they had me gagged and bound up with my ankles tied to the leg of a heavy desk. Then they blind-folded me and left.

I try to stop shivering so I can listen out for any sounds – my hearing and smell are the only senses I have left – but it's hard as I'm still soaking wet and freezing from the rain. What the hell was I thinking, running away from home in a strop like that? I'd do anything to be with Mum right now. She'll be going out of her mind with worry. I've no idea what the time is, but it must almost be Sunday morning by now. My body is stiff and sore from lying here for hours.

'Aaeerggghhh-oooh...' I cry through the gag. I've tried

gnawing at it, but it tastes disgusting – like engines and chemicals – and it's too tough to chew through. 'Mmmm-aaarrggh... eerrraaghh-oooh...'

I'm hoping the child will say something back, perhaps recognise that I'm trying to ask her who she is, if she knows why she's here or who the man is.

'Aaarrgh-uuhhh-aahh-ahhh?' I try to make it sound like I'm asking a question, but all I hear in reply is another whimper.

'I'm scared,' the child says – a girl, I think. She's only young.

I make a noise in reply, trying to sound soothing rather than scary.

'I... I want my mummy,' she whimpers, hiccupping through a sob.

Another sound from me, but it comes out as a croak.

'He's bad man. The bad man took me.' More cries. 'Now the bad man got you.'

I make more groaning noises, wishing that I could at least get the blindfold off or my hands free. I don't even have my phone to call for help anymore – he took it from me – but we might have a chance of escape if only I can get these ropes off.

I keep chewing on the gag until my jaw aches, and sawing and wriggling my wrists within the rope ties, feeling as if I might be making a bit of progress, but it's slow going. I'm scared they'll come back at any moment.

For what seems like forever, I chew and chew and chew... squirm and writhe and wriggle, dragging the back of my head against the floor in case I can slide the blindfold up and off my eyes... chew, wriggle, slide, squirm... I keep going... I won't give up.

I must have dozed off because I'm suddenly wide awake. For a moment, I wonder where the hell I am, why everything is pitch black and why my body aches as if I've been through a grinder. Then I remember.

Wait... there's someone here, someone in the room. They're moving about so it can't be the kid. I'm certain she's tied up too, or she'd have helped me get free by now. I keep dead still, hardly daring to breathe, my ears straining for clues. Then I smell smoke. Cigarette smoke.

When I skipped school on Friday and hid here the first time, that man had dropped a dog-end. It could be him. I think he's come on his own this time. No Zayla. I reckon she's got caught up in something illegal – maybe drugs or county lines – and now I'm caught up in it too. We're always getting talks about that stuff at school.

The smell of smoke gets stronger, and I hear the scuff of his feet nearby. Then the little girl whimpers, making little noises in her throat.

'Yes, please... yes more, I'm hungry...' she bleats.

It sounds like he's giving her food. There's rustling, like cellophane being opened, followed by the sound of someone drinking furiously, making me realise how thirsty I am. My mouth feels like it's filled with sand. Ever so slowly, I try to move to ease the pain in my shoulder, but the side of my head catches on something sharp, making me stifle a cry. I grit my teeth, certain I've probably drawn blood on what felt like a nail or screw sticking out of the desk leg. But it gives me an idea... while he's busy with the kid, I move my head back towards the sharp thing again, trying to catch it on the edge of the blindfold to pull it off.

At first, it feels like I'll never do it, but then the blindfold snags on something, and yes... the fabric moves a bit, turning sideways around my head. Then the fabric slips off the nail, and I have to find it all over again.

The man has finished giving the child food, and now he's clattering about the room, moving furniture or chucking things on the floor – it's hard to tell. God, my heart is pounding so much as I slowly rub my head against the desk leg again and… and there. Got it! Ever so slowly, I pull my head down so the blindfold lifts a little. I don't want it to come right off – just enough to get my bearings and see who he is.

It takes ages for me to get used to the chink of light beneath the fabric, but gradually things come clear. I see a filthy floor, and, across the room, there's a little pair of legs curled up on a dirty mattress with grubby white socks on her feet. It looks as though she's got a grey pleated skirt on. Like school uniform.

Slowly I twist my head around and, over the other side of the room, I glimpse the lower half of a man's legs standing beside another old mattress. He's wearing dirty trainers and jeans and seems to be shaking out something that looks like a sleeping bag. Then he lowers himself down. I hold my breath, convinced I'm about to get a proper look at him. But instead, he stays sitting up, lighting up another cigarette, his face staying out of view.

FORTY-FOUR

HANNAH

DC Bright and DC Starkey keep asking me the same questions over and over and over – though I don't see how grilling me for several hours is going to help find Mila. The guilt from finding out that she's still missing is unbearable.

'You've got to believe me. I have no idea where Mila is.' I'm close to tears, but also beyond them, too. 'No one took me seriously when I reported this over a week ago. I even came back with concerns about the welfare check, wondering if you'd got the wrong child, but I was made to feel stupid.'

Shivani has remained quiet so far, but when DC Starkey assures me that it was definitely Mila they saw at the welfare check, suggesting that I must have subsequently harmed her, or that I acted as an accomplice, we take a break so I can ask her advice.

'There's no way I would ever hurt a child,' I tell her when we're alone. 'The thought makes me feel sick.'

After we've spoken, I'm allowed to use the toilet. I lean back against the cubicle wall with a female officer standing outside, wondering how many criminals have used the same toilet. Is that what I am now, a criminal?

Back in the interview room, I take Shivani's advice.

'I'll repeat the question, Mrs Marlowe. Did you harm Mila Weston?'

'No comment,' I state clearly, hardly able to believe it's me uttering the same words I've seen in films and TV dramas so many times.

'Did you release the child in order for the police to conduct the welfare check?'

'What, no! No comment.' I feel the beat of anger simmering inside me – a red-hot pulse deep within.

'How well do you know the child's nanny, Zayla?'

'No comment.'

'Do you know where she is right now?'

'No comment.'

'Is it true that you found Mila's artwork to be disturbing?' DC Bright asks.

I frown, shaking my head. 'Yes... I...' I glance at Shivani, and she gives me a nod. 'No comment,' I say, remembering the last painting Mila did in my art group – the blood, the shadowy figures in the woods. I told Kim, her class teacher, about it, saying I thought the picture was concerning.

'Do you have favourites in your classes, Mrs Marlowe? Some children must stand out over others, right? Making some more likeable – or *less* likeable – than others, perhaps?'

'No comment,' I say, desperately wanting to answer, but instinct tells me to give them nothing. These questions are leading me down a path I don't wish to take.

'Did you take a dislike to Mila Weston?' DC Starkey asks. He's not been as talkative as DC Bright so far. 'Or have reason to hurt her family?'

'No! No comment.'

'How well do you know Mila's mother, Anna Weston?' DC Bright asks, tapping a pen on the stack of papers in front of him.

'I don't know her,' I say, concerned that *no comment* on

repeat is only going to make me seem more guilty. 'Mila was new at the school last September. She's in the reception class. I think her nanny usually does the drop-offs and pick-ups. I've never paid that much attention, apart from the handful of times when she's not been collected.'

I sigh, deciding to continue despite feeling I've already said too much.

'Look, you've got to believe me. I have not harmed Mila Weston. I don't know who the police saw when they did a welfare check, but if Mila is still missing, it can't have been her, can it?' I take a breath. 'Yes, I was bloody stupid to take her off school premises without permission, but I am not a kidnapper. And I'd never, ever hurt a child!'

If only they knew how much I'd longed to have a baby with Rory, making our family finally complete, and how sweet and precious Mila is in my class. How I've sometimes looked at her for longer than I maybe should, imagining that she's mine – imagining Rory and I holding her hands, swinging her along as we went for a walk along the beach – then perhaps they'd understand. But telling them all that is only going to make me seem more guilty, that I'm unhinged, a psycho driven to kidnap a child whatever the cost.

Then the papers in Anna Weston's study are on my mind again. I really don't think I can tell them about all that, not yet. Not until I can phone the clinic tomorrow. Besides, it would mean admitting that I was snooping around Mila's family home, even if I had been let into the house legitimately by Jan. Under the circumstances, me being in her house alone is not going to look good. But the upshot is, I'm lying to the police.

'OK, let's move on, Mrs Marlowe,' DC Starkey says, opening a file in front of him. Every word of this interview is being recorded, making me even more on edge and careful about what I say. 'Do you recognise this item?'

The detective slides a photograph towards me – an item of clothing spread out on a table beside a tape measure for scale.

'No,' I say. 'What is it?'

I mean, I can see it's a coat – pale-blue and lightweight with a zip up the front. Even without the tape measure, it's clear that it's meant for a child because of the three yellow ducklings printed on each front pocket. There are several rips and tears up one side, with greeny-brown stains all over the fabric.

'It's Mila Weston's coat,' DC Starkey says, rubbing at his chin. 'We know this because it has a name label sewn into the neck. See?' He shows me another photo – a close-up of the collar. Then he sits back in his chair, folding his forearms across his shirt.

'I've never seen it before,' I say, suddenly feeling light-headed as I realise that's not entirely the truth.

I think it's the coat Jodie grabbed from the cloakroom at Anna Weston's house, saying something about giving it to Zayla – who she conveniently happened to be friends with – before disappearing off in Zayla's car rather than coming back with me. I didn't take much notice of it at the time, but I do remember it was light blue.

I stare at the photo, trying to work out what this means. Jodie knowing Zayla, acting oddly, running away after Lewis left, then her disappearing... Something is going on that I don't know about, and I really don't like it one bit.

'Are you sure?'

'Quite sure,' I reply. Another lie, but there's no way I'm incriminating my daughter.

'Have you been along the coastal road in the last couple of days, Mrs Marlowe?' the officer continues. 'Either by car or on foot. Particularly where the road meets the cliffs. There's a picnic spot there with a couple of tables.'

'No,' I say without thinking. *Yet another lie.* Then I quickly add, 'Comment.'

'Have you ever been to Ocean Heights up on the headland?' he continues.

'No... no comment,' I say, wondering if there are cameras along that route, or perhaps they spoke to that woman, Nicole, who let me in there the first time. 'Why are you asking me all these questions? It's not helping to find Mila, is it? And I'm still so worried about my daughter, Jodie. Have you heard if my father picked her up from the supermarket?' I grip the edge of the table, feeling the sting of hot tears as they spill over the edge of my eyes. But the officers don't answer my question. 'Look, there are *two* girls missing now, and instead of looking for them, you're grilling me when I haven't done anything!'

'We're trying to establish a few facts based upon what we already know,' the detective continues. 'The reason I'm asking you about the coat is because it was found on the rocks beneath the coastal path, a little way from the picnic area. It's an eighty-foot drop at least. Were you trying to get rid of evidence, is that it?'

'Oh my God.' I cover my mouth, horrified at what this might mean. It's unthinkable that Mila went over the cliff edge – or worse, that she was *pushed* over. 'No, I swear—'

'Mrs Marlowe,' DC Starkey says, leaning forward and getting in my face. 'Did you kill Mila Weston?' A pause, and then he sits back again, folding his arms and staring right at me. 'Because it's not the first time that a child has come to harm while in your care, is it?'

His comment hits me right in the face, making my head spin.

'No... no comment,' I say, screwing up my eyes.

FORTY-FIVE

Before

There was nothing to watch on the TV, so Hannah picked up a book about French Impressionists from Natalie's bedside table and flicked through the pages. She glanced at her watch – it was only 10.15 p.m. Then she checked her Nokia to see if any texts had come in from Rory, but there was nothing apart from a message from her mum yesterday that she still hadn't got round to answering.

The phone had been a Christmas present from her parents last year, so she could be safe on nights out, they'd said. She couldn't afford even a five-pound SIM top-up right now, so she figured she'd probably better save the last remaining credit for texting Rory. She'd not seen or heard from him in a few days. He'd been in a strange mood these last few weeks, seeming stressed and distracted, and Hannah knew better than to pester him. But she still missed him and wished he'd get in touch. They were good together, or so she'd thought, and he'd been a good distraction after her last break-up.

'Hey, gorgeous girl,' Hannah said to Fleur, leaning over the cot. Having a baby was full-on, she thought, catching a whiff of something. If it wasn't a nappy change, it was a feed or comforting or bathing or entertaining – an endless round of duties. There was a nursery on campus, but she had no idea how Natalie was able to keep up with her studies still, let alone prepare for their final project before they graduated this summer.

It made Hannah wonder if she was doing the right thing, agreeing to be Fleur's godmother. If it came down to it, was she cut out for the job? She'd never even thought about having kids of her own, let alone looking after someone else's.

After Hannah had changed Fleur's nappy, she put her gently back in her cot. The baby seemed content, wriggling about in her cut-off bunny sleepsuit and little socks, wide-eyed as she watched the musical mobile above her go round to the tune of 'London Bridge is Falling Down'. Hannah wound up the mechanism again and Fleur pumped her legs, gurgling up at the mobile as the little furry farm animals twirled around above her. But it didn't last long, and her contentedness soon turned into a mix of grizzles and whimpers, as though she wasn't sure what she was feeling – hungry, happy or tired.

Hannah put the book down and got up again, peering into the cot and making a face at Fleur. 'Oh, you funny little thing,' she crooned. 'You're actually quite sweet, aren't you?' Something stirred inside her – like a rewiring of her heart as emotions she wasn't familiar with crept through her. Was this what broodiness felt like?

Then, for some reason, Rory was on her mind again, causing her to check her phone. Nothing. She caved and sent him a quick message – *Hi, it's me. How are you? Love, Hannah xxx* – and pressed send. Her credit was almost gone.

'You wait here while I get your bottle,' Hannah whispered to the baby, winding up the mobile again. Then she opened the bedroom door, hesitating and turning back to the cot for a moment. She should probably take Fleur down with her, but the baby seemed settled again, staring up at the mobile and making more gurgling noises. It was better to leave her up here, especially with those boys smoking in the kitchen. If Hannah hurried, she'd be back before the three or four minutes of music ran out.

'I won't be long, sweetheart,' she said, heading out onto the landing.

Hannah rushed down the three flights of stairs, annoyed that someone had left an airing rack of soaking wet washing on the landing, blocking her passage. She opened the nearest bedroom, seeing a boy lying on the bed with a gaming device. He barely looked up when Hannah shoved his washing through the door. 'Fire hazard,' she said, feeling like a school matron. But now that she was responsible for Fleur, even if only for a few hours, safety came first. The whole house suddenly seemed like a death trap, and she wished Natalie didn't have to live here. Despite what happened between them, she still cared for her.

At the bottom of the stairs, the hallway had been partially blocked with three muddy bikes that looked as if they'd only just been brought in from outside. Their rain-soaked owners were now in the kitchen pouring copious amounts of alcohol into shot glasses for the half dozen or so lads congregated there. The air was thick with the sour tang of weed and cheap after-shave. She shook her head and tutted as she made her way to the fridge.

'Christ, it's like a crack den in here,' Hannah said. The whole room was filthy and littered with dirty crockery in the sink, empty food packets and bottles all over the table, and an array of football boots and other sports equipment on the floor. Plus, the rubbish bin was overflowing.

At least it was only a few more months until the end of their final term. She didn't know what Natalie's plans were after they graduated, but she'd already told Hannah there was no way she was going back to Norfolk to live with her parents. 'I might give Bristol a go,' she'd said, which had sounded like a cool idea. Hannah wondered if they could share a place together.

''Scuse me,' Hannah said, trying to open the fridge door. A boy was standing in the way, downing a shot. 'Can you move? I can't get to the fridge.'

The lad grunted and stumbled sideways, accidentally slamming the door to the hallway closed. Hannah hesitated, her hand on the fridge – she wouldn't hear if Fleur cried, especially when someone turned up the music. But she was glad she'd left her upstairs. The kitchen was no place for a baby right now.

Tutting loudly, Hannah took the bottle from the fridge and was about to put it in the microwave when one of the boys stumbled against her, knocking it from her hands. As it hit the floor, the lid popped off, sending a spray of milk everywhere.

'Idiot!' Hannah cried, glaring at him as he took a drag of his joint.

Then someone grabbed Hannah from behind, pressing his fingers into her ribs. 'Now, now, play nice,' he said with leer. 'Aren't you Nat's friend?' He purposefully splashed his foot in the milk.

Forcing herself to stay calm and unfazed, as well as knowing that she had to get back upstairs to feed Fleur, she went to the fridge to get the final bottle. She hoped it would be enough to last until Nat got back – she had no idea how to mix up more.

'Yeah, I am,' Hannah replied. 'And I've got a baby to look after so keep out of my way, you muppets.' She put the bottle in the microwave and while it was heating, she grabbed some kitchen paper, dropping to her knees to mop up the mess.

'Your lucky night, Nige,' one of the boys said, ribbing the lad nearest to Hannah. She did her best to ignore him – ignore them *all* – and thanked God that Rory didn't behave like this.

'When's Mick coming?' Hannah heard one of the lads say.

'Dunno,' another replied from behind her as she washed her

hands at the sink, 'but there's another party going down tonight. That house on Pelican Row. You know the place?'

Hannah's ears pricked up. Rory's student accommodation was on Pelican Row. She wondered if he was having a party, but quickly dismissed that idea. If he was, he'd have invited her – of *course* he'd have invited her. Wouldn't he? And now he knew that she and Natalie were on speaking terms again, he'd have invited Nat along too.

Then Hannah had a horrible thought – what if that was where Nat had gone tonight, to Rory's house party? What if he'd decided not to invite *her*, his actual girlfriend? Was that why he'd been so quiet lately – because he'd wanted to end things but didn't know how to tell her? The thought of Nat doing the dirty on her so soon after they'd reconciled made her feel ill.

Watching the final few seconds tick past on the microwave timer, Hannah shook her head, telling herself she was being stupid. That there was no way Rory would do that to her, and when one of the lads said, 'Yeah, it's Richard's party at number three. I've been invited if you wanna go,' Hannah almost burst with relief. It wasn't Rory. Rory was not having a party without her. He was not ignoring her. They were rock solid. She was being stupid. *Oh so bloody stupid.*

Hannah grabbed the bottle from the microwave, giving it a shake. It was tempting to spray it all over the buffoons in the kitchen, who were still ribbing her and getting in her way on purpose, but she held her nerve and, satisfied the bottle was the right temperature, she squeezed her way past the boys and went into the hallway.

She didn't realise it then – and, in fact, she didn't remember until much later when she played the scene back in her mind – but a couple of the bikes had been moved, one of them half toppled over, and the front door had been left slightly ajar, the rain coming in and wetting the front doormat.

It was only when Hannah got up to the top floor, singing out to Fleur that her bottle was ready, that it was time to have her milk and a snuggle, that it wasn't long until Mummy would be home, that she realised something was not right.

The attic bedroom door was wide open. She was sure she'd left it almost shut.

The ceiling light was on. She was certain she'd turned it off – not wanting the glare in the baby's eyes.

The pink cot blanket was lying on the threadbare carpet. She knew she'd left it draped over Fleur's legs before she'd gone downstairs.

The musical mobile had stopped, the fluffy animals hanging limply by their strings.

Hannah walked slowly up to the cot and peered inside.

The baby was gone.

FORTY-SIX
HANNAH

By the time they gave me my phone back at the custody desk, it had run out of battery.

'We're releasing you under investigation,' DC Starkey said after I'd been grilled in two separate interviews and waited another few hours in the custody cell.

Shivani had explained. 'In simple terms, that means you're not being charged, *yet*. I wouldn't advise taking a long holiday, but you're free to leave and continue with your life as normal. They'll likely bring you in for an informal interview or possibly even rearrest you at some point, but it's very much pending their investigation and any evidence that may or may not arise.'

It was a few moments before I took it all on board. 'So they don't have enough to charge me now, but they might going forwards?'

'Exactly,' Shivani said at the desk where I'd been brought in about ten hours ago. The custody officer was processing my release, handing my meagre belongings back to me. After I thanked the duty solicitor, I left the station, pretty much running all the way home.

Now, panting and breathless, I bang on my front door, ringing the bell repeatedly.

'Dad, *Dad*, it's me,' I shout through the letterbox, crouching down to see into the hallway. 'Dad! Jodie! It's Mum, I'm home. Can you let me in?'

I only had my phone on me when they arrested me this morning as I'd given Dad the car keys to drive and the house keys to lock up – I'd only anticipated a quick trip to the supermarket to fetch Jodie.

I ring and knock a few more times, squinting through the letterbox flap to see if Dad's shoes are there – he always takes them off when he comes round – or if Jodie's trainers are discarded on the floor. But I can't see anything. I wonder if they're both having a nap after getting no sleep last night, but when I step back a few paces, I see the upstairs curtains are all open.

'There's no one there,' a voice says. When I turn, it's Mrs Kirk standing in her front doorway, looking at me warily.

'Oh hi, Mrs Kirk,' I say, trying to sound normal. 'Do you know where Dad is?' I'm relieved to see a friendly face. 'Did you see him come home with Jodie earlier?'

Mrs Kirk is shaking her head before I've even finished. 'No,' she states decisively. 'He left shortly after...' She hesitates, clearing her throat and looking up and down our street. '... shortly after the police took you away. He hasn't been back since.'

'Are you sure?' Maybe she missed them coming back.

'Since all the kerfuffle first thing, I've been glued to the window. What am I supposed to think now, the police turning up at all hours and taking you away? Who have I been living next door to all this time?' she says, shaking her head and tutting, arms folded across her chest. 'And then that unsavoury man hanging around, prowling about your garden. I don't feel safe anymore.'

With that, she slams the door and goes back inside.

It takes a bit of persuading, but after a brisk walk back into town, a taxi driver at the market square rank agrees to drive me to Mum and Dad's house on a promise that they will pay his fare when we get there. I know they always keep some cash for a rainy day.

'Look, take this as insurance meantime,' I say, handing him my dead iPhone.

He rolls his eyes but lets me get in, dropping my phone onto the passenger seat while I sit in the back, and, fifteen minutes later we're pulling up outside my parents' 1970s semi-detached house in a suburb on the west of town.

'I'll be back in a moment,' I say, getting out and rushing up the drive. I have a key to their place at home in my hallway drawer and wish I had it on me now, because when I rap the knocker and ring their doorbell over and over, there's no reply.

'This can't be happening...' I bang on the door again, not knowing what to do. The fare is thirteen pounds fifty and I don't have a penny on me. I can't let him *actually* take my phone – I need to charge it as soon as possible to see where Jodie is – but apart from smashing a window, I have no way of getting inside my house to get my charger.

I consider trying to break in here at Mum and Dad's, knowing they keep some cash in a biscuit tin at the back of the food cupboard, but they had all their doors and windows replaced last year with high-security toughened glass, so there's no way I'd get in.

Defeated, I walk slowly back to the waiting taxi, the driver looking less than pleased as he drums his fingers on the wheel.

'They're not home,' I say, pulling a face. 'You'll have to keep my phone. If you could jot down your details, I'll come and pay the fare and get it back, and—'

The driver stares up at me, scowling. 'I'm not a bloody pawn shop,' he snaps, but then I hear another voice calling out to me – a voice coming from a vehicle that's just pulled up behind the taxi – a blue van, to be precise. The driver gets out and comes over.

Lewis.

'What's the problem, mate?' he says, one hand leaning on the roof as he peers in through the open window. 'No need to get annoyed with the lady.' When the taxi driver explains what's happened, Lewis pulls out his wallet. 'Twenty quid cover it?' The driver nods, handing my phone back to me.

'Thank you,' I say, hugging my arms around myself as I watch the taxi drive off. 'I owe you.'

'Trust me, you don't,' Lewis replies, and I know better than to question what he means.

'Anyway, what are you doing down my parents' cul-de-sac?'

'Looking for my daughter,' he tells me, which makes my heart sink. 'You?'

'Same.' I explain what happened after he left yesterday, Jodie running off, glossing over the bit where I was arrested, but he interrupts.

'Get in my van,' he says. 'I'll give you a lift home.'

On the short drive back, I finish my story. 'So, I'm praying that Jodie is with Dad and they've gone for a walk or to get food or something. I dunno.' Before I get out, I drop my head into my hands. 'I can't get in as Dad's got my house keys,' I say, 'but thanks for the lift.' I open the door to get out, then Lewis comes round, holding out his hands to me. When I let out a pathetic sob, his arms wrap tightly around me.

'Hey, hey. It's OK. I'm here.'

Strangely, despite it being Lewis saying those words – the man who was literally never there for me or Jodie – I gain some comfort. Right now, he's all I've got.

'Just tears of frustration,' I say, feeling stupid as I wipe my face on my sweatshirt sleeve.

He takes me by the hand, leading me down the alley by my house. At the side gate, he hoists himself up and over the fence with ease, jumping down the other side. Then he slides the bolt and opens the gate to let me through.

'Lewis, did you...?' But I don't finish, watching as he pulls out his wallet and takes out a credit card, easing it between my back door frame and the door itself, level with the Yale lock. The sun glints off his light brown hair, while the muscles in his back stand out through his T-shirt. I try not to look, try not to be affected by the sight of him, but it takes me right back to the days when I worked in the pub, when I was smitten by his charm and good looks.

'Just give me a second,' he tells me, taking a Swiss army knife from his other pocket, still holding the credit card in place. Using his teeth, he pulls out a ridged tool, slipping it into the mortice lock lower down. With a few deft wiggles and twists and another shove from the credit card, Lewis lifts his knee and presses down on the door handle, opening the door into my kitchen. 'Voila,' he says, stepping back and beaming.

FORTY-SEVEN

HANNAH

'I know you're worried, but she's my daughter, too,' Lewis says, handing me a mug of coffee.

He insisted on making it, seeming to know where I keep everything. But trying to figure out if it's him who's been breaking into my house, taking my things and snooping around, getting up to whatever it is that Lewis has always got up to, isn't my priority right now. I need to find Jodie.

'Which means that fending for herself is in her DNA,' he adds.

'Right,' I say flatly, wishing he'd given me something more hopeful to go on than that. 'I'm just praying she's with Dad.' My phone is on the worktop, plugged in while I wait for it to get enough charge to switch on. I don't know Dad's number off by heart, or I'd have used Lewis's phone.

'And look, I'm really sorry to hear that bloke did the dirty on you,' he says. 'Jodie told me what happened.'

I pause, stunned, my eyebrows raised as I stare at him. 'That *bloke*,' I say, 'is my husband of eleven years. I've known him since I was nineteen – longer than I've known you. He's been more of a father to Jodie than you ever have.'

I feel bad when Lewis winces at my cruel comment, but I need to take my anger and frustration out on someone, and he happens to be nearest. But a voice inside tells me to back off, that until Jodie is home safe, I need an ally.

'Sorry,' I say. 'Look, there's only one thing I'm interested in right now and that's finding Jodie. If you hadn't been... conning her online or whatever you were playing at, then she wouldn't have—'

'Hannah, stop.' Lewis drags out a chair beside me and sits down, his face so close I can see each hair of his stubble, noticing for the first time that there's a smattering of grey in it. 'If I'd turned up on your doorstep asking to see Jodie, or sent you a letter or phoned you to find out how she was getting on, would you have let me see her, let me get to know her? Be honest.'

'After all this time?' I make a pfft sound. 'You let us down one too many times, Lewis. You think you deserve another chance?' I fold my arms.

'My point exactly,' he says. 'I've changed, Hannah. I *swear* I have. Things have happened in my life that...' Lewis shakes his head and looks away, rubs a hand around the back of his neck. 'Things that made me realise what a dick I was when I was younger, OK?'

When he looks at me, I see something earnest in his eyes. For once, I have no smart retort to throw back at him.

'I didn't know how lucky I was when we were together. I was young and stupid, and only realised what I'd lost when it was too late. Back then, I was obsessed with travelling about the country for work, my mates and footie, playing the field. Then it was more work, more women, more boozing. I was spending my hard-earned cash faster than I was earning it, getting deep into debt. I'm not proud, but a couple of times I had to nick food just to survive. I never hurt anyone, but it was that or literally starve. I was too proud to sign on and spent several winters living in my van when work dried up. I was so bloody miserable, Hannah. I missed you. I missed my daughter. I missed the life we never had.'

I listen, hardly daring to breathe, trying not to get drawn into Lewis's eyes, knowing that every time I've ever got lost in them, I've been heartbroken all over again. I made a promise to myself and to Jodie that I'd be strong next time, not get sucked back in. He reaches out and touches my arm.

'I can't do this, Lewis. Not now. Not ever.' I shrug away from him and get up and go over to my phone, pressing the power button. Thank God, the screen lights up. The first thing I do is tap on the tracking app to see if it's picking up Jodie's whereabouts, but it seems to take forever to resolve. When it does, the familiar message that she can't be located right now pops up.

'That's weird,' I say. Lewis comes over, standing behind me. 'Her last known location was at the supermarket, just before I was arres...' I trail off. I haven't exactly been honest to Lewis about being arrested, telling him that the police just wanted my help about an enquiry. 'Before I went to the police station.'

'OK,' he replies, peering over my shoulder. 'So where is she now?'

'That's the thing, I don't know, but her last known location has definitely moved. The grey dot is here now, look. That must be where the app located her *after* the supermarket and before her phone lost signal again. If Dad had fetched her from the shop, that's not the way he'd have brought her home. This location marker is on the road to the old industrial estate just out of town, look.'

'Agreed,' Lewis says, puzzling what it means.

I jump as my phone suddenly lights up with a picture of my father, and *Dad Calling* is displayed on my screen. I swipe to answer.

'Dad, thank God. Where are you? I've been so worried. I

came round to your house, but you and Mum weren't there. Where's Jodie? Did you find her? Was she at the supermarket?'

'Hi... Han... I'm... eh... um... Jodie isn—'

'Dad, stop, I can't hear you properly. It's a terrible line. Say that again, would you?'

There are more twanging sounds as his voice cuts in and out, and I can't tell if he sounds urgent or calm.

'Dad, move somewhere with better signal, can you? Where are you? Can you hear me?'

I wait, but there's nothing. Then I just manage to hear a few clear words that chill my blood.

'Jodie wasn't there...' and then the line goes dead.

'We'll take my car,' I say, chucking my keys at Lewis when he tells me he's low on fuel. 'Will you drive? I don't feel steady enough.' There's no way I'm sitting about at home doing nothing – I need to be out there, looking for my daughter. I'm not stopping until I find her. Dad's call might have been cut off, but I heard enough to know he hasn't got her.

Outside, Lewis beeps my car unlocked. I'm about to get in when I spot the brown leather suitcase that I picked up from Marion's house still lying on the passenger seat.

'Hang on, I'll just shove this in the back.' I grab the case handle and haul it out, but as I'm about to put it on the back seat, both catches pop open, and the contents spill out onto the pavement.

'*Christ...*' I mumble, trying to keep my cool as a load of baby clothes and other paraphernalia fall into the gutter. I silently curse Marion for making me fetch it – for hoarding these old things that I wouldn't want to put on a baby even if I had one.

'Here, let me help,' Lewis says, coming round. He starts to gather up the stuff – musty blankets, old-fashioned baby suits with rusty poppers, stained terry nappies, faded little bonnets and tiny socks – shoving a few things back into the case.

I stare down at what looks like an entire layette that Marion has been saving for the non-existent baby she believes me and Rory to be having. I push down the grief that threatens to overwhelm me.

Suddenly, I freeze.

'Hannah?' Lewis says, getting up when he sees I'm motionless, a tiny sleepsuit clutched between his large hands. 'Hannah, what's wrong?'

His words wash around me as I stare at what he's holding, my eyes narrowing.

'Give... give me that,' I say, slowly reaching out and taking it from him.

I hold up the little sleepsuit, my body gripped with guilt and memories and panic from that terrible night nearly twenty-four years ago.

'Oh... oh my God,' I whisper, not knowing where to start explaining what it is, or what it's even doing in this suitcase – not when I have no idea myself.

It's the little sleepsuit with pink and blue rabbits and cut-off feet that Natalie's baby was wearing the night she was taken. The night I was looking after her.

FORTY-EIGHT

HANNAH

Another night has passed without Jodie. I was *so* close to getting her from the supermarket yesterday morning, I swear that if the police hadn't arrested me, Dad and I would have got to her before she disappeared again.

Later, after I'd been released, Lewis drove my car as we went out searching, while I messaged all the mums on Jodie's class WhatsApp group again, reminding them to let me know if they or their teens heard anything from her. I was beyond caring what they thought of me, that I was a bad parent – I just wanted my daughter back.

It was early evening as Lewis and I were driving around town – scanning every single person we saw – when my phone rang. It was one of the investigating officers on the case, and my heart skipped a beat as I answered.

'Jodie's phone provider alerted us to a ping on her phone at the supermarket around 7 a.m. this morning,' she said. 'A car was dispatched immediately, and the supermarket informed and—'

'But I already told you about this when I was in custody!' I replied, exasperated as my heart sank. Lewis had given me a sideways look when he heard the truth about where I was.

'A response team was sent to search the area, but nothing's come up so far. We've also checked the shop's CCTV but nothing yet. We'll keep you updated.'

I flopped back in my seat, tugging my seatbelt. It felt tight across my chest. Like me, the police had been so near yet so far. 'At least they're still out looking for her,' I said, grateful that Lewis didn't ask why I'd been in custody. Finding Jodie was the priority.

Gradually, darkness had fallen for a second time without my daughter being home. Awful, intrusive thoughts forced their way into my mind, mainly about what I would do if we never found her. But with Lewis beside me as we searched late into the night, the pair of us walking the streets of West Bradport as he shone his powerful torch into every nook, cranny, hiding place and alleyway, I somehow managed to hold it together. But only just.

'Thank you for helping,' I'd said to him when we went back to my house for water and something to eat. As much as I couldn't face food, Lewis insisted I get something inside me, telling me I'd be no use to anyone otherwise. 'Thank you for being here when...' I forced the darker thoughts from my mind. 'When it matters,' I'd said, drawing my legs up on the sofa. We planned on going out again in half an hour or so, but we must have both fallen asleep, because the next thing I knew, Lewis was waking me up with a cup of coffee in his hand telling me it was Monday morning.

I'd sat bolt upright, grabbing my phone to see if there was news – but there wasn't.

'We'll cover old ground first, then start searching a wider area,' Lewis says now from the driver's seat of my car an hour later, his strong hands gripping the wheel. He pulls off a roundabout onto a quieter side road. 'The only thing we know for certain is that she was between the supermarket and the old industrial estate by the river – that's assuming she hasn't lost her phone or had it stolen.'

Lewis's words make my stomach churn. I don't even want to consider that possibility.

'I'm surprised the estate's not been bulldozed and built on by now,' he continues. 'Those warehouses were starting to get dilapidated when I was working on the bypass, do you remember? When we first met?' He glances across at me, but I don't say anything. I'm not in the mood for reminiscing. 'They must be in a bad way by now.'

'I don't understand what Jodie would be doing around here,' I say, staring out at the desolate scene. West Bradport is a lovely town, but this area is certainly its ugly side. 'I'm still not convinced she's around here,' I say, thinking we're fixating on the wrong area. 'She could have been passing through after the supermarket and turned her phone off again.'

I hate the thought of her not *wanting* to be found, but then I hate the thought of her being *unable* to be found. Each option is equally terrifying.

'Maybe she got lost. Or what if...' I can't stand the awful thought. 'What if she got a lift from a stranger? There are loads of vans and lorries parked up around here at night. It's a known stop for long-distance drivers coming off the bypass.' I shudder at the idea of her spending the night with one of them.

'It's a concern,' Lewis says, not seeming so convinced by Jodie's innate survival instincts anymore. He cruises around for a while longer then pulls in at a layby where a couple of vans and an HGV are parked up. He gets out and taps on each of their windows, taking my phone with a photo of Jodie on it to show them. When he returns, he's shaking his head. 'None of them have seen her. Two of the drivers have been parked up since last night, but she's probably long gone from here now. We're missing something, Han. Something bloody obvious.'

Lewis drives to the supermarket and parks the car. 'You look pale. I'm getting you something to eat and drink. I'll ask around if anyone remembers seeing Jodie yesterday or today. You never know, she might have been back in again this morning if she's hungry.'

I nod, sending him the most recent photo I have of her, and close my eyes, leaning my head back briefly. But it's no good. There's no way I can relax with Jodie still out there, two nights missing now, so I phone the school office and tell Alma, the secretary, that I've gone down with the sickness bug and won't be into work today.

Then, while it's on my mind, I look up the phone number of Mayfield Clinic. It's just after 9 a.m., so I'm hoping they'll answer my call – a call I don't want to have to make at all, let alone in front of Lewis. But it needs to be done. I need to know what the hell that paperwork was doing in Anna Weston's study. My palms sweat and my heart thumps as I dial the number, bracing myself for news I'm not sure I want to hear right now.

'Good morning, Mayfield Clinic, Amber speaking. How may I help you?'

My mouth is open, but nothing comes out. I press the phone to my ear harder, screwing up my eyes, imagining the last couple of times Rory and I were at the plush clinic with its velvet chairs and filter coffee in the waiting area. We'd gone in filled with hope and excitement, then, a few weeks later, we'd left with our dreams of having a baby together dashed once again.

'Hello? May I help you?'

'Sorry, yes,' I croak. 'Is there a doctor I can speak to?'

'I'm sorry, our clinicians are all with patients at present. Are you registered at the clinic?'

I'm on the verge of hanging up, but I only have to think of Mila's sweet little face to keep going. 'Yes... yes, I am. I have my embryos stored with you.'

'I see. Would you like to make an appointment with a doctor? I can book you in for a consultation, perhaps later in the week, if you're looking at implanting.'

'No, no it's not that. I... um, this is a bit delicate, but I...' I can't help the laugh – inappropriate and verging on hysterical, but Amber listens patiently. 'I wanted to check my embryos are... I mean, I wanted to confirm that they're safe. That you still have them.'

Silence down the line. Then Amber clears her throat before asking my name. 'I can assure you, Mrs Marlowe, that if you paid for our embryo storage service then they will be safe for whenever you and your husband are ready to proceed.'

I shudder at the mention of *my husband*. 'Would you just check?'

'I can pull up your file,' she says in an appeasing voice. 'What's your date of birth please, and the full name and date of birth of the registered father? Plus, I'll need your address.'

I give her the details and hear her tapping at her computer.

'Sorry, can you just confirm your address again?'

I do as she asks, my heart thundering in my chest.

'Just one moment, please. I'm going to put you on hold.'

It's the longest one moment of my life, my eyes still glued to the supermarket door as I watch out for Lewis returning.

'Hello, Mrs Marlowe?' a different voice says – a woman again, but she sounds older and somehow more in charge. 'I'm Rachel Fieldman, clinic manager. My colleague tells me that you're enquiring about your frozen embryos.'

'That's right.'

'I think there may be a mix up with the details you gave. For security, can you confirm your address again?'

My mind whirrs, thinking back to what I saw in Anna

Weston's study. If what I suspect is true, then I need to think smart. 'Sure, it's Eastcliff House, Ocean Heights—'

'Ah, thank you, that's fine. Thanks for confirming, Mrs Marlowe,' she says, leaving me grateful that she interrupted me before I had to give the postcode. I've no idea what it is.

Then I hear more tapping on a computer and low voices in the background, as if she's covering the mouthpiece.

'Mrs Marlowe, let me just clarify. You're calling to check that we still have your embryos in storage, is that right?'

'Yes,' I say. My hands are shaking, and there's a whooshing sound thrumming through my ears.

'I'm sorry, I'm a little confused,' she continues. 'You had your remaining embryos implanted almost six years ago now, according to our records. You and your husband signed the paperwork, and the procedure was successfully carried out. Is everything OK, Mrs Marlowe? Would you like to make an appointment to speak to a clinician – either here, or perhaps with your GP?'

But I don't bother replying – partly because I'm in too much shock, and partly because Lewis is striding back across the car park. I end the call and let my phone drop into my lap, the woman's words ringing in my ears.

If what she's telling me is true, then it means that Mila *is* mine – my very own precious little girl – which, in turn, also means that now *both* of my daughters are missing.

FORTY-NINE

Hannah stared down into the empty cot. To begin with, she was strangely calm, her brain taking a moment to catch up with the reality of what her eyes were seeing.

Door wide open. Blanket on the floor. Baby gone

That's not right, she heard in her head, as though someone else was breaking the terrible news to her. She bent down and picked up the pink crocheted blanket. Then she stared vacantly at the floor where it had been dropped, half expecting to see little Fleur lying under where it had been. But it was just the threadbare carpet.

She leant into the cot and lifted the corner of the mattress, checking underneath before letting it drop back down. She shook her head then fell to her knees, checking under the cot and then under Natalie's single bed. Apart from a few discarded clothes and a shoe box, there was nothing but dust under there. Certainly no baby.

'That's... so...' She wanted to say *fucking weird*, but went to the door instead, stepping out onto the landing before peering over the bannisters where she could see the hallway three floors below – the bikes against the wall, loud laughter coming from the kitchen, the smell of weed as it filtered up the stairwell. Her stomach tightened.

'Hello?' she called out in a voice that didn't sound like her own. Then she rushed back into Natalie's room and searched everywhere like a mad woman – in the wardrobe, in the bags on top of the wardrobe, under Natalie's duvet, behind the desk, in the desk, turning everything upside down and inside out, not even considering that she was destroying evidence.

She charged down the stairs, bursting into the other bedrooms. 'Have you taken the baby?' she screamed at the boy gaming on his bed.

He pulled off one headphone.

'Where is she?'

'What?'

Then she rocketed into the other rooms – some occupied, some not – but there was no sign of Fleur anywhere. In the kitchen, the lads mocked her at first, thinking she was joking, looking for attention, that maybe she was drunk or wanted to join their party, but then one of them realised she was serious.

'Guys, it's Nat's baby. We need to help. If someone's taken her, they can't have got far.' All the boys dispersed on foot or on their bikes, seeming to sober up as they went off to scour the local streets. Hannah couldn't recall how many of them came back to report that they'd not spotted anyone with a baby, because the police were there by then.

Thinking back, she couldn't even recall phoning 999, but she must have because the call was logged on her phone. The house soon swarmed with uniformed and plain-clothes officers, and shortly after, a white-suited forensic team entered. In fact, that was what Natalie returned to when her taxi dropped her off, slightly tipsy but happy from her night out. Hannah had been asked to remain in the kitchen with a female police officer, and they sat at the kitchen table with two cups of cold tea between them, set amongst the vodka bottles, shot glasses and overflowing ashtrays.

'Blimey, what's going on?' were Natalie's first words as she stood in the kitchen doorway. Her face seemed refreshed – bright eyes, rosy cheeks, a curious smile on her face. Then she looked at Hannah. 'Where's Fleur?'

The police officer stood up, reached out her hand and touched Natalie's shoulder. When she explained, Natalie passed out.

Over the next few days, Hannah didn't see Natalie. After being interviewed several times at the police station, her statement made – as well as all the lads present in the house that evening giving their version of events – Hannah remained in her student accommodation, barely eating, barely functioning. She couldn't face seeing anyone. She was tempted to go home but didn't want to drag her shame back to her parents, having to explain to them what had happened in a way that didn't make her look like the irresponsible and negligent person everyone now believed her to be. And then the rumours started.

I reckon she did it, Nat's friend Hannah. She killed the baby. Jealousy... an axe to grind... that baby ruined things for them... came between them... revenge... payback... evil bitch..

Then, after a few weeks, Hannah became old news to the rest of the world, though not to herself. Every time she woke in the morning, it felt as real as if it had just happened. The police had put out two appeals on television, holding several press conferences with a tearful and almost mute Natalie sitting beside the detective in charge of the case – a balding man in his fifties with sweat patches under his arms. A reconstruction was aired on a prime-time TV crime investigation show. Hannah stared at the actor playing her, wondering where they found someone who looked so similar.

But there was still no sign of baby Fleur. And no contact from the baby's father, either, though rumours were spreading that Natalie didn't even know who he was. No ransom notes or demands came, no remains or items of clothing were found, and, apart from her birth certificate and few belongings in Natalie's room, there was little to suggest that she had even existed.

Hannah wanted to contact Natalie but didn't know what to say. A couple of the other girls in their year suggested they club together to send flowers to her, so they did, with Hannah organising it. In those few weeks of keeping herself to herself, she'd also handwritten a letter to Natalie, reading it over a thousand times before deciding she wouldn't send it after all. Nothing sounded right or appropriate. She'd gone from knowing Nat so well to not knowing a single word to say to her.

Dear Natalie, words can't describe how sorry I am for what happened, and if I could turn back time, I would do anything. I don't expect you to forgive me, but I did not leave Fleur alone on purpose. She seemed content, so I rushed down to make her bottle again. If I can help you through the days until she's found safe and well, then I'll do whatever you need. You did not deserve this, it is so unfair. Hannah xxx

Then she tore up the note into small pieces and chucked it in the bin – just like she'd done with the letter she'd written at the end of November last year when she'd discovered that Natalie was almost six months pregnant. *If only you'd told me, Nat, if only you'd confided in me...* She'd never been able to get past that point with her thoughts, throwing every version of the letter away.

Up until that point, Natalie had hidden her bump well

under loose tunic tops, and it was only when people started to ask questions that the truth had come out about her pregnancy. It explained why she'd stopped coming on nights out and kept cancelling their regular swim and gym sessions that they both used to love. It also answered a lot of questions that had been on Hannah's mind in the few weeks before. *Is Nat avoiding me? Does she not like me anymore? Have I done something wrong?* She'd put the gentle curve of her friend's belly down to a healthy appetite, to not going to the gym. Besides, she knew better than to comment on Natalie's weight.

And then Hannah heard that someone else had gone with Natalie to see a doctor, holding her hand, coaxing her out of the hole of denial that she'd fallen into. By then, Nat had no choice about what to do. That baby was coming into the world whether Nat wanted it or not.

When Lewis gets back in the car, telling me that no one in the supermarket recognised Jodie's photo or remembered seeing her, he finds me with my knees drawn up to my chest as I bury my face from the world. I still don't believe what I've just heard. It's not possible. It can't be true.

Your remaining embryos were implanted... Six years ago now...

The words pound my brain as I absorb what it means.

Not implanted in me! I should have screamed down the line, but instead I just sat here, numb, gobsmacked, unable to say a word.

'Hey... hey, come on now,' Lewis says, doing up his seat belt. 'I got you this to eat. To keep your strength up.'

I hear rustling and then smell hot coffee as he puts two takeout cups in the cupholders. When I look up, Lewis is holding a chocolate croissant out in my direction.

'Eat,' he says. 'You need it.'

I do as I'm told, and, after a few bites, I agree that he was right. My blood sugar must have dropped as, combined with the caffeine, I feel less like I'm about to faint.

'It's all too much,' I whisper, staring out at the supermarket car park, praying that Jodie will walk past at any moment. '*Everything...*' I don't even know where to begin explaining what I've just learnt from Mayfield Clinic, even though I sense Lewis would do anything in his power to make things better for me. I can't deny it feels good to have him here with me, albeit temporarily.

'Tell me how I can help,' he says with pastry crumbs around his mouth. 'I still care deeply for you, you know, Hannah.'

I stare at him, wondering what it would have been like if he'd been in my life all these years, if Jodie had had her real dad by her side. Would life have turned out differently – for better, for worse? I don't know why, but I sense that if he'd set his mind to it, Lewis would have been a great dad – not the absent, excuse-making stranger he became. Seeing him picking up those baby clothes from the pavement yesterday did something to me... but then all *that* is back on my mind again – the baby sleepsuit with the pink and blue rabbits and the cut-off feet. I can't even begin to work out how the hell it came to be in Marion's possession, though I know I need to find out.

'Start the engine,' I tell Lewis, screwing up the paper bag from my pastry. 'There's somewhere I need to go.'

Chapelfields is an old farmhouse set down a gravel drive and where Marion and Frank Marlowe raised their only son, Rory. With this area of Dorset extremely sought-after, it's no wonder Rory has been champing at the bit to get his hands on the place – it must be worth a fortune these days.

'It's my ex's parents' home,' I explain to Lewis when he whistles out through his teeth at the sight of the house. He parks on the sweeping gravel drive, peering out at the property as he pulls on the handbrake. 'Rory's dad made his money in shipping,' I add, pre-empting his next question.

'No wonder you're pissed off Rory left you,' he says, unbuckling his seatbelt and opening the car door.

I resist the urge to thump him and, instead, reach into the glovebox for the house keys that Marion gave me. We walk up to the front door, complete with white roses growing around it. 'Keep your hands to yourself in here, OK?' I say, shoving the big old key in the lock. 'I'm not stopping long. I just need to check if…' I stop, not sure exactly what it is I'm here to check, but I want to have a hunt around in the spare room where Marion had the suitcase of baby clothes stashed, see what other mementos she's got secreted away in there.

I head up the old, creaky staircase, with Lewis following behind me. It's so sad – the place smells musty and uncared for now. The house used to be so full of life and laughter when Frank was alive, when him and Marion lived here. They'd often entertain, having family members from around the country to stay, or they'd host charity events in the garden for village fundraisers. They were such a part of the community. Rory and I would visit regularly with Jodie – how she loved charging around the garden or playing football with Rory on the massive lawn – and every spring, there'd be lambs in the field behind, and she'd delight in watching them frolic.

Times long gone…

'In here,' I say, leading the way into the spare bedroom with the pink and white wallpaper. It feels strange being in here with Lewis when Rory and I had so many nights together in this room – nights trying for a baby.

Lewis peers out of the window, while I screw up my eyes and grit my teeth – the past has no place in my thoughts now. Though I suddenly realise the past is exactly the reason I'm here. I've not seen that baby sleepsuit with the cut-off feet for almost twenty-five years, and for it to suddenly turn up at my estranged husband's family home isn't something I can ignore. *Or* explain. I know I'll have to inform the police about it.

I get on my knees and drag stuff out from under the bed – dusty old boxes and another suitcase, this one full of Frank's old clothes. Clothes that Marion couldn't bear to part with. The boxes don't contain anything useful, mainly bits of old costume jewellery and ancient perfume bottles, items from a dressing table, as well as postcards and a stamp album, some old lace tablecloths and a stack of sheet music. Marion certainly has an aversion to getting rid of things.

Then I pull open the double doors of the antique wardrobe by the fireplace. I'm starting to believe that this room isn't going to contain much else of interest – and I'm right. The wardrobe just has some of Marion's old summer dresses, plus about ten pairs of her and Frank's shoes, three old tennis rackets in wooden presses, and some umbrellas. 'Follow me,' I tell Lewis, and he trails across the creaky landing after me.

'If you tell me what you're looking for, maybe I can help,' he says, scanning around.

'This was Rory's childhood room,' I say, followed by a sigh.

He rests a hand on my forearm, looking at me in a way that makes me pull away. 'What are we searching for, Han?'

'Honestly? I don't know,' I reply, which is the truth. 'Old papers... photos... anything, really.'

Lewis nods. 'This house is like a time capsule,' he says, pulling open the drawers in a chest. 'These boy's clothes look as though they've just stepped out of the eighties.'

'That's my mother-in-law for you.' I open the small wardrobe, my eyes flicking about. When it's clear there's nothing of interest inside, I take a couple of steps back, but my foot catches on something, making me trip and stumble backwards. Thankfully, I land on the bed.

'Careful,' Lewis says, reaching out for my hand and helping me up. 'Looks like a loose floorboard.' And then he's down on his knees, lifting the rug that's partially covering the boards to see what the problem is.

'You don't need to fix the floor,' I tell him, knowing there will be a hundred jobs like that at Chapelfields. Frank would always grumble about the upkeep of the place. 'We might as well go. I don't think I'm going to find anything. I was stupid to think—'

'No, no... I'm not fixing it,' Lewis says, suddenly prising up a section of floorboard. 'But look, you can tell someone's had this up. These are modern screws – totally different to the original nails.' He lifts the loose floorboard right out and turns on his phone torch. 'There's something down there,' he says, shining the beam underneath.

I get down on my knees beside him and peer down into the dusty space. At first, all I see are cables and pipes, plus a thick layer of dirt, dust and bits of old plaster and building rubble that have accumulated over the last three hundred years. 'What is it?' I ask, watching as Lewis sticks his hand down there, wiggling something about.

'Looks like...' he says, straining, 'Like an old shoebox,' he says, finally pulling it out and putting it on the rug. He brushes the dust off the top before lifting off the lid. 'Just a few old newspaper clippings, by the looks of it.'

Being here suddenly feels invasive and disloyal – not to Rory, because he long since lost my loyalty and trust, and even more so after hearing how dismissive he was on the phone yesterday morning, telling me he was on a business trip as if that was the most important thing... like Jodie and I never even mattered to him.

No, being here feels disloyal to Marion and Frank. They were always good to me and treated Jodie as if she was their granddaughter. And now it seems their only son is intent on getting his hands on his mother's inheritance and property – all while she's still alive.

'So this isn't what you're after?' Lewis asks.

'I don't know,' I reply, getting up and sitting on the bed. 'Let's have a look.'

I take one of the newspaper clippings from the box, unfolding the yellowed paper.

'It's probably just Marion keeping pieces about their fundraising,' I say, though I'm not sure why she'd keep them under the floor in Rory's old bedroom. 'They always had the local press round when they did an event.'

Or I suppose it could be clippings that Rory collected and stashed away as a teenager – he used to do a lot of swimming and athletics competitions, often winning county prizes. His love of sport rubbed off on Jodie.

But it's when I read one of the headlines printed across the yellowing columns of newspaper print that I realise it's neither of those things, and it becomes clear why the box has been hidden away.

Mystery of Stolen Baby Continues...

FIFTY-ONE
HANNAH

The last thing I want is for it all to come spilling out in front of Lewis, but seeing these headlines again, reading the pieces written by journalists intent only on shock and sensationalism, sends me into a new kind of emotional hell.

Babysitter or Killer in Student House of Horrors?

There's a large black and white photograph of twenty-year-old me beneath this particular headline, trying to shield my face with a denim jacket on one of the few times I left my student room. Journalists had been hanging around the campus during the couple of weeks after the abduction, hoping to get a lucky photo.

Mother of Missing Baby Tells All on Evil Babysitter

As my eyes sweep over the text in the weekly magazine piece, it's clear that Natalie did nothing of the sort. I know from others in our year that she never spoke to any press about Fleur's abduction, let alone anyone from this trashy magazine.

It's nothing but made-up hearsay gathered from a few dubious contacts. I let the clipping flutter to the floor in disgust.

But it's the next newspaper piece that really tips me over the edge. Back then, I'd made a point of not speaking to journalists about what had happened, and I tried not to read what they'd written. Once or twice, I got wind of the gossip spreading around the university, which made me realise I'd done the right thing by staying out of it. I'm not sure I'd have survived if I'd have read this piece back then.

Babysitter's Shocking Confession Letter

Hannah Bailey, 20, originally from West Bradport and art student at Plymouth University, penned a cold-blooded letter to Natalie Martin, 21, and grieving mother of missing baby Fleur, who was abducted from her cot three weeks ago. Heartless Hannah's missive was saved from destruction in the nick of time when it was recovered from a university dustbin. Torn up and filthy, the Daily Examiner p eced the unsent letter back together to reveal her shocking confession.

Dear Natalie, I am not sorry for what happened. I would dc it again if I could. I did leave Fleur alone on purpose. You deserve this. Hannah

I cover my face, sobbing tears of frustration at the injustice of it all – at the photograph of my wrongly pieced-together handwritten letter from when I'd ripped it up and chucked it in the bin. I had no idea at the time that some desperate journalist would be rummaging through my trash.

Then I blurt everything out to Lewis.

All the things I never told him when we first started seeing each other come tumbling out – what had happened at university a few years before we met, how I'd lived in the shadow of guilt for most of my twenties, how I'd made out to him that my life was...

'...was this perfect, carefree existence that would last forever,' I say, wiping my nose on my sleeve. Lewis grabs a box of tissues from the dressing table, passing one to me. 'Pulling pints, living with my parents, going out and getting drunk. It was all an act. A cover-up. It was all *my* fault Fleur was stolen, and I've had to live with the guilt and shame ever since. Sometimes I manage to hide it. Sometimes I don't. One thing's for certain – the newspaper's right, I *am* heartless. A heartless bitch who doesn't deserve to have—'

'Shhh, enough!' Lewis presses a finger against my lips as I lean into the dip he's making in the mattress beside me. 'Listen, the past is long gone. It's behind you. Don't let it ruin your present, too, Han.' He pulls me close, rubbing his hands gently up and down my back.

'That letter in the newspaper,' I say, looking up at him. 'They've totally twisted it. They put the ripped-up pieces back together in the wrong order, missing loads of it out. You can see the pieces don't even fit together properly. They've made it sound awful, as though I did it on purpose. The letter I wrote was an *apology* to Nat, but I couldn't face giving it to her and—'

'I know, I know,' he says, the deepness of his voice strangely soothing. 'But there's something else, isn't there? Something else that's upset you. I see it in your eyes, Hannah. Don't forget, I *know* you. Even after all this time, I can read you.'

I look away, not wanting to get drawn into talk that is going to unravel my heart, reminding me of all the reasons I once loved him so much. I stare over his shoulder to the little ornaments on the mantelpiece of the small bedroom fireplace – a china elephant, a metal jet aeroplane, a black felt cat in a red hat... Rory's things from long ago.

I give him a small nod, still not looking at him for fear he'll see it behind my eyes.

'Just now, when I said I was a heartless bitch who doesn't deserve...' I pause. Once it's out, I can't unsay it. It will be real, sitting right here between us. 'It's come true... my worst nightmare.'

'Hannah, no, don't—'

'It's karma come back to bite me,' I say, on the edge of tears again. 'I let the most terrible, unimaginable thing happen to Nat's dear little baby, and now the unthinkable has happened to me. My precious Jodie is missing.'

'Oh, Han, don't give up—'

'Not only that, but I found out this morning that my frozen embryos have gone missing from storage, too.'

'Wait – what on earth do you mean? Your embryos have *gone?*'

I take a deep breath before explaining everything as briefly as I can, including finding the paperwork in Anna Weston's study, right up to the call I made to Mayfield Clinic while he was in the supermarket just now.

'Jesus, Han,' Lewis says, falling unusually silent. He rubs the thick stubble on his chin, looking first out of the window and then back to me. 'I mean, are they certain? Perhaps they just got some documents muddled up. I'm sure errors like that happen all the time. A careless entry on a computer.'

'No, I don't think so. I mean, obviously I'll need a lawyer and it will be fully investigated, but until Jodie's back safely, there's no way I can even think about—'

'This woman's house where you found the papers, remind me where is it again?'

I tell him about the gated community and the expensive houses.

He nods. 'Yeah, I know where you mean. Fancy places. But...' He stops for a moment, thinking, shaking his head. 'When I met Jodie at the market square, she was... well, she was really pumped and hyper, and not in a good way if I'm honest. And I'm certain it wasn't because of meeting me for the first time,' he says with a wry smile. 'She told me that she'd just been in a bit of a scrape, that she was a bit wired because of some girl called Zoe or something. No, not that… but it definitely began with a zed. She got in my van, telling me how she'd just been caught up in this crazy—'

'Zayla,' I say quickly. 'Do you mean Zayla? She's Anna Weston's nanny.'

'Yeah, that was it. Zayla. Anyhow, Jodie told me how she'd ended up at this massive sick house – her words – up at Ocean Heights. Apparently, she'd had to deliver something.'

'*Deliver* something?' I say, frowning. 'But Jodie told me she was coming to *fetch* something. A coat…' I stop, my blood running cold. 'A child's coat,' I whisper, remembering the pale blue garment. 'The police found it on the rocks at the bottom of a cliff.'

It's as I'm speaking that Lewis shoves all the newspaper clippings back into the box and replaces the floorboard. Then he takes me by the hand and leads me down to the front door, handing me the shoebox to hold. He takes the keys and locks up the house, then, outside, he opens the passenger door of the car before getting into the driver's side himself.

'Where are we going?' I ask as he swings the car round, skidding on the gravel as he pulls out of the drive.

'To find our daughter,' he replies, not taking his eyes off the road ahead.

FIFTY-TWO
HANNAH

'Lewis, slow down!' I grab the passenger door handle as we take another bend at speed. 'The turning off the main road is coming up soon. Don't forget to—'

'Hannah, please, try to stay calm,' Lewis says, his strong hands gripping the wheel of my Toyota. 'Tell me what you know about this Zayla person. And the woman she works for.'

'Not much, really. Zayla is a bit alternative – think gamer or goth type,' I say. 'She's early to mid-twenties.' I grab the door again as Lewis swings the car down the road leading towards the coast. 'She works for Anna Weston, and looks after Mila, Anna's daughter. Mila is five and goes to the school where I teach ...' I trail off, hardly able to keep it together.

It all sounds so clinical when I say it like this, yet in all probability, it's *my* daughter I'm talking about – the daughter I never knew I had – as well as the woman who has clearly stolen her from me. I can't think of a single reason why mine and Rory's names would be on the paperwork otherwise. Is that why I sensed a bond with Mila in class, knowing there was something special about her, that she needed taking care of, that she was *mine?* How on earth will I ever come to terms with missing out on the first five years of her life?

I try to picture Mila's little face in my mind, wondering how I could have not seen any likeness to me and Rory – she certainly has his piercing blue eyes, and I suppose her nose is similar to mine, but it's hard to tell on a young child – and especially hard to see what's right under your nose if you're not looking for it.

'And the child's mother, Anna?' Lewis asks.

'I don't know much about her. Apart from she's a single mum and had IVF treatment at the same clinic as me.' A strange noise bubbles up my throat – something between a choke and a sob.

I simply cannot accept that everything is lost – that my dreams are over, my final chance at being a mother again is gone. Once we find Mila, I will do everything in my power to fight for my daughter, to get her back. And if it wasn't a mistake by the clinic, then Anna Weston isn't going to get away with what she's done to me.

'Apparently, the mother works away a lot, and given where she lives, I imagine she's a high earner. She employed my good friend, Jan, to design her interior. That's why I was up there on Saturday,' I say, explaining how Jan had invited me for a picnic. 'Slow down, the gates to Ocean Heights are coming up.'

When Lewis pulls into the entryway, he stares at the security code pad. 'That's that then. My breaking and entering skills only run as far as dodgy back doors. You should get a better one, by the way.'

'Seven one eight nine,' I say, double checking it in my mind.

Lewis stares at me, knowing better than to ask questions, then he puts the window down and enters the number. The gates slowly swing inwards, and he drives on through. 'Impressive. Which house?'

'Keep going. It's right at the end. The one with the white

fence. Lewis, do you really think Jodie is here?' What I really mean to say is *do you think she's here against her will* but I can't stand to acknowledge those words. 'Her location never once showed her at Ocean Heights—'

'Honestly? I've no idea, Han. But what we do know is that she was here on Saturday and that she knows the nanny. Does she normally hang out with Zayla?'

'No, that's the thing. Not at all. I was so surprised to see her here. Zayla had given her a lift. I didn't even know they were friends. Jodie said they met online through gaming, which I suppose could be true, but she's a bit older than Jodie, and obviously more streetwise.' I pause, closing my eyes briefly. 'Look, Lewis, there's something else I haven't told you.' The words have been stuck in my throat since we left Chapelfields, since I blurted everything out to him. *Almost* everything.

'Go on,' he says, stopping the car in front of Eastcliff House. He leaves the engine idling.

I take a deep breath, unable to keep it inside any longer. 'Ten days ago, I took Mila Weston home from school without permission. Shortly afterwards, she was kidnapped from my kitchen. It was the most stupid thing I've ever done, so I don't need telling off. God knows, I've done that myself enough times. The reason I took her was—'

Suddenly his hand comes up over my mouth. 'Wait,' Lewis hisses, staring intently at me. 'Shush...'

'What the hell...?' I mumble from behind his hand. But he's shaking his head, his eyes flicking behind me to Eastcliff House.

'Someone just came out of the front door,' he says, lowering his hand. 'A woman, and she's coming over. It must be Anna Weston.'

Slowly, I turn around. My eyes won't focus properly at first, trying to make out her features through the passenger window. My hand comes up to open the car door, and I attempt to get out, to stand up, but for some reason my legs have turned to jelly. I pull myself up, leaning on the window frame, squinting and shielding my eyes as I see a female figure approaching.

Her hair is a soft honey blonde with highlights that glimmer against her tanned skin. Her full mouth is set in an unsmiling line below her high cheekbones and her perfectly made-up eyes. She's wearing a long skirt that trails around her ankles in greens and pinks with threads of gold. Above it, she has on a loose black blouse adorned with lace trim. Her wrists are heavy from the stack of bangles on each arm, and huge gold hoop earrings glint beneath her long hair.

'No...' I say, my words barely there. Lewis has got out of the car and is standing beside me. 'Oh... my... *God...*' I whisper to him. 'That's not Anna Weston.' I can't take my eyes off her.

The woman approaches us, her eyes firmly fixed on me as she stares right back, her glossy lips parting as if she's about to say something but can't quite get the words out.

It's as if the years between us have melted away, no time at all passing since I last saw her on that terrible night.

'It's *Natalie,*' I say, before grabbing Lewis's arm, convinced my legs are going to buckle beneath me.

FIFTY-THREE
JODIE

I wish my dad was here. Lewis, my *real* dad. I can't believe I've waited nearly sixteen years to meet him, then we only got a few hours together before *bam!* – my life is about to end.

I swear the ties around my wrists have loosened. I just need to keep twisting and wriggling my hands.

Dad told me he's been keeping an eye on me over the years, watching me from outside the school gates once or twice when he's been in the area, even following me to athletics practice a couple of times. He was worried that if he made himself known, I wouldn't want to meet him or get to know him because he's been absent all my life, but he was truly sorry for how things had gone. He reckoned Mum would have lost her shit if she'd found out he was lurking about, which is the truth. Not that she's exactly been there for me lately, always distracted and anxious and paranoid about something or other.

It still feels weird calling Shadow *Dad*, because Rory is the only dad I've ever known. Though he turned out to be a total let down. Lewis won't do that; I know he won't. He's my *proper* dad. I wish I'd had more time to get to know him before I end up dead – because that's what it feels like is about to happen, that I'm never going to get out of this godforsaken place alive.

I let out a stifled sob, feeling utterly hopeless that this is it – my life over before I even turned sixteen. I'm pretty sure Mum will have checked the tracking app, but there's, like, zero 4G here, so it won't show her where I am.

There... definitely looser now. I can get my wrists apart!

Then I have a thought... balaclava man grabbed my phone from me just *after* I'd logged back into the app. He tied me up then went off somewhere. If he took my phone with him, there's a chance Mum might have seen *his* location show up briefly if there was signal, giving her enough information to... I dunno, maybe work out a rough area where I am.

Or perhaps she's not even checking the app at all.

Perhaps someone will find my skeleton in twenty years' time.

My only hope is that balaclava man dies of lung disease or liver failure in the next few hours because he's constantly chain-smoking and swigging from a bottle. I still have a sliver of sight beneath the blindfold, though all I can see is the floor and his feet – his trainers jiggling against each other nervously as he sits on the grubby mattress. He's about eight or nine feet away and I think there's a desk and a chair between us, as well as what looks like a stack of boxes and papers or something. It's hard to tell. The little girl has been quiet this last hour or so.

Right now, I'd do anything to get out of here – literally anything at all. Dear God, I promise on my *life* that I'll never bunk off school again, and I'll be helpful to Mum and do my homework the same day I get it, and work really hard for my exams and... Even with the blindfold on, my eyes sting from the tears. A couple escape from under the fabric, dropping down onto the concrete floor.

'Stop crying,' he says in a growly whisper, which tells me he's either got some kind of disease in his throat, maybe from all the fags, or he doesn't want me to know what he sounds like. I hear him come over, standing right beside me.

'Mmmee-aarggg-aayyaa!' I bleat through the gag, begging him to *let me go*...

Then I feel a sharp jolt between my shoulder blades, forcing air from my lungs as he kicks me. I squirm in pain, trying to twist round, making more noises in my throat, but he shoves me with his foot again, harder this time. I try to keep still, to stop moving, but my whole body is shaking so much.

I screw up my eyes under the blindfold, stifling more tears, and keep wriggling and twisting my wrists behind my back. If I keep up like this, I'll be able to slip a hand free soon. Then, suddenly, there's a waft of cold air on my legs, followed by the sound of a chair scraping back.

'Y'all right,' a female voice says – Zayla's voice.

Balaclava man mumbles something through a throaty cough that seems to go on forever. I think he's back on the mattress again. 'Went to the supermarket first thing. Got supplies.'

'More booze and fags, you mean,' Zayla says in a snarky way. 'Any calls yet?' She sounds nervous now. There's a wobble in her voice.

'Nope.'

'Shit. This isn't right.'

More scuffing, and then a sound like a fridge being opened and closed... the crack and hiss of a drinks can being opened.

'What you gonna do?' she asks, followed by a slurping sound.

'I don't fucking know yet. *She's* a problem.'

For some reason, I sense they're both looking at me.

'I want my mummy...' comes a sad little voice, followed by a grizzle. The little girl has woken up.

'Shut her up, for fuck's sake,' balaclava growls.

'Come here,' Zayla says, and I imagine her picking up the child.

Then it dawns on me – the little girl has been *kidnapped*. For some reason, Zayla and balaclava man have abducted her, and I've gone and got caught up in it. The kid's parents must be going out of their minds with worry not knowing where she is, maybe trying to get the money together to pay their demands, the police working round the clock to find her. And then it dawns on me for a second time – it was *me* who delivered the ransom note.

Oh my God... one of my hands is almost free! Just a little more now...

My mind reels as I try to work out what's going on. Was I just in the wrong place at the wrong time, and they got me to deliver the note instead of risking it themselves? I reckon Zayla is taking orders from balaclava man as she doesn't seem happy about any of it.

Bumping into Mum up at that big house was totally unexpected, and I wish I'd asked her what she was doing up there, but I was too busy trying to cover up my own guilt for skipping school. It makes me wonder if she knows the kid's parents or something. Maybe they're from St Peter's and—

Oh Christ, what if this kid is the one Mum brought home from school that Friday afternoon when I skipped athletics? I *knew* she was up to something, the way she kept asking me if I'd seen anything, checking a hundred times that I'd gone straight from school to the track. She was guilty as anything. Is my mother somehow involved in a kidnap?

Surely not. A shiver sweeps through me.

'Want to go home...' the little girl whines again. Then there's more rustling as if a packet of sweets is being opened.

'Try to keep quiet and eat these,' Zayla says in a kinder voice. 'We have to stay here a bit longer.'

'But why?' Then there's more rustling and she falls silent again.

Hardly daring to breathe, I inch my head towards the desk

leg with the nail sticking out and snag my blindfold again, this time virtually uncovering one eye. If they spot what I'm doing, I'm in deep trouble.

'Check your phone again, for God's sake,' Zayla says impatiently. 'We should have had a call by now. I'm getting twitchy. What if she's gone to the police?'

'No signal in this bloody place,' balaclava man croaks. 'I have to keep going up to the main road to check messages. Don't worry, she'll have seen the letter. She'll phone soon.'

'Look, I just want my money,' Zayla says, her voice cut with bitterness. 'You promised it would all work out. I've risked everything for this. You know, I could go to the police myself and tell them—'

'Blackmailing the blackmailer isn't smart, Zayla.' Balaclava's voice is hard to make out because he growls the whole time, but it's unmistakably threatening. 'Just remember, you're as disposable to me as these two now.'

Disposable? Another shudder runs through me.

'OK, look, just give me your phone and I'll go up to the main road to check for messages,' Zayla says. 'What if her mother has already rung to say she's dropped off the cash and you're sitting here getting slowly pissed? This ain't what you promised.'

'All right, all fucking right,' balaclava spits back, coughing as he scuffles to stand up. He staggers sideways, grabbing onto a chair and knocking a bottle onto its side by the mattress. It clinks and rolls across the concrete, the contents glugging out towards me. The stink of whiskey makes me feel sick.

'Shit,' balaclava says, kicking the bottle in anger. 'Here, take my phone. But don't be long,' he growls. Then I hear Zayla leaving through the door back into the warehouse area, locking it again behind her.

Everything is quiet for a few moments, apart from the sound of balaclava man cursing the wasted booze. Then it sounds like he grabs another bottle and opens it, dropping back down onto the mattress before lighting up another cigarette. Slowly, I keep on working the rope, my hands so very nearly free. Then I'll be able to pull the gag off, maybe see something nearby to use as a weapon—

'Oh, fucking hell!' balaclava man suddenly booms, making me jump. He kicks the chair, sending it smashing into the desk. It hits the empty whisky bottle, sending it rolling even closer to me. 'Stupid bitch has taken the wrong phone!' More cursing, then I hear the door being rattled. 'It's bloody locked!' he curses. 'She's got *your* phone...' he then yells in my direction. 'I hope she bloody throws it in the river. You should've just kept your nose out.'

Oh my God – my hands are free... I'm shaking, I'm terrified, but my hands are finally free...!

I daren't move as balaclava's words spin through my mind. If he gave Zayla my phone by mistake, then there's a good chance the tracking app will pick up her location when it gets reception. I send a silent prayer for Mum to log in and check.

When I'm certain he's back on the mattress drinking again, I slowly lift the blindfold fully up. I can't see much at first, but gradually the room comes into focus. My ankles are still bound tightly together, with a short length of rope tying them to the desk leg. The little girl is also tied up, curled in a ball on the mattress. And then I see it. A big, heavy whisky bottle lying about three feet away from me.

I stare at it for a few moments, then judge the amount of slack in the rope there is joining me to the desk. I see balaclava's legs still splayed out on the mattress. After that, it all happens so fast – I figure it's now or never and I need to act before Zayla comes back. I make a grab for the bottle and then heave myself up from the floor, shoving my full weight against the desk, dragging it a few feet across the room with me.

When balaclava suddenly sits up, startled by the noise –

though his reactions are slowed from booze – I smash him over the head with the bottle. When the first blow doesn't knock him out, I do it again and again and again.

Thwack... thwack... thwack... as hard as I can on his skull.

He's too stunned to react and just sits there for what seems like forever, staring up at me, motionless. But he's not balaclava man anymore – he's taken his mask off – and our eyes stay locked, each of us shaking and horrified for different reasons.

Using all my strength, I smash him over the head for a final time, delivering a hard blow to his temple, making him fall sideways off the mattress, his head hitting the concrete with an even louder thud as he goes down. The cigarette drops from his hand as he lies in the pool of whisky, blood spilling from the gash.

I stare at him, my mouth hanging open, but there's no time to think about what I've done or who he is or what the hell is going on. I just need to get my ankles untied, grab the little girl and get us both out of here.

It's as I'm fumbling with the ropes – it's taking ages to work the knots loose – that I smell the first whiff of smoke. Not cigarette smoke this time, but something even more noxious as it gradually permeates the air.

'Oh no... oh *shit*,' I gasp, twisting round to see a stack of papers and cardboard boxes smouldering. The dropped cigarette has caught the edges, setting the pile on fire. Then a second later, there's a whooshing sound, the floor lighting up as the alcohol ignites.

FIFTY-FOUR

HANNAH

'I wondered how long it would be before you showed up.' Natalie stands defiantly in front of Eastcliff House, looking completely out of place around here in her long flowing skirt and flat, strappy sandals. Her mouth curls up at one side – not a sneer, but not a smile either.

'Natalie,' I say, breathless and barely able to speak. I want to disbelieve my own eyes, but almost twenty-five years later, she's hardly changed at all. I recognised her in an instant – still the same beautiful woman I met at university. The same long, straight nose. The same high cheekbones and full lips. The same wayward hair tumbling around her shoulders in high-lighted locks of honey blonde.

'But, why are *you* here? How come you're...?' I can barely speak.

'Hello... Natalie,' Lewis says uncertainly, stepping towards her, clearing his throat. 'We're looking for Hannah's daughter, Jodie. We think she might be here. She knows a young woman called Zayla who—'

'Well now,' Natalie interrupts. 'Hannah Bailey is looking for her daughter.' Her voice isn't filled with anger or bitterness or... or anything really. The way she says it is flat and robotic, but it still delivers a punch to my guts. 'Oh, the sweet irony.' She folds her arms across her chest and widens her feet in a defensive stance.

'Natalie, stop... don't. Look, this isn't easy. You're the last person I expected to see.' Though after the week I've had, I don't think anything will ever shock me again. 'Why are you here? Do you know Anna Weston, Mila's mum?'

'I don't have to answer any of your questions, Hannah, but you're here now. A lot of things have happened since we last saw each other. Why don't you come inside?'

I look across at Lewis, who gives me a brief nod. Please, just tell me – is Jodie here?'

But Natalie has already turned and is walking back towards the front door.

'It's OK,' Lewis assures me. 'I'm here. Come on, let's follow her.'

Natalie holds the front door wide open, closing it once we're in the hallway.

'Welcome to my humble abode,' she says, flashing a white smile at me. It's Natalie but it's also... *not* Natalie. She seems so different to the warm, loving, creative and generous young woman I once knew.

'You own this place?' I ask, confused.

'Of course,' she replies, leading us through to the living area. The sea view is no less impressive today, and I hear Lewis catch his breath. She spins round. 'Does that surprise you? Poor little Natalie who lost everything, who was broken and ruined, now lives in a gorgeous house like this?' She strides up to me, gripping my arms, digging her nails into my flesh. Her smile is a leer as she pushes her face into mine. 'I'm a phoenix, Hannah. A fucking *phoenix*.' Then she shoves me away and walks over to the huge expanse of glass before swinging round again, a demented look in her eyes. 'Not bad for a starving artist, eh?'

'I'm confused. I thought... I thought Anna Weston lives here.' Then it strikes me. 'Is she your partner... your wife?'

Natalie throws back her head, the veins on her neck standing proud as she laughs. 'I was married once – and you'll be shocked. I was married to a *man*, Hannah. Does that surprise you? I took his last name – Weston.'

'Wait... *you're* Anna Weston?' Then I remember, Anna was Fleur's middle name. 'You changed your name,' I whisper, trying to process what's going on.

Natalie shrugs. 'Why not? Being Natalie Martin wasn't exactly working for me, was it? I was only married for a year, back when I was twenty-three. He was much, *much* older than me when we met. Fifty-seven. He died a year after our wedding,' she adds with a shrug, almost as an afterthought and with no emotion whatsoever. 'Heart attack.'

'I'm so sorry,' I say. 'That's tough. Especially after—'

'Don't be sorry. I wasn't. I hated him. He was a lecherous old creep, and I was punishing myself by being with him. After Fleur was taken' – Natalie sucks in a breath, sticks out her chin as if she's used to defying the world – 'I went back home to Norfolk to grieve. But my parents drove me mad, so I hotfooted it to London and got a job in a casino. Drugs and alcohol helped me forget. That's where I met Tony. A few months later, we married. And twelve months later, he dropped dead. I knew then that the universe wasn't ever going to let me love or be loved, but Tony was rich, had no children with me or anyone else, so I inherited the lot.'

'And that's how you bought this place,' I say, instantly regretting it.

'Christ no,' Natalie says, pacing up and down by the huge window. 'I pissed Tony's money up the wall within a few years. Alcohol, drugs, fast cars, designer gear, skiing, wild villa holidays in Europe for crowds of people – all paid for by me.

'When the money ran out, I was empty and broken, so to

save myself, to save my sanity, I started painting again. It took a while, but gradually I started to sell a few pieces. To the States mainly. I was living in a squat in London, finally being true to myself.'

'You say you had no children with Tony, but...' My mouth is so dry, making it hard to get out what I need to say about Mila. The papers in Anna's – *Natalie's* – study... the IVF... my embryos... The sum of my thoughts is unthinkable, unspeakable, but I've got to find out what happened. 'So who is Mila's father?' I ask, wondering if she's married again and that's how she's been able to afford Eastcliff House.

'My daughter is *missing*,' Natalie spits, swinging round so her skirt and hair flare out. '*Again*.' She whistles out through her teeth, shaking her head. 'And you of all people expect me to answer a question like that?'

'I'm sorry, it's just...' How the hell do I bring up the IVF papers or push her about Mila's conception at a time like this – not when the daughter that she's convinced is hers, the child she *stole* from me, has been kidnapped. 'Listen, it's important, Natalie. I need to know... Just tell me if—'

'Look, Hannah's daughter is missing too, Natalie,' Lewis says, interrupting. 'It's why we're here. Have you seen her? She's about five foot seven, long hair a similar colour as mine, freckles...'

But Natalie ignores him, her attention focused on me. I have no idea if she knows I work at Mila's school, or if the police have told her I took Mila home – but from the thunderous look on her face, I'm assuming they must have.

'Jodie is fifteen,' I say, hoping she'll be sympathetic. We're both going through the same thing. 'I think she's friends with your nanny, Zayla. Do you know if they've gone off somewhere together? Maybe they're even with Mila. I'm so sorry this has happened to you again, Nat.' I go up to her, my face crumpling from worry, my arms outstretched, hoping she'll take hold of my hands. 'It's not fair that—'

'I hated you for what happened, you know,' she spits at me, recoiling. 'I've never *stopped* hating you. You were my first proper love, Hannah Bailey, and you destroyed me. Destroyed my entire fucking life.'

I stagger backwards from her cruel words – it feels as if I've been shot.

When first loves end, it can feel as though nothing will ever be as... as special or intense again...

The therapist I saw years ago was right about that, at least. I suddenly feel eighteen years old, back when I first set eyes on Natalie. It took until the second year at university for us to go from best friends to lovers, but when we did, it felt so natural, so obvious, so seamless and meant-to-be that nothing and no one else in the world mattered.

Natalie had a magnetic aura, making her the most perfect woman in the world – the same woman who stole my heart. We were so in love, and along with our art, it was all we needed to get through life. We had everything planned out.

Until I wasn't enough for her.

'Now stop!' I yell. 'That's just not fair!'

I don't know what's come over me, but it feels like she's pressed a button – a button I've had my own finger on since that awful night.

'I've punished myself enough over the years, and God

knows I've driven myself to distraction with self-hatred, but this has got to end somewhere, Natalie. You're right, it *was* my fault that Fleur was taken, but I still have my life, and I can't live it under this... this awful shadow of doom anymore. If you continue to hate me and punish me, then the only person you're really hating on is yourself.'

Natalie falls silent, swaying from side to side, her long skirt wafting around her ankles. Then it strikes me.

'It was *you*, wasn't it? You took my car from the garage. You picked up my dress from the—'

'Did you like the rose?' she asks. 'To think you thought they'd make everything better.' She makes a spitting sound at me. 'A bunch of fucking white roses. You really believed that sending flowers was a good substitute for my baby?' Natalie shakes her head, then stares directly at me – her piercing eyes boring right through me. Right back to the past.

'It wasn't meant to be like that,' I say, remembering how a few of us sent Nat flowers after Fleur was taken, to let her know we were thinking about her, that we'd help her any way we could.

'I wanted to mess with you, maybe even feel what it was like to be you, Hannah Bailey, living your perfect life with your perfect daughter doing your perfect job at the school. Or should I say, Hannah *Marlowe*. You and Rory finally got together for good, I see. Last I heard was that you'd split up after university. I've been watching you for a while. I even came into your house a few times. It's quite... cosy.' Another laugh. 'I wanted to unsettle you. Disturb you. To make you think you were going mad, and—'

'Enough now,' Lewis says, stepping between me and Natalie. 'None of this is helping find the girls. The pair of you can deal with this later.'

'He's right,' I say. 'We can talk, but later.'

Natalie glares at Lewis, then surprisingly she nods in agreement. She heads off to the kitchen and returns a moment later with her phone and a packet of cigarettes. She pulls up a photograph of what looks to be a handwritten letter and passes her phone to me. 'I don't usually do this inside,' she says, lighting up a cigarette. 'But it's not a usual day.'

I stare at her screen, shaking my head then glance back at her. 'Oh my God... this is terrible'

'It was waiting for me when I got home yesterday,' she says flatly. 'It's a ransom note for Mila. The police have the original now, but it was left on my kitchen counter. I've been away for the last ten days. A forensics team has been here since yesterday and only left an hour ago.'

'Yes, Zayla told the school office that you were overseas,' I say, realising there's no point trying to conceal where I work now. She knows everything about me. I force myself to stay calm at the mention of police forensics, knowing there'll be traces of me here to crossmatch with the DNA sample they took at the police station.

'Zayla wasn't exactly telling the truth about where I was,' Natalie continues. 'I wasn't at home, but I wasn't overseas either. I was only twenty miles away. Zayla knew I didn't want anyone bothering me.' The skin under one eye twitches as she lets out a sigh. 'This place doesn't always feel like home to me. After losing Fleur, nowhere does, and sometimes I need to get away. Just take off and hide. I have an old caravan in a remote spot by a river. Nothing flash, but it gives me peace and somewhere to paint. Time alone to think.'

I can't imagine doing such a thing, leaving Jodie with a nanny for days on end when she was only five, but then I've not been through what Natalie has.

'I knew Mila would be safe with Zayla – well, at least I *thought* she would. If I'm away, I speak to her on the phone often to find out how her day was and say goodnight. But then Zayla told me Mila was poorly, that she was off school with a bug. She said Mila was sleeping a lot but getting better, so while I was concerned for her, I didn't worry too much when we didn't speak for a few days. Zayla sent regular updates.' Natalie paces about, sweeping her hand through her long hair, making it even more mane-like than it already is. She lets out a whimper. 'Oh God, I can't believe it's happening again...'

'Try to stay calm,' I say, forcing myself to overlook how much she still hates me – so much so that she saw fit to break into my house, steal my things, make me think I was losing my mind. And not only that, but she's bought the same plot of land that Rory and I once dreamt of owning. That's when it hits me – there was nothing random about it. She *knew* Rory and I wanted to live here. But how? 'The police are out looking for Jodie and Mila. I'm sure there'll be news soon.'

'Let me see that note,' Lewis says. He reads from Natalie's phone. 'Fifty-thousand pounds in twenties. Deposit in waste bin at picnic spot layby, coast road to Bradport within twenty-four hours. Wrap in black plastic bag. Text back to confirm. No police or Mila is dead.' He blows out through his teeth. 'I'm sure the cops will be tracing the phone, but it's probably a burner.'

'The deadline is this afternoon,' Natalie says, sucking on her cigarette. I never once saw her smoke at university.

'Have you got the money?' I ask.

'I don't need your help, if that's what you're implying,' she replies. 'Anyway, the police have advised me not to pay it. They're planning an operation but said that I must wait for a next move from the kidnappers. They're sending surveillance officers to the area and will set up here in the house later. They said it's likely there'll be another note or maybe even a phone call. There's talk of depositing fake money so they can monitor the site, but it's very exposed up there. There's nowhere for the police to watch without being seen. They mentioned using drones.'

'I'm sorry to have to ask this,' Lewis says, 'but is Zayla entirely… trustworthy? Might she have—'

'Trustworthy?' Natalie interrupts again with a snort. 'I always thought I was a pretty good judge of character, but maybe you should ask Hannah about being trustworthy.' She strides away again, standing at the huge window.

'Nat, *don't*,' I say, knowing exactly where her thoughts are leading her. 'We can discuss it all you want later, but let's just get the girls back safely first.'

She spins around. Suddenly, she seems young again, just like the carefree girl I knew and loved in Plymouth. We told no one about our relationship. That was my choice, I'm ashamed to say. I'd never even considered being with a woman before I met Natalie, but she did something to me, igniting me as though she was my missing piece. I know I did the same to her.

'You do realise that we'll be together forever, painting our pictures in a little cottage by the sea with twenty cats, don't you, Han?' she'd said one evening as we sat outside a pub by the waterfront, half a cider each and a bowl of chips to share.

For the last couple of weeks, she'd been even more sentimental and loving than usual, not wanting to leave my side, telling me how much she adored me, that she'd never intentionally do anything to hurt me. I'd sensed a change within her after she'd had a big night out, wondering if something had happened, though I wasn't sure what. But whatever it was, I liked the romantic, soppy version of the woman I adored.

'I'd be mightily disappointed if we *don't* end up like that,' I replied, wishing I had the courage to tell my parents about her – get them used to the idea of me being with a girl. Neither of them would take it well. Natalie had been out since she was fourteen so was entirely comfortable with who she was. For me, it was all new.

It was about four months later when I discovered that Natalie had cheated on me. We were getting ready for a mutual friend's birthday party and Nat was grumbling she didn't have anything to wear. I offered to lend her my skirt – the one she loved and often borrowed – but when she slipped into it, there was no way the zip was doing up around her belly. At first, she told me she was bloated, that she'd eaten something dodgy, that she'd put on a bit of weight. But we both knew it was more than that.

We didn't go to the party that night. Instead, I sat alone on my bed, staring at the wall, wondering how the hell Nat had got pregnant if she hadn't cheated on me. Cheated on me with a *man*.

'Hannah!' I hear someone say urgently – Lewis. 'Hannah, your phone. Check your alerts.'

I snap back to the present and dig my phone from my pocket. There's only one notification on my screen, and the sight of the blue and white tracking app logo makes my heart thunder in my chest.

Jodie's phone is now online. Last known location updated 30 *seconds ago.*

'Oh my God, it's Jodie!' With a trembling finger, I open the app and wait for the map screen to resolve. The green dot with my daughter's name above it makes my heart pound. 'Where is she? Where *is* she?' I zoom in on the map.

'There!' Lewis shrieks in my ear, pointing. 'Near that bloody industrial estate again!'

'It looks like she's on the move. The dot is heading that way towards...' I zoom right in and screenshot the road she's on. 'She's heading to the warehouses, by the looks of it. God, we even drove around that area a few times. We were so close.'

'Right, let's go,' Lewis says, taking the keys from his pocket and grabbing my hand, leading me out to the car. I don't take my eyes off my phone screen.

'I'm coming too,' Natalie says, following on behind. But

then my heart sinks when the green dot turns to red and, once again, Jodie is offline.

FIFTY-SIX

HANNAH

Lewis drives like a madman, cursing the gates at Ocean Heights's entrance as they seem to take forever to open. When we're out on the coast road, Natalie grabs the door handle to steady herself as the car hurtles around the downhill bends. She's sitting in the front, and I'm in the back, clutching onto the front seat with one hand while holding my phone in the other, praying the green dot comes back online. Praying harder than I've ever prayed before that we find Jodie.

Lewis barely slows down as we enter the thirty-mile-per-hour zone in West Bradport, weaving between cars, taking a couple of shortcuts, and even running a couple of red lights. A few minutes later and we've reached the bypass roundabout between the supermarket and the road that leads down to the industrial estate.

'Keep your eyes peeled,' Lewis says. 'This is where the app located her.'

Natalie has remained silent for the journey, but her shoulders are tense and her knuckles white as she grips the door. She twists round to face me. 'Have you got a photo of your daughter?' she asks. 'I never did anything to hurt her, just so you know,' she adds, her face pale and emotionless. 'It was *you* I wanted to scare.'

She gives me a look – a look that tells me she was hurting so much *herself* that she needed someone to take out her pain on. And that person was me.

I reach out and touch her shoulder. *I know*, I mouth before showing her a photo of Jodie.

'She looks like you,' Natalie says with a brief smile. 'When we first met.' Then she gives my hand a squeeze before turning round again.

'There's no one about,' I say, peering out of the side window. Even the laybys where the vans and lorries were parked up are empty now. 'Drive around the warehouses,' I suggest as we pass the entranceway strewn with old To Let and For Sale boards, along with more recent Keep Out and Danger warnings. Lewis cruises about for a while, but the whole place seems deserted.

'This is useless,' he says, stopping the car at the side of the road. 'There must be twenty or thirty warehouses between here and the river. If Jodie's in one of them, how are we supposed to find her?'

'We should search on foot,' Natalie says, undoing her seatbelt and getting out. 'Mila! Zayla! Jodie!' she yells, striding off ahead, cupping her hands around her mouth. She turns back to us as we follow. 'Let's split up,' she suggests, so we each take a different route.

I head off down towards the river, briefly wondering if I saw someone dart for cover behind a row of skips. I run over but find it's just a couple of seagulls scratting about in the rubbish.

'Jodie, it's me, Mum!' I call. 'If you can hear me, please come out! Jodie... Jo-*die*!'

I keep walking and yelling until my voice is hoarse and my throat hurts. I turn and look back up the road to see Lewis striding between a couple of old buildings further up, shaking his head and giving me a thumbs down signal. I carry on, almost at the river now, suddenly getting a whiff of something on the breeze.

What is that?

I stop, sniffing the air, wondering if someone has got a bonfire. I could ask them if they've seen anyone hanging around. But it smells more like old tyres burning or something noxious rather than someone just burning wood or cardboard.

And then I see it. A plume of black smoke rising from one of the warehouses near the river.

Christ... What if Jodie is inside?

'Here! Lewis! Come quickly!' I scream. 'Hurry! Get down here!'

Lewis appears from between two buildings with Natalie following on. They charge over to me. 'There's smoke, look... Over there. It's coming from that warehouse.'

Lewis runs off with me and Nat following close behind. When we're beside the building, there's smoke billowing from a couple of broken windows, too high up to climb in through.

Further along, Lewis is trying to wrench open a steel sliding door, but it's either stuck or locked. He bangs on the walls, screaming out as he goes further down. 'Jodie! Are you in there! *Jodie!*'

At first, there's no reply – nothing at all. But then, as we reach the far end of the warehouse, my body turns to stone.

'Did you hear that?' Dear God... it sounded like a scream. And it was coming from inside. 'There it is again.' I run up to the metal wall, pressing my ear against it, feeling the heat from within. 'We need to call the fire service,' I say, fumbling my phone from my pocket. 'Bloody hell, still no signal!' I dial the number anyway in case it connects through another provider.

'My network has one bar,' Natalie says, tapping the three nines. She gets through faster than me and gives the call handler all the details, begging them to hurry as we suspect there are people trapped inside the burning warehouse.

'You two go round the other side of the building, see if there's another way to get in,' Lewis calls out. 'I'll keep trying this door. Maybe I can get up to one of those windows. Cover your faces,' he yells.

Natalie and I head off together, running down the length of the building and skirting back round to the roadside. 'Look,' I say. 'Let's go down that alleyway.'

'OK, but be careful,' she calls out.

I pull the neck of my T-shirt up over my face, not that it's going to provide much protection from the smoke that's now billowing down the passageway, while Natalie covers her face with her scarf. The area is filled with weeds and rubble, and smoke is seeping out of the joints in the rusted metal side of the building, making us cough even out here.

As we reach the end of the alley, I stop, spotting a metal door. I give it a couple of shoves with my shoulder, and it slams back against something inside. Immediately, we're hit with a wall of smoke, though thankfully I can't see any flames in this part of the warehouse.

'Jodie! Mila!' I scream, hearing a distant yell. 'It came from over there,' I call out, pointing towards what looks like an office at the other end of the warehouse. 'I think there's a door,' I add, grabbing Natalie's hand as we pick our way across the factory through the smoke and semi-darkness.

When we reach the other side, I turn the metal handle, but instantly recoil. 'Shit! Give me your scarf,' I say, wrapping it around the door knob. 'It's locked,' I shriek above the roaring sound coming from inside. Smoke pours out from under the door, so I give Natalie back her scarf as we head further along to where there's a window looking into the office.

I peer through, though it's hard to see anything because of the dense smoke, but suddenly something moves. Something –

or, rather, some*one* – rises up from the floor. I see my daughter's terrified face through the murk just at the same moment she sees me. Her mouth is wide open as she screams, her eyes red and bloodshot as she coughs, her hands pressed up against the glass.

'*Jodie!*' I cry, banging my fists on the pane. 'Oh my God, Jodie! Get out! You've got to get out!' But then she drops down out of sight again.

FIFTY-SEVEN
JODIE

'*Mum!*' I scream until my throat burns. I can't breathe... there's no air left in here, just thick, black smoke. My limbs feel weak and my head heavy and throbbing. I've not heard the little girl make a noise for a while, either. I've called out to her, tried catch sight of her, but there's no reply. 'Mum, help us!' I yell, terrified she can't see or hear me. Her face is pressed up to the office window, but I only got a glimpse of her when I sat up. I had to drop back down to the floor again because it's easier to breathe down here – and I need to get these ropes off my ankles.

My hands won't stop shaking as I fumble with the tight knots, and I have to keep my eyes closed because the smoke stings so much. One side of the office is completely ablaze now, and the partition wall is alive with flames and spewing out foul-smelling smoke. The ceiling tiles are alight, too, and I reckon we've only got a couple of minutes left before we all die.

Though... oh my God... he's dead already... I screw up my eyes even tighter as I imagine him lying on the floor, thinking about what I did. Even if I get out of here alive, I'll be going to prison for murder. I bet they'll be able to figure out it was me who killed him. But I can't think about that now. I just need to get my ankles free.

Suddenly, there's a pounding sound on the glass, getting louder and making my ears vibrate – dear God let it be the fire brigade.

'Come on, come *on*...' I curse, tugging at the knots.

Then a whimpering noise comes from where the little girl is lying. 'It's OK,' I call out to her, coughing. 'We'll be out of here very soon.' I pray that's true.

Then more pounding and battering on the window, followed by an almighty crack and the sound of shattering glass. *Thank God.*

'Jodie!' Mum screams, her voice panicked. 'Where are you?'

'Over here. Behind the desk. I can't get the ropes off. *Help me!*' More coughing.

Then there's clattering and grunting. The sound of Mum scrambling in through the broken window. She falls into the room, knocking over a couple of chairs. I hear her coughing as she makes her way over to me – but then there's another voice I don't recognise.

'Mila! Mila! Are you here? Zayla!'

I quickly draw a shallow breath. 'The little girl... she's over... over in the far... corner,' I say, followed by more coughs. Then I feel something at my feet – a pair of hands pulling at the ropes around my ankles. 'Oh... *Mum*,' I cry, my smoke-filled eyes smarting from tears. 'Mum, help, I'm so sorry... Mum, *please*...' I cover my face and break down into a series of sobs as I suddenly feel her strong hands beneath my shoulders. She's got my legs free.

'Can you stand up?' she yells above the roar of the blaze. But before I get to answer, there's a loud cracking and splintering sound above us. The entire office is alight.

'Watch out!' the other woman screams and, with half a second to spare, Mum drags me over to the window, narrowly missing a blazing beam falling on us as it comes crashing down from above.

'Nat, have you found Mila?' Mum yells, dragging a chair over to the smashed window. She helps me up onto it, then bundles me through the hole, shards of glass scraping and tearing my bare legs and arms as I virtually fall back through it – but I don't care. I'm out of that inferno and in the main warehouse, which is quickly filling with smoke.

'Mum?' I call back through the window. 'Mum, you've got to get out! Please... hurry!'

'*Natalie?*' I hear Mum scream from inside the office. 'Nat, where are you? Mila? Zayla?' More coughing and the sound of furniture being shoved aside, then another crash as something else falls from the roof.

'Mum, now... you've got to get out! *Please...*' I cough until I feel myself retching, doubling up as I stagger backwards. One whole side of the warehouse is up in flames, and if Mum doesn't get out now, before the entire roof caves in, then... then... oh God, I can't stand to think what will happen.

I stop, listening out, trying to stifle another coughing fit. Above the panicked screams coming from Mum, over the roaring of the fire and the creaking timbers, I hear the distant sound of sirens... and they're gradually getting closer.

I'm driven back by the heat, stumbling away from the smoke spewing out of the office, sobbing for Mum. I can't bear to leave knowing that she and the others are in there still. Suddenly, I'm jolted as a pair of hands grabs me from behind. I swing around.

'Oh my God, *Dad!* You're here!' I shriek, burying my face against him. He's got his sweatshirt pressed over his mouth and nose. 'Mum's in there,' I cry, pointing back at the broken window.

'OK, but you've got to get out now!' he orders, shoving me in the direction of the side door. The door I should never have stepped through in the first place.

'Please, *please* save her, Dad!' I wail. 'There's a woman and a little girl in there too... and...' I break into another coughing fit, keeping low as I run to avoid the smoke, hating that my dad has to risk his life to save Mum's. And it's all because of me. Dear God, let fire service get everyone out.

In the semi-darkness, I find the exit door, almost falling through it and out into the alley between the warehouses – also filled with black smoke. I run along its length, finally emerging onto the road gasping and coughing and staggering over to a grass verge, where I fall down, exhausted and weak at the same moment three fire engines come screaming down the road, stopping a few feet away from me.

'Four people in there...' I say weakly, pointing to the warehouse as one of the firemen crouches beside me. 'My parents... a woman and a girl... office at back... no, actually... *five* people...'

I don't remember much after that as everything becomes blurry and unreal. I feel myself slipping in and out of what seems like the deepest sleep ever, but suddenly it's not and there's noise and panic and commotion around me and my heart is pounding and my head throbbing. And then I'm being moved, and I feel sick and there are more sirens and yelling and arms underneath me and kind voices and I'm being carried because I see the sky above me moving, the trees swaying, and a column of black smoke reaching up into the sky.

'Where am I?' I ask, not knowing if it's days or minutes later. A woman's face is beside me – someone I don't recognise wearing a dark green uniform. She says something, but I don't know what because suddenly I'm not here again, and when I am, when my eyes open, I have an oxygen mask over my face and someone telling me to breathe normally, asking me if I can hear them.

I give a little nod and that's the last thing I remember until I wake up in hospital, bright strip lights overhead, the sound of beeping from a machine beside my bed, and a nurse nearby writing something on a clipboard. I try to sit up.

'Did... did they get out?' My mouth is so dry, and my throat is sore. 'Where are my mum and dad? And the others?' I ask, but the nurse rests a hand on my shoulder, guiding me back down onto the bed.

'Just rest now,' she says, a pitying look on her face that tells me everything I need to know.

FIFTY-EIGHT

HANNAH

I don't know how long it will be until there's a funeral. I don't even know if there will be one.

A detective came to see me while I was still in hospital – though the respiratory consultant tried to discourage me from exerting myself, saying I should wait until I'm discharged. But I insisted that I was strong enough, that I wanted to give an early statement to the police. Somehow, telling them what I knew – or rather what I was choosing *not* to know – seemed safer under the watch of the medical team. I had an excuse to get rid of the officer if things didn't go the way I wanted.

'DC Bright,' I said quietly, glancing up at him as he stood beside my bed. 'Can't speak very well yet,' I whispered. Each syllable felt like a razor blade in my throat.

'I'm so sorry about what happened to your daughter's father,' he said, bowing his head. 'And I'm sorry for your injuries. You've been through a lot.'

I nodded in reply. None of it seemed real to me yet.

The detective asked me a few questions, and I did my best to answer, but it was when he got onto the specifics that I wanted to set things straight.

'I understand your daughter was held captive in the warehouse for almost forty-eight hours,' he said, deciding to sit down in the hospital chair next to my bed after all.

I nodded, staring straight ahead. I can't even begin to fathom what Jodie went through during the time we were searching for her. I'd managed to have a brief chat with her earlier in the day when I was allowed to get out of bed for the first time, taking my oxygen cannister with me to the paediatric unit. We were both on oxygen therapy for several days, following chest X-rays and various blood tests. She was doing well.

'Yes, that's right,' I said, wheezing.

'The man in question, Jodie's father... It's early days in the investigation, but he appears to have suffered a blunt trauma to the head.'

I nodded, picturing the scene. Picturing it so well, in fact, I was able to describe it in detail to the officer. 'Yes, a... a beam fell on him. I saw it all with my own eyes. One minute I was trying to help him, the next he was crushed.' I couldn't help the shudder as my mind played out the scene.

'Did your daughter also witness this?'

I shake my head, coughing again. I have to be so careful. 'No, thank God, she didn't. I'd got her out into the main warehouse by that point.' I breathe in more oxygen, taking my time.

Jodie sobbed against me when I sat on the edge of her hospital bed earlier, telling me everything that had happened to her – what she'd done to escape, how terrified she'd been throughout her ordeal. She could barely get the words out, the tears were flowing so fast. I did everything in my power to convince her that if she hadn't acted, she wouldn't be alive now.

'But I killed *Dad* – I mean... I killed *Rory*. He's dead because of me.' she wailed, sobbing against my shoulder. 'The police, they'll find out, and I'll go to prison...'

'Jodie, shush now,' I said, putting my finger over her lips.

We were alone, thank God, but I didn't want anyone to over-hear her. 'Please don't talk like this. You didn't kill anyone, darling, OK?' I couldn't have her believing that for the rest of her life. I replayed in my mind what she said she'd done – smashing the bottle on his skull over and over and over.

When she described how she'd overpowered him, her words had spun around me, making me reel – just like when I'd seen Rory's ashen face staring up at me blankly through the smoke, his eyes wide open, his lips the colour of a purple bruise.

I'd already got Jodie back through the broken window and into the main warehouse, and I'd been screaming for Natalie when I tripped over Rory's body lying semi-prone on the concrete floor. Blood was congealing from a gash on the side of his head. I knelt down to check for his pulse, though the real reason why he was in the warehouse hadn't yet dawned on me. When we'd briefly spoken on the phone the morning before, he'd told me that he was away on a business trip. Yet another a lie, I now realise.

For a stupid moment, I wondered if he'd somehow located Jodie and had come to rescue her, but then Natalie's screams had sent me clambering over debris and furniture to help get Mila out. It was only when Jodie confessed to me in hospital that she thought she'd killed him that I realised he was her *captor*, not her rescuer, that I knew I had to cover up what she'd done. No way was my girl going to prison, not when she'd been forced to defend herself against a monster.

'By the way,' I told the officer by my bed. 'Lewis Dunn is Jodie's real dad.'

'My apologies,' DC Bright says. It's obvious he's trying to tread carefully – a thin line between upsetting me and getting the truth. 'I'm glad to hear that Lewis is being discharged later. A brave man, by all accounts, helping you all get out of the warehouse.'

He asked me a few more questions, but I'd already told him

what I needed – that a beam had hit Rory on the head, that when Jodie escaped the building, he was still alive. The police could think what they liked after that.

'I'll never trust anyone again,' Jodie told me, hugging me tightly from her hospital bed, oxygen tubes under her nose.

'I thought that once, my darling,' I told her, hugging her back. 'Time will heal everything... and we have plenty of it.'

But I was starting to think that there *was* someone I could learn to trust again – someone who'd changed, someone who'd finally showed up for his family at just the right moment. I'll never forget the way Lewis saved Mila, scooping her up and passing her through the broken window to Natalie, the flames searing around us. But as he handed her over, the little girl froze, staring down at Rory lying on the floor, a terrified expression on her face.

'I... I don't want him to be my daddy anymore,' she wailed, making my blood run cold. 'He's a bad man, and he hurted us...' She curled up against Natalie holding her tight as she ran through the smoke to freedom. My heart ached as I watched them go.

'Now you!' Lewis yelled at me. 'We've got to get out, Hannah!' He glanced up at the ceiling where more timbers were creaking and groaning.

But I was rooted to the spot. 'What Mila just said...' I was shaking, staring down at Rory. '*He* did all this. He kidnapped Mila and Jodie...' I couldn't stand to think about what Mila meant by not wanting Rory to be her daddy anymore, but a burning building was no place to work it out.

'Come on, we've got to get out!'

'Lewis,' I said, grabbing his arm. 'Wait... Rory is still alive. I felt for his pulse just before. He's still *alive*,' I screamed through the roar of the flames, doubling up from more coughs.

Slowly, from the floor, Rory turned to look up at me, his eyes meeting mine through the smoke.

In that briefest of moments, I saw a man I didn't recognise anymore, yet somewhere, hidden behind his bloodshot eyes and his blackened and bruised face, there was a glimmer of the man I fell in love with – the funny, clever, caring guy I met at university with his googly alien antennae and penchant for green fur. I choked back a sob for everything I'd lost, but it turned into another coughing fit as I saw something else in his eyes as he stared up at me. He reached out a hand towards me, his fingers twitching as he silently begged for my help, his lips parting as he tried to speak. But above the roar of the flames, it was hard to hear what he said.

She was ours...

I was consumed by rage at the sight of him – wanting to hurt him as much as he'd hurt me over the last ten months.

'You stole my happiness, you evil bastard!' I screamed through the fabric of my T-shirt. 'I hate you for what you did to me and Jodie! You left us – and now you took our daughter! What is wrong with you?!'

The anger inside me reached boiling point, and I couldn't stop myself from grabbing the empty whisky bottle lying on the floor beside him. I raised it up over my head, about to give Rory what he truly deserved, but suddenly there was a firm grip around my wrist.

'No, Hannah – for God's sake stop!' Lewis yelled, glancing up. The beam above us suddenly dropped another couple of feet, making a loud creaking and clanking sound from the heat. 'We've got to get out of here!'

The bottle fell from my hand, smashing on the concrete just as Lewis grabbed me and shoved me towards the broken window, helping me climb back through with him following close behind. We turned just in time to see the beam collapse on top of Rory, bringing the remainder of the burning ceiling down with it.

FIFTY-NINE

HANNAH

Jodie and I are released from the hospital three days after the fire with a clean bill of health and a whole load of gratitude. Thankfully, Lewis has also been allowed to go home – not that I know where that is, exactly, though I suspect it's the back of his van.

The doctors told us how lucky we are, that we'll make a good recovery, though we should take it easy for a while. They've kept Mila in for few days longer as a precaution given that a young child's lungs are so much smaller. Natalie is staying at the hospital with her even though she's officially discharged, too.

I'm on my way to the children's ward to see them, taking a colouring book and some felt-tip pens in for Mila. It was Nat's idea to visit, saying that it would be a new start for each of us – time to unknot everything that has happened. Unpick from the beginning. It feels as though she wants to forgive me for what happened with Fleur, but I'm not anywhere near ready to forgive her for what she's done to me – stealing my embryos, claiming my daughter as hers. I'm not sure I ever will be ready for forgiveness, but I need to know why mine and Rory's names were on Mila's IVF papers, how she managed to take my unborn child. It's time to get the truth.

Can't lie, I'm nervous about seeing her. I don't trust myself not to thrash everything out in anger, even though I know the children's ward isn't the right place to do this. I'll have to hold myself back, though for now at least, we have a common bond – our precious daughters are safe.

'Now you can do some art while you're in hospital,' I say to Mila as I sit beside her bed, watching as she rips open the packet of pens, beaming up at me.

She takes out the black one and opens her colouring book. 'Thank you, Mrs Marlowe,' she says, sitting cross-legged on top of her bed. Natalie has brought in some pyjamas for her, as well as her fluffy bunny wearing the tutu. I close my eyes for a beat when she calls me that, imagining she called me *Mummy* instead...

'Why don't you try another colour?' I say. 'You could use green for the trees instead of black,' I add, giving Natalie a look. 'And maybe a nice blue for the sky.'

'But *my* trees are black,' Mila replies, chewing on the end of the pen. 'Mummy told me black is her bestest colour.'

I look at Natalie, wondering if she's been teaching Mila about different tones and shading, but mainly I'm trying to hide my sadness at hearing Mila call Natalie *Mummy*. It virtually kills me inside.

When Lewis rescued Mila from the fire, she seemed to truly believe that Rory was her father – her words *I don't want him to be my daddy anymore* have haunted me ever since. But there hasn't yet been a right time to demand the truth from Natalie – not when we've all been in hospital, and Mila is still getting treatment. It hasn't even been a week since the fire.

Natalie laughs – one of her wide-mouthed, I-can't-help-it laughs, exposing her straight, white teeth. She tips back her head, making a grab for the blue baseball cap she's wearing over her long hair before it falls off. It has *Captain* embroidered across the front.

Seeing it on her reminds me of when we were younger. She had quite the collection of caps when we were at university. Despite her bohemian style, the hats were more practical than anything, keeping her wild hair out of the way, and a leftover from her sailing days out of Blakeney when she lived in Norfolk with her parents. I was always borrowing them.

'*Sea Ya...*' I whisper as it suddenly dawns on me, watching Natalie help Mila with her colouring. Of *course* – it was Natalie's cap in my house. Another knot to unpick.

But it leaves me with a burning question: Was it Natalie who took Mila from my kitchen? It would have been her right to do so, after all.

'Sorry, what?' Natalie says, turning to me. 'You're not going already, are you?'

'No, not yet,' I reply, my thoughts racing. 'I was just reminded of something.'

Natalie stares at me for a moment, a smile spreading on her face, though I don't have it in me to return it. Her eyes narrow in thought.

'Help me colour in,' Mila says, vying for Natalie's attention.

'Now, doesn't that tree look nice coloured in green?' I say to Mila, leaning over to see the picture.

'Not really.' She looks up at me, then at Natalie. 'Mummy says black is the best colour. I told you, it's her favourite.'

I raise my eyebrows at Natalie. 'Maybe Mummy forgot that her favourite colour is purple,' I say, passing her a mauve felt pen. 'Do you like purple too, Mila?'

Mila gives a little cough, then shakes her head, scowling as if she has no idea what I'm talking about.

'Mummy's favourite colour is not purple, it's black,' she says again. 'That's why I painted black trees – from when Daddy made Mummy go in the woods behind the house. It was dark and scary. I saw them when I was on my swing in the garden. Daddy made Mummy cry.'

Mila wipes her hand across the back of her nose, so Natalie passes her a tissue. 'What do you say?' she says, when Mila snatches it from her.

'Thank you, Nat-nat,' she replies, wiping her nose on it.

I stiffen, wondering if I heard her right. *Nat-nat?* Where has that come from?

'That's why I made the forest black, Mrs Marlowe,' Mila continues. 'You said we could painted things that made us sad or scared. And I was sad *and* scared because Daddy Rory hurted Mummy and made her cry. And I think that's why black is her favourite colour.'

'You're a very brave girl,' I tell her, thinking she sounds confused. I make a mental note to tell Natalie about the support school can offer, as well as recommending a child psychologist if she wants to go that route.

After my visit, Natalie follows me into the corridor outside the children's ward, telling Mila that she'll only be a moment.

'*Nat-nat?*' I say, my arms folded as we stand facing each other. 'Why on earth did she call you that?' I'm desperate for her to tell me everything, demand answers and for it all to come spilling out, but the hospital corridor hardly seems the right place. There are nurses and doctors everywhere.

But Natalie never gets to answer because we're interrupted by someone approaching. I turn, surprised to see Zayla standing beside us, her face ashen and her eyes heavy with guilt. She's wearing jeans and a grey zip-up hoodie and has no make-up on. Her streaked hair hangs limply around her shoulders.

It's the first time I've seen her since the fire. From what I've heard, Zayla wasn't there when the warehouse had caught light, but she'd been lurking nearby, too scared to make herself known.

'How is she?' Zayla asks in a sheepish voice.

'She's doing really well,' Natalie replies. 'Go in and see her. I'll be back in a moment.'

Natalie holds the door to the ward wide open, and Mila looks up from her bed. A huge smile spreads across her face when she sees Zayla coming over.

'*Mummy!*' she squeals, holding out her arms for a hug.

It turns out that the hospital canteen ten minutes later *is* the right time and the right place for it all to come out. And it's Natalie who suggests it. I get us each a coffee, though neither of us really wants one. We sit at a table for two in the far corner.

'I hate hospitals,' I say.

Natalie stirs her coffee. 'You and everyone else,' she replies, followed by a cough. 'I've given up smoking, by the way,' she says. 'Doctor's orders. After the fire, I didn't take much convincing. I was stupid to have started again, though it's only been for the last year or two. It's the stress, you know?' She bows her head. 'It all got too much.'

'Can we just cut straight to it, Natalie?' I say, leaning forwards. 'I think you've got a hell of a lot of explaining to do. I need to know the truth about Mila.'

I brace myself, convinced that she's about to confess that Mila is *my* child – mine and Rory's little girl. A part of me hopes she's about to reveal that Mayfield Clinic made the most awful error imaginable, that she didn't steal my embryos on purpose, rather it was all a terrible mix-up by the doctors. But she doesn't.

Instead, she says, 'I lost another baby.'

My hand automatically reaches out to hers, clasping her

fingers. Despite everything that's happened between us, I feel her pain. I *know* her pain. 'Oh, *Nat.*'

'I was pregnant, Hannah. Pregnant again. And I lost it. I was only twelve weeks.'

'I'm so sorry, Natalie. You did not deserve that.'

I see the agony in her eyes – the once emerald green dulled to a murky brown. The light inside her has long since gone out.

'That's the thing, though. I think I probably did.'

'No, no… oh, Nat. No one deserves that, and believe me, I would know.' It isn't the time to tell her about my own losses.

'Hannah… the baby I lost was yours.'

SIXTY

HANNAH

Mine?

The hospital canteen blurs around me, the world spinning like I'm on a carousel. I feel sick, yet there's no way to get off.

'What do you mean, the baby you lost was mine?'

Mila is safe. Mila is up on the ward. I saw her with my own eyes... This is what I tell myself to stay grounded, to keep a grasp on reality. Nothing makes sense.

'After Fleur was stolen, I was angry at you, Hannah. Angrier than you can ever imagine. My life was filled with red-hot rage morning till night. Not that there was a night, because I rarely slept.' Natalie sits perfectly straight in the plastic chair, her shoulders square and her head held high. 'Not unless I'd drunk myself into a stupor.'

She starts shaking then, a tremor coming right from her core.

'The police never said as much, but I knew they believed my baby was dead. Six months later and they downscaled the investigation. It was like she'd never existed.'

'Nat, I—'

'Shush,' she says. 'Just listen.' She fiddles with the teaspoon in her saucer, staring down at her coffee as it goes cold. 'I wanted to hurt you, Hannah. Hurt you in the most unimaginable way possible. The same way you'd hurt me.

'Of course, deep down I knew it was irrational to blame you, that I should have directed my hatred towards the person who'd abducted Fleur, but there was nothing rational about it. For years and years, I planned what I would do to you, and how I would do it. It consumed me. But of course, I didn't. I was too busy getting married, being a widow, living a drug-fuelled lifestyle to try to hide my pain.'

'Nat, I'm so very sorry you went through all this.' I have to say something, even though it feels as if I'm falling apart inside.

'The money ran out, but my torment didn't. I don't know how I got through those years, but it culminated in me tracking you down. I thought that if I could just see you, maybe see how pathetic you really were, it might dispel my obsession with you. Because that's what it had become – an obsession.'

It's hard to hear all this without reacting, without accusing her of being utterly insane, but I don't want to interrupt her as I'm certain she's on the verge of telling me the truth.

'But that's the thing – when I found you, you *weren't* pathetic, were you?' she continues. 'Seeing you all loved up with Rory in your perfect cottage with your perfect family, your art teacher job – it did something to me. I wanted to destroy you even more, in the same way you'd destroyed me. And I started by taking your husband away.'

'*What?*'

'It was easier than I thought to get his head to turn. A friend from London did it for five hundred quid and a long weekend by the sea. I mean, I was hardly going to do it myself, was I? I was with Tony for his money, not his body. That marriage was like an act of self-harm.'

'You mean... you had Rory set up? Like a honeytrap?' I try to imagine him falling for another woman's charms, and at one

time I'd have said *no way, that's not my husband*. But now...
now, I'm inclined to believe her. She has no reason to lie.

Natalie nods. 'I've plenty of video proof. She got him drunk
in a bar after he'd been on a night out with colleagues. They
went back to her hotel.'

'Then you blackmailed him?' I hardly dare ask.

'He buckled surprisingly easily,' she says. 'Though he
almost had a heart attack when I met with him a week later,
when I told him it was me who'd set him up. After that, he was
putty, saying he'd do whatever I wanted. Though give him
credit, he was very insistent that I mustn't hurt you. I guess it
was testament to how much he loved you.'

'Fuck...' I don't know whether to throw my coffee over
Natalie or what. 'Go on,' I say instead.

'Back then, it wasn't actually money I was after,' Natalie
says. 'That came later. Instead, I asked him what it was that you
desired most in the entire world, because *that* was what I
wanted to steal from you. Without hesitation, he told me that
you wanted a baby.'

It takes all my strength to listen to her, but I know I have to.

'He was drunk when he told me about how you'd been
trying to conceive, how many miscarriages you'd had, how you'd
spent all your money on IVF treatments. He even told me that
you'd recently frozen your final three embryos. It was quite
touching. And it was perfect – not only could I hurt you by
taking your chances of a baby away, but I could replace what I'd
lost all those years ago because of you.'

I stare at Natalie, not knowing who she is anymore.
Wondering if I *ever* knew her.

'You should have seen me – I made a wonderful Mrs
Marlowe. Rory and I were the perfect couple when we
attended Mayfield Clinic together. He easily got them to
change the address on your file to mine at Ocean Heights,
pretending we'd moved house. Rory made sure we saw a

different clinician to your usual one, but with him bringing your ID and other papers along to confirm my identity, and me darkening my hair colour to match yours, playing the doting wife, no one knew that I wasn't Hannah Marlowe. Not a single person challenged me when I said I wanted my – sorry, *your* – frozen embryos implanting.'

I will not cry… I will not react… I will not break down…

'Everything went to plan – my little baby growing inside me, knowing I'd taken what you wanted most in the world, and finally having a baby again – until it didn't. Like I said, I lost your baby. At twelve weeks.'

I have no words. I can't fathom the level of deceit that I'm hearing. My voice comes out as a whisper, and I can hardly breathe from shock.

'My *God*… Natalie… I don't believe that you *did* this to me—'

'Rory didn't know about that part, of course – that I'd miscarried. I'd gone back to my London life, pregnant and happy, while he breathed a huge sigh of relief convinced I'd got what I wanted, praying that I'd never come back or darken his door again. I left him panicking about how he was going to dissuade you from ever having your embryos implanted, but that was his problem.

'My only regret was that I wouldn't get to see your face when you found out that your embryos were gone, already used up, knowing how desperate you were for a child. But then I lost the baby and that's when things changed. Once again, I had nothing.'

'Who even are you?' I say, pulling back my chair. I've had enough. 'You cheated on me at university – with a *man*! – then blamed me for what happened to Fleur. And now this. I mean, I know—'

'Is that what you really think?' Natalie says, half standing up as she reaches across the table, grabbing my arm. 'That I *cheated* on you?' Tears collect in her eyes as she slowly shakes her head, staring at me. Then she shoves me away. 'Sit down. I'm not done yet. Apparently I need to spell this out for you,' she says, her eyes blackening as she glares at me. 'It happened after a night out with friends. You weren't there – you'd decided to stay home and paint. Yes, I was drunk. And no, I shouldn't have walked home alone so late at night. But did I deserve what happened? No. No, I fucking did not. And I certainly didn't deserve the lifetime of shame that has haunted me ever since. It was so dark, and he came up behind me, so I didn't even get a look at him. I still have no idea who he was, and I didn't tell a soul what he'd done to me. I doubted the police would believe me, anyway. I could barely function in the weeks and months after. Then, when it was too late to have a choice, I found out I was pregnant with Fleur.'

A hand comes up to my mouth. I'm stunned by what I've just heard, I can't speak, I can't cry... I can't do anything. Natalie didn't cheat on me – she was attacked. I watch as she wipes a finger under her eyes, sniffs back her tears and plasters a fake smile on her face. She looks over my shoulder.

'Zayla's coming,' she says quietly, waving her hand in the air.

I twist round just in time to see her approaching our table, a small smile on her face when she sees Natalie. She pulls out a chair and sits down beside her.

'Hi, Mum,' Zayla says, giving Natalie a little hug.

SIXTY-ONE

HANNAH

'I know what you're thinking,' Natalie says, looking at me. 'And whatever it is, you're wrong.'

I shake my head, my eyes flicking between Zayla and Natalie, not knowing *what* to think anymore.

Mum... I'm speechless for a second time, trying to work it out.

'Mila is my granddaughter,' Natalie says, making me catch my breath. 'And Zayla is my daughter.'

I can't move – for what seems like an eternity, I'm frozen to the spot. Not capable of a single word.

'Coffee, love?' I hear Natalie say, but Zayla shakes her head.

'*Grand*daughter?' I eventually whisper. 'Mila? Why... how...?'

'Mum doesn't look old enough to be a grandma, right?' Zayla says, unaware of the conversation we've just been having.

'No, no she doesn't,' I say. 'So... but... I thought you and Tony didn't have any children.'

Then it occurs to me. I'm not certain of Zayla's exact age, but what if Tony forced himself on Natalie when he found out about her sexuality, that she'd only gone with a man because she hated herself so much?

'We didn't,' Natalie replies. 'Tony is not Zayla's father.'

I pause, thinking, then turn to Zayla. 'Mila called you Mummy on the ward. I mean...'

'No judgement, yeah? I've heard it all before. I had her young. I was eighteen when I got pregnant. Had to give up college and everything.'

'No, no I wasn't going to judge you. I'm just confused.'

'If it wasn't for Mum here, God knows where Mila and I would be living. Think I will go and get that coffee after all,' Zayla says, heading off to the serving area.

'Natalie, will you just tell me what the fucking hell is going on?' I glance back over my shoulder, but Zayla is far enough away not to hear.

'She was really struggling. She'd raised Mila alone for almost four years and had no idea what she was doing. They were both feral.' Natalie stares across the canteen at her. '*She* found *me*, you know. And she decided that she hated me before we even met, but I guess that's understandable. She'd been told I'd given her up for adoption.'

I shake my head. 'I don't understand.'

'Fleur. She found me, after all these years. She wasn't dead, Hannah. She was just lost.'

'Oh my God.' I clap my hands over my mouth. My head is spinning. It can't be true... can't be possible after all this time – can it? I have no idea what to think. It's all too much.

'She found me through a DNA website – the one where you can also do your family tree. I'd registered my details eight years ago. It was my parents' idea. They'd always believed Fleur was out there somewhere. It's just a shame they never got to meet her. They died before she found me. Zayla said she'd always known that something had happened to her when she was little, that her past wasn't what people were telling her, so that's why she did the DNA test, to see if she could trace any family members. And here I am.'

'Wait, you're telling me that Zayla is *Fleur*? That she's not dead? That she's... she's been found?'

'Yes.'

I look back over my shoulder, staring at Zayla in her skinny jeans and black hoodie as she orders her coffee.

'One hundred per cent certain, before you ask. I had another private test done. But we've not gone public with it. I couldn't stand the press attention all over again. I've not even told the police, and no one has ever made the connection. I'm trusting you, Hannah.'

'Jesus Christ, Nat... this is all too wild.'

'The thing is, Zayla came as a package. She already had a child. She'd been at college and got herself pregnant with some lad. Oh, the irony,' Natalie says with a small laugh. 'It turned out that Mila was almost exactly the same age as the baby I'd miscarried, within a month or two. *Your* baby, Hannah. It was an easy switch to make, and when I told Zayla there'd be some money in it for her, she happily agreed to changing Mila's last name to Weston. When I got back in touch with Rory again, he had no idea that she wasn't his child as I'd been out of his life for a few years. But suddenly, I was back in the game.'

I take a few sips of my cold coffee in the hope it might ground me – that or wake me up from this terrible nightmare.

'Before Zayla comes back,' Nat continues, 'I just want to say that she's far from an angel. In fact, she's a total nightmare to live with. She's been through the care system and had a turbulent childhood. She grew up believing no one wanted her, and that included me. I took her in – of *course* I did – I wasn't about to lose her again. It's been so hard, but the pair of them, they've given me a purpose again, Hannah, a reason to carry on. Thing is, I had no money. And I wanted to give her and Mila a good life. They deserved that much from me. So that's where—'

'That's where Rory came in,' I finish for her. 'You black-mailed him again.'

'I'm sorry if that made things tough for you this last couple of years. Though in the end, Rory fought back, turning the tables by kidnapping Mila. He spun Zayla all sorts of lies about me, promising her a load of money if she helped him. Though for Rory, it wasn't about the ransom – it was just about getting me to stop. I believed him when he told me that his mother's money was running out, that he'd used up all his own savings, and if I kept pushing for more and more, he'd have to sell Chapelfields. He said it would all come out then. Thing is, school fees aren't cheap, and a house like Eastcliff costs a lot to run – he should have realised that. He designed and bought it for us, after all. Or I suppose, technically, Marion paid for most of it. He bled her dry.'

I cover my face, wanting to block it all out. This can't be happening. Simply can't be true... though I know deep inside that it is.

'I think it all got too much for Rory. At one point, I was concerned he was going to take his own life,' Natalie tells me. 'He was terrified that you wanted to have one more try at getting pregnant, but he knew if that happened, you'd discover the missing embryos – *and* find out that he was broke and in huge debt.'

I close my eyes, looking back to see if I'd missed the clues, if I could have seen this coming. But there's nothing.

'So... that's why Rory left me, so he didn't have to confess what he'd done,' I whisper.

'Pressure drives people to do crazy things, Hannah. And for a while, he did act the part of Mila's father, truly believing she was his child. He'd come round and play with her, read her a story. Sometimes phone her at bedtime, telling her that he loved her. He thought she was his daughter, after all, so I allowed him that much.'

I remember overhearing Rory on the phone by the harbour. *I love you so much, my darling...*

'After he left you, he fell into a deep depression, drinking and smoking, partly living at his mother's empty house, sometimes staying with me. He even told me that he'd slept in abandoned buildings, and I let him use my caravan for a while. He had to sign off work long-term sick. I'm ashamed to say that my obsession with hurting you ran so deep that I stole his keys to your house. But I always locked up after I'd been inside.'

'You're mad, crazy!' I say, half standing up again. 'You can't just go around ruining people's lives like this...' But I stop because suddenly, Zayla comes back.

'I got some biscuits if anyone wants one,' she says, sliding them between us. 'I was thinking,' she adds, looking at me. 'You're that woman whose car broke down, aren't you?'

'It seems fine now,' I say, trying to dodge her question. I don't want Natalie knowing I was up at her house, and certainly not that I was there with Jan. But everything she's just told me explains why my clinic paperwork was in her study. I'd wrongly assumed that Natalie's IVF pregnancy had gone full term, that Mila was hers – or, technically, *mine*. But Mila belongs to Zayla.

'Anyway, I think Zayla has an apology to make to you,' Natalie says. 'Don't you, Zay?'

'Oh, yeah,' she replies, suddenly seeming vulnerable.

I can't take my eyes off her, hardly able to believe that she's the little baby I looked after that night, whose milk I went to heat up, who disappeared from her cot.

'I'm sorry for coming in your house and taking Mila,' Zayla begins. 'I was running late to fetch her, and I'd just arrived at school when I saw you holding her hand and taking her out of the playground. I knew you weren't really supposed to do that, but thing is, because you were her teacher and stuff, I... I let you. I followed you to your house, so I knew where you'd gone, but... I... well, I just needed a bit of a break to be honest.

'I wasn't coping with looking after Mila. It was hard to take care of her properly, especially when I only feel like a kid myself half the time. I reckon people thought I was neglecting her. Like, Mum had gone away for a while, and it was all a bit much for me. I only went into town to get a Coke, to clear my head, but then that guy, the one who thought Mila was his, the one who wanted to get back at Mum, well, he phoned me saying I had to bring Mila to him right away. That it was time for our plan—'

'You mean Rory?'

'Yeah, him. Look, I was well pissed off with Mum. Things had been tense between us for a while. I mean, I'm not really her nanny, right? We just told everyone that. I was raging at Mum because Mila was getting this amazing childhood in a huge house with tons of money and... and I'd got dealt a shit card and grown up in the care system. I was twelve the first time I ran away and lived on the streets.' Zayla took a long breath. 'I was jealous of my own daughter, I guess. And I blamed Mum for not protecting me when I was a baby.

'When Rory approached me behind Mum's back a couple of weeks ago, spinning a load of lies about her as it turns out, he said I could earn a load of money if I helped him out. I figured if I did it, I'd be able to afford to rent a little flat of my own to get away. All I had to do was help him make it look like Mila was missing for a few days, deliver a ransom note, and he'd pay me ten thousand pounds in cash. I thought it might teach Mum a lesson.' Zayla fiddles with her fingers – her nail polish black and chipped, her bangles jangling on her arms. 'I know I've been stupid. I was a mess and wasn't thinking straight, and... I don't know what I'd do without Mum frankly. She's been amazing and forgiving.'

'So that's how you were able to take Mila to the police

station for a welfare check,' I say as it dawns on me. 'Mila wasn't at a sleepover at all. She was a prisoner at the warehouse.' Poor, *poor* Mila – they must have primed her what to say.

Zayla hangs her head. 'I feel bad about Jodie getting tangled up in it. But when Rory found her schoolbag in the warehouse, he went mental, convinced she must know something. He never mentioned that he was her stepdad. I just thought she was some kid hanging out and bunking off school. He said it would be better if she delivered the note, save us getting caught. I agreed, not wanting to deliver the note myself. It didn't occur to me that he was using Jodie – incriminating her rather than us, and not caring if someone witnessed her at the house. She seems like a good kid.'

'She is indeed,' I reply, thanking my lucky stars that I have her. I check my phone, seeing a message alert on my screen.

All fine here, Mum. Just chilling. See you soon. J xx

SIXTY-TWO

HANNAH

Six Weeks Later

Rory sits in the car beside me.

I glance over at him as I drive, not able to think of a single word to say to him. I fetched him half an hour ago, phoning Natalie as soon as I'd picked him up.

'I'm on my way,' I told her, hanging up.

Fifteen minutes later, she's sitting in the back seat.

'How's Mila doing?' I ask, glancing in the rear-view mirror. I see her smile, the fond look in her eyes. 'And Zayla?' I force myself to hold it together.

'Mila's enjoying the school holidays and having fun with her mum. Things are going well for them.'

It's only a short drive to where we're going, and when we arrive, Natalie and I get out, leaving Rory in the car. I'll deal with him later, but first I've got some things to show Natalie. I've been putting it off these last few weeks, especially as it's taken time for everyone to get over the aftermath of the fire.

We sit at a picnic table bench, the wind whipping around us on the clifftop. 'We'll have to watch these don't blow away,' I say, pulling down the cap I'm wearing so it doesn't fly off. *Sea Ya* somehow seems appropriate, especially given the crashing waves below us.

I put the shoe box that Lewis and I found under the floorboards in Rory's old room on the wooden table between us, explaining to Natalie what had happened, why I'd gone looking for clues in the first place. Then I tell her what the first item is, so she can prepare herself mentally.

She gives me a nod.

I open the lid and take out the tiny sleepsuit – the one with the pink and blue rabbits and the cut-off feet. I'd put it in there along with the newspaper clippings to keep it safe.

'Oh...' she says, tears pooling immediately. 'Oh, no...' She brings it to her face, the fabric crumpled between her fingers, pressing it against her nose. I already know it smells musty from being stored under the bed in Marion's spare room for so long, but I imagine that won't matter to Natalie. To her, this sleepsuit is as fresh as it was the day Fleur – *Zayla* – wore it.

'There are some other things, too,' I say, taking out the newspaper clippings. Natalie casts a quick eye over them. 'Some photographs,' I tell her. 'Plus the letter I mentioned.'

They took some finding, but Lewis helped me, turning Chapelfields inside out for more evidence. We had to clear out and pack up the place ready to sell, anyway – it's the right thing to do for Marion. It's all she has left to pay for her care now most of her money is gone, though when I say *gone*, it's starting to feel like it's been put to good use. Natalie, Zayla and Mila seem to be thriving at Eastcliff House these last few weeks, and Jan has offered her decorating services free of charge. Nat might own her own home, but she still needs to be careful with what she spends. It's early days with the New York gallery, but she's already sold several paintings, and they're planning an exhibition for her.

A part of me is happy for her – especially after knowing

what she went through. But the bigger part of me is... well, I'm still bitter as hell about what she did. I'll never know if my embryos would have implanted successfully and gone full term in me – Natalie took that chance away from me. I'll never forgive her for that.

'Take a look at this picture,' I say, handing her a photograph of a woman in her sixties. She's posing under an apple tree, holding a baby in her arms.

Natalie takes it from me, her lips parting as she studies at it. Then she looks up, a frown between her eyes.

'It's Rory's mother, Marion,' I explain. 'When she was younger. Twenty-four years younger, to be precise. Taken in the garden at Chapelfields.'

'And the baby?' Natalie asks hopefully.

I give her a single nod, our eyes locked together. 'Yes, it's Fleur.'

'*Oh my God...*' she whispers, but the breeze carries her words away. She traces a finger over the baby's pink shawl.

'Here's the letter I told you about,' I say, handing her an old, unsealed envelope. 'Marion wrote it but, for some reason, she never sent it. Maybe she was worried it would be intercepted. It's pretty incriminating.'

I've already alluded to the contents, not wanting her to be too shocked when she reads it for herself. Natalie lifts the flap and slides out a single piece of cream folded notepaper. Marion's writing is a slanting scrawl, but neat enough to read. I've read it so many times, I almost know it off by heart.

September 8th, 2001

Dearest Rory,

Chapelfields is not the same now you've left. Gone off to study for your master's degree. My boy... we're so proud of you, darling. It was such a perfect summer, having you home for a few weeks after graduation, the four of us happy together. Three generations here at once.

Being a parent isn't easy, and we know you didn't want to be a father in the first place. And we know you did your best under the circumstances. Anyway, it sounds like that girl wasn't a good mother or partner – no one upsets my boy! But, darling, we also know what you did. Bringing your baby home at the end of May... we can pretend all you like, but it was all over the news for weeks. The mother didn't know you'd taken her, did she?

After you'd gone, after you'd left Fleur with us, we were so worried someone was going to get wind of her being here. Realise who she was. Wonder why an old pair like us had a baby. I'm certain we'd have been reported to the police.

Besides, Dad and I aren't getting any younger. We did our best for her, darling, but it came time to say goodbye. I know you're busy and can't look after a baby you didn't want in the first place, but we couldn't take care of her either. We could hardly give her back to her mother! We were scared the police would somehow work it out, realise what you'd done, and arrest you straight away. And I couldn't have that. Why you went with that wretched girl in the first place, I don't think I will ever fathom, but then it's not a mother's job to know everything about her children. Just to protect them at all costs. Whatever they were, you must have had your reasons.

So we did what we must. Your father and I drove through the night to Manchester, a long, long way from home. The baby had clean clothes and a full tummy when we left her at the hospital in her bassinet. Don't worry, I wore a headscarf and dark glasses, and Dad parked a short walk away. We left her outside the maternity ward with a little note – Please take care of me because Mummy can't. I was born 3rd April 2001 at home in Manchester. *The wrong information, of course, and enough to throw them off the trail, we hoped. I just prayed the system never put the pieces together, that they had no reason to suspect anything other than she was an unwanted foundling.*

I will sign off now, Rory, dear, and please know that you are always in my heart. Your father sends his best.

With love, always,

Your mother.

Natalie sits back, looks up at the sky. Her chest rises and falls with her shallow breaths as she takes it all in, her eyes narrowing in thought.

'Oh my God.' She puts a hand to her throat, as if it's hard to speak. 'It was *him*... Rory... He... was the one who...' She can't get the words out. 'The one who attacked me. All this time and I've been angry at the wrong person for Fleur's disappearance, and all this time I knew the person who raped me,' she says, imploring me with her eyes. She brushes a strand of hair from her face as a thousand thoughts sweep through her – everything from realisation, confusion, anger, pain and sadness. Her eyes glisten before a single tear rolls down her cheek. 'I should never have blamed you, Hannah, but I didn't have anyone else to be angry at. That bastard – he stole my happiness not once, but twice. He stole from us *both*.'

I reach out a hand, not knowing what to say. Sometimes words aren't needed – just the understanding and realisation as it settles between us.

When the police spoke to Natalie in the aftermath of the fire, she lied to them, saying that she'd given me permission to take Mila home from school that Friday afternoon, that there'd been a huge misunderstanding and miscommunication, and that her message allowing me to collect Mila hadn't reached the school office. Natalie told the police that she felt terrible because of all the trouble she'd caused while she was away and that no further action should be brought against me. She even convinced them that I'd overreacted about the whole thing, that I was hysterical and not thinking straight when I turned myself in for abducting Mila – that my anxiety made me believe I'd committed a crime. The police had implied as much themselves anyway, so they took her at her word. And as far as anyone else is concerned, Mila is still Natalie's daughter, and Zayla is her nanny.

In return, as much as it pained me to do so, I promised I would keep what Natalie had done to myself. She'd prevented a child abduction case being brought against me, after all, allowing me to keep my job and my reputation, so I convinced myself that reporting her to the police for stealing my precious embryos and blackmailing Rory would not change anything or bring them back. It was a precarious stalemate that we were each prepared to accept, an undeniably bitter pill to force down. But we'd been through worse.

I look at Natalie. Natalie looks at me.

'Is it time?'

She nods.

We walk over to the car together and put the shoebox in the boot. Then we go round to get Rory from the passenger seat, lifting him out together.

Back on the clifftop, we open the lid of the urn.

There will be no funeral. There will be no words to mourn his loss, or heartfelt readings or hymns or flowers. There will be no tears shed, and there will be no grave to visit or memories to share. No sandwiches and cups of tea at the wake, and no long-lost relatives huddled together. No hushed voices saying what a wonderful husband and father he was.

No one to witness the agony he's caused Natalie and me.

Between us, we tip the plain metal urn on its side, allowing the breeze to take Rory's ashes out to sea. It's more than he deserves, but I didn't want to keep him.

Jodie didn't want to come, saying she'd rather spend time with Lewis. He's taken a job with a local building contractor, and even got himself a flat in town. This weekend he's helping Dad put up a new greenhouse and painting my parents' living room. When he comes round to visit, he tells me it's to see his daughter. But I'm almost certain it's to see me too.

'Done?' I say to Natalie.

'Done,' she replies, brushing the dust off her hands.

As we walk back to the car, I drop the urn into the rubbish bin at the picnic spot, a little smile spreading across my mouth before I drive Natalie back to her family.

Then I go home to mine.

EPILOGUE

'That's a lovely painting,' I tell Mila as she mixes up another bright colour.

My Friday afternoon art group is almost at an end, and I can't help feeling twitchy. I've been waiting for a phone call this last week or so, ready to dash off at a moment's notice.

'Who is it of?' I ask, though I already know.

'Mummy, of course,' Mila says, pointing to the figure's huge belly. 'The baby is in her tummy.'

I can't help the inner smile, knowing how excited Mila is about having a little brother or sister. And Natalie can't stop going on about how over the moon she is that Zayla is pregnant, that she'll be a grandmother again – not that she looks the part at forty-six. She's just got back from an exhibition of her work in New York that was a sell-out within the first week, with dozens of private collectors desperate to get their hands on her art.

I'm pleased for her. I really am. Honestly.

So very pleased.

Or that's what I've been telling myself these last few months.

But the truth is, I'm not pleased at all.

She betrayed me in the most unforgiveable way. And she might think all is forgiven – but she should never have been so stupid.

'Are you going to take the picture home?' I ask, writing Mila's name on the back.

'It's a present for Nat-Nat,' she tells me. 'She's so happy that the baby is coming.'

Mila doesn't know how much her words mean to me.

'It's fate, Han,' Natalie said to me one morning recently when we had coffee together. At her request, we've been keeping in touch. 'It's a second chance for me to have a baby in the house. Zayla has no idea who the father is, but I don't even care. I get to relive my life the way it *should* have been lived. I'll take care of this baby as if it's my own. I'm so bloody excited!'

I smiled sweetly when she told me, seeing pure happiness in her eyes.

After art class is over, I write a few words on the back of Mila's picture – *A little reminder for you* – knowing Natalie will read it. I hope she pins it on the wall.

The phone call I've been waiting for comes three days later as I'm packing up the art studio at school.

Breathless and panting, Zayla tells me it's time, that she and Natalie are already on their way to the hospital. Thankfully it's late on a Friday afternoon and Jodie is at home when they drop Mila off with her on their way to the maternity unit. Lewis is there, too, making dinner for them all. He's been staying over a lot lately.

Baby coming, I text him before I drive off. *So excited. So nervous. Will keep you posted xx*

Then I speed off like a madwoman.

The next morning, Zayla cradles a perfect little baby boy – seven pounds four ounces, born six hours ago. His searching eyes gaze up at the three women looking adoringly at him – Zayla, Natalie and me. Perhaps he's wondering which one of us is his mother.

'He's so beautiful,' Natalie says, fighting back the tears. She looks at me, grinning, so happy, though behind her eyes, I see all the memories flooding back. Her room in the student house, the filthy kitchen, the battered cot, the rabbit sleepsuit. Her baby gone...

'May I hold him?' Natalie asks, itching to take her grandson.

'In a moment, Mum,' Zayla says, giving me a glance. 'Hannah, will you take a photo?'

I nod, aiming my phone at Zayla as she holds the baby against her chest, his mop of dark hair partially covered by a tiny white hat. Natalie leans in close to them.

I pause. 'No, just Zayla and baby,' I say, feeling a bit mean when Natalie looks upset, but it's for the best.

Photos done, I open another app on my phone and do what I need to do. A moment later, Zayla's phone lights up on the table beside the bed. I catch a glimpse of the notification.

Bank deposit: £10,000 sent from H. Marlowe.

Zayla glances at her screen, then at me. She gives me a little smile and a nod. I've already paid her five thousand pounds to cover her initial expenses, and this completes the transaction. My solicitor has the Parental Order ready to file at court, to which Zayla fully agrees. That order will make me the baby's legal mother.

'May I hold him *now*?' Natalie asks again, holding out her arms to Zayla. There's a nervous look on her face.

Zayla turns to me, watching as I stand up and slip on my jacket. 'Is there time?'

'Not really,' I say, giving Natalie a glance. 'Sorry.' Then I hold out my arms.

Zayla gives the baby a quick kiss on his head before handing him over to me, a nurse watching on. The medical staff have all been briefed. I will never get my embryos back, but with Lewis being the baby's father – Zayla falling pregnant the first time she used his donation – my beautiful baby boy easily fills the hole in my heart.

I look at Natalie, her face a picture of shock as I cradle him in my arms.

'He's mine now,' I tell her, reaching out to squeeze Zayla's hand. 'It's all legal. I'm taking him home. You stole my future, and now I'm taking yours.' Then I turn and walk out of the ward.

Dear Reader,

Thank you so much for reading *I Took Her First* – I really hope it had you turning the pages fast! If you'd like to be kept up to date about my new books, please click on the link below to sign up (your email address won't be shared, and you can unsubscribe any time you want).

www.bookouture.com/samantha-hayes

Writing a book about every mother's worst nightmare – a child being taken – isn't an easy task. But I wanted to up the ante with this one, and so started to explore ideas around someone stealing a child – but then have the child stolen from the abductor.

All sorts of 'what ifs' started to crop up, and once my characters came to me with all their backstories and traumas and histories and fears, everything slotted into place.

I love writing stories that are centred firmly in the present day with urgent and dramatic scenarios playing out for my (poor!) main characters, but I also love nothing more than delving into the past and uncovering secrets that my cast are harbouring. And this lot did quite a good job of keeping secrets, don't you think?!

While writing, I really felt for my protagonist, Hannah, as I got to know her story. Deep down she's a good person, but I couldn't help throwing lots of curveballs right into the middle of her life from the get-go (sorry, Hannah!), though she came out of it strong and determined and got what she wanted in the end.

I really hope all the twists and turns along the way kept you guessing and took you by surprise. I've written some questions for you or your book club to ponder, and hopefully, you'll find them thought-provoking for some juicy book group chat with your reader friends!

If you loved this book and have a moment to spare, I would really appreciate a quick review on Amazon to help spread the word – just a few words are fine! Thank you so much.

As ever, I'm already making progress on my latest psychological thriller, and I have a large backlist on Amazon for you to enjoy if you haven't read all my other books.

With warm wishes and happy reading!

Sam x

www.samanthahayes.co.uk

 instagram.com/samanthahayes.author

 facebook.com/SamanthaHayesAuthor

 x.com/samhayes

BOOK CLUB DISCUSSION QUESTIONS

1. Did Hannah do the right thing by taking Mila home from school that Friday afternoon? How did her emotional state and recent relationship problems feed into this? What could she have done differently, and how would it have altered the course of the book?

2. How much did past triggers affect Hannah's actions in the present day when Mila went missing from her kitchen?

3. Mother-daughter relationships can be hard to navigate, especially when teenagers are involved. Do you think Hannah and Jodie have a good bond? What could either of them have done to bridge misunderstandings that arose between them? What do you think their relationship will look like going forwards?

4. Natalie and Hannah have had a complicated and tumultuous relationship over the years – beginning as friends, then lovers, followed by estrangement and finally brought together again as 'frenemies', albeit with a glimpse of understanding emerging between them. After reading the epilogue, how do you see their relationship in the future? Do you

think they will grow their friendship again, or is Hannah's final revenge a step too far?

5. What could Rory have done differently to close down the chain of events that led to him being blackmailed by Natalie? His crimes reach far back into the past, building up after Natalie rejected him at university. Do you think Rory deserved to die? Even though he's gone from her life, how will Hannah feel about her past relationship with him now she knows the truth?

6. How much do you think Rory's parents are to blame for what happened to Fleur? Discuss how things could have played out differently.

7. Lewis is a 'loveable rogue' but was never there for Hannah or Jodie in the past. How do you see the trio's relationship going forwards? Do you think Lewis has changed? Do you think he will finally step up and be a dad to Jodie, as well as to the new baby that Zayla carried for Hannah?

8. Which characters did you love or relate to in some way and why? And which characters did you love to hate?

I hope your book club enjoyed discussing *I Took Her First*.

ACKNOWLEDGEMENTS

It goes without saying that a massive thanks is owed to my lovely editor, Lucy Frederick. Your clever insight and drive to help me make this book the best it could be is something I value hugely – so thank you for everything you've done. I really do appreciate all your hard work.

And grateful thanks to Sarah Hardy and all the publicity team at Bookouture for spreading the word far and wide about my book, as well as to Laura Gerrard for copyediting, and to Jennifer Davies for proofreading, and Lisa Horton for the wonderful cover design – I really appreciate everyone's input and hard work. As ever, my sincere thanks to the whole team at Bookouture.

Big thanks always to Oli Munson, my brilliant agent, for looking after me, as well as everyone at AM Heath. And big thanks are also due to Richard King and the fab rights team at Bookouture for helping lots of readers around the world get their hands on my books.

Finally, massive thanks are always due to all the fabulous bloggers, reviewers, and readers who shout out about my books, whether I know you in real life or online – I truly appreciate you spreading the word. Couldn't do it without you!

And last but not least, all my love as always to my amazing Ben, Polly and Lucy, who keep me going – keep sending the cat pics!

Sam xx

PUBLISHING TEAM

Turning a manuscript into a book requires the efforts of many people. The publishing team at Bookouture would like to acknowledge everyone who contributed to this publication.

Audio
Alba Proko
Sinead O'Connor
Melissa Tran

Commercial
Lauren Morrissette
Hannah Richmond
Imogen Allport

Cover design
Lisa Horton

Data and analysis
Mark Alder
Mohamed Bussuri

Editorial
Lucy Frederick
Hannah Wilson

Copyeditor
Laura Gerrard

Proofreader
Jennifer Davies

Marketing
Alex Crow
Melanie Price
Occy Carr
Cíara Rosney
Martyna Młynarska

Operations and distribution
Marina Valles
Stephanie Straub
Joe Morris

Production
Hannah Snetsinger
Mandy Kullar
Nadia Michael
Charlotte Hegley

Publicity
Kim Nash
Noelle Holten
Jess Readett
Sarah Hardy

Rights and contracts
Peta Nightingale
Richard King
Saidah Graham

Dear Reader,

We'd love your attention for one more page to tell you about the crisis in children's reading, and what we can all do.

Studies have shown that reading for fun is the **single biggest predictor of a child's future life chances** – more than family circumstance, parents' educational background or income. It improves academic results, mental health, wealth, communication skills, ambition and happiness.

The number of children reading for fun is in rapid decline. Young people have a lot of competition for their time, and a worryingly high number do not have a single book at home.

Hachette works extensively with schools, libraries and literacy charities, but here are some ways we can all raise more readers:

- Reading to children for just 10 minutes a day makes a difference
- Don't give up if children aren't regular readers – there will be books for them!

- Visit bookshops and libraries to get recommendations
- Encourage them to listen to audiobooks
- Support school libraries
- Give books as gifts

There's a lot more information about how to encourage children to read on our websites: **www.RaisingReaders.co.uk** and **www.JoinRaisingReaders.com**.

Thank you for reading.

www.ingramcontent.com/pod-product-compliance
Lightning Source LLC
Chambersburg PA
CBHW030528190726
48283CB00006B/1823